THE REAL DRAGON COLLECTION

Tales of Science Fiction Romance and Adventure

PAULINE BAIRD JONES

ISBN: 978-1-942583-62-2

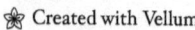 Created with Vellum

About this collection

Mayhem, romance and adventure runs through them...

Together for the first time in one volume, Pauline Baird Jones' science fiction romance short stories (with a little bit of steampunk swirled into some of them just for fun).

Join Emma as she tries to puzzle out the mystery of her past, with a little help from her (mysteriously returned and talking) bearded dragon.

Journey to Nebula Nine Station with Special Temporal Agent, Jane Jones, as she works with the handsome security chief to prevent a tragedy.

Take a leap into the past with Prudence Pinkerton and sort out the mystery of the specters in the storm.

Find out why going home for the holidays isn't all cookies and eggnog.

Dive into the two *Project Enterprise* short stories—a murder mystery with an alien twist, and join Ani as she faces down an automaton outlaw gang in old time Texas.

And as a bonus for buying this digital collection, fall into a time trap with Briggs (from *The Key* and *Girl Gone Nova*), Madison, and the mysterious Sir Rupert.

Pauline Baird Jones is known for writing smart, quirky, funny fiction. Grab your copy of this collection today!

The Real Dragon

By
Pauline Baird Jones

About The Real Dragon

Emma Standish didn't think her day could get any worse. Her dad is marrying his boss, her dragon suddenly came back talking and typing, and it's her fault the Earth, or at least ten square miles of Texas, is going to be destroyed. That's what happens when you forget something very, very important. Luckily for her, she's got the love of her life that she can't remember and her dragon by her side. Who needs to worry when you're having a day like this?

This short story originally appeared in *Pets in Space*. This now out-of-print anthology was picked as a *Library Journal* e-Original Best Book of 2015.

~

Chapter One

My dragon came back the day my dad told me he was getting married again.

I found him—my dragon, not my dad—sitting on my desk with his front legs on my computer keyboard.

Typing.

Of course he's not typing. Just because it sounded like he was typing, didn't mean he was *typing.* His head turned my direction and he blinked. I closed the door behind me and saw what seemed like recognition in his deep, dragon gaze.

He lifted a front leg—usually a sign of submission in a bearded dragon—and waved his claw at me, or possibly at the computer screen. "I hope you don't mind?"

I stepped over to the bed and sank down just before my knees gave out. Peddrenth shifted so he could still see me, his beard flaring black for several seconds, like I'd annoyed him. Bearded dragons make great pets, but male bearded dragons like to dominate, and, despite the submissive paw waving, he'd ruled our shared roost long before he disappeared. I shook my head, closed my dropped jaw and said, "I don't...mind."

Minding wasn't even on the list of what I felt. Beyond the shock, the disbelief, the awe, and freaked out, I realized the one thing that didn't surprise me. How he sounded. Kind of gravely, with a slight lisp. Like, well, a dragon.

He turned back to my computer and symbols began to flash on the screen. My dragon *was* typing.

Gobsmacked, I stared at the screen without seeing it at first, but then I realized some of the stuff he was putting on there looked vaguely familiar, if I had time to think about it. Which I didn't. I had all these questions bouncing around inside my head. I needed to herd them into an orderly queue before something exploded in there. I set my purse down on one side, my brief case on the other, and eased off my shoes. This familiar, post-work day ritual helped. A little. Okay, not that much. But at least my feet were happy.

I rubbed my temple, then the bridge of my nose. I pinched myself. I seemed to be awake. If I was dreaming, I wanted to wake up. Except for having Peddrenth back. I wouldn't mind if that was real—with or without the typing and talking. I'd missed him. He'd been my companion, my best friend for ten years, until—

The typing stopped and Peddrenth slithered around. His paw waved, like giving me permission to speak. So I did.

"Where have you been for the last eight years?" I sounded more curious than freaked out, which surprised me, because I was pretty freaked out.

He shouldn't even be alive. A bearded dragon had a max life span of twelve years. I got him for my eighth birthday and I would be twenty-six in a couple of days. You do the math. On the other hand, he wasn't supposed to be typing or talking so the life span thing felt moot.

"Away," he said significantly.

"For eight years." He'd disappeared the same night as the accident. My fingers curled into my palms. I didn't remember much about that night, except that when the dust settled, Peddrenth and my mom were both gone. Losing them had changed my life almost beyond recognition, but whatever. I'd moved on. Without actually moving on, since I still lived at home with my dad.

"It is true that eight of your years have passed..." His paw waved again.

Maybe he was trying to use the Force on me. It had that vibe. Which might explain why I only just noticed his mouth wasn't moving when he talked. Just in case things weren't weird enough.

Was I having a breakdown? In which case I was hallucinating

because...oh, wow, it feels lame to think I might be that upset over my dad remarrying. I considered it and decided it wasn't the marrying part. It was the who part. My dad was the stereotype of the absentminded inventor slash scientist. And he was about to marry Iris. Of all the women who'd tried to get his attention since my mom died, he picks his dragon-lady boss?

My dad was marrying his boss.

And mine.

Just because I found her more personally annoying than just about anyone else in my life, I needed to not lose sight of the fact that if this happened, I stood a good chance of getting my life back—after eight years of being Peddrenthless when I needed my pet dragon the most. "*Where have you been?!*"

"You are conversant with faster than light travel."

Ice trickled down the center of my back. "How could you know that?" No one knew about her dad's super-secret, faster-than-light project.

"For one thing, you have geek plastered all over your Facebook and Instagram profiles."

I opened my mouth to ask how he knew that, then noticed the tabs on my browser. My dragon had checked out my social media.

"And it has long been your dream to travel in space."

This was true, but how—oh right. I'd told him everything before he disappeared. "I...didn't know you understood me."

He might have looked aggrieved. "You told me I was the only one who did."

"Yes. And I meant it." For a teenager, "you understand me" is the same as saying "you let me talk all I want and never tell me I'm wrong," but this didn't seem like the time to tell him that. That I knew this gave me hope I'd matured, even if I did live at home. Then I wondered why I was talking out loud when my dragon wasn't. *Can you hear me?*

No response from my dragon.

"How come I can hear you inside my head but you can't hear me?" I felt a d'oh from him.

"You lack the implant that gives me a telepathic voice."

Implant. My dragon had an implant that made him telepathic. Okay. And where—it was starting to sink in that my dragon had been...I couldn't think it. Not yet. I was a geek. I should be excited, not—

"So you took," I sort of managed another dry swallow, "a...a...space trip?"

I had a sudden flash of memory. Like a movie still frame. The bright light stabbing out of the dark that put us at the center of a spotlight—but that was just a weird dream. A weird, reoccurring dream. It had to be, because if it wasn't then...then...

"You observed my departure."

I looked away. "I don't remember much about that night." I rubbed my face with both hands, leaving them over my eyes. Now I saw the flash of headlights. This time not in still frame. They moved erratically, the glow bouncing off the dense trees that lined the road. The squeal of tires—and then nothing. Just this vast blank ocean inside my head that was awash with guilt.

My dad had been devastated about losing mom, but it had been eight years. In the Old Testament, even Jacob had only served seven for Rachel, unless you counted the seven extra years he got tricked into serving, but I didn't want to count those. Eight was bad enough. And I hadn't even got a date out of my eight years, let alone a spouse or two.

You don't have to leave, my dad had told me today after dropping his bombshell, *Iris and I want you to stay, to keep working* with us.

Yeah, sure, I'd love to play third wheel to my *dad* and his wife. I didn't tell him I'd rather poke out my own eye. I didn't have to. He was clueless but not that clueless. He'd almost seemed startled by his words, then he'd smiled at me, tempered with a bit of wry and something almost...puzzled. I'd hugged and congratulated him and came upstairs to...a typing, talking dragon. I lowered my hands.

I had to know. "Were you...abducted by...aliens?"

"I wasn't abducted." His beard flared black again. "It was an accident."

My next thought was totally inappropriate, but one can't always help that.

Why didn't they accidentally take me, too?

～

"So, you're not dating Ted?" Peddrenth broke into what had turned into a long silence.

It wasn't that I'd run out of questions. I think I had maxed out my ability to process his answers. Here I sat in my bedroom, dealing with the fact that my dad was getting married again, my dragon had taken an accidental trip to space and back, and all I had were book boyfriends. I glanced around. And a bedroom that hadn't been updated since that night. And who was Ted?

I started to ask, but then I remembered. The me before the accident had thought Ted might ask me to the senior prom. He hadn't, of course. I'd been in the hospital with a concussion. And our "dating" had been as imaginary as my book boyfriends.

"No...I'm not dating Ted."

"That is well."

Why? I directed a penetrating look his direction, but he had a tough hide. I was curious he was curious about Ted, no question, but it didn't seem like the main point, which was...

"Why did you come back?" I hesitated. "Are you really back?" I'd need to restart his bug order. It had really impressed my friends that I bought bugs and had a dragon for a pet, I recalled a bit vaguely. Was this what shock felt like? Cold and fuzzy around the edges? I grabbed the lap quilt at the foot of my bed and wrapped it around my shoulders.

"Mazan would like to talk to you."

"Mazan?"

My dragon studied me with a peculiar intensity. "You truly do not remember?" I shook my head. "That perhaps would explain—"

"Explain what?" I felt a strange dread, as memory tried to pierce the thick fog hiding whatever happened that night eight years ago.

"There is a problem with the launch."

There was nothing in my nondisclosure agreement about talking to a dragon, but it still felt disloyal. "Launch?" I tried to look clueless. Which should have been easy since I pretty much was.

Peddrenth couldn't raise his brows, but it felt like he did.

"Okay, so there might be a launch—which you didn't hear from me—what of it?"

"There is a leak."

"A leak?" I jerked upright in alarm. "In the fuel tanks? On the team?" Exploding space vehicles and corporate sabotage were both a real worry. "What?"

"You. You are leaking."

Chapter Two

I t shouldn't be that hard to wrap my brain around making first contact with an alien. It's what all of us geeks dreamed of and hoped for. Perhaps we didn't hope for first contact by dragon, but still, I should have been ready.

I didn't feel ready.

The almost full moon was up, but mostly hidden by puffy clouds left over from an afternoon storm.

With Peddrenth riding on my shoulders, we took the path through the woods just like we used to do. It didn't feel like it had been been eight years since I'd taken Peddrenth into the clearing to hunt for free range bugs...why had we come this far, I wondered now? There were bugs closer to the house, further from—

My heart began to thump like it wanted to jump out of my chest as this path wound ever closer until the one place road and path crossed.

The spot where my mom had died.

On that night I can't remember.

She died instantly, they said. It wouldn't have helped if the other driver had stayed. The shrink told me my need for closure, for justice, was what kept me from remembering. I guess I believed him, since my degree wasn't in psychology. Oh wait, I didn't have a degree. I gave it up to help my dad. That probably sounds bitter and I'm not. Mostly I'm bewildered. And I didn't understand why dread coiled in my chest like a snake. Or why my throat felt closed, and the humid air felt thicker than usual. Why did I taste metal on my tongue?

Why was I afraid?

It wasn't the place. Dad and I passed the spot every day on our way to work. Some days I didn't even think about it. I certainly didn't have a panic attack, which was good since I drove. But now I wanted to turn tail and run home.

I didn't. I couldn't run. I couldn't hide. I couldn't flinch from thinking about that night. Not anymore.

I needed to know what happened. I needed to remember.

I might not be a genius like my dad, and no, I didn't have that college education, but I'm not stupid. It had to be more than a lack of closure fueling this choking dread. There was something I didn't want to face, something buried deep inside my head. Only it wasn't buried, maybe it never had been. It had ridden on my shoulders for eight years, it was riding there now, with Peddrenth.

I glanced his way, found him watching me. He almost looked worried. Or I was projecting.

I swallowed to wet my dry throat and asked, "Is he, you know, humanoid?"

"Mazan? Of course."

What was "of course" about it? This alien had accidentally collected the dragon, not the human.

"Does he look like...I mean, is he purple or something?" I had a feeling if Peddrenth could have rolled his eyes, he would have.

"You..." he stopped, as if reconsidering what he'd meant to say. "You all look similar to me."

If I could have chuckled, I would have. I did manage a smile that felt wry, but it didn't last. "The implant, they didn't hurt you, did they?"

He actually shook his head, well, his head swept left, then right.

"The implant was a gift, so we could communicate."

"They wanted to talk...to you?" And not me. Was I jealous of my dragon?

There was another pause. "The Draze are like that."

The Draze. I didn't know anything about the Draze, did I? And yet...there was something almost familiar about both words. Mazan. Draze. My panic eased. "Did I meet him that night? The night you left."

Peddrenth hesitated, then said, "Put me down here, please."

I opened my mouth to tell him I usually waited until we crossed the—

The road. Until we crossed the road. It was just a road.

I crouched and he left his perch. I straightened as he crawled out of sight, his tail twitching from side to side. I clenched my hands into fists and followed my dragon.

And there it was.

The road.

Right where it was supposed to be, looking like it always had. At least, it looked like it had a couple of hours ago when we drove home. Still, it felt different looking at it from here. It changed my point of view. Standing, not speeding by, I could see the spot—though brush had grown back where her car hit the tree. The skid marks were long gone, too, of course. Time was supposed to heal everything, wasn't it?

I didn't feel healed. I felt...not healed. To my core.

All was quiet, peaceful even in the low light from the nearly full moon. I looked both ways, even though ours was the only house this far down the road, and I would have heard a car coming from quite a ways off—I tensed but the twitch of fear didn't produce an image to go with it—so I crossed. I was relieved to get to the other side. I felt a chicken joke wanting to happen inside my head and quickly followed the path into the woods to escape it. The trees and bushes closed in fast, narrowing the trail so sharply, I couldn't see that far ahead.

Instead of dread, now I felt eager, excited, like a good geek should.

I pushed a particularly large branch aside and there it was.

My jaw dropped and in my amazement the horizon spun around the ship, but not in a bad way. More like a flourish. I moved forward, because it was too cool to fear. Straight out of a bigger budget scifi movie, its sleek, aerodynamic lines made my geek heart go pit-a-pat with happy. Big enough to fill the clearing almost from edge to edge, it was thickest at the center. It was so much what I'd expected it was almost a cliche, except it wasn't because it was there. It was real. And it glowed *the* shade of green most associated with alien encounters. Seriously, it was like that green had been matched to this ship. I drew close, my hand lifting because I just had to touch it, but a crack appeared in the side closest to me, a crack that rapidly turned into a lowering ramp. I froze with one hand half lifted. Just visible at the top of the ramp, I saw booted feet. Brown boots. A bit buccaneer-ish. Sassy. I would buy those boots.

I thought that before. For the first time, I believed I had been here, that I'd felt this, seen this. But then the boots started moving toward me...

This wasn't a movie. This was real. I backed up as the horizon began to spin around me again—and this time not in a good way—with the ship at the center, as if it needed to keep pace with my suddenly racing heart. I wasn't worried, not about meeting Mr. Boots. There was something else, some other worry that made panic build...

The horizon spun faster, blurring it into an impressionist painting. Then it tilted to one side as my suddenly weak knees hit the dirt. Oddly enough I was more worried about landing in a fire ant bed than the alien wearing the boots a few inches from my nose. I tried to put a hand out to touch them, but my hand didn't move. The spin of the horizon narrowed to a pinpoint. And then went dark.

A pinpoint of light pierced the black and grew slowly bigger. Memories played pinball wizard inside my head, all disconnected and weird as the smothering fog hiding that long ago night began to shred, letting bits and pieces of the past escape.

I opened my eyes and there he was.

A familiar stranger.

Someone I knew, but didn't.

His worried eyes were the color of a stormy sea, with streaks of purple and turquoise in the gray. And his lashes, do not get me started on his lashes. So not fair that a guy got those lashes. He had a narrow face, with tufted brown brows and hair with a mind of its own. Kind of *Harry Potter* without the glasses. His body was long and narrow, too. He wasn't handsome, at least not in a movie hero way. I knew, without knowing, that he was clever, that I used to love his smile—which was nowhere to be seen. That I used to love—I shut that thought off. I couldn't finish it, not now with memories playing bumper car inside my head and refusing to connect properly. When I backed off, the pain eased, as if to reward me for being good...

"Are you feeling more satisfactory?"

His voice wasn't deep, or especially low or high, but still managed to be very distinct. I knew it, I knew his voice. He had a slight exotic accent that made my toes want to curl. *Had always made my toes curl...*

"Mazan?" I made it a question, though it was more of a mental confirmation as at least one piece slotted into place. I knew the name, knew it belonged to him. Why he had mattered, why he did matter to me, was less clear.

His lips curved up, but it wasn't a full smile. He thought I was leaking something, I remembered. But what?

Moving slowly, carefully, his fingers wrapped my wrist, his fingers settling on my pulse. I looked down, startled at the sight of his hand, his skin against mine. And yet...not surprised either. His fingers felt cool, but not like he was cold. More like that was his normal temperature. There was an "otherness" about him. No sparkles and no sign of prominent incisors between his lips. I know it was silly to even think it, but he was seriously pale.

I flexed my fingers, trying to connect this present with the pieces drifting in and out of view inside my head. To figure out this mystery, wrapped in the past and happening...inside an alien space ship.

"Will I," I had to clear my throat to finish it, "live?"

His smile widened and his hand dropped away, leaving my skin feeling suddenly cold. "I believe so, my friend, Emma."

His friend? My heart hurt a little, like there'd been more between us.

Mazan looked away and his shoulders rose and fell in what looked like a sigh. He turned to face me again, sadness and yes, disappointment in his gaze. That hurt as much or more than being called his friend. I struggled to a sitting position, letting my legs hang off the edge of what I realized now was some kind of bunk bed affixed to the wall. It was just high enough that my toes barely brushed the metal floor.

I pushed my limp, damp hair off my face. "What?"

"Why did you do it?"

"Do what?" I didn't have to try to look bewildered.

"She does not remember," Peddrenth said, a bit too patiently, like they'd covered this ground already. His beard flared black for several seconds.

Mazan's gaze probed mine for what felt a long time. My eyeballs dried. I wanted to blink, but I didn't dare. If I blinked, he'd think I was lying and I would never lie to him—

"How—" he stopped. He pushed his hands through his hair,

which probably explained its charming disorder. And that's when I saw something new enter his gaze.

Hurt. I'd hurt him.

"I was in a car accident eight years ago. My mom—" I had to look away then. It took two tries for me to get it out. "My mom died. I hit my head." Those first words felt like rocks coming out, but the rest came easier, faster. "The shrink says I have hysterical amnesia which is kind of funny because I haven't been able to cry. Not once in eight years. Don't you think that crying is a prerequisite for hysteria?" I rubbed my face fiercely. I had to...I had to...what? It was as if there was this voice in my head telling me I couldn't. Couldn't what? I didn't know what I wasn't supposed to do or say, but if I did or said it, something bad would happen. I almost laughed at that last thought. What could be worse than this half life of guilt and fear? This sudden realization that I'd lost more than my memories of that night?

I lowered my hands and looked at him, met his gaze with my chin lifted a little. He could believe me or not. Didn't know why I wanted him to believe me, except that I seemed to be in trouble. And I did want him to believe me. A frown pulled his crazy brows together. Made him look just a touch mad scientist. My heart did this little flutter. Apparently I liked mad scientists.

"This news is...well, my friend, Emma, it is heart-breaking. It is—"

At least we were still friends. But that didn't explain why *he* was heart-broken. It's not like he knew my mom.

"She is lost, gone, and we did not know." He turned away, causing more disorder in his hair with frantic hands. He paced away, then back.

"Are you talking about my mom?"

He looked surprised then. "Of course. She was a great hero to our people."

"Hero?" I croaked. To his people? "My mom?"

"Yes, she was the Deliverer."

I felt my jaw go slack and couldn't do a thing about it.

~

So I was back to gobsmacked.

Neither Mazan nor Peddrenth appeared to notice. Mazan had adopted a tragic pose over by the door, like he needed something to hold him up. Peddrenth, well, he sat there staring at Mazan with his tail twitching back and forth, looking very wise and remote.

She was the Deliverer.

My mom. The Deliverer. A hero to his people? She'd driven car pool and made cookies and bandaged my knees and bought me Peddrenth and nagged me to take care of him. She delivered mom-ness, not hero-ness. There had to be some kind of mistake. Only... somehow, don't ask me why, I knew it wasn't a mistake. I didn't believe it...but I did. It was there, I decided, buried somewhere in my missing night with all the other stuff I couldn't remember. Or...was I afraid to remember?

I sat there because I didn't know what else to do, other than finally get hysterical, and honestly, I didn't have the energy. Looking at Mazan was unsettling. More than memories started to stir inside my head. For the first time, I was also starting to realize how little I'd *felt* for the last eight years. As if all of me had been wrapped in some kind of emotion-damping fog. Seeing him made my heart hurt. Like a limb coming back to painful, tingling life—I looked away, studying my surroundings instead. It was more of the familiar unfamiliar. Like I was on the other side of a movie, watching me, seeing this without being part of it.

The small cabin was very ship-like and also very space ship-like, because it had that curved edge on what was probably the outside wall, and there were space-stuff fixtures. The bunk where I sat had been tucked into that curve, which saved the straight wall for a small desk area, some shelves, and a sink. There were two doors. One stood open giving me a glimpse of the corridor and the other, I suspected, was for a commode. No, I knew it was. Why could I remember peeing here but not being here?

Bits of memory drifted just out of reach, taunting me, daring me to look. Was it the whole Deliverer of her people thing? But why would I freak out and get amnesia over that? If she really had been a Deliverer of an alien people, well, logically, that could have played out in a lot of different ways. But it wasn't logic that made me know how it **was**. Okay, more weirdness to realize my mom was an alien. I made myself repeat it. *Mom was an alien.*

That would actually be more cool than having a dragon for a pet, particularly at the cons.

Oh my freaking heck. If my mom was an alien, then I was one, too. At least half a one.

Still not enough for amnesia.

Okay. Even the doctor admitted that something traumatic had happened that night. He believed it was the driver of the other car that I was afraid to remember. I knew he wasn't wrong, but he also wasn't completely right. There was more. Something huge and ugly lurked just out of sight inside my head like a bad dragon, the mythic kind that hides in storm clouds over the ocean and dives out to eat sailors. My dad—

My brain twitched with a sudden stab of pain. I mentally jerked back, wanting—no, needing to go fetal and forget again. But I wasn't seventeen. I was twenty-freaking-five about to turn twenty-freaking-six. It was time to woman up. And that meant facing the dragon in my head. No matter what—or who—it was.

Okay, it was unthinkable that my dad would, so just think it, I told myself. Because if it was unthinkable, then it wasn't true. My dad couldn't have been in that other car. He wouldn't have left us there. Unbidden came the memory of my dad's haunted eyes, his strained gray face. Okay, what if he had?

There. I'd thought it.

And the world hadn't stopped turning.

My brain hadn't exploded. Or given up the Big Secret.

It was still there, just out of reach and fighting me. It was weird to feel detached from me but to also feel this rising panic. My heart pounded and my breathing came in shallow pants. I forced myself to hold in a breath, then another, to slow it down. The little stars circling my vision faded. I flexed my tingling fingers, then looked at Mazan. He'd turned back to face me, looking sober, sad, but calmer.

"This is sad news for our people, my friend, Emma, but—"

My eyelid twitched. Oh right. "*Our* people?" If my mom was alien, then I was half alien. So that made his people half my people. My other eyelid joined the twitch-fest.

His brows arched. "But you know this, my friend—"

"I don't remember." It was the truth. I didn't remember. I'd just connected some really obvious dots.

"Just that night. You said you do not remember **that** night," he protested.

I shook my head and he stopped talking, his head tipping to one side. I knew that pose, that look. He was...seeking to understand.

"You can call me just Emma, you know," I murmured, as little bits and pieces, small Mazan moments drifted in and out of view. "We *know* each other."

"Of course, just Emma—"

"I mean, we knew each other before that night," I interrupted, pushing back at the pain and resistance building inside my head. "We met...when..." my gaze shifted to Peddrenth. "...when I got you."

"Yes." Mazan nodded, his expression lightened some, but also puzzled. "Peddrenth is a Draze Dragon, genetically engineered to look exactly like a species native to your world, your bearded dragon. He is your Companion." The way he said it the word had a capital C.

I looked at my dragon. My Companion? Who had accidentally left me behind? I opened my mouth to ask or accuse, but the look in his eyes stopped the words. He looked like I felt. Betrayed.

"You know this—"

"But I didn't, I don't, I mean, that's part of what I forgot." I looked at him, fighting to keep my breathing even again. "Why would I forget you? This?" And remember Peddrenth? But not the part about Peddrenth being a Companion, and now it was coming back to me in bits and bites how he'd always been able to talk to me like the best invisible talking friend a young girl ever had. "What happened that night? Why did you take Peddrenth and leave—" ...me behind, is what I wanted to ask. We were young, but we meant something to each other. I didn't know a lot of things, but I felt this to my toes. All the way through my heart. I touched my chest. It felt like I could see the cracks in it. He left me. For eight long, miserable years. I hadn't known it, but I'd *known* it.

"You told me to leave, just Emma."

"Emma," I corrected, absently. Like the crack in his ship as the ramp lowered, a breach appeared in the wall inside my head. And it was a wall. I'd thought it was an ocean covered in fog, but it was a wall. High and solid, scary to approach and painful to touch, to try to breech. "Why would I tell you to leave?"

"Someone came. A car. We could see the headlights on the road. There was a risk *The Entireer* might be seen. It was protocol. You told me I must not risk discovery. I cloaked the ship and launched."

Regret was in his eyes, in the tone of his voice. There had been a cost to him, too.

"But...they told me I was in the car with her." It was like trying to fit together pieces from two different puzzles. If the car we'd seen was my mom's, the pieces might fit—but if she'd picked me up where the path met the road, she wouldn't, she couldn't have been going fast enough to hit that tree with lethal force, even with a nudge from another car. I didn't remember another car. And that meant...I don't know what it meant. I looked at Mazan. I needed to move, to get ahead of the flight instinct trying to send me back out into the forest, back to hiding from the past. I backed away from the wall, just a little. Maybe if I focused on something else... "Let's walk while you tell me what it is that I'm leaking."

Chapter Three

It took three circuits of the inner corridor for Mazan to explain, and one more for me to process it. He spoke the truth. I knew it in my heart, but my brain, well, there was that ugly wall of resistance. What lurked behind the wall shouldn't be life threatening, but it felt like I would die if I remembered. Took the fun out of walking around in an alien spaceship—which you've already done, I reminded myself. *Focus*. It was a strange feeling, having the old and new kicking around there.

As we did one more circuit, the ship got more and more familiar. This corridor circled the central core where the FTL drive was housed. Everything else required was located in the outer dish, except the bridge which was up top and the cargo hold in the lower belly of the ship.

Mazan stopped at the galley. "Do you require something to drink, Emma?" He stumbled a bit over the single name, which was interesting. Had he been calling me "my friend, Emma" for all those years? *All those years*. It had been years if I met him when I got Peddrenth. But why—*The Entireer* had been my...school. I came here to learn, but no one had told me it was because I was half alien. I thought I'd been picked because I was special. Pause to be grateful I was no longer quite that needy and clueless. Chagrined, possibly, but not needy and clueless.

"Thanks." I didn't really want something to drink, but the circuits were making me a bit dizzy. Or the memories swirling in my head were doing it. I followed him into galley. It was more functional than cool, but still cute in a *Tiny House* kind of way. Peddrenth hadn't joined us. He'd gone to hydroponics, I thought absently, and then was surprised by the thought. He had a friend or friends there...

All of the sudden I found it hard to look at Mazan and had to resist the urge to curl my hair around my finger or do some other flirty thing. This was a Serious Thing, not a boy-girl moment. I stole a look at him when he handed me a cup of water, his alien scent drifting close enough to tease my senses, comparing this Mazan to the bits of memory still forming inside my head. He hadn't changed as much as I had, I decided. This ship hadn't just been my school. Mazan had been my teacher, then my friend, and then my more-than-friend—at least for me. He shifted from one foot to the other and tugged at the neck of his space suit. Not as indifferent as he appeared? I hid a totally inappropriate-to-circumstances smile. Apparently I could face the dangerous deep and still go shallow. Great.

I wrapped my hands around the cup and propped a hip against a counter, took a sip and said, "So I'm half alien, my mom is some kind of war hero that you thought was dead until she hacked a NASA satellite and sent you a message." The words emerged from my mouth a lot calmer than they felt inside my head. In there they were all in caps and accompanied by lots of "oh, my hecks!"

"But by the time you answered her message, she'd married my dad." I had to pause here to try process the fact that *my dad had married an alien*. "...and she had me. So instead of going home, she asked you all to educate me so that I could choose where I wanted to live when I got old enough. You've been coming every year—" I broke off the frown. "Except for the last eight years? What happened?"

"Your mother would send a safe signal, my—Emma. We did not receive this signal."

"Okay." That made sense, but... "...there was no signal this year." Since my mom was gone. "Why did you come back now?"

Once again he shifted from one foot to the other, but this was different shifting. The guilty conscience kind.

It took me a minute, which was kind of embarrassing, but I got there finally. "The leak." I went back out into the main corridor and looked around. TFTL's ship wasn't the same, but there were signs of my leaking. Their ship was like a distant echo of this one. I looked at Mazan. "But...that's my dad's research. I'm just his assistant."

He shook his head. "It is not possible for your father to know the things he knows, to do the things he's done."

"My mom—"

He shook his head again. "He did not know."

"He didn't know he'd married an alien?" My voice rose a bit on the end.

Mazan half smiled. "He knew. He did not know about this." He gestured around him. "And the Deliverer would never have given him our technology. It would not have been safe to give it to him."

"Why not safe?"

He looked at me through those ridiculous lashes. "There are... those who closely monitor the development of technology in backwater star systems. It is illegal to accelerate technological advancement. There are severe penalties."

I let the "backwater star systems" slide past. It was not relevant to the moment. Even if it stung a little. Instead I considered my dad. Would he have been able to resist the temptation to use what he'd learned? Or even have remembered he wasn't supposed to use it? Probably not, I had to concede. "But I did know?"

He nodded. "It was part of your education."

"You gave advanced technology to a teenager."

"You understood the boundaries and each level of knowledge came after you proved you could keep it to yourself—"

"—until I got knocked on the head and forgot." My head hurt like I'd whacked it again. I rubbed my temple. "But if I didn't remember, then how did I leak it?"

Mazan looked troubled. "Perhaps it was a subconscious thing. You did not realize you were helping."

It was possible, I supposed. What—the stab of pain felt like a needle in my eye. What the heck? When it subsided some, I tried again. *What did I know*— oh yeah, that question was like some kind of mental trigger. I backed off and relaxed, letting my mind drift and something emerged from the fog.

"The Kruvox," I said. "That's who my mom fought, right?"

Mazan looked pleased. "Yes. They are evil."

"Did they have technology or something to manipulate memory —" I yelped when this pain hit, like a punch inside my head.

"What is wrong, Emma?"

23

I gritted the word out past the pushback. "Kruvox?"

"There were rumors of such things, but—" He frowned. "But the Kruvox are not here. Your mother destroyed their fleet."

My mom, the driver of carpools and bake sales, had destroyed a fleet. A Kruvox fleet.

"By taking out their leader, you said?"

"The Opposer, yes."

I glanced around. My mom had done that and set this up. She'd always known—I thought it was my special secret, one shared only with Peddrenth. Wow, shone a whole new light on my teen years. But not on the big, black hole inside my head. Not yet. If she could do what she did, then her daughter could face the past and get over herself. I gritted out. "How did she do it?"

"She was not just a great warrior, Emma," he looked at me with glistening eyes, "she was a great scientist as well. She used her knowledge to create an explosion—"

"—that didn't destroy her ship," I felt compelled to point out. It was the crash here on Earth that did that. I felt a little miffed at his hero worship. Of my mom. My mom the hero of the Draze.

"We learned later that the explosion created a chain reaction that opened a wormhole. It pulled both ships in. Her ship was damaged. The Opposer's ship did not survive transit."

My brain gave a kick, sharp and painful, like a memory trying to kick through that wall. "You sure he didn't make it?"

"He?" Mazan looked surprised. "The Opposer was also female."

There is no way I can explain the chill that went through me. The pushback inside my head was almost more than I could stand. There was both pain and the sensation of an iron hand closed around my throat, trying to choke off my words. I reached up a hand but there was nothing there.

"Do you have a picture, an image of this Opposer?" I croaked.

Mazan looked surprised, but went to the wall and touched something. A computer-looking thing swung out and he tapped. Then tapped some more. The screen filled with bits of color that slowly resolved themselves into a face.

Huge cracks appeared in the wall, but I didn't need to see the other side of the wall to know.

Tomorrow evening, my dad was going to marry the evil Kruvox Opposer.

At least now I knew why I didn't like her.

~

Mazan now looked as shell-shocked as I felt. "We must warn him."

"He won't believe me." I blew out a sigh, one hand gripping the armrest of the pilot's position. It was everything I'd ever hoped for in an alien ship's bridge. And I couldn't enjoy it. All the flashy lights, the cool looking switches, the shiny were no help at all in solving the problem of Iris. No wonder my prospective evil step-mom didn't want me to move out. And knowing my dad, he hadn't told her that would never happen, that I would never live in the same house with that woman. He wouldn't know how much keeping me around mattered to her. How could he know I was her ticket to ride home? Which I would be if we couldn't figure out how to stop her.

"You are his daughter. Of course he will believe you."

I bit back a sigh. How could he understand? I wanted to pat his hand, say, "There, there," and kiss him on the mouth—I yanked my gaze away. *Focus, Emma.*

"I had to see a shrink, a doctor, about my memory loss. The shrink told him I was mentally fragile." I hadn't been meant to hear that. It stung then, still did, I admitted grudgingly. I'd known I wasn't hysterical or fragile. I'd known something was wrong, but I wasn't old enough back then to fight their belief. All I could do was try to prove I wasn't fragile. It hadn't worked. Dad hadn't noticed because of his whole absentminded professor deal. And he didn't know my mom, his *alien* wife had done the equivalent of the Kobayashi Maru. She'd saved her people and Iris was using me to get back there, maybe to even undo what my mom had done. If she escaped on a ship I helped build, however unconsciously... "We have to stop her. *I* have to stop her."

He took my hand again and this time his smile was different. More personal. More grownup to grownup. I hoped it wasn't hopeful thinking, but whatever. If I was going to take on evil, I needed hope.

"So, the wedding is tomorrow and the launch is the day after." Only my scientist dad would think that was romantic. And logical. "Somehow we have to stop the wedding and, what, sabotage the launch?"

Mazan suddenly avoided looking at me.

"What?" I asked suspiciously.

"I have already taken care of the launch."

I arched my brows.

"I was ordered to stop the launch."

"Show me." I gave the order, but was surprised when he did. It's not like I was in charge.

He swiveled his chair to face the control console and moved things. Tapped things. Like before, it started as little bits that gradually formed into something I understood. It was not unlike the language Peddrenth had used on my computer. I was about to ask what it meant, when I realized that I knew.

"Mazan, this won't just stop the launch. It will leave a ten-mile crater in Texas! You'll take out the whole facility and then some!"

I stared at him as his gaze slowly returned to meet mine.

"That's the plan?" I shoved my hands through my hair. "You're going to blow up my dad." My eyes got wider. "You were going to blow up me."

He didn't look away this time. It was the look of a man who knew exactly what he'd done. Or had planned to do. The stern line of his lips and jaw, the steady seriousness in his gaze, well, it was kind of sexy. Despite this, or because of it, I glared at him, but I had to concede, "You didn't know I hadn't betrayed you."

I still felt hurt. He should have known. Even if there was no way he could have known. I looked at him, my eyes wide and dry, my heart, well, my heart wasn't happy. "You were my friend."

His lips twisted a bit wryly, as if I'd hurt him. "Yes, I was, I am your friend. But you...you are my love, Emma."

I felt my eyes widen.

"And still I would have done it."

He'd just used the l-word. It kind of helped. I felt older. I tipped my head and asked, my tone different. "Why?"

"It was you and your ten miles of Texas, or your whole world."

That sobered me really fast. "Okay." Those monitor aliens, I guessed. I looked away, then back at him. "You love me? Do you know what that means here?"

He took my hands again. I'm not sure how a guy with his core temperature managed to warm me up, but he did. He didn't pull me closer or kiss me, which was a bummer. But since I was all grown up, or getting there fast, I sucked it up.

"I know what it means. I will be there with you."

"With me?"

"When the ten miles goes away."

I didn't jerk my hands away, but I did give his a shake. "We're not blowing up." Not now that I knew he loved me. "We're going to figure this out." I adjusted my grip so I could squeeze his hands. "And then..."

"Then?" His lips twitched.

"Then we'll figure *this* out. Us, I mean." Just because my brain was an on-steroids video game with most of my memory offline didn't mean we couldn't.

It just meant it would be a little challenging.

Chapter Four

"So if Iris thinks she's got a ticket off this planet using my leaking, why is she marrying my dad?"

Now we were in a little version of a boardroom. There was even a board, well, a screen for me to write on with this nifty pen looking thing. Sadly, it was still blank. I faced that board, because looking at Mazan, not to mention hearing the clock inside my head ticking down to us blowing up, made it hard to focus.

"You have not reached your maturity age as yet."

I swung around. "I blew past that five years minus two days ago." I'd thought it was cool my dad's company had scheduled the launch on my birthday. Now...well, I still thought it was kind of cool.

"On Draze the age of maturity is equivalent to twenty-six of your Earth years."

"So?" I shrugged.

"Draze is a matriarchal society."

"Really?" I needed to think about that. But not now. "Why does that matter?" Because it clearly did.

"As long as you are under age, as your father's wife, she would be the head of your family."

"For one day," I pointed out, though I will admit I started to feel uneasy.

"If she marries your dad and you died before you reached your maturity, she would control your inheritance."

"I...don't have an inheritance." He gave me a look, but didn't speak. I lifted my hands. "I do not want to know."

I turned back to the blank screen, my disordered thoughts spinning in un-pretty patterns. Okay, we had suspicions, but what did we know? I wrote "Dad" in the air, and then "Iris." With a mini flourish, both names appeared on the screen.

"The company hired my dad within a few months of the accident." I added the date under my dad's name. "They were a new start-up, but well funded." I looked at Mazan over my shoulder. "I never heard their pitch." I frowned. "Dad told me I could work for him for a while if I wanted to." I bit my lip. "I thought it meant he needed me to be there to help him. I mean, I knew he was worried about me, but he was so devastated by mom's death, he got kind of clingy." In his absentminded way. I shook my head. "It all felt so normal. Even when my friends asked questions about why I wasn't going to college after all, but even then it felt normal. Right."

"Was The Opposer there?"

I shook my head. "She didn't pop out of the woodwork for two years." I wrote that date on the screen, more for something to do, than because it was relevant or helpful. My hand trembled a bit, skewing the words. I felt closer to knowing something, but the push-back in there was painful. Someone or some thing didn't want me to remember. Was the someone me? Or her?

"It was not long after that my dad had his first breakthrough." How did she do it? How did she pick my brains? How did she make my dad believe he did it? "But they came very slowly."

"If she is The Opposer, then she knows the intergalactic laws for this star system. She had to be careful. The penalties are severe, not just for her and this planet, but for the Kruvox."

I swung around to face him. "But she wasn't careful enough. What happened?"

"I did not know this when I was pulled out, but they left monitoring in place." I must have looked annoyed, because he added, "With what you knew, it was necessary."

And a good thing, I conceded. If they hadn't, what would Iris have done? Could she have talked my dad into taking a ride to the stars? Maybe she already had. He was a geek, too. Would I have agreed to go with them? That was harder to answer. It was one thing to dream about it, something entirely different to just up and go—particularly when it was my dad's honeymoon trip to the stars. Ugh.

So she'd have had a plan that didn't require my consent, or could force my consent without my knowledge. And before the end of my birthday, I'd have had an accident. I shivered but shook it off and focused on Iris.

This plan had been a long time in the making. She'd had years to figure out what she wanted and how she was going to get it. And we had hours to figure how to stop her. Okay. At first, she'd have focused on surviving, figuring out how things worked. Dad and I weren't on her menu then. She'd have had to find out about my mom in some way—

The mental fist hit so hard, I gripped the edge of the table to stay on my feet. I had to push the words out past the block. "She was here."

He frowned and shook his head. "Here?"

"That night. She—what she did—it's the reason I can't remember. I didn't just lose a night. I lost everything related to you." I waved my arms. "I lost this. She did that. Somehow she did that." I licked my lips as a far off echo of "Run, Emma!" slipped through the cracks in my memory wall. "She...must have killed my mom. She would have killed me, too, but somehow she realized I could help her. So she took my memory instead."

And now my dad was about to marry that evil, murdering inheritance-stealing dragon lady.

"My dad has already married one alien."

We'd been bouncing around ideas for what felt like hours. My screen was a mess, filled with notes, some crossed out. I don't know why I didn't erase them. But I didn't. Since the wedding was first, we'd focused on that.

"He's not going to dump his boss without proof." And what if she'd done something inside his head, too? He couldn't be...complicit. Not my dad...could he?

We didn't have proof. Okay, we had this ship and the records on its databases but, if she'd messed with his head—or his loyalty was at all divided—that might open this ship up to her, too. And, I glanced at Mazan out of the corner of my eyes, attraction was a powerful force. Just looking at him made it hard to focus on not getting blown up. I didn't know how badly my dad wanted to marry Iris. It made my stomach queasy to even think about that. But he was a guy. She was a gal. I hated her, but she'd kept herself up pretty well. She'd made sure I wasn't around her a lot, but when she did swan by, heads turned, even young guy heads. She had "it" despite her dragonlady, fist-of-iron deal.

"And he might actually, you know, like her." No matter how grownup I'd suddenly become, I couldn't use the word "hots" and "my dad" in the same sentence. Okay, I did it inside my head and it made my eyes twitch again.

Mazan's lips twitched. "You mean in the way we *like* each other?"

I looked at him then and kind of lost the plot for a few minutes, because even when things are about to blow up and evil is about to triumph over good, love still makes the world go round. As first kisses went, this one was epic. The truth was, I'd pretended to have a crush on high school Ted so I wouldn't accidentally slip and tell my friends I was in love with an alien. Like my father before me.

If the shrink had only known how truly messed up I was...

The longer we kissed—it was as if sensation, feeling returned to my world. And color. I was on a basically gray ship but it was an awesome gray. A vibrant gray. The best gray ever. My toes curled and possibly some other body parts. If the world ended now I'd be—if the world ended it would be my fault.

I eased back and inch or two and smiled at him, then sighed. As delightful as the kissing was, we were steaming up his view screen. And we had a world to save.

I had learned something, though. If my dad's brains were this scrambled, an appeal to reason wasn't going to work. Would we have to blow him up? That assumed I managed to survive his wedding night. Oh wow, wish my brain hadn't gone there.

At least it cleared my head. I stared at our screen and for some reason, this time I began to see a pattern in the chaos.

"You don't need your plan to take out the company," I muttered, rubbing both my temples. "She's already got a plan in place."

"To blow it all up? But—"

"Not blow it up, but she doesn't want us to have that tech. It's all for her. And you said she knows the risks of accelerating our tech. She's not taking any chances." There wasn't as much pushback inside my head, because this was new knowledge, not old, or so I postulated. "Want to bet she also got the cloaking technology from me?"

"It does not appear on the ship's specifications," Mazan pointed out, though thoughtfully rather than in a tone of denial.

"The ship will appear to blow up, so there won't be extra scrutiny from whoever does that. I'll bet she's even got some debris ready to scatter around. And what the team knows—it won't be complete. It isn't complete. The whole project is compartmentalized to cut down the risk of corporate espionage. We'll have a launch. There'll be a big boom and everyone will think it's just another private industry failure." There'd even be some reason all of us were on board. Or were killed by falling debris...

Mazan nodded as comprehension broke over his face. "Of course. That is the best way for her to avoid an investigation into the launch. But the ship—"

Which meant... "All we need to do is stop the wedding. And make sure the launch fails to happen." Could we manage to modify the ship just enough to make it look like it wasn't quite there yet? Remove the unearned tech and leave the ship? Though the thought of blowing up Iris...I sighed and let it go. We had to make sure Iris never left this planet.

I explained my idea and he nodded again.

"I can manage that part, but not until after the wedding. If we fail—"

He didn't have to spell it out.

"At the wedding, though—she would recognize me as Draze. I can't assist you very much other than to be there with my personal cloak." He looked adorably worried.

"We'll have to make it work," I said, rubbing a spot on my temple as the something inside me fought this old knowledge question. "How did she get it out of my brain?"

"It?" Mazan shook his head as puzzled took over his expression at the sudden shift in topic.

It was so cute I almost lost the plot again. "The illegal knowledge? We know she must have got it from me, but how?" Had she implanted something in my head? In my dad's head? This wedding was so far out of character—

Suddenly all signs of daze left Mazan. His expression turned grim and older. "We need to run a scan of your brain."

The one thing you loved to hear the man you loved say.

Chapter Five

There are things you should never know about your parents. It makes it really hard to face them across the breakfast table. And it is especially hard when that breakfast is on your dad's wedding day. The wedding I needed to stop so that Mazan didn't have to blow up ten square miles of Texas. Or they didn't give those galactic monitors an excuse to take out Earth.

"So," I stirred my cold cereal around in the bowl, "your big day. You nervous?" I know I was.

He met my gaze for a couple of seconds, then nodded. "The wedding. Of course."

Had he forgotten for a moment it was his wedding day? Words wanted to flood out my mouth, words like, "Don't do this," and "Are you freaking crazy?" I managed to hold them back. My discomfort was not helped by the knowledge I had a Kruvox implant in my brain. The analysis of it had delivered complicated and inconclusive results. One thing Mazan was sure about, it was a patched together affair with a somewhat unstable power source. Yay.

Mazan was reluctantly impressed by the jury-rigged device. And was unsure of the level of penetration Iris had achieved inside my head. If she could have seen through my eyes, she'd have already shown up at *The Entireer.* This made us cautiously optimistic she couldn't completely read my thoughts. The implant seemed to "encourage" me to avoid certain thoughts by causing me pain and rewarded me for doing what it wanted with endorphins. Which explained a lot and creeped me out. Without removing and examining it, there was no way to know if it depressed my memories or if there was some kind of subliminal hypnotism, also messing with my head. And Mazan didn't want to remove it until he found a way to stabilize the power source.

I would like to say I was getting used to the killer headache, but I'm a terrible liar. With a headache.

I know the smile I directed at my dad was over-bright because my face hurt. "I was thinking I'd pop out and buy a dress for the, um, ceremony tonight."

His eyes widened a bit and then he nodded slowly. "Perhaps Iris—"

There must have been something in my expression that breached even his level of absent-minded. "I know this is happening very fast, Emma."

Sometimes you just have to rip that bandaid off, is what I wanted to say, but I managed not to. I looked away. "It's...she's my boss, so yeah, it feels a little weird." I hesitated, then met his gaze. "I want you to be happy, dad." And for neither of us to die, possibly horribly at the hands of the Opposer. "Are you...happy? Do you love her?" Amazing how much push back I got from those questions. Did I see a struggle in his eyes? Or just the discomfort of a dad who was about to remarry?

He cleared his throat a couple more times. "There are...different kinds of...affection, Emma."

So that was a no, then.

"I'm...surprised you're doing it before the launch." I opened my mouth but couldn't say honeymoon without gagging.

His gaze slid away from mine. Did that make him embarrassed or did he know he was planning to honeymoon in outer space? How could I know the answer to that question? He was my dad. I knew daughter things about him, not...guy things.

"Iris was, well, she liked—" his words trailed off, as if he didn't know why they were getting married today.

I nodded. "Do you want me to drop you at work or are you taking today off?" He just looked surprised, so I pushed my chair back. "I'll drop you off then."

"Iris will—I'll see you at the chapel then." A look of anxiety crossed his face. "You won't be late?"

I shook my head. "No, I won't be late."

Chapter Six

I reached up to adjust my dad's bow tie, not able to meet his gaze. It was cool in the vestry, but that's not what made me shiver.

Mazan and I had a plan. Not a good one—since most of it hinged on me—but it was a plan. Okay, it was the outline of a plan. Hopefully it would achieve plan-ness before my dad said, "I do."

Peddrenth didn't seem worried. Not that I expected him to be worried, but—the truth was, I didn't know what I expected, other than a horrible death. Mazan was clearly not worried. They'd been over the ship and knew how to stop the launch, but I had to stop the wedding first. Otherwise the ten square miles were going to blow. For now, all they had to do at the wedding was to boost my morale.

Up off the floor.

I took a deep breath to steady my nerves and ran the plan over again inside my head. I had to engage in battle with the Opposer inside my head without tipping off the wedding guests that there were aliens among them. Iris had had eight years to learn how to dig around inside my head and I hadn't even tried to get inside hers for fear of tipping her off. It had seemed easy on Mazan's ship, gazing into Mazan's eyes, and dreaming of a future with the alien who loved me.

Now I faced the reality of playing happy daughter, slash, employee, while mentally gas-lighting the evil Opposer of the Draze. All the while hoping she didn't get annoyed enough to blow up my brain with that implant. Which would actually be better than ending up on a dissection table at Area 51 if the word got out that I was half alien.

I was excited about getting my own little Kobayashi Maru moment. Who didn't want to be an un-sung hero of her own world? Or a dead—

If I fail, Mazan...

She does not wish to involve the galactic monitors either, Mazan reminded me. *She will have to take care in how she responds to you.*

That was the lone bright spot. Mazan had figured out how to tap into my implant, and link it to Peddrenth's, so that he could hear and talk to me, too. It was like getting mental hugs—hugs I badly needed.

I repositioned my dad's buttonhole, moved his tie a millimeter left, then back to where it had been, gave it a pat.

"You look good." I stepped back. In his sober black suit, with the white carnation, he could get married and buried—

He grinned. "For an old dude?"

I managed not to wince at hearing my dad say "dude." He patted my hand.

"You look lovely, Emma."

"Thanks, dad." It all felt so natural, I figured Iris was sending me endorphins as a reward for being obedient.

Our minister, the painfully named Reverend Wolverscampton-wood, who had presided over my mom's funeral, poked his head in. "We're ready for you, Dr. Standish." His gaze flicked to mine, equal parts compassion and worry in there. "You look well, Emma."

I cranked up the edges of my mouth. "Thanks, Reverend Wolver-scamptonwood. I am...well." Getting his name out without a stumble gave me the confidence to gesture to my dad. "After you."

Dad hesitated a minute, then followed the Reverend out into the main part of the chapel, with me trotting obediently in their wake. Dad moved into the groom spot, then glanced around like he wasn't sure why he was there. Neither of us liked the limelight, I reminded myself, even though I hoped it was a sign his brain had been messed with. There was a minor rustle from the guests—about fifteen coworkers who looked a bit lost—and then the soft murmur of voices faded away as the organ began pumping out the familiar march. Iris popped into the door at the back, inappropriately eager to get on with the wedding and the killing.

Dad tugged at his tie as she beelined his direction, just a bit ahead of the tempo.

I tensed, even as a heightened sense of calm flooded through me. A false calm for sure.

Be strong, Emma. Peddrenth's voice inside my head was comforting.

We will be victorious, Mazan added. He was in the upper gallery that overlooked the chapel, hidden by his personal cloak. I wished I was with him. I saw a flicker of reptile tail near the last pew, then a snout poked out from behind the wooden base. I looked away as Iris closed on us. What was Peddrenth doing? Wasn't he supposed to be cloaked with Mazan?

Iris reached my dad and gave him a coy smile as she grabbed his arm and almost yanked him around to face the minister.

It was a good thing I hadn't expected to enjoy my dad's wedding.

~

With a last, somewhat discordant, wheeze, the music stopped. In the silence between that and the minister clearing his throat, I felt the wrongness of what we planned to do. Though the chapel was small, it was a sacred space, with a majesty that wasn't just about the religious fittings and soaring ceiling. Light shone through the stained glass windows, painting their patterns on stone and wood. I remembered feeling comforted by the sight of them at my mom's funeral—

When do you wish to begin?

The sound of Peddrenth's voice in my head jerked me out of the past. This was not the time to lose the plot. And surely this was a place where it was right to try to save my life, my dad's, some Texas acreage, and, possibly all of Earth.

The slow, solemn words of the wedding ceremony filtered softly into the serious silence. I glanced at my dad. Beads of sweat stood out on his forehead. He glanced at me and his lips moved soundlessly. Was it my imagination that he mouthed the word, "Help?" Or did I just want to believe that?

Let's do this. I think the words were more for me than for them.

As if on cue, I heard the minister say, "Should there be anyone who has just cause why this couple should not be united in marriage, they must speak now or forever hold their peace."

I opened my mouth, felt my throat close, and my thoughts slowed and thickened. She was stopping me—

I have just cause.

I almost let my surprise show at the sound of Peddrenth's voice in my head.

Iris jerked violently. "What did you say?"

The Reverend looked confused. "Um, should anyone have just cause—"

"I heard that." Iris snapped. "You don't have to repeat it."

My dad cleared his throat nervously. "Is there a problem my, er, dear?"

Iris looked around, saw everyone was staring at her in confusion, and gave a fake smile very much at odds with the fire bolts shooting out of her eyes. And possibly some smoke out her nose. "Bridal nerves." Her titter sounded like chalk on a blackboard. With a last, suspicious glance at me, she said, "Please continue, Reverend."

He opened his mouth to continue, but before he could speak, one of the guests gave a small shriek that rapidly grew in volume, swelling into quite the echo, thanks to the vaulted ceiling.

We all spun around. The offending lady encountered a look from Iris and stammered out, "I'm so sorry, I thought I felt...something... cold...brush against my leg..." Her voice trailed off, she looked down, then up again. "I'm so sorry..."

Another woman gave a gasp. "I felt it, too!"

The guests were shifting, stirring, looking down. Pretty sure I knew who was doing the brushing. I hoped the shadowy spaces under the pews would give him enough cover. Did I imagine the faint click of claws against the stone floor?

"I thought I saw—" This time it was a guy, one of the engineers who spoke.

"What do you think you saw?" Iris asked in a deadly tone through gritted teeth. It was weird, because she seemed to swell and her shadow against the wall was kind of dragon-like...

"Eyes..." The word echoed around the room and a flush stained his face. "Nothing. I didn't see anything."

I did. Eyes peered out of the shadow beneath the front pew. His snout hovered between a secretary's nylon-covered legs, so close I wondered why she didn't feel his breath on her ankles.

Iris's gaze swerved toward me. I swallowed. "Maybe you have a mouse, Reverend."

He opened his mouth make some kind of answer to me, but Iris impaled him with her steely gaze. His mouth moved several times, liked a landed fish, but no words came out.

"We came here to get married, not—" Her mouth worked, as if she held back a slew of expletives with an effort. "Could you continue?" Her harsh tone bounced around, building briefly before fading. She managed something sort of smile-like. "Please?"

"Of...of course." He glanced down at his book. "Dearly beloved—"

"We've done that part." The gritting of her teeth sharpened all the lines of her face, erasing her man-bait "it" factor like it had never been.

My dad looked at her in some alarm.

"You are right, of course. We were objecting, I mean, we were asking for objections, I mean—"

"What exactly do you mean, Reverend?"

Her deadly tone drained the ruddy color from his pendulous cheeks.

He is objecting to this marriage. Everyone objects to this marriage. Peddrenth sounded firm, very dragon-like. There was something symbolic about my dragon taking on the dragon lady.

"This is not funny." Iris's eyes kind of bugged out.

It was funny, but I managed to hold back the giggle, because her looks might actually kill.

Iris stared at my dad. "Surely you heard that!"

"Um, what did you hear, um," the Reverend glanced down at the sheet with their names on it, "Miss Smith?"

She stared around the room. "You can't stop this wedding. There is no *impediment*." She spat the word out.

"Im—uh—pediment?" the Reverend asked, his eyes going side-to-side in that way people do in the presence of crazy.

Her fingers curled into talons. I think she snarled. Or growled. No actual words. Just bared teeth.

I felt a need to look around because her expression was scary. I think I managed to look puzzled despite the bubble of laughter and yes, fear, trying to crawl up and out my throat.

"There's no, um, impediment, is there?" My dad sounded kind of hopeful.

"That's what I said!" Even Iris seemed startled when her words echoed back on her from all corners of the chapel. Her mouth worked for several very long seconds, then twisted up in this half snarl, half smile. "Let's just—"

In almost slow motion, the secretary in the front pew glanced down and saw Peddrenth's snout sticking out between her ankles. Her shriek rose, traveling up and up, increasing in intensity and coming back in waves as echo met echo. She jumped up and then up onto the pew. I couldn't see Peddrenth anymore, but I could track his movement as person after person leapt up on the pews.

One guy, a physicist, added fuel to the panic by yelling, "That's not a mouse! It's too big and scaly!"

I had to give the Reverend chops for not running and jumping up on something. He did cast a longing look at his closest up point—the pulpit. My dad just blinked. Iris looked incredulous. Her gaze swept the room as Peddrenth kept the panic going. And then I think she snapped.

The temper tantrum was impressive and sucked all the angst out of the room, leaving only her frustration and rage. When she finally stopped, and the echoes finally faded, the silence was not a happy one. I think even my heart quit beating.

She pointed her red laser gaze at each guest in turn. One by one, they sank down, though no one put their feet on the floor.

Iris's face was so red, her eyes so bugged out, she looked like she'd escaped from a graphic novel. And I'd swear her nose tried to extend into a snout.

My breathing stopped when her crazed gaze settled on me. Her chest rose and fell. Her lips pulled back in a snarl.

"You," she said. "You did this."

I felt my jaw drop, because yes, I planned to do something, but I hadn't actually done anything yet.

"Iris?" There was a sternness to my dad's tone that I remembered from my younger days.

With a decided twitch, her gaze flicked at my dad. "This is between Emma and I, isn't it, *dear?*"

It took all my self-control to not let even an eyelash flicker on my outside.

Why yes, it is between us, you Kruvox bitch.

I didn't know she'd heard me until her arm lifted back and swung toward me. My dad caught it two inches from my face.

"Iris?" Not just stern, but shocked now.

She shook him off, her gaze never leaving mine.

"Don't play games me with me, little girl."

I'm not a little girl anymore.

"I'll crush you like the little bug you are." Her lips stretched back, revealing sharp canines. There was an echo of Smaug-ness about her and I felt a fellow sympathy with Bilbo, who had also awakened the sleeping dragon. I felt, distantly, the unease that rippled through the benched congregation—did they see or just sense what was happening? I didn't dare look away to find out.

Bug? You're the cockroach inside my head and you call me a bug?

"It's...it's not the done thing, to...to..."

I had to give the Reverend chops for trying. Iris ignored him and another protest from my dad.

Her fingers flexed, then curled into an upturned fist, almost cutting off my oxygen supply. Somehow I managed to keep my arms at my side. I stared at her, then mentally reared back and slugged her. It felt like a real hit, sounded like one, too, though only inside my head.

She reeled back with a shocked look. The hold on my throat eased.

"Excuse...me?" Maybe it was the lack of oxygen making me light-headed. Or an adrenalin rush. Or maybe I just liked hitting Iris. Inside my head, I took up a mental boxing stance, watching her closely. She swung at me, the physical blow not even close. I mentally ducked and hit back. Then hit her again.

I don't know why she took physical shots at me. I just know it was both comical and scary watching her punching the air and staggering around from my hits.

My dad backed away, though protectively toward me, which gave me a warm fuzzy. The Reverend was less gallant, but I couldn't blame him. This was a lot of crazy to process.

She took a couple more swings. I dodged all but the last one. Managed to not rock back on my heels, though it hurt like a son-of-a-gun. I had a feeling I was going to have a real black eye.

"Do you think you're strong enough to take me on?"

My mom kicked your ass and I will, too.

She kicked off her shoes and took her version of a boxing stance, dancing to one side, then the other.

"Your mother was weak. I killed her and I should have killed you, too," she snapped.

The words echoed and re-echoed around the chapel. She froze. A look of panic twisted her face. It seemed like it took longer for the echo of the damning words to fade away.

She looked left, then right. She had no friends left in this room.

Malice replaced panic. "I'll take you down with me you little mongrel spawn of—"

I mentally punched her in the mouth and her head jerked back, a trickle of blood tracking from the side of her mouth. She wiped it away. In the fraught silence, I heard the distant sound of approaching sirens. Someone must have called the cops.

Her head jerked to the side, tilted to listen. I could almost see her trying to figure a way out. Her gaze tracked to my dad. "Did you tell them about her? That she was from another plan—"

I didn't have to think about this hit. My mental fist connected so solidly, the shock of it shuddered through me. Her eyes rolled back in her head and she dropped.

I liked the thump her head made when it hit the stone floor.

Chapter Seven

I stood next to my dad and watched them wheel his former fiancé out the double doors to the waiting ambulance. My headache was gone and my memories were back, the good and the bad. The EMT's thought she'd had a stroke. I knew better and wondered what would happen when she woke up.

We will deal with that later, Mazan told me. He'd gotten Peddrenth under his cloak and had slipped outside in the confusion. They were going to disable the ship and then—well, I wasn't sure what happened next.

I was glad to feel whole as my dad and I finally escaped the church, both divided and united by our secrets. Overhead, the now full moon—which brought out the crazies, according to one of the cops—both taunted and beckoned with what might have been.

I realized my dad was staring up at it, too.

"What's going to happen to the launch?"

He sighed "It will be cancelled."

I glanced at him, but the night hid his expression from me. "I'm sorry," I said, shifting from one foot to the other.

He looked at me then. "Are you?"

I wasn't. But I was. It had taken eight years to get him to this point. "Are you?" It was a question I could ask in the dark.

He didn't speak for several seconds. "I should be." He sighed again. "There is no fool like an old fool."

His words gave me an out. We could slide past this. Get back to

—yeah. Neither one of us could go back to that shadowy status quo. It was weird to realize now that I hadn't known, but I *had*. I'd felt it and just buried my head in the work. I'd let the days slide by, not living my life. So much time lost. Was I really prepared to lose even more? Or not live the days we had left?

I faced him. "No, dad. You aren't, you never were a fool." I glanced around. We were alone, but I lowered my voice anyway. "She...Iris...did something to you." And to me, but I wasn't sure he could handle that right now.

He turned to stare at me, the moon's light now full on his face. His gaze met mine and I saw the person, not just the dad. He'd been young once, had lived, had loved an alien—if we lived through this I really wanted to hear that story—lost her and...gone on. He'd put one foot in front of the other day after day after day. He'd stood between me and Iris, or thought he had. He loved me and I loved him.

Relief broke the shadows in his eyes. We stood there smiling at each other and I realized that even if Iris tried again, we'd won. She'd lost. Dead or alive, she wasn't going home. No one would believe anything she said after her little breakdown in the church. At least my mom hadn't died for nothing.

"Your mom would be proud," he said, almost as if he caught my thought. He went silent again and I could almost feel the wheels turning inside his head. Finally he sighed. "If she did something— then it's not over, is it?"

I shook my head. "No, it's not over yet."

I don't know what he saw in my eyes—or if he could see anything —but he was a genius. He nodded slowly, his shoulders straightening just a bit. Then he looked up at the round, gold moon. "I would have liked to take a ride around the moon."

I looked up, too, started to agree. Stopped. "Maybe we can."

Dad looked at me, his brows arched. I grinned.

"Well, I am my mother's daughter, too."

You would think that someone who had married one alien, had almost married another alien, and had spent the last eight years building a space ship, would be a little less shocked by Mazan's space ship. Of course, he'd had a more than few shocks in the last twenty-four hours.

"You...wish to fly around your moon?" Mazan had that "seeking to understand" look as his gaze tracked between me and my dazed dad.

Dad looked from the cool tech to Mazan to me. I think he wanted to say something, but instead he indicated the command seat and lifted his brows as if to ask if he could sit down. After a brief hesitation, Mazan nodded.

I stepped up to Mazan, my hand on his arm, our faces close together.

All my memories of him were back, too. I couldn't believe I had forgotten him. No wonder he'd looked so hurt. My heart ached at the thought of our lost eight years. He was my other half. No wonder I'd been a travesty of myself, a lost ghost-like creature drifting through a monochrome life. If I'd fought back sooner—no, now was not the time to look back. But wow, what a difference a day makes. Not just color, but Technicolor had returned, full and vibrant, but also bittersweet because I didn't know how much time we had left. No one was going to call us when Iris woke up. I'd probably know before they did anyway. So I smiled at Mazan and said out loud, "Yes, we really would like to fly around our moon." Inside my head, I told him, *I'm so very sorry. Can you forgive me?*

He blinked, his hands coming up to cover mine, his touch both cool and comforting.

When you look at me like that, I can forgive you anything. But what—

For letting her steal my memories of you. I smiled, totally forgetting my dad was watching. *I love you.* I inhaled his closeness, his familiar alien scent, trying to take it as deep as I could, to live as much as I could in this moment.

His hand tightened on mine. The implant that might kill me linked us together with an intensity that brought tears to my eyes. I felt his love, the loss he'd felt, his joy we were back together, his fear it wouldn't last.

We stared at each because we needed to see each other for as long as we could. The moment was perfect except for lack of kissing, but with my dad a few feet away...

He smiled, taking my breath away. It was the smile I'd missed a few days ago during our second first contact. "I will take you to the moon. To Mars. To the next galaxy. To where ever you wish to go, I will take you there."

And then he kissed me even though my dad was there and I didn't care because wow. As second kisses go, it was a whopper. I felt connected to him in every way two people could be connected, all of it heightened by that crazy implant.

Such a pity that dragon-lady Iris chose that moment to wake up.

I don't know if we actually staggered. It felt like we did as fire burned into us, a howling hurricane of rage that rode the implant from me to Mazan and back again. It hurt that she attacked him through me. It helped that she had to fight us both. We drew strength from each other. But...

She had nothing left to lose.

I felt it to my aching toenails. She would rather die than be stuck on Earth in a mental institution or jail. And she planned to take us with her. I couldn't look at my dad, couldn't see him, couldn't tell if she was after him, too. It took all my focus to hold my ground.

And it wasn't enough.

Cell by cell fire burned deeper and deeper into our minds.

It was too bad we really did use all our brains. If I'd only had to protect ten percent—

I think I felt an arm come around my waist. Not Mazan. He still gripped my hands. My dad? Had he joined us in the link—or he been there all along? I didn't have time or focus to be embarrassed by what he might have overheard.

He stopped Iris's progress, but even with dad's help, we weren't regaining lost ground.

Iris was pretty pissed. Her rage gave her power.

Or it helped her maximize the link.

I didn't know. Didn't really care. I wanted to win. I wanted to beat her.

I wanted to believe we could because love should conquer all.

Our love has conquered, Mazan told me. *She has lost.*

He'd come here expecting to die with me, I remembered now. He'd been prepared. I was behind that curve. I felt her find knowledge of his ship in our heads. She could still take out Earth if she exposed it to those monitors...

Did I feel an actual shudder under my feet? Had she somehow managed to take control? No, if she had the ship, she wouldn't be so mad. Her rage built as she felt the ship lifting off.

Who's...flying... I managed the question, barely. It felt like the edges of my mind were starting to disintegrate in the heat of her dragon fire.

We tumbled to the floor as the ship accelerated, the nose pointed toward the stars. I felt air rush out of Mazan and my dad as they tried to cushion my fall.

We were flying.

And dying.

Anger gave me the strength to push back. It surprised her for a few seconds, but she'd had a long time to be mad.

She was both old and evil. I felt her jerk at the word "old" and took pleasure it throwing it at her again and again.

Might have been bad move, since she came back with lots of pissed.

Die....die...die...

We were going to die. All three of us. I tried to protect my dad and felt, I don't know, as if he shifted me aside and stood in front of us...

A hero, like my mom...

I am so sorry, Emma...

Not your fault...

This darkness closing in was not an escape to a merciful release. It was thick and oily and malignant and so hot—it surged and sucked and licked at us, looking for and finding our weak spots. It raced around, digging in here and there and rising to break over us in a fiery wave. We cowered, clinging to each other and bracing for the end...

I love you.

I don't know who said it, me, Mazan, or my dad. Maybe it came from all of us.

In an odd counterpoint to the black slime, I thought I heard Dean Martin singing *Fly Me to the Moon*. That had to be my dad. Huge Dean fan. He always hummed that song when he was really focused...

As one, we faced her. She could kill us, but she couldn't break us—

And then, from behind her, I thought I saw a wave of light. Charged like lightning, but crackling around bright points, rather than the more typical stabbing, jagged lines. It rushed at her, at us.

This is going to be bad.

No one disagreed with me.

Not that anyone could.

I closed my eyes. Didn't matter.

Light met dark.

Even with my eyes closed, I saw it. Light shooting up like a brilliant wall. Dark rising to meet it.

The impact was kind of like touching metal after crossing carpet.

If I'd walked about a thousand miles of carpet, then touched a thousand metal bars.

I flew backwards.

Hit something.

Pretty sure I died.

~

I did not know it could hurt this much when you're dead.

For some reason, I'd expected better from the afterlife. That didn't mean I wasn't curious to see what it looked like so I opened my eyes. Big mistake. Who knew eyelids could hurt that bad? Made me want to cry, but my tear ducts were, like, no way. That will hurt even more.

I winced involuntarily and it felt like all my cells cried out in protest and then were suddenly not silenced.

A gray expanse, like the bulkhead of a spaceship, met my sore gaze. The unforgiving metal underneath my cringing back cells felt like a space ship, too. I blinked. That hurt bad enough to make me gasp—

Wait a minute. I inhaled. Exhaled. That felt like breathing. The dead didn't breathe, did they?

Maybe I'm not dead. Maybe this is Mazan's spaceship and not the afterlife.

I considered this possibility, while studying as much as I could without moving more than my eyeballs—which didn't like moving any more than the rest of me—and was forced to conclude that I was probably not dead. Was reserving judgment on whether that was the good news or the bad.

My pained gaze found Peddrenth perched in the command chair. Peddrenth...looked like he was flying the ship. My dragon was flying the ship? That was some sassy implant they'd give him. Or Draze dragons were a species smart enough to fly a spaceship.

It seemed kind of right. Dragons should fly, shouldn't they? Well, good dragons. Iris, there at the end, it was almost as if she turned into a very bad dragon—

Out the front screen of the ship, a planet hung in space. The

50

moon? It was. Not the distant moon, seen from Earth. This was the moon up close and personal. A little bit of Earth was visible against one curve. Earthrise on the Moon.

I opened my mouth to ask or say something, but all that came out was, "Ow."

Someone groaned next to me. No, not someone. *My dad.* In painful inches I turned my head his direction. He looked pretty hammered, and I think I saw little wisps of smoke coming off his head. I couldn't be sure, but his eyebrows looked a bit crispy on the ends.

The sight of the moon appeared to revive him. He struggled into a sitting position, managed to pull himself into the co-pilot's chair. With a hand that visibly shook, he reached out, as if he needed to touch the moon to believe it. That he couldn't was another indication we weren't dead.

"Hello," Mazan said, his mouth close to my aching ear.

I looked his way, not sure I believed what my ear was telling me. It hurt to smile, but I did it anyway. And touched his cheek with my own very unsteady hand. He grinned, then winced.

"I do not believe there is a nerve in my body that does not hurt."

Despite this he managed to scramble up, then reached down to help me. I needed the help. Oh, yeah, everything hurt. Even the ends of my hair, which seemed to be smoking, too. I sank into an auxiliary station seat and blinked.

Was it over or was this just a reprieve? Before I expended energy on rejoicing a possible happy ending or did any kissing, I wanted to know.

Mazan kept hold of my hand as he sank into the seat next to mine. That hand was pretty much my only happy body part. My head felt oddly empty. Had Iris fried my brain?

"Your father is very fond of the moon," Mazan said, looking puzzled by this.

"He's been trying to get here for a long time," I explained.

Peddrenth turned, leaving one claw on the helm. *I hope you do not mind?*

It seemed Peddrenth was of the "seek forgiveness rather than permission" type of dragon. Which was fine with me. I'd wanted to get to the moon, too.

The edges of Mazan's mouth twitched. "No. I do not mind."

My dad turned and looked at Mazan, then at Peddrenth, then at me. He looked like he wanted to ask, but couldn't manage it.

I remembered that feeling from...was it just yesterday? No—I looked at my watch—it was the day before yesterday. Today was my birthday. The birthday girl had lived. For now.

I made a little gesture, which I quickly wished I hadn't. "This is Peddrenth, dad."

Peddrenth moved his head and waved a paw. Pretty sure it wasn't an act of submission since his beard flared black.

"Didn't you used to have—"

"—a bearded dragon? Yes, I did. He left and then he came back." But I wasn't bitter.

Yes, you are.

Okay, yeah, I was. "Sorry. It's not your fault."

My dad blinked. "Is he...talking?"

"My dragon?" Dad kind of nodded. "He's thinking. Telepathically. He has an implant." I turned to Mazan. "Speaking of, what about the implants in our heads?"

Mazan shifted around to his station and started tapping things. He stopped and spun slowly around to look at us. "According to the latest scans, both of your implants appear to be non-active."

I leaned over and took a look. "The circuitry has been fried." I thought about the wave of light I'd seen. Or thought I'd seen. "What did it?"

I could almost see the wheels turning inside my dad's head.

"The full moon," he said and looked out the view screen. "If we passed through the Earth's magnetotail..." He paused, considering.

The magnetotail extends beyond the orbit of the moon, Peddrenth's tone was musing. *It can cause electrostatic discharges, particularly strong ones when the moon is full.*

I blinked. "Electrostatic discharge?" I asked. I looked at my dad, who shrugged, so I turned to Mazan. "Would that do it?"

"They were constructed out of inferior materials, unlike Peddrenth's," Mazan said. "That is why I was reluctant to attempt removal when the power source was active and unstable."

"Did you think that an electrostatic discharge might destroy our implants?" I asked Peddrenth.

Peddrenth regarded me with much solemnity. *Your parental unit told me to fly you to the moon.*

I opened my mouth to press the issue, then decided not to.

Whether he knew what he was doing or not, we'd been saved from the dragon by my dragon. Very cool.

"We should be able to safely remove them from your brains now," Mazan said.

He sounded awfully cheerful for someone talking about digging around in my head. My dad looked as dubious as I felt.

"Can you, um, beam them out?" I asked, tacking on a hopeful smile. I tried to remember if my years of Draze schooling had covered implant removal.

Mazan tried not to smile. "It will only hurt a little."

I opened my mouth to protest and realized he was teasing me. Mazan was teasing me. The edges of my mouth curled up and a small chuckle slipped out. An actual laugh would hurt too much. But there was a nice lightness born of relief bubbling in the air around us.

"It's over." My gaze connected with his. "Isn't it?"

We'd stopped the wedding. Kept Earth from blowing up. Defeated the Kruvox Opposer. Ridden to the moon. We had not died.

Happy birthday to me.

Mazan smiled. Peddrenth's beard flared black, but in a happy way. He turned back to the controls.

I recall a promise to take you to Mars...

His claw wrapped around the helm control and moved it. I stole a look at Mazan. Caught him looking at me. His brows arched and he indicated the hatch. I looked at my dad. He was staring at the view screen, his jaw just a bit dropped, as the moon started to dwindle. I grinned and nodded.

Mazan pulled me upright and yes it hurt, but this looked a lot like a happy ending and a happy beginning. There was still stuff to sort out, but for now...

Mazan's arms closed around me, his head bent, his lips finding mine...

Third time was the charm, I thought a bit hazily, especially when it came to kisses...

Nebula Nine

About Nebula
Nine

Lives at risk. Time out of whack. Is it a test? Or a trap?

Special Forces Temporal Agent, Jane Jones finds the thrill of going where she'd never gone before giving way to wondering what is wrong on Nebula Nine Space station. Is the Agency testing her loyalty? Or has she jumped into a trap? As her doubts grow, so do her fears of destabilizing her own timeline and disappearing from existence. And who is Ryder Jaxon?

Ryder Jaxon doesn't trust anyone. And he sure doesn't trust things that only he can see. So when he starts seeing visions of the station blowing up, and he has to work with a woman he *wants* to trust, he wonders if he should take a long vacation.

It's a trip into crazy for both of them as they race to stop a madman intent on destroying the station. But when they realize how completely they have both been betrayed, they must make a choice that will change more than their past history.

≈

Chapter One

J ane Jones, Special Forces Temporal Agent, dumped her pack on the bunk and sank down next to it, rubbing her eyes. It didn't erase the transit-migraine-induced halo from her vision, so she applied pressure to the back of her neck, wincing as her icy fingers found the knots. That helped enough for her to rip open the pack and find her meds. The berth was so small, she didn't have to get up to reach the sink. The Agency had gone super cheap for this gig. Good thing she didn't suffer from claustrophobia.

She pulled a cup from a dispenser and waved it under the miniature faucet. Bright green fluid spurted into the cup. She sniffed it, which was totally pointless, since her sense of smell would be MIA for at least half an hour. It was a hard habit to break, she thought wryly. The time jumpers called it fog head. Not only were her senses messed up, but fog head blunted the wonder of time traveling, left her feeling remote from herself and her surroundings. She tossed back her meds and washed them down with the green stuff.

"Not that bad." A little peaty with a hint of metal aftertaste, but that was probably the fog head. Everything tended to taste like metal after a jump. At least the meds hit the pain centers fast. The halo around her vision reduced in size. Too bad the meds made the fog head worse. Some agents liked to sleep right after a transit. Some liked to work, or walk it off. Jane tended toward the latter, since she had trouble sleeping out of her own time and space. And this out-of-time was in a whole different star system. She'd been a history, not a science, teacher before being recruited by the Agency. She'd never expected to travel through time, let alone make it into space.

For some reason, the fog head felt worse this transit, tired tugging at her lids. She eyed the bunk, mentally measuring herself against it. Not even slightly her length. She perched on the edge, distantly aware the mattress had no give. She rubbed her eyes again, then extracted the cylinder from the specially sealed pocket in her pack. She fingered the long cool tube before keying in her personal code. The metal side rose with a soft purr. Inside was a paper roll with her final instructions and a small media chip. The roll was thinner than usual—which should have been a good sign, but even the fog head couldn't keep a frown from forming as she read the few words. What the—

There had to be more than this. She turned the paper over, but the reverse side was blank. She took the chip and inserted it in her wrist band. The hologram wasn't that much more informative. Five faces. Five names. And a location. The station's casino? That would explain why there'd been so much focus on the casino security footage during her prep for the mission. But she could count on one finger the times she'd been in a casino in her life. When they sent her in, butts needed kicking—occasionally with extreme force. Jane had been surprised at her aptitude for ass kicking and suspected her teachers had been as well.

Which brought her back to what the heck was she doing here?

She turned off the holo, but left the chip in place. It was possible that the techs at the Agency would go back in time and update it with more data. She inserted the roll back into the cylinder. The side whirred back into place. There was a soft sizzle, followed by a puff of smoke as the paper disintegrated. She frowned again. Why did it feel like she should have kept the scant instructions?

The narrow walls closed in as unease she couldn't quite access bubbled behind the fog head. All she knew to do was to go forward. She jumped up and yanked open the hatch door. Outside on the narrow walkway she almost bumped into a couple headed toward the bank of lifts that hugged the central core of the space station. She pressed against the metal wall to let them pass, then turned to follow them, but had to stop as a wave of something breached her fog head. She grabbed the railing, staring down at her hand. It was her hand. But not her hand. Her skin prickled, lifting the hairs on the back of her neck.

Had to be a memory bleed-through. Who knew how many times the Agency had had to reset this time line?. Only—that tended to manifest more like *deja vu*. This felt as if she were inside a stranger— a familiar stranger. It faded as quickly as it came, but left questions stabbing at the fog, trying to breach her detachment.

When the fog cleared, would she find answers or more questions?

Chapter Two

Jon Lee wondered who they would send this time. Would it be someone he knew? The Agency tried to limit interaction between agents, but they couldn't completely cut them off from each other. They'd all go mad without someone to talk to that understood. It didn't really matter who they sent. No agent could hide from him. There was a protocol to be followed upon arrival, a protocol that could be seen if one knew what to look for. And he did. It was almost too easy. The agent would arrive. Do just what he or she had been told to. And the jaws of his trap would snap closed. That's when the real fun began. It was ridiculously easy to spin them into destabilizing and erasing themselves from time.

It was ironic that the better trained they were, the faster they went down. Thanks to the Agency's "training," they had no defense. Some did better than others, but none had provided more than a mild challenge. Almost, he wished for a real challenge. He was so bored, he almost came to this time iteration as Jon Lee—just to see if anyone at the Agency would notice. But in the end, caution prevailed. The security chief, Ryder Jaxon, was too good for this backwater space station.

Should have chosen a different site when he realized. Oh well, everyone made mistakes. Choosing Nebula Nine for his anomalous time event was a minor one compared to joining the Agency, compared to signing on their dotted line for their "adventure of a lifetime."

But they'd made a bigger mistake when they'd recruited him.

And now he could clean up all the mistakes. His and theirs.

"You in or out, Green?"

Lee looked up from his cards, pretended to consider, because that's how the game was played. It didn't matter that he knew all the plays, all the hands, for all the days until he reset this time again.

"Raise." He could have cheated. But he didn't. It wasn't worth the risk. Time Travel 101 insisted that even small changes could ripple around in unexpected ways. So he kept his play as consistent as possible. Besides, this game didn't matter. It wasn't the game he was here to play.

Under his lashes, he studied them. Did any of them remember dying over and over? Or playing this hand, living this day, again and again? Bleed-through was a real risk when one did multiple time resets. He didn't need his poker partners getting nasty *déjà vu* and changing their play.

He glanced beyond the table, what he could manage to see without moving or creating a "tell." Like an errant breeze, he felt—not enough of a something to call it unease. Not actual change, but possibly the prelude to change?

It couldn't be a full response team. That many people arriving here would cause more than a flutter in time's fabric. And he'd kept his game clean. Kept himself off the Agency's radar, other than the trap, of course. If he was wrong, he wouldn't have time to know it.

Deletion. So much more neutral sounding than kill. Destroy. Erase. Because they wouldn't just delete him from the moment. Once they knew who he was—the desire to tell someone was an acid eating at his resolve that he fought every time reset—they'd try to go back and excise him out of existence. At some point, someone had to notice the Agency was shrinking, not growing.

He'd bought the company line at first. Believed the garbage about protecting the time line, hadn't realized until it was too late what was really going on. They didn't have the right to decide who deserved to exist and who didn't. No one did. Well, they erased the wrong person. He couldn't bring her back. But he could make them pay. He would stop them before they stopped him.

Time started a slow spin and he reined in his thoughts. Didn't need to get disoriented in the middle of an operation.

He did a careful survey, but everything looked exactly the same. Which brought him back to wondering, was the agent here? Had they told him or her how many agents had already failed to take him out? He smiled to himself. Oh, right, they couldn't. Because there was no record of deletions they hadn't sanctioned.

He played with the tiles in front of him, then tossed one into the center of the green table.

"Call," he said.

Chapter Three

R yder Jaxon was a practical man, as grounded as one could be living in a great big spinning top in space. He didn't believe in anything he couldn't see with his eyes, couldn't shoot with currently available weapons. Granted, he couldn't see his instincts, but they were as real as his sight and sound and smell. His gut, his instincts, had been honed in the field against the enemy. He could smell trouble coming.

What he didn't do, what he never did, was see things that weren't there. Didn't see dead people. Didn't see explosions that hadn't happened. Didn't have premonitions or *déjà vu* or any of that other shit.

Until today.

He'd opened his eyes this morning and the station exploded into flames around him. It had been so real, he'd thought, "I'm dead." Only he wasn't. The vision faded leaving him sitting up in his berth with his heart hammering in his chest. He'd shaken it off. But it kept happening. In the shower. In the lift. Inside the security center the flames had surged up through the floor, stopping him in his tracks for several seconds. Luckily no one had noticed. He mostly trusted his team, but this was, well, he didn't want to get hauled off for a visit to the head ripper.

When he couldn't take sitting down any longer, he left his office. That wasn't unusual. Sometimes he needed to walk, to think, to remind himself why he'd come here, and remember that being bored was a relief after too many years of not being bored. His team knew he liked to to prowl the station. That he liked to get his real eyes on what was happening. So no warning flags would go up.

But this was the first time he'd walked with images—visions or hallucinations, he wasn't sure which—of the station blowing up. Again and again. He tried to ignore it, but this wasn't something he could ignore or will away. Maybe he'd spent too much time out here. Needed to get dirt side for a while.

He'd almost decided to put in for leave, to book the first transport out—but what if it was a premonition or something? Keeping this station safe was his job. He took a deep breath and headed into the heart of the fire.

Chapter Four

J ane was pretty sure Space Station Nebula Nine had never been sleek or aerodynamic, and a hundred years of refinements had only exacerbated its ungainly lines. It had began its existence as a modest research station and had been randomly expanded to become a defensive platform when war broke out. It somehow managed to survive long enough to become a sort of way station serving travelers coming into or leaving the system. It was not a prime—or a minor—location. More like a middle-of-the-space-lanes stopover lurking near a minor nebula.

Despite that, the history teacher Jane had been felt an irrational affection for it. *I could be happy here.* Okay, that was weird. She was happy. Wasn't she? Well, not just at this moment. The strange feelings had to be a side effect of—well, a side effect. Just because this particular effect had never happened before—she pushed that thought away. At a junction she hesitated, casting a longing look toward the station proper. Would be fun to play the actual tourist and take a tour. But she had a job to do.

As she walked, the fog began to recede. Her sense of smell came back, too. Not exactly a blessing. The scrubbers were as old as the station, it seemed. The air was on the stale side, with notes of sweat, food, old perfume, and some kind of fuel. She passed a small bistro with a few tables clustered around the entrance and had that odd, out-of-body experience again. Her steps faltered as she remembered sitting there, the fork lifting something to her mouth, and someone sitting across from her. Someone she needed to see—

Jane felt a bump, heard a muttered apology. She looked around, yanked out of the memory-but-not-a-memory, but whoever had bumped her was already lost in the crowd. Lots of people teemed along this shop-lined corridor. Jane's hands curled into fists. Why had a knot formed in her throat? Why did fear once more push against the remnants of fog head?

Nothing about this mission felt right. She started forward again, but her steps were as slow as her thoughts.

Right was a mission brief that had *details*. Details such as the how, the why and the who, not to mention a, "this is how we expect you to fix this." Always, always her mission brief was detailed and specific, so specific sometimes it was annoying.

She checked her chronometer. Three days. More time than usual, but was it enough time to assess this mess, let alone figure it out?

What the heck was going on? She stopped again. Unless...

Was this a test? She'd heard of agents getting sent on fake missions designed to test their commitment to not going off script. But there was no script.

So...a setup?

The prickle at the back of her neck worsened as the fog thinned some more. Now she considered the run-up to her mission. Let herself recall and consider the reactions of the techs helping her get ready. They'd seemed the same, for the most part, but had there been more tension than usual? An extra edge of unease emanating from them? Why would she even think about being set up? Did she doubt the Agency? Did she doubt her mission?

She'd seen the explosion start, she reminded herself, in the security videos the advance team had collected. The explosion would happen in three days if she didn't stop it. That wasn't a vague unease. It was reality.

Maybe she had a particularly bad case of transit sickness. She rounded a corner and heard music and the muted, but still shrill, sounds of lots of people talking. Her head started to ache again, dully but a pain holding its ground against the meds. Why her? She wasn't a gambler. Okay, it wasn't unheard of for an agent to use future knowledge to beef up their retirement nest egg. But all she could do was recognize slot machines and a roulette table, and the only thing she'd ever done with a pack of cards was play Solitaire. Surely there was a middle ground between clueless and addict?

Her headache throbbed in time with the clock ticking down to the big boom. The very big boom. Remembering that was a dash of mental cold water. Green cold water? She almost smiled and that helped her regain her balance somewhat. Time to focus on why she was here.

The closer she got to the casino entrance, the louder the crowd noise. Now machine sounds could be heard. She actually recognized the slot machine racket, from that one time in a casino. That was kind of funny. Not funny were the bright lights that stabbed into her pupils. Suddenly the child-sized bunk looked pretty appealing. But... three days. She made herself go inside and look around. Lots of glitz and glitter, but also signs that this place was as tired as the station that housed it. Now she felt time's flow here, felt this reality meld with the video she'd watched. She knew these faces. She'd seen them, seen this place from every camera view possible, watched hours of security footage right up until the moment it was blown out of existence.

It was the same. Only it wasn't. Now she was here. She was part of it. She wasn't one of them she told herself. Her tech kept her from completely integrating with this time and would yank her out just before the blast if she failed her mission. Only she didn't feel separate. Not anymore. Again that sense that this mission was different washed over her.

Test?

Setup?

Something else?

There was a slight tremor to Jane's hand as she traded credits for casino chips—did they still call them that? She didn't plunge into the melee. She knew what she was supposed to do. If this was a test, then that was exactly what she should do. But if it was setup?

The prickle raised the hairs on the back of her neck as flight or fight kicked through the remaining shreds of the fog head. She calmed her breathing, her clenched fists out of sight in the pockets of her time appropriate attire. When she felt she could, she stretched out her time senses, taking a sounding to see if this time felt off.

It was, seriously off, but there was more. She felt it. And then smelled it. Acrid. Nasty.

Malice. Possibly more. Her brain flinched back, but her brain named it. Evil.

Like an oil slick on water, she sensed something riding on the conditioned air. Someone? The presence felt male to her, but she couldn't be sure. Just knew he sought her. Wanted her. Wanted her gone. The instinct to flee built as adrenaline surged, but her knees lacked the integrity. Through a haze of red, she looked around, saw a slot machine close by. Somehow she reached it. The feel of the cold handle helped. She fumbled for one of the coins they'd given her, managed to get it in the slot and pulled the handle down. Her body pressed against its solid length. She clung to it, slowed her breathing, though it took an effort. Only then did she take a careful look around.

And saw them.

All five suspects seated at the same table?

And one extra man, with his back to her. He tossed some chips in the center of the green table and looked to his left, his profile bland to the point of ordinary. And yet, a memory flickered at the back of her mind, a memory that refused to fully surface. She did remember feeling the same flick of malice she sensed now.

Her five suspects all together with the dubious unknown?

Was going to have to go with trap, not test.

Chapter Five

Ryder followed the visions, curiosity trumping his distaste and unease. In the past, he'd only seen the aftereffects of explosions. Against his will, he found it interesting to study the blast from the inside, to follow it back to its source. Though as he got closer to what appeared to be the epicenter—the casino—the frequency of the visions began to decrease. If he hadn't seen the explosion flow backwards into the casino, he might have thought he'd lost the trail. But he could see it, though once inside he lost the path.

Ryder wasn't the right kind of gambler to enjoy the casino. And the owner had his own security in place. He didn't like him treading on his turf. He went in sometimes, so they'd know he could. This time was different. It was almost a relief to go where the visions, apparently, couldn't or didn't want to follow. Though it bugged him to lose the trail.

He started around the perimeter, had almost made a complete circuit without a single vision. Was beginning to wonder—when he saw her standing at one of the slot machines. What caught his attention first was the long pause between pulls on the handle. And she wasn't looking at the screen, the spin of the fruit. Instead she stared toward the poker tables. She was a tourist, slight of build, with brown eyes and hair. He was at enough of an angle from her to see the hint of lost in the eyes, to see her lower lip tremble before the line of her mouth straightened and thinned. And then, as if she felt him watching, she looked his direction.

A buzz started inside his head. His throat tightened. Felt like it took too long for her gaze to connect with his...

And then they stared at each other.

The buzz ramped up, so loud he couldn't hear, couldn't see...

She turned abruptly and walked out, the way she moved at odds with the bewildered tourist bit. There was a hint of ex-military in walk—she stumbled, and he wondered if he was getting paranoid. He gave an internal shake but didn't take his gaze off her until she passed out of his sight. And then he wondered why he felt a stab of — what? He didn't know her, so he couldn't miss her. Who was she? If she was ex-military, she should have been flagged during arrival screening. He'd look her up on the security vids. Should be able to get a name.

A shrill burst of laughter cut through his distraction, jerking him back to the present. The present? Where else would he have been? Damn, maybe he did need a break. So she'd been looking at the poker tables. What had interested her there? He studied the section, not seeing anything unusual.

It was just a twitch, but hardcore gamblers tried to avoid any kind of tell. Other than the actual play, they didn't move, almost didn't blink. Except for the twitcher. Which was no big deal—

The table where the twitcher sat with five other men erupted, a geyser of flame rising from the center of the table and spreading like lava toward him. He took a half step back, as the fingers of fire reached out for him—

Then the blast faded as abruptly as it had appeared.

Which brought him back to, what the hell?

Chapter Six

Damn the man. What had brought Ryder Jaxon to the casino? The security chief's passage caused ripples in time, like something solid tossed into a still pool. A pebble or a boulder? Hard to say. For a few seconds, he'd felt something, but then Ryder showed up. At least Ryder had moved on without looking at him as if he'd tagged him for further study. Not that Ryder would signal that. So Jon waited to see how his time bubble would react to the unexpected intrusion.

Gradually Jon relaxed. No sign of big changes. Not that he could get a really good look around from his place at the table. For the first time, its limitations irked him. But cards were going down exactly the same. And he'd feel a big change with his time sense.

Where was the agent? Every other reset, someone had showed up by now. He allowed himself a stretch of arms and shoulders between hands. Signaled for something to drink, which gave him a better look around. The sight of everyone doing exactly the same thing annoyed him. Made him want to set the bomb off and move on.

But he had the pieces in play. Changing it now, that might be more of a tell than just playing this last hand out to the end. Someone had to be here. What was he or she waiting for?

Chapter Seven

Jane didn't remember leaving the casino. One minute she was there staring at the man, the next she was back in the corridor. She got bumped again and managed to move to the edge of the flow, finding a blank wall to lean against. Her knees felt gone and her heart thumped in her chest. Inside her head, her brain felt like glass with cracks spreading across the surface, leaking pain from some hidden place that she hadn't known was there.

She stared straight ahead, feeling again the moment when she saw him. That was the blow that had cracked her memories. She'd been clinging to the handle, frozen as evil crept closer and closer to sensing her and then—the breath of clean and crisp had blown past her, sending malice back to its owner.

Her breathing shallowed. She made herself take deeper breathes, as fear of what lay hidden deep inside her own head dried her throat.

Who was that man? Why did it feel like he mattered? She'd never seen him before—at least, he hadn't been in the security footage she'd seen. Was he a time deviation? But even if he was, the sight of him shouldn't put her into shock. Her skin was clammy and she clenched her teeth to keep them from chattering. She saw a few glances cast her direction and straightened. Forcing upright, she forced herself to saunter, at least she hoped that was how her walk looked. She still felt unsteady.

She saw the museum gift shop, almost empty, and turned toward it. Wove through the aisles until she was at the back, standing in front of a model of the space station. She reached out, lightly touching one of the arms sticking out from the ungainly thing.

"You're not supposed to touch the model," a deep voice said, off to her right.

She jerked around and there he was again. Broad, pulsing with leashed power, his blond hair brushed back from a high, proud brow. His eyes were impossibly blue and shattered the barrier inside her head. Time pulsed around him. He wavered in, out, then back into view.

He flashed something badge-like. "I need you to come with me," he said.

The words echoed inside her head. She felt her knees losing integrity as a black hole formed at his back. His hand gripped her elbow, but he couldn't save her as the hole sucked her in.

Chapter Eight

The med tech looked up from the cuff monitoring Janet Williams—if that was her real name.

"She should wake soon, sir."

Ryder thanked him, then jerked his chin toward the door. With some surprise, the tech left, the door sliding closed behind him.

The patient looked better than she had when she'd collapsed in the gift shop. He'd barely caught her before she hit the floor. He'd felt a moment of unease, wondering if her collapse was a trick to get close to him, but her ashen color was no trick. Her skin had been icy, her breathing rapid and shallow.

With his arms around her, he almost—but that was crazy. He didn't feel anything. Ever. Feeling was for fools. He frowned. Where had that thought come from? He'd never let a woman close enough to be played for a fool.

She could make him one. He flinched, shoved the thought away. She shouldn't be *on* his station. He'd run her face through the software for days back, while he waited for her to regain consciousness. She sure as hell hadn't come in through the front door. She had a lot of explaining to do.

As if she heard his thought, she shifted, sighed, and opened her eyes. First she looked away from him, then her head began to turn in his direction. He felt that strange sense of waiting and of time slowed. Why did it take so long for her to look at him? Her gaze hit his like a stun shot, almost rocking him back on his heels. She blinked once, then again. More color appeared to leech from her face. Her mouth opened. Closed. She pushed herself up, letting her legs hang over the edge of the table and studied him.

He'd thought her eyes were brown, but now he could see green and gold in there as a slew of emotions came and went.

"I'm Ryder Jaxon, head of security for Nebula Nine." He hesitated, but felt he had to ask, though he made the question perfunctory. "How do you feel?"

She looked down at the med cuff, then tugged at it until it released and set it next to her on the table, her lips twitching. "I'm fine, thank you."

Was there a bit of irony in her thanks? The husky sound of her voice ignited a familiar—and inappropriate—response in his gut. The almost smile faded to a frown that pulled her neatly arched brows together. She studied her surroundings.

"I was in...the gift shop."

"You collapsed." He hesitated, but he had to know. "I need to know how you got on my station without passing through security screening."

Beyond the name she'd used to register, another name drifted just out of reach. Had he run into her during an op? It didn't feel like that. His go-to emotion was suspicion, but it wasn't coming online like it was supposed to. He tried for dispassionate as he stared at her. His connection to dispassionate was sketchy, too. It shouldn't—it *didn't* matter that he liked the sound of her voice. Or that this close she looked less ordinary and more interesting. Her scent drifting on the recycled air was light and pleasant. She reminded him of what he liked about women. Worse, there was something about her that invited...trust.

Only he couldn't accept that invitation. She might be the source of his problem. This was not the time to think he could like her. And then a worse thought popped inside his head. *I did like her.* That was impossible, was as impossible as the visions appearing and disappearing around them both. For whatever reason, the visions had returned during his retreat from the casino.

Her legs swung gently as she studied him with frank curiosity, her head tilted to one side. The colors in her eyes kept shifting, getting more green, then more gold, then sliding back to brown. The silence didn't appear to make her uncomfortable, but he'd activated tech to monitor her vital signs and this showed she was not as calm as she looked. Not afraid, his monitoring geek told him via his comm. She was uncertain. Why wasn't she afraid? As if she heard that, the edges of her mouth twitched again.

"How did you get on my station?" he asked again, his voice harder than before.

"How." The edges of her mouth twitched. "You wouldn't believe me if I told you."

"I'd believe the *truth*." The thought of her lying to him twisted something in his gut. Like an old wound had been hit. What old wound?

"Would you?" It wasn't said like a question directed at him, but more as if she asked herself if she believed him.

At the assessing nature of her gaze he bristled. He wasn't the one who'd snuck onto Nebula Nine.

Her gaze reconnected with his, held it for several seconds. He saw, or felt, her reach a decision. Felt a need for her to tell him the truth that was out of proportion to the situation.

"The truth then."

Against his will, he felt relief.

"For your ears only." When he just stared she added, "You need to turn off monitoring."

"Bad idea, sir," his geek said in his ear.

She shrugged, as if to say, "Take it or leave it." But her eyes told him this truth was for his ears only. Considering the crazy visions, he couldn't disagree with her.

"Do it," he said, flicking off his comm and removing it. Felt a jolt of shock at himself. It was crazy. Out of character. He didn't trust—but he did. He trusted his team. And he trusted her. Or he would if she didn't kill him. She had no weapons on her, though a good operative didn't need them. He shifted to a more alert stance and was obvious about it.

She grinned, the laughter springing into her eyes and sparking them with gold. His heart jumped in his chest, which should have felt uncomfortable. But it wasn't. His hands curled into fists at his sides. He didn't move. Or smile back. Wasn't easy. Because he wanted to move toward her *and* smile. For a second, a memory flashed at the edges of his mind. A memory where he had done both those things before...before...he shook the memory away.

"I'm kind of flattered you think I can," she said, her gaze doing a run down, then up his person. She lifted her hands, palms out, then pointed to her top. "I need to get something out. Or you can get it." A provocative edge changed her grin to something that lit a small fire in his mid-section.

"Keep your hands where I can see them. Just lift the edge until—" His throat dried.

Her eyes warmed behind the amusement. With hands and fingers in full view, she lifted the edge of her shirt until a pale belly button came into view. He wanted to tug at the abruptly tight top of his uniform. He didn't. At first he didn't see why all the—

His gaze jerked up. Her brows arched, but nothing else moved. She just waited. "Peel off one edge," he directed, his voice hoarse. Whoever had done the match with her skin...well, they knew what they were doing. He didn't expect the stab of—something that followed that thought. The thought of other fingers than his touching her skin...

His fingers flexed, closed. He straightened them.

Again, taking great care, she lifted one edge, until another ID folder appeared against her skin. The color was familiar. Too familiar.

"Give it to me."

She extracted it with her thumb and index finger and held it out. He took it. Warmth from her body still clung to the blue surface. His gaze flicked down, then back up at her. He flipped it open and glanced down. He looked up again. Jane Doe. Seriously? Who named anyone that? The IGSF wasn't usually that obvious. "Don't remember you from the IGSF."

"I don't remember you either," she said, that grin quivering at the edges of her mouth again. A grin quickly followed by uncertainty.

The Intergalactic Security Force kept cells compartmentalized. And she looked young. He'd been out for five years.

She gave a small, puzzled shake of her head. "Not from there..." She frowned, her gaze speculative as she studied him once more.

As if his brain had been waiting for a break in his defenses, memory flickered again. That sense of...the memory faded, leaving a sense of frustration behind. A sense of...loss. Could the IGSF have messed with his memory? Could they do that? This memory felt... different. Not part of his time in the service. It felt like it was part of...this time. That was crazy, but he still tried to retrieve the memory. Only the more he tried, the more it retreated.

Her gaze was intent, as if she were waiting, but for what? He looked down, closed the ID and handed it back to her.

"It's a fake." A good one, but it had to be a fake. He didn't know why he knew. He just did.

"It's for real," she qualified.

"But you're not."

She looked pleased. She shook her head. "No, not IGSF but—" she stopped and looked uncertain now. "I am here to help." She glanced around, even behind her at the solid gray wall. Her lips compressed and then she almost appeared to brace herself.

What did she think could happen in here? His mouth settled in grim lines. "Thank you," he didn't try to modify the irony, "but I think we—"

"I have credible intelligence that a bomb is going to be detonated on this station."

Her words shook him, not because of what she said, but because of what he'd seen. He'd hoped, well, he'd hoped it was stress or something. She could be wrong, lying, he reminded himself, but he looked at her and he knew she wasn't lying. He always knew. But just because she believed her words, that didn't make them true.

"And does your *credible* intelligence mention who? Or where? When?"

Instead of getting defensive, she sighed. "It should. Usually it does, but this time..." She half shrugged.

He frowned. His frown usually made the targets of it tremble and go soft at the knees. She didn't even blink.

"Who do you work for? What's the source of your intel?"

She hesitated again, flicked that glance around as if she expected someone to leap out of the closet and yell, "Stop!"

She bit her lip for a long moment. Sighed. "The Agency. I work for the Agency. Or I did." A slight shudder shook her small frame.

He thought he knew the names of all the major intelligence services. But she still wasn't lying. Yet, he reminded himself. He arched his brows. "Did?"

"Telling you about them is a violation of my terms of employment," she admitted.

They sent her in alone? With sketchy intel? Sounded like a job she needed to get out of. "What's their purview?" Why would they be interested in a bomb out here? he wondered.

She hesitated again. Looked down, then up. "Time."

"Time?" he shook his head. "What?"

"I'm a Special Forces Temporal Agent."

She believed it. He could see that. He didn't look away because you weren't supposed to with the crazy ones, or so he'd heard. But how did she get her hands on an IGSF ID? That took a special level of crazy. Oddly enough, he believed she was SF. She had the air of someone who knew how to walk the walk. No one could fake that.

"I told you that you wouldn't believe me." Now she sounded amused. And a bit relieved. "But ask yourself, how did I get past your security?"

"I'm asking *you*."

"I came via a time portal." She sounded almost apologetic. A bit resigned. "When they approached me to work for them, I didn't believe them either."

"So, convince me," he challenged. "Show me something."

Her grin was wry this time. "I wish I could, but my tech is pre-programmed, probably so we won't play with it. I think, I'm pretty sure, it won't pull me out in time to avoid the blast, which it's supposed to do. I'm already too late." Her gaze lifted to his and the look in them shook him. "Something is wrong with this operation. Very wrong."

She believed it. And she was scared. He didn't need monitoring tech to see it. To feel it. To feel something more, something he hadn't felt since he left the IGSF.

Evil.

Not from her, but from somewhere out there. He'd told her he'd know if she spoke the truth. Hadn't seen the trap coming. Could he believe *her* truth? As he stared, the vision came again, red and gold and blue and green erupting through the floor between them and spreading out. He'd have flinched if he hadn't seen the same thing all day. He must have twitched. Her eyes narrowed.

"You see it, don't you?" She didn't wait for him to agree or disagree. She half leaned back, shaking her head. "That means someone is doing resets, but why?"

"Resets?" he heard himself ask.

"Resetting time. It happens, has to when you want to fix something, but there are strict limits on how often you can do it. Memory begins to bleed through and that can cause even more problems. Paradoxes and other crap." She rubbed her face. "It's kind of brain bending. Time, well, yeah. It makes your brain hurt if you think about it too much."

He believed her. His brain hurt.

She lowered her hands. "But if you can see it, then maybe we can track it to the source."

He hesitated. If he said the words, he didn't just believe the crazy, he became a part of it, became an accomplice to crazy. But if she was right and the explosion he kept seeing was real, then he had to act. He had to use the means at hand to stop it. Even the crazy means at hand. It felt harder because he wanted to believe her. He wanted her to be not crazy. He wanted to trust her. And so he hesitated. This time probed his heart, his gut, his instincts. This was too important for him to get it wrong.

Around them the explosion faded once more, the room was still there, still boring. For now. If he failed, she'd die too, or so she claimed. He didn't know why that was the tipping point. It just was.

"I already have," he said.

Her back straightened. "You saw where it starts?"

He nodded. "At a table in the casino, but I don't know how—what explosive can take out the whole station?"

"It's from the future. That's how we, they knew it was wrong. That's why I was sent in. At least, that's what they told me."

"You don't believe them?"

"I did." That frown pulling her brows together again.

"And now you don't."

Her gaze lifted to his, worry clearly present in her eyes. "And now I don't."

Chapter Nine

Something was wrong. Jon bent his head to his cards, suddenly sick of it all, the game, his companions, this place. He glanced around, trying to feel where the threat came from, but nothing was different. He should know. He'd been here so many times.

This would be the reset. He'd take down this agent, then let this station blow up and stay blown. Move on. Find a new place to craft his trap.

He didn't have to look at his hand as he put the cards down, one at a time. If everything was the same, why did it feel like it was different? There was no unusual interest—

He stiffened, his gaze sliding slowly toward the middle of the table where he knew a surveillance camera was positioned. Could he...no, it was a she this time, though he couldn't have explained how he knew. He looked where he thought the camera was and smiled.

Clever girl.

Chapter Ten

J ane jerked back, as if the so-called Roger Green could see her, could see them.

"He knows," Jane said.

Ryder frowned at the video screen but didn't disagree. "Do you recognize him?"

She hesitated. "I think I saw him once in passing. Not sure if he saw me."

She glanced at Ryder, still amazed he was on board, or mostly on board. He still had doubts. It was as if the more time she spent with him, the more in tune to him she became. It was...uncanny and unsettling, but also...somehow right. She hadn't known she felt wrong, hadn't known about the hole inside her until she saw Ryder. She kept having flashes of something that looked like memories of someone else, someone she didn't know—but did know. She wasn't sure how it was possible, but she knew this man. And, well, knew he'd mattered.

It was impossible, but so was time travel.

Jane had known the Agency had studied her prior to recruitment. It only made sense, but for the first time she wondered if they'd only studied her. What if they'd—she stopped. What did she fear they'd done? Like creeping toward a bigger bomb than the one that might take out the station, she let the questions form inside her head. Had they interfered in her life? Her real life? Shaped her experiences for their own purposes? Removed people from her life so she'd be more open to their offer? But...Ryder lived over a hundred years in the future. Unless—pain grew in her head, pain trying to push back the thought. She fought it, mentally pounded against the wall inside her head. She didn't know how it came to be there, just that it tried to keep the memories buried—what if this *was* her time? What was real? Was her dad? Her mom? Had her life happened or had they—had the Agency—planted those memories in her head when they took her away from home. She snuck a look at Ryder, the name coming so naturally into her mind, she knew that somehow, some way, he had been part of her real life, whatever that was. The very thought seemed to crack open her mind even more. But it also increased the instability of time around her. Was this why they told them not to think about the past? She didn't know what was true and what wasn't. But she did know one thing. She didn't trust the Agency. Not anymore.

But...if the Agency had, ugh, harvested her from here, then why send her back? Unless this was a test, as she'd halfway suspected? If it was, she was flunking it. If they came after her, she shuddered at the thought of losing the bits of herself that she was finding here if they came after her, but if they could do it to her once, they could do it again.

Did Ryder feel any of this? She couldn't tell. His face was hewn out of rock. She'd already freaked him out. He'd come this far. She didn't want to undo it all. She needed him. There was one thing she could do to try to stave off the Agency. She opened the fastenings on her jacket.

"I need a change of clothes," she said. Her tech was woven into her clothing. She'd been told she'd lose her time sense, would not be able to feel when it was off. Whatever. She didn't believe them, not anymore. But she wasn't sure she believed them anymore. She'd never taken her gear off outside the base. She hoped removing it would inhibit their ability to track her. "Do you have access to an EMP?"

This was the future. Surely they'd have one sitting around.

His brows arched.

"My tech is woven into my pants and jacket. And I might, well, I wouldn't mind making sure that's all the tech I have on board." She shrugged her jacket off, shivering a little as cool air reached arms bare to above the elbows. She met his gaze squarely.

After a pause, he nodded and said something into his comm. Then he looked at her. "So how do we take this guy down?"

She stared at Green playing poker like it was the only thing he cared about. "I might know a way," she said slowly and, if he only knew, reluctantly. Talk about going out on a time limb.

She'd read about it during her training. No agent was ever supposed to do more than a couple of re-sets, but apparently it was possible for unintentional resets to occur, resulting in endless causality loops inside a time bubble. And if she were say, a rogue agent who wanted to cause problems—or set traps for an agent—or multiple agents? Multiple time resets would be a good way to do it. So someone had come up with a way to fight back. Based on what she read, a clean reset would result, once the bubble was popped. It wasn't recommended except in extreme cases. She wasn't thrilled about reports of pieces of agent showing up on the recall pad, but blowing up involved multiple pieces, too.

The worst part? The fly was going to have to go into the spider's parlor. She wouldn't have minded if she could have just kicked his butt.

She looked at Ryder. "Can you teach me how to play poker?"

Chapter Eleven

Jane knew Ryder wouldn't like her plan—what she'd told him of her plan—but in the end he agreed. Neither he nor his team could go in without being recognized. Normally their tech made it possible for agents to sense each other's presence. At least taking it off hadn't sent her back to her own time—if she had an "own time"— or resulted in rapid aging. Yeah, she was that shallow. She'd felt a shiver of something when she shed the tech but didn't feel like she completely integrated into real time until she took an EMP blast. Not that she was sure. She was free falling now. She did feel a settling of something inside and more memories pushing against the wall inside her head, widening the cracks.

She wished she had time to process the memories that had escaped the pit, to feel fully herself, before going head-to-head with this Green character, but, even without her tech, she felt the differences in this time. Maybe the time sense was hers and not just the tech, like they'd claimed. She and Ryder had altered the time line and the changes were still rippling forward. No way to know how much or how far. The bomb could go off in three days or three hours. Everything was fluid now except her. She was solidly back *in* time, or rather in the bubble, and as vulnerable as anyone on this station to explosions and time resets.

Her challenge would be to trigger a disorientation event in Green before he could realize what she was doing and generate a reset. If

Green had been doing this as long as she suspected, well, the odds weren't in her favor.

She eyed the unfamiliar face in the mirror of her tiny berth. One didn't need makeup or up-dos in the time service, but she needed both right now, as much to prop up her bravado as to fit in to the casino atmosphere. She tipped her head to one side. The world hadn't seen that much of the girls for a while. Hopefully their modest slope would give her some help at the table of guys. The dubious Mr. Green would be suspicious of anyone approaching him, but with her tech gone, she hoped he'd be just enough uncertain to give her an edge. Or even a sliver of an edge.

An impatient buzz of her door told her that Ryder was getting restless out there in the corridor. She reached for the release but hesitated. He might not remember her, but he felt something. It was there in his eyes, in the way a pulse beat at his neck—in the way he trusted her against his better judgement. That was the biggie. She knew, she didn't know how, that he didn't give trust easily. Had their separation done something to his ability to trust? Could she have willingly left him? She hoped not, but she didn't remember that yet. All she could do was hope that they would find themselves again. And that she'd have the sense to not mess it up this time.

If the Agency had messed in their lives...no, she pushed that worry away. Deal with it later. For now, focus on this problem, she scolded the familiar stranger in the mirror. If they survived, she could think about how to keep the Agency from messing with her—them— again. She sighed and slapped the release. Gave Ryder what she hoped was a confident smile.

Heat flared in his eyes for several seconds, before his gaze hooded. That gave her confidence a boost, even though he didn't say anything. His lips parted, but compressed again. She suspected he wanted to argue, but there was nothing to say that hadn't been said. He'd shed his uniform for more casual wear, and the sight of it dried her throat. Well, that and fear. But focusing on the fear felt like it would open a destabilization spiral beneath her feet.

He crooked an elbow and offered it to her. She took it. Not having worn heels for a long time, and because panic fluttered in her chest, she needed to hold on to something solid. The arm was more than solid. It was warm and the muscles twitched at her touch. She flicked a glance at him. Yeah, that pulse was pounding in his neck. A comforting male scent drifted her way, riding on the filtered air, pushing out the metal tang of the old station.

His voice was calm though. "Once you're in the game, I'll start moving my people in." He hesitated. "McGraw, their head of security, will probably notice."

"What will you tell him?" Jane asked the question more to see if her voice still worked. Ryder would handle it. *He always did.*

"I'll think of something." He steered her into the lift and punched a button.

Later.

If there was a later. If not? She glanced at him. She was where she should be, where she needed to be. Doing what needed to be done. It was the best she could hope for. Whatever the Agency may or may not be, saving this place was the job she'd signed up for.

Chapter Twelve

Jon felt the change, felt time shift with something new and looked up, prickles of unease running down his spine. He knew every face in this casino after so many resets.

The woman, moving slowly past people and tables, was not one of his regulars. Was this the person who'd been on the other side of the camera? The time agent he'd been waiting for? Or something else? Someone else? He didn't sense the tech, but he felt a rising sense of anticipation. Why?

She wasn't that special, though he liked the graceful way she moved. The red dress hugged where it should, flared in the right places for maximum impact. Her hair was artfully piled to exposed the smooth sweep of skin of her neck and draw the eyes down to the rounded curve of her breasts. The vibrant red turned her skin white. She didn't have a lot up top, but what she had was balanced. He liked that.

And he liked a woman in red. Almost it made him wonder if he could...

She might be the worth the risk. Not forever. He'd tried that, but for tonight? The music, dimly heard above the noise, had a beat that she seemed to sway to. She was light on her feet. Like a dancer.

Or Special Forces.

His glance hooded. He absently called his hand.

She paused by a roulette table, watching the ball bounce around before finally landing. A man turned and smiled as he gathered in his winnings. He was telling her she'd brought him luck, Jon decided cynically. Was probably offering her a drink. She hesitated, then laughed and shook her head. Her smile was friendly, even as she moved on, her hips swaying one direction to avoid a table, then the other direction so she could slide by an empty chair.

He could be wrong. She could be a spacer taking a break and looking for action, at the tables and in the bedroom. He studied her. Not really giving off available vibes, despite the red dress. There was something...he shook his head, still not sure. He needed to be sure. A distraction could be dangerous, to him, to his plan.

Now her gaze swept the clusters of poker tables. Was she looking for the five men in the trap? Or something else? Her pauses stretched his nerves. He wanted to know. More than that, he wanted her to make it to his table. Wanted her to be the one. He'd been bored. Now he wasn't. She paused by the table next to theirs and his gut tightened. So close...

At his table, four of the five folded their hands. He tossed his cards in, too, was only vaguely aware of Number Five gathering up the chips he'd just won in the latest hand. Jon had felt weary from the long session, but felt a surge of energy renew his sense of purpose.

She glanced his direction, her gaze tracking around the table.

"I think I'm done," Number Five said.

Usually Jon talked him into playing another hand. This time he didn't. It was risky. Even the small change made the time bubble quiver. What was he doing? Risking everything for a woman? She saw Number Five rise to his feet. There was nothing but curiosity in her gaze, nothing to show that the five men meant anything to her. Still no sign of tech.

He stood and gestured toward the free seat. "Looking for a game?" The risk could be managed. He knew what the cards should be, could steer the play for minimum impact. He ignored the voice whispering that he couldn't control her play, that she was a wild card. Look what he'd done so far. He'd evaded the Agency's enforcers and taken down four of their top agents. He could change the play and win. He was smarter than all of them.

She hesitated for what felt like a long minute, her gaze going from face to face. Finally, when he thought she'd decided to move on, she drifted over to the empty chair, her hand resting on the back, indecision on her face and in her voice. "What are you playing?"

The four guys still seated around the table straightened, making vague movements to tidy their clothing.

"Five card draw," Jon said. "If you'd prefer something else..." He showed her the deck, tensing though he tried not to. If she changed the play too much...

She shook her head and pulled the chair out, sinking onto the seat. The edges of her mouth curved up. "Five Card Draw sounds interesting. It's almost...old school." She set her chips down and arranged them randomly in front of herself, her gaze doing a lazy circuit of the players once more.

What did she look for, he wondered? Her voice was soft, with a husky timbre that trailed down his spine like the gentle drag of a fingertip. He licked his lips, felt sweat bead along his top lip. He hadn't noticed how warm it was in here. Or realized how long since he'd been with a woman. If she wasn't the One, maybe she could be the one for tonight.

She rested her hands on either side of her chips, the white slope of her shoulders relaxed. Her stillness radiated out, affecting the other players at the table. They visibly relaxed. Number Two even stopped playing with his chips.

Jon shuffled the cards without taking his eyes off her. She didn't look at him. Her gaze slide to the right, the slight lift of her brows getting first one, then all four men to cough up their names. Might even be their real ones.

"And you are?" one of them asked.

Her lips curved slowly up. "Call me Jane," she said.

Jon chuckled. He hadn't had this much fun since his first time jump.

"Aces are wild, Jane," he said, dealing the first card.

Chapter Thirteen

"You look good. Relaxed and ready to play. You had good training in that place."

Ryder's voice in her comm sounded amused and a bit bemused. What would he say if she told him she'd learned to fake being calm, not from her Agency training, but while facing a room full of middle school students? A teacher could show no fear or she'd get eaten alive.

She'd felt the tremors of disorientation when the subject of her name came up. It had subsided some when she said, *call me Jane.* Why had the words, *I'm Jane* stuck in her throat? Made the tremors increase?

One card, two, three and finally all five cards were in front of her. She picked them up, careful to position them so that Ryder could see. If this guy was resetting time, then he'd know what cards she held. The trick for her was to change the play enough to destabilize time without having him guessing what she was doing and jumping out. If he initiated a reset, it might put her back to her arrival on station or even worse, back at the base with no memory of all of this.

Ryder's teammates were positioning themselves to take him when they saw her signal. But the timing had to be just right. If she pushed the destabilization too far, it might speed up the explosion. If she moved too soon, that might launch a reset. Or so the study she'd read claimed. She was inclined to trust it. It hadn't been part of her class-work. Librarian had snatched it back when she realized Jane had it.

Too bad for them she was a fast reader. That thought was comforting as she pretended to study her cards.

A king and queen of diamonds and ace of spades with a couple of low numbers.

"Not a bad hand," Ryder said. "Pity you're playing to lose. You'll want to appear to arrange your cards so that the ones you want to keep are together. When it's your play, discard two, one of them the king or queen."

Jane arranged her cards as he'd directed. Then looked up. Green could probably arrange his cards with his eyes closed. Gradually all of the other men looked up, too. The man to the left opened, tossing two red chips into the center of the table. The play moved around the table to her.

"You have a strong hand. You can match or raise," Ryder said.

All she had to go on were her instincts. And her time senses, she reminded herself. It was both easy and hard, this scene she played. She'd seen this movie, so she knew how to look as she tossed two red chips into the center. What was hard was not tensing as she waited for time to react. Or not react. And for Green to react. A tiny, very tiny crease flickered between his brows, a "tell" she was sure had nothing to do with poker. Her time sense agreed, though the quiver was as slight as his "tell."

She'd changed something. What would he do? She kept her lashes lowered, watching him covertly as he sat there, like a Sphinx.

"You're a conservative player," he said, finally, his smile tight and a bit feral.

That was true. She hesitated, then decided it wouldn't reveal much, and nodded. The disorientation tremors seemed to ease some. That was interesting. Contradicted what she'd been told. *Never tell the truth. It is dangerous to you, to the time line you are trying to repair.*

"You from this sector?" the man on her right asked.

She looked in his direction and pondered her response. As before the tremors ramped up when she thought about an evasive response. A bit cautiously, she shook her head. And the tremors eased. She felt a bit like a diver on the edge of a cliff leading to a nasty fall or—what if what she'd been taught was a lie?

Ye shall know the truth and the truth shall make you free?

Could it be that simple? She smiled and mentally jumped.

"I'm from Earth." The tremors vanished like they'd never been.

"Do you have a last name?" Green asked, a hint of malicious in his voice.

She tensed. A name, a real name was a road someone could follow to one's beginning, could be used as a deletion point. But—once again—any thought of evasion made the tremors ramp up again. Her lips quirked up at the edges.

"I don't know." It was the truth according to the tremors. She didn't know the name of the person in the flashes of memory. The name she thought was hers. It felt more of a lie than her smile.

"Really?" The guy next to Green looked startled. "Were you adopted?"

Jane sorted through her responses, picking the one that eased the tremors but didn't give away too much. "I was lost." She put down her discards. "I'll take two," she said.

Time—not the tremors this time—quivered. Green twitched, this tell bigger than the last. If he jumped out now—but it was too soon for her to signal Ryder's team. She felt it in her gut.

"I didn't catch your name." Her gaze caught Green's, held it captive.

His eyes widened and then she saw him fight against the same disorientation she'd been dealing with. The truth was a trap for him. She waited for a few seconds, then lifted her brows just a bit.

"And since we're all sharing, are you planning to blow up this station?" She lifted her arm to give the signal, but his disorientation happened too fast. It was as if his side of the table came to boil, the ripples of it crawling up his body. His mouth opened, round and shocked. If any sound came out, she couldn't hear it. The furious waves went up and over his head, and then shot out in a shock wave that knocked her on her back.

Chapter Fourteen

Jane opened her eyes and stared blankly at the gray metal ceiling behind the big, bright light. She'd been here before. She tried to sit up but a hand pushed her down.

"Take it easy," he said.

Ryder. She was almost afraid to look, but her head turned before her brain could make a decision.

He looked a bit white around the edges, the line of his mouth grim.

"How do you feel?"

Like I have no clue what just happened. If anything happened.

She flexed her legs, moved her arms, then her neck. "I feel...okay." Some twinges and sore spots, but happy to not be dead. Or back at the Time Base. She could remember everything that had happened. But did Ryder? Were they back to her passing out in the gift shop? She realized that Ryder's hand was still on her shoulder. Her *bare* shoulder. She looked down. The red dress. She relaxed, well, relaxed some.

"What happened?"

Ryder rubbed his face. "I'm not sure. Even the security footage is —warped." He lowered his hand. "Green is gone. It's like he was never there. The guys at the table don't remember him at all. His cards are gone. No record of him checking in or any sign of him on the security cameras."

That was a pity.

"I...destabilized him. I think." She sat up and this time he didn't push her down. "What about the," she glanced around and then mouthed, "bomb?"

"We've evacuated the casino—no one is happy about that—and I have people dismantling that table, but if he was never here—" His comm trilled. He listened, his face turning so grim she thought it might crack. He looked at her. "They found something."

Chapter Fifteen

The bomb, if that's what it was, looked like nothing Ryder had ever seen. It fit neatly into the table's central support and had the requisite wires and blinking lights. What was new was the way the space around it was distorted, for maybe a one inch perimeter. When his bomb guy tried to touch it, his hand bent. He yanked it back.

"That burned, sir," he said, massaging his fingers with his good hand.

"It's not in this time. Yet," Jane, now dressed in coveralls, was pale and her eyes were wide and worried.

A good thing. It was...distracting and he didn't have time to be distracted. *Time.* If she'd told him the truth—and so far it looked like she had—then it was, well, he didn't know what it was. Ironic, maybe. Except she'd been right about something else. It made his head hurt thinking about time.

"So how do we stop it?"

He didn't like how close she was to the bomb. She'd crouched just shy of the warp field, staring at it like that would make it go away. She half shrugged.

"At some point it has to integrate into this time to—" she stopped and glanced at him.

To explode. "Can we disarm it then?"

"If I'm reading the timer right, we'd have about five seconds."

He rubbed his face. "We could try to evacuate the station."

They didn't have enough ships, but with the escape pods, they could ninety percent clear. He and his team couldn't leave, not until everyone was safe. Just like he knew she wouldn't leave either.

She half nodded. "Yeah, but..." she bit her lower lip.

"You have an idea?"

"I have a," she half grinned and flicked one of the playing cards that had fallen to the floor. "A wild card to play that might work."

"What do you need?"

"The clothes I was wearing. And your smartest, best geek. Or geeks."

Chapter Sixteen

It wasn't just a wild card. It was a crazy wild card. But give Ryder credit, the geek was good. He'd almost salivated over the tech embedded in her jacket. Thankfully Jane knew where the return controls were, since they had to be scanned prior to launch. The Agency didn't show them anything they didn't have to. Her slight knowledge might not be enough, since they didn't know when the bomb would integrate into their time.

"Please don't mess with anything but the timing," she cautioned. "I know you want to," she added when he looked up.

He grinned. Then sighed. "Yes, Ma'am."

He'd needed the super magnifying glasses that turned his eyes into huge bug eyes. As he studied the mechanism, then worked to carefully expose the guts, Jane felt a timer ticking over in her head. Actually, more like a pounding in her head. Bam, bam, bam.

Time. Either too much or too little.

Could he reset the recall time on her suit?

What had happened to Green?

Did he still have the power to reset this time?

Or had she popped the bubble?

Her time senses told her nothing. The rest of her instincts were screaming to hurry, hurry, hurry. Instead, she curled her hands into fists, took slow, deep breaths and prayed. She didn't even care if the memory of prayer had been planted inside her head by the Agency.

When Ryder's geek finally leaned back and looked at her, his eyes enormous thanks to the glasses, she stopped breathing. "Well?"

He half shrugged and lifted the glasses, returning his eyes to normal size. "I think I got it. When you're ready, push there."

She memorized the spot, then lifted the jacket into the container and fitted on a lid. Ryder came in then, his gaze going to the container. She and the geek shrugged at the question in his eyes. He was deep in grim, his skin verging on gray, which increased his resemblance to rock. He lifted the container and told his guy to get to the escape pods. He strode out and she followed him to the lift.

"I've got one of my people—a volunteer—monitoring the device," he said. "If it, well, we'll have a few seconds warning."

"How is the evacuation going?"

"We've got most of the women and children off. I'm concerned that the escape pods won't get them far enough away, though. They were designed for less explosive force."

These were big changes in this time line, and now that she wasn't focused on the tech, she felt their impact. She wished she knew what those changes would do to the time line, or the bubble—if they were still inside it. Her tech would have helped her answer that question, but she didn't dare wear any of it. The Agency could suck her back and let the station go. They wouldn't care what happened to it, just that Green was gone. He wouldn't be back and they wouldn't like what she'd learned in the encounter.

They wouldn't like the truth setting her free.

The lift stopped at the casino floor and the door slid open. They reached the casino entrance when Ryder's comm shrilled. As one, they leaped forward. His volunteer, a woman, was whiter than snow as she backed away from the table. Jane ripped the lid off the container and grabbed the jacket, running toward the bomb. Ryder might have shouted something. She didn't—couldn't hear anything. There was a rising whining sound. Lights were flashing now that the warp was gone. She pushed "there" and tossed the jacket over the bomb, not sure she got the right spot or that they'd be in time.

She didn't run. There was no where they could go in the couple of seconds left to them. Ryder stopped next to her, took her hand and turned her to face him. He smoothed the hair back from her face and said one word.

"Daci."

The door on her memory exploded, memories flooding in and overflowing. Not a bad flood, though. A relief. She smiled up at him as the white light flashed.

Chapter Seventeen

This time Jane, no *Daci,* didn't wake up in medical. She was still in the casino. And flat on her back. She stirred and then wished she hadn't. It hurt. At least she was still here. From her vantage point, it seemed like the whole station might be on emergency power. She pushed up onto her elbows, managed to achieve a sitting position. Paused there to let the pain waves subside.

Next to her Ryder was stirring. He groaned and opened his eyes. "Daci?"

She crawled closer and helped him sit up. He rubbed his face, looked around, then grinned at her. "We're still here."

Relief on his face. Relief surging inside her and pushing out pain. He grabbed her, looked at her like he couldn't quite believe it, then yanked her close. Body to body, mouth to mouth. It wasn't so much passion as relief. They pulled back, grinned and then he hugged her again. It hurt but she didn't care.

"We're still here," he said again.

"We are." For now, she was still here, too. She wasn't sure what it meant. Memories of two lives bounced around inside her head, but she figured the ones with Ryder were the real ones, so she clung to those as hard as she clung to him and tentatively reached out with her time sense.

So far, so good, she decided. With Ryder's help, she got to her feet. He hugged her again, and then they both turned toward the table, exchanging worried looks, before cautiously approaching it.

Other than the top bent back into a molten piece of deformed plastic, everything appeared the way it had before the bomb went off.

"This might be hard to explain," she said, after a long silence for processing.

"We found a device, we disarmed it. That's my story—"

"—and I'm sticking to it," she finished, with a chuckle. Ryder appeared more relaxed. He wasn't just relieved and a bit banged up. His eyes had lost their bleakness. He caught her watching and grinned.

Then he sobered. "Who did this to us? The Agency?"

"It had to be them," she said. She straightened a chair and sank into it. "I have two completely different lives inside my head. What about you?"

He shook his head. "I had a missing chunk that I didn't realize was gone. Who does that?"

"The Agency," a voice said behind them.

She jumped up and they both whirled, Ryder's hand going for his weapon. The woman was unarmed and not wearing an Agency uniform. She appeared unfazed at having a laser blaster pointed at her.

"I'm impressed. How did you do it?"

"Why should I tell you?" Daci shot back. She might not be in uniform, but she'd come here via time portal. "I won't go back," she added.

"We—I don't want you to go back." She nodded toward the remains of the table. "Not even he wanted that."

"Green's dead?" Ryder asked sharply.

"I don't know. Destabilizing someone creates unpredictable results. He could be gone. He could be injured. He could be..." she shrugged. "He could be fine, just a little banged up. Won't know until he tries again." Something in his face must have caused her to add, "He won't be back here. But he might be curious enough about you to make another attempt at trapping you."

That sent a chill down her back. She moved closer to Ryder. "Who are you?"

The woman smiled. "Who I am is irrelevant—and dangerous, as you well know. What I am is a resistance fighter. I was recruited by the Agency, eventually realized they weren't as advertised, so I signed on to fight them."

"And now you want me to sign on? After being messed over by the

Agency, I should trust you?" Daci didn't try to hide her scorn.

"They won't leave you alone. They'll find you and run you through the system again. You'll be back where you were only they won't make the mistake of sending you here. You'll never see each other. With us, you have a chance."

Daci shivered. Ryder's arm came around her again, pulling her close against the warm, solid wall of his body. She cast him an anxious glance.

"This time—" he began.

"Time. It's tricky. As long as you're in real time, they can find you. I'm surprised I got here before they did."

"They are probably a little...startled right now," Daci said dryly. "I sent the bomb to them."

The woman's eyes widened, then she laughed with genuine amusement. "Yes, that might slow them down a little. We could use someone who thinks on their feet like you." Her gaze shifted Ryder. "You, too. You'll be more interesting now. They'll know—"

"Know what?" Ryder asked, his hold tightening.

"That you're her weak link."

Daci drew in a sharp, painful breath. "Why me?" Would she believe this woman's answer? She didn't know. But she had to ask. "Why would they mess with our lives?"

The woman looked surprised. "Your time sense. It's rarer than they want the agents to know." She studied Daci. "Yours is strong. Yeah, they'll be back for you. Sooner, rather than later."

Ryder frowned. "Then why send her back here? Why bring us back together?"

The woman frowned thoughtfully. "That's a good question. It might have been a test—of you or their memory processing."

Daci shuddered at the thought of being "processed."

"Or they didn't have a choice. Our recently departed poker friend was hard on their supply of agents. We've been tough on them, too. Our ranks are growing."

Daci glanced at Ryder. Suspicion clouded his gaze.

"We'll need to talk about it," Ryder said, his voice hard. "Privately."

The woman held out a small device. "This will bring you to me, but it's on a timer. The invite won't be there for long. Can't risk the Agency getting their hands on this."

Daci shrank back. "Just put it on the table."

She laughed. Set it down and looked at Ryder. "You know I'm not lying. You always know, don't you?"

A flash and she was gone.

Daci didn't even pretend to be brave. She burrowed into the comfort of Ryder's embrace. "We weren't just in love. We were married and they...they..." She wasn't destabilizing so much as coming apart at the seams as her memory realigned.

His arms tightened to the point of painful, though to be fair, that wasn't hard to do. He gently pushed her chin up. "I didn't know...but I did. I never even got close to another woman. It was like I knew I was taken. And there was this deep...sadness...no reason, but just..."

That made her the angriest of all. They left him with pain and her empty. Rewritten. Processed. She hadn't been interested in anyone either, but it was like they'd turned that switch off, left her unable to feel love at all.

"It's evil, as evil as Green." She stared at him. "I'd rather be dead."

His face tightened and so did his hold. He kissed her again and this time there was more. Passion, longing, relief, desperation. It was familiar and strange and wonderful. It healed places she hadn't known were broken. He eased back finally and glanced at the device.

"We have to go. That's the only way to get away from them."

Her heart, her soul cried out at this. But she nodded. It was death or...trust that woman. Together they went to the table and he picked it up. There was a single button on it.

Daci felt time shudder around her and cried out. "Push it! Now!"

She saw the team and then she and Ryder vanished in a bright, white light. Time elongated, stretched and contracted. Daci knew this part, but Ryder didn't. She held on tight, hoping her love would help with his first time ride. As abruptly as it started, it was over. She didn't let go, only studied what she could see without moving. The recovery pad wasn't as fancy as the one at the Agency. That was a positive sign. The base, or whatever this was, looked more beat up than Nebula Nine.

The woman was there. "You cut that close. They almost had you." She tipped her head to one side. "The first time transit is the roughest. Let's get you to medical."

"Where are we?" Ryder asked, his voice strained.

When Ryder didn't move, the woman half sighed. "You're everywhere. You're nowhere. Welcome to the rebellion, Mr. and Mrs. Jaxon."

Specters in the Storm

About Specters in the Storm

Specters, Automatons & Evil, oh my!

Dr. Ernest Warren is done with love. Losing his wife in the Great Storm of 1901 left him with questions only science and interstellar travel can answer. When disturbing storms begin to brew again, he reluctantly turns his airship back to where he lost his love in hopes of finding answers.

Prudence Pinkerton has been following Ernest's multi-dimensional career from the future and knows she has to meet him.

When he reluctantly accepts her help, Prudence doesn't waste time. She knows time is running out and the world is on the cusp of life-altering change.

Prudence must overcome his distrust of her if they are to save Earth from the evil hiding in the heart of the storm.

Pauline Baird Jones' is known for writing smart, quirky, funny fiction. Check out her venture into a time-bending paranormal detective story with *Specters in the Storm*.

Chapter One

He saw the fog first, then the storm looming above, its dark expanse occasionally cut by flashes of light. The fog rode the storm's wake, billowing and curling like diaphanous bits of feminine clothing. In places the fog wrapped around the storm, long white fingers reaching out, then spiraling back in to cling to the dark mass. In constant motion, the storm itself spun in rotating shades of black and gray, except where the lightning pulsed, like a heart beating in its center. The white fog ebbed and flowed at times, teasing with glimpses of where the storm rode over the strangely calm sea.

As his airship drew closer, the salt-tanged air also brought a hint of metal that left a bitter residue on his tongue. And a hint, no more, of burning wood teased his nostrils. There must be another ship out of sight, he concluded. If his calculations were correct, they were one to two days from making landfall.

The sight of the sullen storm off the prow of his airship, and the oddness in the air lifted the hairs on his arms and sent his instruments into a frenzy of random readings that made a mockery of his many months of careful observations, not to mention his belief that Science could provide the answers to all questions.

Dr. Ernest Warren lowered his spyglass, handing it to his automaton ship handler to hold while he extracted his log book and noted his observations. All of them, even the ones that offended his sense of logic, were recorded. His task was to observe and report, not to pass judgement on the data he did not like. Later he would attempt to find points of similarity buried within an admittedly incomplete historical record, or in the findings of colleagues. One thing his travels had taught him, the true scientist does not ignore anything, particularly he does not ignore the data that did not fit one's thesis.

He extracted his pocket watch to note the time. But it was as useless to him as his instruments, the hands tracking around the face at close to twice their normal speed. Despite these unusual observations, *The Weatherman* steamed forward with only a moderately increased instability as it rode the air currents. Below him, the waters of the Gulf of Mexico appeared mostly indifferent to the storm, as if sky and water operated separately from one another.

Ernest had not believed the reports that reached him in Europe, had reluctantly turned his airship toward his native soil when the reports became too numerous for a serious weather scientist to ignore. The more lurid of the reports he put down to fear-driven mass hysteria and the remnants of superstition. But when a respected colleague such as Dr. Sebastian Masterson wrote him about the storm, Ernest felt compelled to take note. If this was what his friend had seen, Ernest could see why he was so, he paused his thoughts in search of the right descriptive, disquieted. This storm certainly had many unusual characteristics. But, he reminded himself, serious scientific weather observation was a somewhat modern undertaking. In his studies, he had come across mentions of weather events that he had not personally observed nor had they occurred in his lifetime. That he had never read of a storm such as this one did not mean it had not happened before.

He had the heart and mind of a scientist, but he could concede that Mother Nature was intransigent and precocious. She would lull one into complacency with her sameness, then vary her theme rather violently and abruptly. She did not liked to be ignored or taken for granted; hence, the reason she was a Mother and not a Father. Despite this, he still believed that she didn't act without warning, even though it seemed so from their too limited knowledge. He would find the key to her secrets. All of them, so that never again—

His thoughts flinched away from *that* storm. The past that had driven him from his quiet life as an inventor to his quest to finally and completely understand the vagaries of the weather. To defeat its irrationality and its random cruelty, or at least provide warning when Mother Nature was about to go on the the rampage so that adequate precautions could be taken.

He pocketed his notebook and extended his hand for the spyglass. Once secured, directed it at the storm, tracking slowly from side to side, then up, trying to gauge its height. When he could not, he moved his attention to the gap between the storm and the surface of the water. If his eyes did not deceive him, the seas beneath the storm were as calm as those they rode upon.

"Curious," he said aloud.

"Yes, sir," Niles said, with no inflection in his voice. He'd not been programmed for curiosity.

Ernest considered the benefits and risks of a closer look. Though his instrumentation was not behaving, *The Weatherman* itself appeared unaffected by the storm. If it was the storm causing the problems with his instruments, it could be completely unconnected, he reminded himself.

Concluding too quickly closes the mind to further, possibly critically important information. Never assume you know, even when you know. Words of Dr. Masterson to newly anointed weather scientist-to-be, Ernest recalled rather wryly, wishing Masterson were here with him now.

The lightning flashes interested him, and yes, they tempted him. Early testing of his Blizablighter 3000 had been promising, but limited by his inability to get beneath enough lightning strikes for sufficient energy collection. He'd rather hoped to encounter a moderate storm during the crossing, but how accurate would the results be in an atypical storm? This storm was bigger than what he'd looked for as well. If his device collected too much charge, could he safely discharge it when water was so highly conductive?

"Let's reduce altitude, Niles," Ernest said, lowering the spyglass. He was most curious about the perceived gap between storm and water. Did his eyes deceive him? The sea liked to play tricks on those who dared to cross it.

"Yes, sir." His automaton used the speaking tube to contact Crispin, his automatonic counterpart, in the engine room.

This change in altitude triggered a threat response in Winston and Fred, bringing them up on deck. Winston still wore the apron of a valet and Fred that of a cook, but those were side functions. They were both higher functioning automatons, primarily programmed to act as research assistants and bodyguards. At the sight of their calm, blank gazes, Ernest found he missed—for the first time—human companionship. Someone who could share the complicated mix of messy emotions roiling his insides. The desire to understand warred with the need to flee this unknown. One might take a vow to be a scientist first and always, but one was, in the end, still human.

"Is there a problem, doctor?" Winston inquired with unruffled calm.

Ernest opened his mouth to explain, but closed it again. They did not have the programming to understand. He did not have that programming. He studied them. "Are you both functioning normally?"

They were also instruments, even if higher functioning than a watch. Both automatons showed the slight eye movements associated with system checks.

"Yes, doctor," Winston said, this echoed by Fred.

Would they know? It was true that the automatons had surfaces resistant to the atmospheric changes and to electrical shocks, but it still seemed odd that they appeared fine, while his other instruments were clearly not.

"Is there a problem, doctor?" This time Fred asked the question, the tenor of his voice pitched just enough different from Winston's so that Ernest could tell them apart.

They had been programmed to be persistent. This worked for Ernest most of the time, but today, less so. He looked at Winston, then Fred. Was there curiosity in the question? Nothing showed in their eyes, but their programming had been designed to adapt and change within certain limits. He'd needed them to learn if they were going to be any help. And they had been considerable help. They'd saved his life more than once, and they were able to store input for him, both visual and auditory, allowing him access to much more data than his own senses could provide.

"This storm may prove to be a problem," he finally said. "It is not behaving...predictably."

Both automatons turned to observe the storm as the airship continued its gradual descent.

"It does have unusual features," Winston said.

Fred nodded agreement, adding, "I am experiencing difficulty in processing the data. It falls outside known parameters."

"I am aware," Ernest said, somewhat dryly. Is this what Mother

Nature did to one experiencing hubris? He would not have chosen to return to the Gulf Coast, not now or ever. But it was to this coast that Masterson had asked him to come. Masterson knew his story. He would not have asked were it not important. The invitation to lecture at the Institute of Meteorological Knowledge in New Orleans had come from Masterson, he suspected. He could not think how else they would have learned of his research. Four years of weather research did not make him an expert by any standard of measurement. Ernest had left these shores, not to satisfy the curiosity of men, but to save lives. He'd been certain that research could and would triumph over dogma and superstition. What price for all his efforts now?

He frowned, considering his options. He'd set this course to avoid Galveston—his brain flinched again—hoping to make landfall at Mobile or Biloxi, then cutting across to New Orleans over land, thus avoiding the locus of his loss. But each time he'd adjusted course to fly around the storm, it had seemed as if it shifted to block his path. It was an illusion, of course. Storms lacked the ability to self direct. For whatever reason, the storm was in his way. He studied the "path" beneath the storm. The fog thickened and thinned, alternatively revealing and hiding the apparently calm seas beneath. It appeared that the gap between water and storm was sufficient for the passage of the airship, though it would leave little maneuvering room for them between sea and sky if something changed unexpectedly.

Was it possible that the storm truly did not interact with the ocean surface? He felt a stirring of scientific excitement, one tempered by the reports he'd perused about the storm. They were troubling and caused him to hesitate. However, the reports he'd read were from land-based encounters. He almost let himself get side-tracked into wondering how it was possible for the storm to appear and disappear in such a wide variety of locations. And why did some people vanish while others were untouched? Such reflections were fruitless and would not get him to his destination. He hated to admit it, but curiosity warred with fear, a wholly natural fear based on learned respect for the forces of nature.

There was one other immutable reality. His fuel reserves. He lacked enough to make it back to Cuba. And if he attempted to fly over the storm and failed, he might not have enough left to attempt passage beneath.

He gave the order, then turned to study the storm again. Would he, he wondered, see the specters in the storm? Or—his personal preference—would he find the proof to dispute the clearly exaggerated reports.

Chapter Two

If Franklin Pinkerton had had the foresight, he'd have never named his daughter Prudence. He had known about the family business, however, which seemed to make it an ironic choice—something that Prudence didn't typically associate with her dad as dad or as the Big Daddy of the Agency. Perhaps he'd lost his sense of irony when he took over from his dad who had died in mysterious circumstances—which might make Prudence the hopeful choice, now that she thought about it.

If her dad had hoped she'd be prudent, hope must have died a painful death when Prudence exhibited early signs of the Talent. According to Dr. Masterson, she had it stronger than any Pinkerton since her grandfather. The one who disappeared. At sixteen, Prudence had been flattered and intrigued by finding out she had the jets Talent-wise. At twenty-five, well, it was all Fat City until someone lost an arm during a botched dimensional transit. Or disappeared in mysterious circumstances.

At least she'd made this scene with all her body parts intact, though the transit had been a rough one. The 1905 threads covered the bruising from her dimensional travel, though that was the only good thing about them. Prior to her introduction to the corset, she thought her brassiere was the worst item in her closet.

She should be used to the corsets. She'd lost count of how many versions of 1905 she'd visited while pursuing her Master of Dimensions thesis, which she'd privately dubbed The Ernest Project. With the encouragement of Dr. Masterson, her advisor, she'd postulated the existence of Fixed Inter-Dimensional Iterations and had initially been excited when it appeared that Dr. Ernest Warren fit her construct. Dr. Masterson had cautioned her about the risks of focusing on a single research iteration, even while being equally excited about the research possibilities inherent in a fixed iteration. He'd been right about the risk of getting too close to Ernest. But if she hadn't had her eyeballs on him, she might have missed this aberrant version of Ernest. And the Agency might have missed The Storm until it was too late. If it wasn't already too late.

She patted her nest. Man, the hairdo was almost as bad as the corset, and she needed to get into her bit, inside her head and out, or she'd be popping out the wrong slang at the wrong time. Ernest had the brains to figure her out. She frowned. Had her dad picked this timeframe for her study to keep her in the prudent zone?

If he had, it had backfired. Both the storm and the Ernest had stirred up all kinds of excitement and worry within the Agency, though the worry quickly burned down the excitement. Despite years and dimensions of study, inter-dimensional science was filled with lots of theory that was hard to prove or quantify. Each time someone thought they'd proved something, a dimension would pop up disproving that theory.

Like an aberrant Ernest. A deviating iteration.

Her father had wanted to send her brother to check him out, but Dr. Masterson pointed out, rightly, that Prudence knew the terrain, knew Ernest. Masterson's gaze had betrayed serious worry, she recalled, though he had still supported her getting the bit—the assignment, she reminded herself. At the time, she'd thought his worry was all about The Storm, but now she wasn't so sure. She realized that her hands had curled into fists. With some effort she straightened them, flexing them several times to ease the cramping. Had he suspected her lapse in protocol?

She did indeed know Ernest. It was both a gift and a curse. She knew a hundred variations of him, all of them persistently the boss with the jets to rock his time. Of course, he was a nerd in every dimension, either circled or snagged-and-about-to-be-circled by his one true love, Ophelia. She made a gagging sound because she could. That Ophelia kept seeing the cutie beneath the nerd was amazing. Prudence wasn't sure which of them was the more predictable. She could plot their lives on a board. In ink.

Until this one. She should be annoyed he was on track to disprove her thesis.

But everyone was more worried about why the aberrant Ernest and The Storm had appeared around the same time—give or take some math formulas and plus-or-minus cross-dimensional errors.

So that was the gig, er, mission. Find out if the divergence had caused the storm. Or the storm had caused the divergence. Or if they were entirely unrelated.

The divergence. An iteration.

Terms were used to give them distance, to keep them from getting emotionally involved. To keep them from remembering that a divergence was a life-altering event, an iteration a human being with gray eyes and this straight nose that quivered—

Don't go there, Prudence. It's not...prudent.

Here, at the top of the Sand Island lighthouse, she could admit she'd been—excited instead of annoyed. That she was intrigued by this one Ernest who had taken his rocket off road. Curious to see for herself what was different—and not just for science and her thesis. Even without The Storm she'd have found a reason to come. She'd made tracks for Mobile, figuring he'd avoid Galveston, but when the storm blew up, she ran the numbers and decided the lighthouse offered the best chance of intercepting him. Everyone needed a lighthouse in a storm. Was it *a* storm, or The Storm? And how ironic was it that it had come between them? Not unlike the hundreds of Ophelias Ernest had fallen for again and again and again—

But she was over that. She hoped. She couldn't afford to be more than curious. Not now. There was too much at stake, particularly if this was The Storm.

Whichever storm it might be, it was still out of her sight, though her instruments showed it out in the Gulf of Mexico, tracking slowly toward landfall just ahead of Ernest's airship. As the sun began its descent in the west, her view from the lighthouse was tranquil, even soothing, after her rough passage. The lighthouse keeper had been happy for the break, for a chance to take the wife ashore for the night, so Prudence was alone, but she still looked around before she lifted her arm. Her instrument panels were built into decorative leather banding on her sleeves, everything triggered by fingerprint recognition and a cognitive sensor on her pulse. She had to be alert and aware for anything to work. She activated the hologram that would stream the data from the drone she'd launched as soon as she arrived in dimension. She'd collected enough data from his stopover in Cuba that she was confident it was *The Weatherman* she could see steaming steadily forward, now on a direct collision course with the storm. He'd adjusted course twice, possibly attempting to go around the storm.

Both times the storm had appeared as if it shifted to block him.

It really was a lot like Ophelia. She bit her lip. In her own time, she'd have had other options for plucking Ernest out of the path of the storm. Her brother would have let the storm have him. Lewis was pragmatic to the tips of his boots. *People get lost at sea all the time,* he would have said. Letting it happen was one way to find out if Ernest and The Storm were connected in some way. But Lewis wasn't here. For some reason, he hadn't been able to transit into this dimension. No one had liked that, but they needed the data, so she got the go ahead.

As the one on the scene, it was her call. She felt in her gut, which she hoped was right and not biased, that giving The Storm what it wanted was a bad idea. There was also the risk that removing him from play in this dimension might spawn more dimensions, giving the storm more places from which to draw energy. The truth was, none of them had ever seen a cross-dimensional storm quite like this one, so they were all winging it. What they needed, what they hoped for from her mission, was information. Data was the lifeblood of the Agency.

No one wanted to say it, but this time it might be the saving of the Agency.

Assuming her gut was right, if The Storm did have designs on his person, she only had one option that might get Ernest where she needed him to be. She unlatched the door and scrambled out onto the high balcony that ran around the lighthouse. Yesterday, when she'd come out here, there had been a stiff breeze coming in from the Gulf. Now the air was still and heavy. It smelled different too, a wrongness to it that lifted the hairs on the back of her neck. The menace, sensed but not seen, set off a flight-or-fight response, and she had to take several deep breaths to close down the dimensional portal that tried to form in front of her.

When the portal faded to a faint shimmer, she looked seaward. Could she see clouds on the distant horizon, or did she see them because she knew a storm was there? She watched *The Weatherman* dot for a couple of seconds more. Adjusted the angle. Did it seem as if it had reduced altitude? She'd heard of ships flying over a storm, but under? She shut down the holo and switched over to communications, took a deep breath, and keyed in the code that would connect it with its counterpart on her familiar.

"Octavius? Baby, go fetch." She launched the pre-loaded data that would help him home in on *The Weatherman*.

Out in the waves just off the shore, the water boiled as Octavius surfaced just long enough to wave a tentacle at her. She waved back, watching the rounded dome sink out of sight, then a wake appeared, the crested "V" pointing straight out to sea. To Ernest. If the octopus made it past this storm.

As far as they knew, The Storm had shown no interest in nonhumans. As far as they knew.

They knew so little. She prayed for his safe passage. If she lost Octavius—she shook off the fear as a portal tried to form again. Pulled up her holo-tracking. All the data they had indicated that The Storm spun above both land and sea, the gap both inexplicable and puzzling. It had to touch down sometimes, though, since people had disappeared in the places it had appeared. No one understood why The Storm took this person, but not that one. Or why so few land grabs. Why it preferred the sea and those who sailed it. There seemed to be no pattern to where it appeared, or why it disappeared just as abruptly. Their difference engine computers had tried every combination of the data collected. Even the so-called link to this dimension, to this Ernest, was a tenuous one.

The stories of what those not taken had seen, well, none of their kind could confirm or disprove the specters in the storm. Or even theorize what they could mean. Her brother had volunteered to ride out The Storm, when it popped up in their home dimension, but it had vanished before he could get under it. That left this dimension, with this aberrant Ernest, as their only hope. No one was certain there was a connection. Or that there wasn't. But it was the only dimension not showing stress from The Storm. If this was The Storm, she reminded herself.

It wasn't proof positive, this storm shifting to block his path, but it was troubling.

An atypical Ernest and now an atypical storm.

Was it stalking Ernest? Or worse, was his aberrant iteration the cause of The Storm, as her father and others believed?

Chapter Three

E rnest didn't position Winston at the prow, though he'd been
tempted. It was their function to occupy high risk places, but
he needed human eyes and instincts, his human responses, as they
cautiously chugged toward the edge of the storm. Below them, the
sea appeared to grow more calm—almost becalmed—as they pierced
the first edges of the trailing fog. Wisps of it wrapped around their
stacks and trailed along the sides of the airship like very long,
exploratory fingers.

There was a small bump, as if they'd passed through something
resistant, then a jerk as the airship's speed increased slightly. It
almost seemed, after that initial resistance, that something now
pulled them forward faster. Alarmed by that thought, he rapped out
an order and the engines slowed. To his relief, so did their forward
speed. Conversely, he now wished he hadn't slowed. A pure scientist,
he had not believed in anything outside his sight and sound, but he'd
learned the hard way that there were other senses, ones that warned
of danger before it was seen. If he'd trusted it back then—

He snapped off the thought that threatened to pull him into the
past, distracting him from this very present peril.

The only sound came from the engines and those sounded
muffled, as though the thick air acted as a dampener. Even the sound
of his own breathing seemed muted, felt labored, as if the thick air
entered his lungs reluctantly.

When they were fully under the storm, the fog fell away, drifting back toward the outer edge once more. There were probably air currents he could not feel, he told himself, currents caused by their passage. He needed the rational in the face of the irrational. It was darker under the storm, but it would be. Though the water ahead was calm, the storm showed an observable circulation, at least from what he could see through the murk. The shape of the storm was that of something viscous pushed through a funnel, the spirals thicker at the edges, then thinning as they approached the center. He was too far from that center to see if there was a defined eye, though this storm appeared to lack other recorded characteristics of a cyclonic storm.

The smell of burning was stronger now, and the air tasted coppery. He was reminded, he frowned, of a blacksmith's forge. Fire and brimstone. It did not fit the general conception of hell. Fire and water were, for the most part, mutually exclusive. Unless there was something in there...his skin crawled, and he felt an urgent need to turn back. He suppressed it with an effort.

The stacks shuddered slightly, as if they'd come into contact with something. The top of the dirigible was lost in the dark clouds, so he ordered a few more feet of descent. The sturdy airship drifted lower, skimming along just barely above the surface of the almost motionless water. The shudder stopped.

They moved forward with more ease. It became easier to breath. Once more he resisted the urge to increase speed. It would be unwise to expend too much of their fuel reserves when there was so much he didn't know about what might be ahead. Their progress was steady and unimpeded. He should have felt better.

He didn't.

The sensation of being watched crept over him. He needed to look up. He feared to do so. Off to his left, the setting sun sent rays of light under the storm, though this light did not reach them. It acted more as a distant beacon. And indicated that the storm had limits, an end, if only he could reach it. The sight of the distant light eased the growing panic, gave him hope, though the sense of being watched did not ease. If anything, it became worse. The sensation was one of animus, but more than that. He felt fear in there. Anger, malice, nothing positive. His hands gripped the gunwale until his knuckles turned white. He tried to speak, but his throat turned dry and tight, as if something gripped it to hold in the call for assistance from his automatons.

He wanted to claw at that hold, but he couldn't let go of the gunwale. Couldn't move. His chin started to lift, as if impelled. When he could fight no longer, when he thought he must look and die, he was distracted by movement along the surface of the water. He blinked, sure it must be an illusion. But the sight of it, for whatever reason, eased the sense that he could not move or speak.

"Winston! 'Ware!" He called out the alert command. This was not his imagination, he realized. It was very real. The wake made a perfect "V," like an arrow pointing straight at him, with waves falling away from the edges of something just under the surface. It came on, swift and straight as an arrow.

A sort of howl, like the wind, but not like it either, sounded above him, then the surface of the water came to a boil. Out of the maelstrom, he saw—

Tentacles?

A different kind of panic rose inside him. Giant tentacles.

He started to back from the edge as two of the monstrous things reached up, sliding along the bow, then gripping the gunwale close to where he'd stood.

"Ware!" he called again, the sound more a croak than a call.

A huge red dome rose from the water and giant eyes regarded him for a long moment.

There was another howl, like a wind he couldn't feel. A jerk. Then a jolt as *The Weatherman* slammed into the surface of the water, yanked downward by the tentacled grip.

Ernest flew backwards, hitting the deck hard enough to knock the wind out of him. Just before his head connected with wood, he saw what he'd feared to see...

...faces...

Thousands of them.

The specters in the storm...

His eyes widened as he saw one he knew better than his own. She drifted just out of his reach. There was another wail, but this one vibrated inside his head, as if he had made the sound. He reached out, but his head hit wood, and the darkness closed in, taking her away from him again.

Chapter Four

Prudence waited on the lighthouse's balcony until her tracking screen showed contact between Octavius and *The Weatherman*. Now together, both raced toward her position. Octavius could haul tentacles when he had to. Or when he was scared. Anxious for him, she went down the winding stairs and outside where tumbled granite blocks surrounded the lighthouse. She glanced back at the light keeper's cottage. Prudence had left a lit lantern on the porch, certain she'd need the light by the time Octavius returned with *The Weatherman*.

The tide was out, she noted. Usually there would be seagulls checking out the small pools left between the chunks of granite by the retreating water, but all was quiet as a grave. She picked her way as far as she could across the large chunks. Now she could see the water line where small waves rippled ashore, much smaller than normal. Of course, what was normal for the twenty-four hours she'd been in the area? She'd done a bit of cramming before her transit, but didn't know then what mattered and what didn't. Or that she'd remember the right things. This Ernest had caused her all kinds of headaches. She should be angry, not—

She checked tracking. Octavius was still within the boundaries of the storm, but moving at his top speed. The setting sun was almost parallel with the water now, sending beams of gold and orange across the almost still surface.

If they didn't show up soon, she'd have to go light the beacon.

Another crash course, this time from the light keeper. Hoped it went well.

Octavius had the ship, but did he have the passengers? The storm had not changed speed, at least not enough to register on her equipment. She was about to turn back when she saw it.

A dark speck that rapidly grew larger against the horizon.

It resolved into the shape of a ship skimming along the surface of the water, and just ahead of it, a hint of a rounded red dome. Red. Something had made Octavius angry. At least he wasn't scared. One of them shouldn't be.

There was still enough light for her to see a figure at the helm, but there was a stillness to it that hinted it was an automaton in power conservation mode. Octavius reduced speed, churning up a counter wake. He released the airship, and it drifted towards her, just above the water. That brought the automaton back to attention. He steered it gently around the rock outcrop, and then toward the pier. Prudence followed it, taking the rope when tossed and securing it. Its dirigible balloon kept the airship above the water, when the engine cut off. It bumped against the edge of the pier.

Octavius drifted in close and waved a tentacle at her. She was relieved to see his natural color had returned. She waved, said into her wrist, "Thank you, sweet baby. Good job."

One tentacle touched his rounded dome, as if in a salute, then he sank into the water until just his eyes and round dome were visible. Beyond him, and not her imagination this time, the horizon darkened. Whatever it was, storm or Storm, it was incoming.

"Be careful out there," she added, lowering her arm once more. It was a pity one couldn't debrief an octopus. He'd been in the belly of the beast. And he'd turned red in anger, not white in fear. That meant something, she just wasn't sure what. She sighed and turned toward the airship. If she turned colors, it would be white right now. What Ernest would she find on there? If she found one. She studied his airship. Looked like a sweet ride, for an airship. Ernest, being Ernest, had probably made some modifications. His iterations had done some interesting things to his steam car. She wished she could check it out.

Perhaps later, if there was time. It was one of the ironies of their kind, that they could travel through dimensional time, as long as it was not their own, and yet still be limited *by* time.

From her vantage, she could see along the length of this side of the airship, but part of the stern of the ship was obscured by the main cabin. She saw a booted foot poking out from behind the cabin, a slackness to it that was a worry. The gunwale was low enough for boarding even with the multitude of skirts, so she gathered them up and climbed aboard, proceeding cautiously toward the foot. She cleared the cabin and stopped. Two automatons crouched protectively next to the prone figure. She didn't have time to study him too closely, not with a couple of alert automatons watching him, but there was no question he was *an* Ernest.

The rise and fall of his chest was a relief. It wasn't a surprise Octavius had delivered Dr. Warren in an unconscious condition. Most people reacted to the sight of the giant octopus by fainting, though, based on the traces of blood on the deck, Ernest had been knocked out before he could pass out. That might help. Men hated to faint. Not that they loved getting knocked out. Or giant octopuses. She wasn't too worried, because there was so much more to come that he wouldn't like.

She stopped, opting to give the automatonic guardians time to assess her threat level. Thankfully they didn't have the ability to do that, at least not accurately. Prudence knew how to look harmless and helpful. Not to mention how to do helpless 1905 lady. She gave a dramatic start and covered her mouth with the tips of her fingers.

"Oh." She widened her eyes and made a couple of ineffective hand gestures, learned from watching Ernest's vapid fiancé through far too many dimensions. "Is he all right? Oh my goodness sakes alive." She fluttered her lashes.

"He is unconscious," one of them finally said.

Prudence pressed a hand to her chest now. "Gracious! Should you leave him there?" She gestured toward the shore. "Would you like to bring him inside the cottage? There is a bed you can use." The quarters were spartan, but they could have been worse if she'd had to time her arrival, say, a year from now when a hurricane would take out the cottage.

The automatons would not find it odd to find her alone and in charge of a lighthouse, or at least they shouldn't. What programmer of a difference engine would waste precious storage on unlikely scenarios like that? Asking the question, though, instead of just ordering it, would give her a sense of how complex their programming actually was. The automaton who'd been at the wheel stumped to the edge and looked down on them from the wheelhouse. Another one came up from what she assumed was the engine room. The situation clearly exceeded their programming. They visibly stalled in place, their eye movement tracking up and down.

The other two showed signs of "thinking," their metal eyes moving from side to side.

"There is a storm incoming," she adding, hoping to tip the balance to cooperation. If their programming perceived her as an ally, everything would be easier, well, less hard, she amended. She'd left easy in her own dimension when her Talent manifested.

The mention of the storm appeared to be the right nudge. One moved to Ernest's head and lifted him by the shoulders, while the other secured him about the knees.

Bodyguard automatons. Normally their programming would make them want to keep him on the airship, but recent events, an octopus —still visible out in the water, its eyes appearing and disappearing as it rode the small waves rippling ashore—combined with the storm threat, would alter that imperative, sending them seeking the closest secure structure. The lighthouse was the sturdiest thing around, but the cottage had better amenities. As she turned, she gave Octavius a quick wink and another out-of-sight wave.

The light was fading fast, the lantern she'd left on the cottage's porch a cheerful beacon. She navigated the gunwale, certain the automatons wouldn't care about proprieties. She stepped back so they could clamber off, casting a last look of regret at the airship. The two ship handlers made no attempt to follow them, though they might become active if she came back without Ernest. He would have needed to secure his retreat during his travels. This world, this time in its history, had many treacherous places. Had this Ernest been seeking redemption or a brave final solution in his travels, she wondered?

The two automatons headed for the light, following the narrow boardwalks, first taking the one that led to the lighthouse. She followed them, finally letting herself study this Ernest as the last of the light fell on him, let herself look at the one Ernest whose life had not followed the pattern of all the others. His face was very tanned, not a surprise since he'd been roaming around studying the weather. Otherwise he looked the same. The face was thin and narrow, with a high, intelligent forehead and a grimness about the mouth, apparent even in his unconscious state. It was, she knew now, his look of repose. And when he thought. Which he did too much, except around Ophelia when he thought too little—

She clamped down on this. His dark hair was untidy and in need of a trim. He also needed a shave. This was new. She'd never seen any of the Ernests anything but meticulously turned out. He was a scientist, but not of the crazy or absentminded bent. He applied the same attention to his attire as he did to his studies. Of course, he had been knocked on his backside by an octopus.

His frame was long and somewhat leaner than the others, his travel clothing more tidy than his hair, despite his tumble. His eyes would be gray under the lids. When they lifted, what expression would this Ernest's eyes have?

She'd known the others felt it. It wasn't just her. At first she'd been shocked and retreated because of *rules*. But then—she'd started looking for it. That moment when he realized that he could want more. His pupils had dilated. His pulse had quickened. There'd been other signs, that had clearly embarrassed and troubled the oh-so-loyal Ernests. Because none of them could stand to be wrong, they'd opted for manufactured dislike. She'd let them push her away. One couldn't fight for what one couldn't have. So she'd faded from their lives, wondering if any or all of them ever thought of her after she was gone...

But this one...

She kept a tight hold on hope, because she was not only out of his time, but also out of his dimension. That didn't mean she couldn't wonder what might be different about an Ernest who had loved and lost. One who couldn't have Ophelia. One who had had four years to heal...

The automatons turned onto the boardwalk that led to the cottage.

"Take him inside. You'll see the bed," she directed. "I need to light the beacon." She had to do it, she'd promised the light keeper. She just hoped she wasn't painting a target on them for the storm.

Chapter Five

———————

When she'd lit the beacon, Prudence made her way to the cottage. The two automatons had stationed themselves against the wall on either side of the head of the bed, their mechanical gazes turning toward her as she entered. Since they could not show emotion, their blank gazes gave no indication of what their next moves would be.

"How badly is he injured?" Automations liked questions, if they could like anything.

"He hit his cranium," one of them said.

"He has been unconscious since the attack," the other added.

Attack? She preferred to think of it as a rescue. Interesting that, while they looked identical, the automatons voices had been programmed to sound different.

"Do you have designations?"

"I am Fred."

"I am Winston."

Names, not numbers. Another divergence from the other Ernests. This Ernest had fled his grief and mostly eschewed human contact—but had given his automatons names. In all the other dimensions, he was at home in Galveston with his wife. All of those Ernests and Ophelias had survived the storm of 1900. Only in this dimension was it the Great Storm of 1900, resulting in a devastating loss of life, including that of his fiancé and her father. The loss of his Ophelia had spawned more differences in Ernest's observable life, but so far these had not resulted in the formation of new dimensions. This went against known dimensional science. And in an interesting dichotomy, there was The Storm, which had appeared across all dimensions—though not in the same places in each—which was again not typical of what was known. Or believed to be known in a science even more imprecise than she'd realized.

This was the first dimension where the storm had appeared in the Gulf. And it was only in this dimension that Ernest had left Galveston. If the storm wanted an Ernest, it could have easily found one of the predictable Ernests. Instead, it appeared to want this one. He'd traveled the world for the last four years. The storm had also cruised around. Had their paths crossed at some point? Or not crossed, but intersected? Was there a connection between this aberrant Ernest and the storm? If that was The Storm heading toward them. It could just be *a* storm.

That was the question she'd been sent to answer. The hope being, that in the answer lay the way to stop The Storm. Because it didn't just appear in all dimensions. The Storm seemed to be drawing energy from the other dimensions, degrading and destabilizing them, eating at the edges like acid. What was different about this dimension? Or was she looking at that difference? Or was the difference something he'd learned in his travels?

She took a deep breath and looked at the automatons. "With the storm coming, I'm sure Dr. Warren would like his gear and instruments, all his research material, secured from the airship." She gave them time to process this information, then added, "The safest structure in the storm is probably the lighthouse. Stow it in the area below the lamp. That will be the safest place."

Prudence wasn't sure about up being safe if it was The Storm. It might put them up in the very heart of it. But she hadn't been sent here to do the safe thing. And the lighthouse walls were some thick. That should help. Because she hadn't been sent to die either.

She looked at the one called Fred. "Perhaps you could stay with the doctor and Winston could secure the ship and the doctor's things? I'm sure his ship handlers would help?" She'd pitched her tone to be authoritative, but hopefully not too much. Bodyguard automatons were tricky.

After a processing pause, Winston nodded and left the room. Prudence waited until he'd thumped out of the cottage and then said, "I'll get some water for his injury."

146

~

Ernest woke with an aching head and a significant gap in his memory. He'd been on *The Weatherman* and now he wasn't. How had that happened? He kept his lashes down and studied the woman from under them, not ready to confess he was awake until he felt more certain what he was waking to.

So far there was just the woman, but that did not help with his unease.

He avoided women. Women reminded him of what he had lost. Or worse, tried to console him. Tried to fill the empty place. It was best to just avoid them as much as possible. Only this time, he couldn't get away, couldn't avoid.

There was something about this one that bothered him more than usual.

She was attractive, he acknowledged with extreme reluctance, felt an immediate stab of guilt at this disloyalty. His friends told him he couldn't, shouldn't mourn forever, but he'd lived while she died. It should have been the other way around. She'd been so bright, so full of life, he couldn't believe she'd agreed to marry him, a dry, dull inventor, over all the other more interesting suitors who'd vied for her hand. But she had. He'd sensed the signs of a possibly dangerous storm, despite the lack of concern by those who should have known. He'd shared his concerns, had asked her to leave with him. She had listened to her father and the other "experts." He tried to find her in it, but the storm won. It beat him back. Kept him from doing his duty. She and her father had died. All he could do for her now was remain loyal. Never forget.

He wouldn't have looked, noticed this woman, if he'd not been at such a disadvantage, he insisted to himself. Any man, alone in a bedroom with a strange woman would be unsettled and off guard. She looked at him like she knew he watched her. There was sympathy and humor and something else in her eyes. In an effort at regaining control, he lifted his lashes, trying for dispassionate distance, to see her as a scientist might. What was she doing here? He looked around. Where was here?

The room was spartan, spare. Some effort had been made to personalize it. A few photos. Some of those things women made for the tops of dressers. They were close to the sea, based on the humidity in the air and the faint smell of ocean.

Because he could not help it, his gaze wandered back to her. Brown eyes and hair, no way to assess her height while she sat. She was dressed for travel. Her corset was leather and durable, her boots sturdy and sensible. She'd left off her hat but goggles hung about her neck. Her sleeves below the elbow sported intricate brass and leatherwork, the panels running down the top of her arms. An odd conceit in an otherwise practical ensemble.

Why did he sense impatience, restlessness when she sat with outward stillness, her hands folded, unmoving. A slight tilt to her head presented a jawline that was clean in its lines with a hint of stubbornness. There was intelligence in her eyes and humor softened the line of her mouth.

His gaze lingered on her mouth until it curved up.

He jerked, his hands clenching on the coarse blanket. A gentleman did not—

"Does your head hurt very badly?"

Her voice was clear and cool, like the mountain streams after a storm—he pulled himself into a semi-sitting position, for the first time becoming aware of Henry to one side. The automaton moved to assist him to sit, tucking the pillow behind his back before retreating again.

Pieces of memory began to return, as if sitting up had shaken them loose in his head. The storm. There'd been a strange storm. Had he dreamt that? He must have, because there'd also been a giant octopus—

"I'm sorry that Octavius startled you. He's young and he got a bit excited, a little over enthusiastic. He's still learning to manage all those arms." She shrugged and moved her arms like tentacles.

"I didn't dream it." He didn't know whether to be relieved or angry or something in between.

Her elegant brows rose. "No. Octavius is quite real, though not at all malicious. He was the best available option for getting you clear of the storm, you see, or I wouldn't have risked his life."

The storm. The specters in the storm. Had he really seen Ophelia just before—

"I promised Dr. Masterson that I'd try to make sure you made it safely ashore." Her mouth curved up a bit ironically. "I should be more careful what I promise."

Perhaps he had not yet waked from his strange dream. Light

filtered down from above, as well from a lantern. He could smell coffee, food of some kind. If this was a dream, it was most vivid.

"Where am I?"

"This is the Sand Island, off Mobile Bay, and we're in the light keeper's cottage."

He processed this for a few seconds. Then frowned. "How long was I unconscious?"

She consulted a watch extracted from a pocket on her leather corset vest. Gave it a slight shake and restored it to its pocket. "I'm not really sure I noted the time, but you've been out an hour since you arrived here."

His frown deepened. "But...I was some distance from making landfall." He no longer felt certain of his calculations. He looked at his automaton. Before he could ask, she spoke again.

"Octavius is a very fast swimmer. Octopuses are, you know. They can't swim fast for long periods, but he didn't like the storm." Something in her eyes changed. She shifted in her chair. "What was it like?"

He did not want to talk about that. And he felt acutely the disadvantage of being prone, even if she was seated. This—none of it made sense. More than he needed for his head to stop aching, he needed to reach a place where something made sense. Anything. He shifted his legs to the edge and lowered them to wooden floor. It helped to get them on something solid, though his head swam unpleasantly. He rubbed his face. It did not help, so he looked at her again.

"I do not wish to be rude, but who are you?"

Her eyes widened. "Oh, I'm sorry. I forgot you haven't met me."

Why did her words seem to imply she'd met him? He blinked. That was not possible. And yet...there was something familiar about her.

"I'm Prudence Pinkerton."

He'd heard the name Pinkerton, heard of the detective agency, but she was a woman, a female. And if she were a detective, what would she detect here? Not that she'd claimed to be one. She'd asked about the storm, but a storm would not be of interest to a detective agency. Vaguely he knew the Pinkertons dealt with crimes, such as train robberies and the like, or so he'd heard. Why would Masterson have dealings with them? Or have sent this woman to help him make it ashore? Masterson could not have known about the storm.

He felt slow and stupid, feelings he did not like. Men were not slow and stupid in the presence of women. They were—he slammed his thoughts down. He was through with women. Masterson knew this and still he'd sent this one. A woman with a giant octopus. Did Masterson know about that? He cast her a look of suspicion.

Her lips twitched, as if she read his thoughts. Ophelia used to call him a closed book, but this one appeared to read him easily enough.

"I could tell you how I came to have Octavius, but it wouldn't help."

She seemed oddly comfortable with being alone with him. She appeared respectable, but there was also something not...not that she looked like a loose woman, it wasn't that. He studied her. Her ease was more of that between two men, as if they were equal. Was she a suffragette? He avoided those as well. Where had they met?

"You are," he paused, adjusting his assessment to something more polite, "most unusual."

She grinned. "Yes, I am." Her head tilted to one side as she gave him an equally direct survey. "So are you, Dr. Warren." She paused, then added, "I've never met anyone being stalked by a storm."

He stiffened. "It is most atypical, but—" He stopped when her brows rose over an abruptly ironic gaze. His mouth set in a stubborn line. "Storms do not stalk people. While it may appear to have been on the same course, there will be a logical explanation for it."

She rested an elbow on the arm of the rocker, then rested her chin in the palm of her hand. "And what is that logical explanation, Dr. Warren?"

He opened his mouth. Closed it. Finally muttered, "If it is following me, which I doubt very much—"

"It changed course after Octavius collected you. It's following a straight line that will bring it to this location by morning, if it maintains its current speed. Sooner if it speeds up."

He blinked, trying to figure out which part of this was the most unbelievable. "How could you know its current speed or course? Did your octopus tell you?"

She looked amused. "No, Octavius does many useful things, but that isn't one of them." She hesitated. "I could tell you how I know, but you'd have to believe six impossible things before breakfast. Can you do that, Doctor?"

Chapter Six

Prudence had been sure she'd *know*, once she saw Ernest, once she looked into his eyes, and she did know one thing. He had not consciously caused the storm. He was not evil or even misguided. He was bewildered. What she didn't know was if he was the reason for the storm, which was a different way of being responsible. He could still have done something to trigger it. Or this dimension could be the problem, and he was a side issue.

Did she need to kill him or recruit him? Could she execute the Final Option? Her heart said no. Her brain said she had to if—but didn't think she could do it either. She wasn't a killer. They all knew that and they'd let her go, so they didn't think she'd have to either, she reminded herself. She knew what she wanted to do, but what if what she wanted to be true blinded her to what really was?

She should have told her father that she wasn't unbiased enough for this mission, but if she had, she wouldn't have just lost the mission. She'd have been out of the Agency. Do not get emotionally involved with dimensional iterations was one of the rules an agent couldn't break and remain an agent, the line that couldn't be crossed. Ever.

Someone should have told her why the line shouldn't be crossed. It might have made a difference. Maybe. Knowing how much it could hurt might have headed her off. It was human nature to risk pain, to pursue the unreachable, to dream big and try harder. Being an agent, required all of those things. She'd broken bones learning to navigate dimensions. It hadn't stopped her. A broken heart, well, that was a different kind of pain, particularly in a hopeless cause. If she'd known, she'd have tried not to let it happen, wouldn't she?

Only she had let it happen. And she'd come to protect Ernest. She knew it, even if she didn't want to admit it. Not because she thought that this time she'd get him, but because she couldn't let him die unless—but what if she had to? He was one Ernest in thousands —only, he wasn't. He was an aberrant Ernest. And therefore unique. Special.

Against special there was only the fate of innumerable dimensions. Billions of lives, including those of her family, depending on her to make the right decision. To do the right thing.

No pressure.

She needed more information, but it wouldn't be easy. This Ernest was like the others in one essential way.

He was a scientist. He probably couldn't believe one impossible thing—let alone six—if she had a month of mornings to spend. Which she didn't.

She had one night to get him from skeptical to helpful. And she could only think of one way to make that happen.

Break the other unbreakable rule.

Never tell an iteration they are an iteration or that dimensions could be crossed.

Since she was already in for pound, why wasn't she spilling the beans?

Because a part of her, a very small part of her, wasn't sure she was right. If Ernest was a bad guy very good at pretending to be good and she told him? Well, it wouldn't just be bad.

It would be catastrophic.

Six impossible things. Was this what it was like through the looking glass? There was a small one tacked to the wall, but Ernest didn't go to it when he clambered to his feet. Instead he made his way, somewhat shakily, to the slightly opened window and looked out. An unfamiliar, diffuse light revealed chunky blocks of stone, and sea. From here it appeared that the house stood in the sea, was surrounded by it. As unsettling as that was, what still struck him the most was the silence. He should have heard something. The sound of gulls. The slap of water against rock. Something. Here was one impossible thing he had to believe, whether he wanted to or no. And it was true that the storm behaved like no storm he'd observed. Or read about. He turned from the window, from the silence, but not toward her.

Losing Ophelia had not been the impossible. People died. It was a fact of life. He'd seen it before. He'd seen it after. Seeing her in that storm—his hands clenched at his sides. It had been Ophelia, but not the way he remembered her. Her eyes when alive had been, well, he could not recall exactly. But not like the eyes in the storm. Those eyes, that face...had not been...

A faint shudder shook him.

"What did you see in the storm, Doctor Warren?" her voice was soft, but something in it, an urgency perhaps, made him turn around and face her.

He opened his mouth, but could not say the words.

"You saw her, didn't you?"

After a pause, he gave a short, sharp nod. "How did you know?"

"You're not the only one to see the specter of a...loved one in the storm." Her gaze shifted away from his, but not before he caught sight of sadness in them that he recognized.

"You have lost someone."

She nodded.

"In the storm?"

She shook her head. "I've read witness accounts." She looked past him, in the direction of the storm. "This will be my first contact with it." Her gaze shifted seaward. "If that is The Storm."

"Why are you here?" Why had Masterson sent her? Why had he sent a woman? And what did she—or he—expect to happen?

She didn't speak for so long, he thought she wouldn't. Finally she stirred, her lips curving wryly up. She looked at him once more. "To stop the storm."

Her tone said it was obvious. His brows shot up, even though some part of him was, strangely, not surprised. "That would be one of the impossible things I am supposed to believe?"

She smiled, transforming her face in a such a way that it caused his heart to thump oddly.

"Only five more to go."

Chapter Seven

Ernest was recovering. He was thinking. That could be good. That could be bad.

He was like the other Ernests, but also different. His wanderings in his airship had altered him. She'd like to think he'd grown, matured, become less rigid. She wasn't sure, though. She might be, not just hopeful, but dangerously hopeful.

She still found it hard to believe that all those Ernests had loved all those Ophelias. In an effort at impartiality, she'd spend some time with some of them, trying to see what he saw. That had only made it harder. Some were not so bad, but none were what she'd call worthy of great devotion. Most had started to make their Ernest unhappy on the heels of their wedding vows. The Ophelias weren't outright evil, and they did show some sense in wanting Ernest, even if he was totally wrong for them. The main problem was they couldn't leave well enough alone. They wanted things for the Ernests that the Ernests didn't want for themselves. Like wanting him to work for her daddy and give up that crazy inventing. They couldn't see what he was, because they were too focused on what they wanted him to be. It should have helped her get over Ernest, because he'd done the proposing, but to be fair, how did a man of his time—or all the times when women were limited so severely—find spouses who were a match for them? Even in her time men—even smart men—fell for the pretty face without looking any deeper and sometimes regretted it. Within the Agency she had sometimes felt the sting of being judged as a girl instead of for her Talent, though not as much as at school. All that had mattered in high school was her poodle skirt and who thought she was a cutie. And the guy who thought she was a cutie had to have a souped up dragster or having a guy wasn't enough to make one cool. Inside the Agency, she had a future, but without it? Her guidance counsellor had urged her toward nurse or school teacher or secretary. If he could see her now? He'd probably cry like a girl.

Though to be fair to him, it also bothered him when she rolled up to his car on her skates. He had wanted better for her and couldn't know she needed a for-show job that let her do her real job.

Honestly, she didn't know if she was a cutie or a dog. She'd been told her looked like her grandmother, the one married to the missing grandfather. She'd never met either. Didn't want to cause a paradox. Those didn't get you kicked out, because most likely you'd erase yourself from history before they could kick you out. The problem with popping through dimensions, you didn't get a lot of time to date. And if one made the mistake of getting a crush on an iteration? Yeah, that tended to kill your love life, too.

She knew she didn't feel comfortable with the idea of seeing herself through someone else's eyes, letting that dictate how she saw herself. So that put her out of step with her peers, too. Even though she pined for Ernest, she didn't *pine* to the point of despair. She tried to keep it wistful, though she had to fight a bit of melancholy after a mission. But she'd always known she couldn't have him. If you started out with no hope, the only way to go was up. At least in theory. But she couldn't remember ever wondering what was wrong with her because it was obvious the problem lay with Ernest. And guys in general who forgot to use the correct brain when choosing a life's companion.

There was a clink as Ernest set down his utensils and the scrape as he pushed his chair back from the rough hewn table. He'd agreed to eat, perhaps hoping she'd be a better cook than his automaton crew. Oh well. He'd eaten. She could have done better in her own time, of course. She'd taken Home Ec. But it didn't prepare one for a wood stove.

He studied her now, with his scientist look back on his face. She'd seen it before this meeting, over and over again on the faces of the other Ernests. She held the look without flinching or blinking. She could have held it in her sleep, except then her eyes would be closed. He looked away first, though his gaze quickly returned.

"No one can stop a storm," he said flatly, as if he'd been thinking while he ate and drank. Which he probably had. All the Ernest Warrens were brilliant scientists, ahead of their time, which made the Ophelias not just wrong, but blindly stupidly wrong. All of them but this one had directed their brilliance toward inventing things, though all of them had allowed the inventing to become after work hobbies. Only this one had turned his attention to the elements, but he still invented things, according to Dr. Masterson. This iteration, this Ernest, focused on inventing weather instruments that he hoped would help him figure out the weather. Was that a clue to the storm's interest? Maybe he'd invented a way to stop it, but didn't know it?

"This is not a normal storm," she pointed out, her tone mild. She rose and began clearing the table, partly because it was expected and partly to avoid that look of distrust in his eyes. She set some dishes in the big farm sink and turned around.

"You are saying this storm is man made?" He could not keep the disbelief out of his voice.

"I did not. I don't know what's causing the storm," she added before he could ask. She crossed her arms over her chest. "You've seen it up close. Is it normal?"

He glared at her, then looked away again. "It is atypical," he conceded some ground, but not all of it since he used the word "atypical" again.

"It is unnatural," she asserted, because he needed to get that far if they were going to make any progress toward those other impossible things he needed to believe.

"The study of weather—"

"Science may not be ready to admit this is unnatural, doctor, but you know it with your other sense. Your instinct." She rested her hands on the table and leaned in. Could she say gut in this time? The need hadn't come up before. He should have good instincts, after wandering around the world for four years. "Your mind may dispute this because minds don't like the unnatural, but you *know* in your gut and in your heart." Did he still have a heart? Was it still broken? The distrust in his eyes was more than the others, but this one had better reason for that distrust.

His mouth straightened into a thin, tight line. But he gave a short, sharp nod that might have been a concession.

"But if you don't know what is causing it, then how do you propose to stop it?" He didn't try to soften his scorn.

"Ah." He'd put a finger on the painful crux of the matter. But still she stalled. Still looked for the right words. Or sure knowledge? Stalling for time, she returned his serve. "You're the weatherman."

"Is this another of your impossible things? I have just begun my research on weather phenomenon. A mystery such as this one is well beyond my skills."

"Maybe, but the storm doesn't seem to know that."

"What?" The single word was snapped. "What are you talking about?"

"It's following you. Either you're attracting it—" she paused, with the sense that she was close to knowing something, just not close enough to know what she knew...

"Or?"

"Or you have something it wants." She frowned. What could a storm want?

"What could a storm want?" He echoed her thought, but with even more scorn than before.

"That's a very good question." She said it slowly, her thoughts spinning, but with a stronger feeling of something important just out of her reach. She sighed. "Let's start with this."

She reached for the map she'd left leaning against the table leg, pushing aside the cutlery and dishes she hadn't cleared, so she could spread it out on the surface of the table. Against his will, interest sparked in his eyes. For a map. She sighed a little inside.

"What is this?" He bent over it, studying it as if he couldn't wait for her answer. He must figure it out for himself. His turn to frown. "It's a map of the world. A most detailed map."

Definitely better than anything he had access to, but hindsight was twenty-twenty.

"What are these marks?" he asked.

"Those are storm sightings."

"I didn't realize there'd been so many."

There hadn't been. In this dimension. But he wasn't ready to hear that.

He looked at it without speaking for several minutes, then frowned, his gaze narrowing. "But—"

"I know. Our people have studied it, too. The dates, the places, there doesn't seem to be a pattern." She looked up, meeting his gaze.

"It doesn't move in what we'd call a logical manner. It pops up, disappears, then pops up half a world away. If the reports are even slightly accurate, the first sighting was in Russia. Then it moved here to Canada. Then to Egypt. Persia. Lots of appearances over oceans. And well, you can see it for yourself."

"I can, but this makes no sense." He'd forgotten to be annoyed with her. Now he was puzzled. Curious. "What are these additional notations?"

"Places where people were missing after the storm. The ones we know about." Sometimes there weren't people to say if people were missing.

His gaze dropped. "So not every time?"

"That we know about." She hesitated, but it had to be asked. "Were you at any of these places? No—I know not when the storm was there, but at any other time, before or after?" Yeah, it was straw grabbing, but straws were all she had right now.

His finger touched the map, tracing a path only he knew. He'd written Dr. Masterson about the weather, but hadn't really mentioned where he was, or outlined his route. It was as if his mind had become hyper focused. So much so that when he'd gone airborne, only the weather had mattered. Where he was for that weather was incidental. Only he knew exactly where and when he'd been. His finger tracked up to New York—he'd met Dr. Masterson there and bonded with him—then across the Atlantic. The only thing they knew for sure, he'd avoided this continent, particularly avoided Galveston and the Southern United States. For four years. And had only been coaxed back by The Storm and Dr. Masterson's urging. It had taken some tricky dimensional travel, getting Dr. Masterson here in time to meet Ernest the first time. She still wondered what the good doctor thought of him, though this was his only Ernest.

Finally his finger stopped moving.

"Here. This is the only place both I and the storm have both been. But my visit was long before the storm, months before."

She leaned over. "Persia." She rested her elbows on the map. She could tell by the way the symbol was rendered that The Storm had been not been in Persia in this dimension. Which was, well, puzzling. "Okay, after Persia the storm tracked toward England. But stopped off the coast." This time in this dimension. "A ship was lost at sea that may or may not have been because of it. There were no survivors to talk to. The *Covington*."

He frowned again. "What's the date?" He bent to look for himself, then sat back with a frown. "There was a geological expedition that I spent some time with in Persia. One of them was from England. I think, I could be wrong, but I feel like I heard that ship mentioned. Maybe by him." He looked up. "This is ridiculous."

He was right, but it was the first time there'd been even the faintest sign of anything. "Isn't that how science works? You start with an inkling, a theory, and then follow it until it leads to something else or fades to nothing?"

He made a move that could have been agreement. "This is something less than inkling. Even for science." He frowned deeply. "That you consider it one tells me you have very little."

"I think saying we have very little is being wildly optimistic of you." She grinned at him, and he almost grinned back, before he caught himself. "Look at the other locations. Any of them related to your expedition? Or your travels? What about the people?" She handed him a list. "This is very incomplete, but any of the names ring a bell?"

He was quiet for long enough, she felt hope wane. Then he spoke, slowly, almost absently. "They were from all over, but I don't know precisely where—possibly Canada. Mexico. England...I wasn't overly interested in their names or where they came from as I was in what they were doing. They were geologists, surveyors, drillers—they were looking for petroleum reserves for the Shah."

So it was easy to keep them at a distance if he didn't know their names and stories, keep it all from getting too personal. Personal led to personal questions. Questions that would remind him of what he'd lost. He'd surrounded himself with automations to get away from the personal.

"What prompted you to stop there?" He was going to have get over answering questions, even personal ones.

He shot her a look. "I was in Tehran getting supplies. Someone, an agent maybe, asked me to check on them. They'd missed a meeting or something. Might be low on supplies. I had room, so I took some things for them, in addition to my own, in case I ran across them."

Prudence straightened. "Really?" She didn't remember enough to know when they'd started hunting oil in the Middle East. Hadn't needed to know. An Agent had a crap load of stuff to remember, and what they couldn't remember got loaded into the gear, but it wasn't like all of it could be stored there. They had to pick and choose. Her upload had focused on the meteorological, not geology. "Was it a company or individual behind it?"

The question was more rhetorical, so she surprised at his reaction.

He stiffened first, then shifted in his chair. "They weren't saying, it was confidential, to prevent speculation, but one of them slipped and mentioned a name. I gave them my word I'd forget."

Which would be the one thing to make sure you never forgot.

"Person or company?"

Ernest's lips thinned again.

"We need a name."

"I gave my word."

"I promise not to speculate." She waited a few seconds. "It could be important."

Still he didn't speak. Men and their word. Just then Winston appeared in the doorway.

"There's a gentleman to see you, sir."

Ernest blinked. Prudence was more like stunned. They were on an island, for Pete's sake. How had he come? Airship? Boat? Magic carpet ride?

"To see me? How—" He stopped, obviously realizing the automaton wouldn't have an answer to the question. "Did he give a name?"

Winston held out a calling card. Ernest took it, stiffening. He looked up. "Tell him we'll be with him shortly."

Only after the automaton had left did Ernest hand her the card. Prudence read it.

"Lord Henry?" She started to shrug, then it hit her. "Him? He's the guy?"

Ernest nodded grimly.

Prudence tapped the card against her thumb, her brows pulling together in a frown. How she'd have loved some time with the Agency's main difference engine. "Interesting."

"Interesting? I didn't even know I'd be here. How could he—" His voice rose a bit. "It's impossible—"

"Number two on our impossible things list?" Though not the number two she'd been expecting. His arrival was very interesting. And disturbing. Profoundly disturbing. She might, just might, be in more trouble than she realized.

Chapter Eight

L ord Henry's threads said he had the bread to splash around, though in this time it wasn't that hard to know what was cool, so Prudence wasn't impressed. What he couldn't buy was the build to be boss. He was a black scarecrow, with his stick arms making awkward lines and angles. Even the sassy cane looked out of whack.

He was a bit too everything for the shabby drawing room. And his arrival had thrown her off balance enough to let the slang creep in. She tried to get her head into 1905, while he did the polite—greater to lowers—bow, first to her and then to Ernest.

The way he looked at Ernest was a bit too cranked—too—well, she didn't know what they called it in this time. Crazy maybe or unnaturally excited. Whatever it was called, it kinda creeped her out. But his lack of distinguishing attention to her, gave her time to eyeball him. Goodness, the guy was downright hideous. Oily, coarse nest on top of that misshapen head. Hair sticking out in all directions. Pocked skin and a nose and mouth in fierce competition for ugliest. With his ears edging into a close third.

He was kind of a caricature of himself, one that had accidentally come to life.

"Dr. Masterson thought you might be here, Dr. Warren." He paused, letting his gaze trail briefly around the space, arching his brows just a bit, as if he wanted to ask why but was too polite to do it. His accent was upper class British. "I am pleased he was correct."

And apparently the doc had a crystal ball. If Masterson had sent

Lord Henry here. Anyone with money could follow the crumbs between Ernest and Dr. Masterson. It was the same calling card she'd used. Copycat. So far she wasn't buying what he was selling. Significant to her, without offering clarity, there'd been no sign of a Lord Henry around the other iterations. Didn't mean there was something wrong with the guy, even if she really wanted to think there was. Cat could be creepy without being creepy.

Ernest stared at him for several seconds and then muttered, "The storm..." He gestured vaguely toward the Gulf. He opened his mouth, probably to ask how either man could have known he'd be here, but closed it, most likely caught in the 1905 manners trap.

Prudence would have liked to know, too. She hadn't told Masterson where she planned to set up shop.

As if he became aware of her, Lord Henry looked her direction, and she discovered there was one thing about him that wasn't ugly. His eyes. Though cavernously deep set and dark, there were lights in there that were kind of mesmerizing. They saw what they looked at, which eyes didn't always do, particularly when directed toward women in this time. Or her time, she reminded herself a bit wryly. There was a fathomless quality to them, leaving her the sense that if she looked long enough and hard enough, she might learn something. Maybe something amazing. Find out deep secrets. Become...better. She felt herself leaning and rocked on her heels.

That woke her up. She dropped her lids over her eyes and took a couple of deep breaths, her clasped hands tightening briefly. The dizziness faded. The wood beneath her feet firmed once more. Carefully, cautiously, she raised her lids, though not all the way up.

Lord Henry extended a claw-like hand her direction, giving Ernest a look of inquiry.

Ernest jerked at this nudge to his manners, but Prudence beat him to it, the instinct to hide her true name well honed by her many dimensional transits. That she'd told this Ernest her real name was another protocol breach, but she hadn't thought it would matter. "Prunella Smith."

Lord Henry had his eyes on Prudence, so he missed Ernest's jerk. Prudence hid a sigh. He was brilliant, but not subtle.

Prudence let the clammy claw close round her hand. At least his slight bow gave her break from the eyeballs. The small shift of air brought her the scent of him. The first wave was pleasant, but the follow-on, not so much. It wasn't bad enough to repel, but there was something about it that made the hairs on her arms lift. She didn't like him, so it wasn't easy to decide if that made him dangerous or just one of those guys women didn't like, well, because. He made a great alternative to Ernest as the bad guy.

No wonder they didn't want agents to get emotionally involved.

"Please," she gestured toward a wooden chair next to a small couch. "Won't you be seated?" She clasped her hands back together and added, hoping it didn't sound too afterthought-ish, "Can I get you some refreshment?" Jeez, she hoped he said no. Though maybe one of the automatons would know how to manage that?

Lord Henry sank gracefully onto the wooden seat, one hand still clasping the cane, but shook his head. "No, I thank you."

Something in the way he glanced around seemed to hint that he couldn't imagine good refreshment in this place. He had a point. Even the water was on the brackish side.

With a look at her, Ernest went to the bench. She followed him, and they sank down together.

The silence grew slowly awkward.

Prudence liked awkward silences. There were things to be learned in them, if one didn't get sucked into awkward. Ernest didn't love it. She knew that without looking at him. Lord Henry didn't like it but didn't seem to fear it. She could almost see wheels turning inside those eyes, his brain searching for a way past the current impasse without him being the one to give ground.

Lord Henry finally cleared his throat, as if acknowledging someone had to do speak. Shifting slightly so that he faced them more fully, he said, "I am glad you made it safely ashore, Doctor."

"Thank you." As if even Ernest realized this was not enough, he added, "I was rather concerned." Another pause. "And relieved. To make it, I mean."

Not a great example of clever, though ultimately just as unrevealing. Prudence had to lower her lashes quickly and keep a firm grip on her lips to hold back the grin.

"I understand you spent some time with my expedition while you were in Egypt?"

"They were...I found them very...they were most kind."

A very slight smile curved the edges of Lord Henry's thin mouth. "I believe you were the one who was kind. They were in need of resupply. I am grateful for the assistance you provided." A pause. "And I am grateful you did not mention my involvement. Your discretion is most appreciated. When it is known that one is willing to fund expeditions..." He made a gesture with his hands that seemed to say he'd like to fund them all but couldn't.

"I imagine...they didn't..."

Lord Henry held up a hand. "Cleveland was worried, but I assured him that I did not mind you knowing. In fact, I am most interested in your researches, Doctor. I have my ticket for your presentation at the Institute."

He moved the cane to a position between his legs, resting both hands on the head. Between his hands, the silver gleamed, something that could have been beak or possibly a muzzle stuck out of the gap created by his palms. Did she see jeweled eyes? Okay, her imagination might be running a bit wild.

Prudence felt the slight withdrawal from Ernest at the mention of the Institute. Lord Henry saw it, too.

"You are going to speak, are you not?"

With an effort, Ernest nodded. "Of course. I just wonder how useful my research is..." His voice trailed off and his focus shifted as the scientist came forward. He looked toward the Gulf, toward the incoming storm.

Lord Henry's eyes gleamed. Was it her overactive imagination that the cane head's eyes did, too?

"So the storm you ran into was The Storm?"

Ernest still resisted. It showed in the tightening around his mouth, but he admitted, "It did exhibit some unusual features."

Lord Henry leaned slightly forward, the knuckles of his hands turning white. "I've read about it, but have not yet experienced this storm."

Stick around, Prudence wanted to tell him, even though she didn't want him to stick around.

"You may have the opportunity," Ernest said, "if it persists on its current course. Though, from what I've read, it can dissipate quite suddenly and without warning."

Lord Henry leaned back again, with an effort at calm or so it seemed to her. "Yes, I have this as well." He too looked in the direction of the Gulf. His gaze returned to them, tracking between them as if trying to figure out their relationship.

He looked at Ernest. "I had come to offer Dr. Warren a share of my modest hospitality..."

There was a hint of a question in the comment, but also some irony, Prudence noted, fighting a grin once more. It would be hard to get more modest than this.

"I am, it is most kind, but..." Ernest shifted on the wooden bench.

"It's very hard to separate Dr. Warren from his airship," Prudence said, to help him out and to add an element of respectability to the situation. Not as much as Ernest would have liked, but as much as she could give him. "Though I believe he was glad to have a break from sea rations."

"Ah," Lord Henry relaxed some, which was interesting. Why did he care?

The air in the room was thick with nuances and tension and questions. All kinds of crap. So much it was hard to sort through. There was menace in there, too, but she wasn't sure it came from Lord Henry or the storm tracking so steadily toward them.

"When do you think The Storm will arrive? If it does," Lord Henry amended.

Ernest hesitated, a frown creasing his brows. "Possibly by morning."

Lord Henry rose, prompting them to rise as well. "Then, with your permission, Miss Smith, I would like to return in the morning? I can imagine no greater pleasure than experiencing it with a scientist of Dr. Warren's caliber."

Prudence did not want to be here to greet the storm, didn't want to face it with those eyes watching her, but what could she say? She glanced at Ernest, then managed a polite smile. "Of course, sir. We'd be pleased to have you join us."

Chapter Nine

E ven after Lord Henry's departure, Prudence didn't speak. Ernest liked how quietly she sat. It was unusual in a woman. The crease between her brows seemed to indicate that she was puzzled. He agreed that there was much about the meeting to puzzle, even without the strange storm heading toward them.

"He was," Ernest finally broke the silence, "most unusual."

"Yes."

Ernest waited for her to say more and when she didn't, he shifted to look at her, only just realizing how close they sat on the uncomfortable couch. Her scent, something light and as unexpected as she was, came to him, for once the reminder that she was a woman not causing him pain. He didn't try to discern why. The situation had pulled him out of the past, out of pain, out of everything familiar. Into the unknown. Into the impossible. He found he didn't mind as much as he should.

"You didn't trust him?" The question surprised him. He had not realized he felt distrust until he asked it.

"No."

She looked at him, her face close enough that he could see all the colors in her eyes. And the curve of her lips...

"Did you?"

The question pursed her lips just right for—

He looked away. He shook his head. "No." He frowned. "I'm not sure why." He looked at her once more.

"He's creepy," she pointed out. She sighed. "That doesn't make him the bad guy."

"Bad guy?" He shook his head.

"The villain of the piece."

"Oh." Ernest looked at the door where Lord Henry had left. "He would be excellent on the stage." He frowned as something in his gut twitched. A sense that he'd said something that mattered.

"Do you think he was acting?"

The direct question startled him. "I'm not good—"

"Do you think he was acting?" she persisted, leaning in so that he couldn't look away.

He frowned. "I'm not sure that was—no—not acting so much as he doesn't seem...authentic." He rubbed his aching head with frustration. "That's not right—he was too—"

"Was he," she hesitated long enough he had to look at her, "too real?"

He considered this, then nodded slowly. "Yes." He studied this notion and felt the correctness of it. "How strange. Can one be too real?" One was either real or one was not. Or so he'd always believed. He could concede that his notion of reality had been tested in the last few hours.

She tipped her head to one side and seemed to seriously consider the question. Then she made a face. "Before today, I'd have said no, but today we're working on believing impossible things."

Impossible things. It was the first indication that she experienced difficulty with them, too. How many had he been forced to deal with so far? He rubbed his forehead. "It is stuffy in here." He was used to fresher breezes, airship life. This place felt closed in, confining. His thinking processes felt as clouded and confined. "I need to walk." To pace is what he meant. How many miles had he logged pacing the perimeter of his airship?

"Let's go for a walk. With the beacon lit, it's clear enough out there, though we'd better stick to the boardwalks." She sighed. "Pacing sometimes helps with thinking."

She appeared indifferent to the proprieties. Technically they were not alone in this cottage, since the automatons were close by. Her confidence in his integrity both pleased and puzzled. It implied, once again, equality between them. Not assumed either. Expected was closer to what he sensed from her.

She didn't speak again, not until they strolling along the boardwalk toward the lighthouse. The tide was still out. In the diffuse light from overhead, he could see the high water lines on the rocks. He dimly perceived the hull of his airship, almost motionless in the unusually still air. The pier jutted out from the other boardwalk, the one from the lighthouse. It looked to be sturdy, as was his ship, but if the storm turned severe...he wished he could move it. He frowned. He could have his ship handlers take it into Mobile, but if the storm moved inland, they did not have the programming to react suitably to the threat.

"You're concerned about *The Weatherman*."

Did she read minds? He nodded.

"I am concerned about all of us," she admitted, with a sigh. "I wish we had time for a tour. It looks to be a fine ship."

He opened his mouth to offer, but closed it again. In the dark— no, that was taking proprieties too far. He realized she was the first woman he didn't mind boarding his airship. Because he didn't feel guilt, he looked up, anxious to change the subject.

The glow from the lighthouse beacon was different from moon or starlight. The light was softer. Brighter, then softer as the Fresnel lens turned in its unique pattern, so that ships would know which lighthouse this was. He studied it, interested to note that it created a sort of umbrella of light overhead, the effect quite interesting. He'd only ever seen a beacon from out over the ocean, he realized. The change in perspective was intriguing. That thought made his instincts twitch. Or flinch. His perspective of many things was currently being challenged. A change of perspective was also the reason he'd left, or so he'd told himself. How much had it actually changed, he wondered now.

"I've become quite fascinated with lighthouses," she murmured, her gaze also directed upwards. "They are beautiful and...hopeful."

Hope. He'd been hopeful once. Felt it stirring inside now. In this light, with her chin raised like that, she was quite beautiful. For the first time in four years he felt no guilt at admiring another woman. She was so different it was impossible to compare, he told himself. She turned, her chin lowering as her gaze met his, and he had the most extraordinary feeling that he'd been here, in this moment, with her, before...

He swayed as the horizon tilted, and she grabbed his arm to steady him.

"Are you all right, Er—doctor?"

He covered her hand with his, and with the horizon in a slow spin around them, said, "You called me Ernest....before."

The pause was long, but she didn't look away or appear startled or any of the things she should have. Instead she looked intrigued. "Did I?"

"But—" he rubbed his head. "How can I have this memory when I know this is the first time we have met? Or met here...I have certainly never been here before."

She steered them toward a spot where a mass of granite offered seating. He sank down, needing the respite for knees that did not feel like his own.

"Your...memory is specific to this place?" she asked.

He examined it and finally nodded. "Yes, though it makes my head hurt thinking of it." He looked at her. "How can that be?"

"That would be another impossible thing," she said ruefully. "I call them the impossible possible, since they clearly happened."

"You don't remember?"

She shifted a bit, her mouth pursing for almost a minute. "I don't remember, no, not yet, anyway. Time is, well, fluid. That makes us uncomfortable, so we call it *deja vu* or past lives or—" she grinned, "a knock on the head. It's only if we open ourselves up to the impossible, that we begin to accept...more and be surprised less."

He stared at her, not wanting to believe—his mind whirled, but his heart said he knew this woman. Against logic and science. Knew her and—as if in a dream, he lifted his hand and touched the side of her face. She didn't flinch or move back. Just watched him, with curiosity in her gaze, but something more. He looked deep and found cautious hope in the brown depths. Hope. It was quite...contagious tonight. He thought he'd discovered all the colors in her eyes, but he found more in the beacon light. Golds. Greens. Darks and light. So much more light than dark.

In some strange fashion, he felt she *saw* him, all the parts of who he was, even those he was less enamored of, and still liked him despite...

His hand slid along her cheek, then around to the back of her neck. Her skin was softer than the finest silk, the stroke of her hair to the back of his hand sending light into his long darkened, hopeless heart. *Hope.*

He didn't think. Instead he bent toward her, noting that her head tipped to accommodate his approach, angling just enough so that they came together, it felt not new, but as if it had always been like this between them. It felt more natural than he'd ever felt with Ophelia...

The rightness of holding her, of kissing her shocked him. He pulled her closer, diving deeper into the kiss—he demanded, and she did not seem to mind—

There was the sound of wood against wood, as if something had hit the pier. He jerked back, waited for the guilt, but still it stayed at bay. His hands lingered on her shoulders. She stared at him, her chest rising and falling rapidly, her eyes big enough to fall into again.

A wave hit his legs, drenching him to his knees. She looked down, so he did, too.

"The tide is coming in," he said.

She frowned, shook her head. "It's not time for the tide. And it shouldn't reach us up here in any case."

"Then what?"

"Could be storm surge. Must be."

Storm surge? "Do you refer to stormtide?"

Before she could answer, they heard footsteps thumping on wood. The sound changed some when it moved to the boardwalk. Now they felt the vibration of the steps on the wood under their feet.

"Sir?"

Ernest huffed out a sigh and let his hands fall away from her. "That's Niles. One of my ship handlers."

"Niles." Her lips curved a bit, as if something about the name amused her.

The boardwalk shuddered. Like it had been waiting for his attention, the wind freshened. Only instead of the scent of the sea, it carried the brimstone smell and taste he recalled from the storm.

She rose to her feet, and turned to face the Gulf, her chin lifting toward the dark horizon. "I think your storm is almost here."

"That's not—" He stopped. He would have to come up with a new definition of "possible," it seemed.

The automaton came into the light cast by the lighthouse beacon.

"One moment all was quiet and then," he blinked. "And then it wasn't, sir."

"Crispin?" Ernest asked.

"He was below deck."

"Is *The Weatherman* all right?"

"It was intact when I left it, but..." the automaton stopped, lacking the programming to explain what had happened, Ernest surmised.

"The water is rising fast," Prudence said. She glanced back toward the cottage.

The glow from the cottage windows somehow appeared further away than logic said they could be.

Ernest studied the horizon again. His impulse to send Niles back in for his counterpart died. Outside the beacon-cast light all was deeply, ominously dark. "It almost appears that—" he stopped, unable to say the words.

"Like the beacon is keeping it back," she finished for him. "That wasn't on my impossible list." She sighed. "If it is holding it back, we'd better make sure it stays lit until—"

He looked at her. "Until?"

"We come up with a plan."

It was, he realized, possible to admire a person's optimism and be astonished by their apparent insanity. One did not plan for this. One fled storms. If one could not, then one rode them out hoping, praying to survive. And then one dealt with what came after. The guilt, the pain tried to come back, but there was not time for either. That would also have to wait for after...

Chapter Ten

"If the water keeps rising, the cottage will not be high enough," Ernest said. He looked around them, as if he expected another dwelling to appear.

Prudence agreed with the unspoken wish, but yeah, this island was going, going, almost gone, even before this crazy storm. This storm surge, if that's what it was, wouldn't help with the erosion problem.

He glanced back in the direction of his airship, but said, "We should seek refuge in the lighthouse."

"Yes," she agreed, her mind still kind of stuck on how he could feel like he knew her. She hadn't seen that coming. And how was it possible that he remembered her calling him Ernest? He'd never allowed that liberty in any of the other dimensions. And he believed it was place specific. That seemed to indicate some kind of time shift, something she'd read about in some of the more obscure texts in the Agency library. But that didn't explain how he could remember something that hadn't happened yet.

She backtracked some, trying to find the right research branch. Been easier with the difference engine, but oh well. Okay, what if Ernest wasn't *the* anomaly? What if the whole dimension was a... closed system? She thought that was the term she'd heard used. Masterson had written the tract, at least she thought it was one of his. The little she remembered, he believed there were dimensions that didn't spawn other dimensions. It was all theory because no one had traveled into one. Or gotten out if they had? Why did her thoughts keep wanting to circle back to her MIA grandfather? It was unusual for their kind to disappear without a trace. Odds were, even if an Agent got lost in a dimension, someone would stumble on signs of them eventually.

But if she'd met Ernest before, then that seemed to indicate, her mind hunted for a word that would fit, a different type of anomaly. What if it wasn't so much about time travel, but a time...repeat? With some memory bleed through? But why would time replay? She didn't even ponder the how, because she was already way past the known unknown.

Okay, say it was repeating, or replaying? Replaying until—what? Well, The Storm was seriously messed up. Or something was. What if this were some kind of correction loop? Early Pinkertons certainly believed in a Higher Talent. Some skepticism had crept in through the years, but the principle of doing no harm was still the standard of conduct within the Agency. She'd heard rumors of rogue Talents, but stuff like that was not on her reading list. No one said so, but it had to be the reason Agents traveled with weapons.

This Storm was doing damage across dimensions. If there was a Higher Talent...or time itself was trying to self-correct? Or man-made tampering gone wrong? Did it matter what had caused this?

It was all pretty far-fetched, but people in the Agency had postulated stranger things on less data.

"I wish I had my gear," he frowned, "though I'm not sure it would be of any use. It was not functioning normally before I went under the storm."

"I had your crew move your stuff ashore while you were unconscious. It's in the lighthouse." She said this somewhat absently, lifting her sodden skirts higher as a wave crashed just behind them, the water splashing in a high arc as it hit rock. "We need to burn rubber, or we're gonna get creamed."

She got a weird look and realized she'd lapsed into her time talk. She grimaced. "We should hurry." She gathered her skirts into an untidy bunch and legged it. It wasn't as bad as it could have been. She had her working uniform under the 1905 duds. Ernest kept up, half lifting her up the porch stairs as water tugged and boiled across the boardwalk. Niles managed to keep up with them, which was a bit surprising. Running was a fairly complex activity.

Inside the cottage, Ernest called to his other two automatons.

"I'll be right back," she told him. She dashed, well, dragged herself and her sodden skirts, into her bedroom, tugging at the various things keeping the now amazingly heavy skirts attached to her person. Luckily the snaps and such weren't of this time, so they were easy to disconnect. She let the mess drop with a thump, stepped out without even trying to kick them aside. She'd probably break something. She dug under the bed for the weapons she'd hidden there and quickly strapped them on. The rest of her gear was easy to stow in the bags attached to her utility belt. Ernest was about to get shock round—what round was this? She'd lost count—when he saw the pants, but she was not going to battle with a storm in a dress.

She took time to check on Octavius. He seemed to be all right. Looked like he'd gone deep. The connection wasn't solid though. That worried her. If this was an anomalous dimension, and she lost her familiar, she and gramps would have more than the Talent in common. Her father had been worried when she bonded with Octavius. It was very unusual to have a sea-bound familiar. In fact, the only other person to have one was that MIA grandfather. Not a good time to think about that.

Back in the parlor, Ernest waited by the door with his automatons. His eyes widened, but the sudden howl of the wind made the structure shake. He didn't have time for shock or questions. He gestured toward the door, then seemed to realize this was not the time for ladies first. Not that she wouldn't have been okay. She was likely more physically fit than he was. She studied his rear aspect. All wet like that she could see what he had. Okay, after his travel around the world, make that almost equal in the toughness stakes.

Prudence took a position to one side of the door and nodded. He yanked it open, and the wind rushed in like it had a mind and a purpose. Ernest stepped into the gap and it threw him back, almost knocking him off his feet. His two bodyguards moved to help, kept him on this feet. He looked at her and gestured toward them. She nodded. The automatons should be able to make headway, even against the high wind. Or they'd all tumble together. It was pretty much a do or die moment.

On his order, they moved into the doorway and waited, their aspect a bit bent against the force of the wind. Prudence got behind one, while Ernest positioned himself behind the other. Ernest grabbed her arm and the belt of his automaton. Prudence did the same with hers. Niles came behind them, a hand on each of their shoulders. The automatons linked arms and pressed forward.

It was crazy bad outside and, out on the porch, the automatons ability to block the wind diminished as it grabbed at them from first one direction and the other, though it did help to have Niles steadying them from behind. In the canopy of light from the beacon, the waves tumbled over themselves in the hurry to block their path. The wood of the boardwalk was slick and treacherous as waves crashed over it. Good thing it was a straight shot, since it made it hard to see the boardwalk. Out on the water, visible because of the beacon, the darkness really looked like it beat against the light. She'd seen some weird crap in her various transits, but this took the prize for sure. She heard a new sound. A sort of weird roar and flashes of orange light flickered against the beacon canopy. Lightning? No. Something was up there. Its shadow moving—no, had to be flying over the canopy. Didn't have the right shape for an airship, unless it was a crazy weird one. It was the right incentive to get her moving faster. She didn't want to be out here if whatever it was found a way in.

Linked together they made their way through the fast rising water to the lighthouse. Weird that the steps weren't under water, but also good. The climb seemed high and inside, the climb would be higher. This was one tall lighthouse. The wind sound rose in a shriek when one of the automatons managed to open the door. They almost fell inside, then it took all three automatons and Ernest to close it.

The sudden silence was not as comforting as it should have been. Both she and Ernest were panting from the effort. She looked up. The stairs wound up and up the side of the lighthouse, visible from light spilling down from the beacon. She knew from personal experience that there were a lot them.

"While I would like to wait and regain my breath, I am not sure it is wise," Ernest gasped out.

In the dim light filtering down, Prudence saw something coming under the door. She crouched down and cautiously touched it. It felt like water, but...not. It burned her finger tip. Wisps like steam or fog curled against the frame, as if seeking a breach. She stood hastily and retreated.

"Yeah, we should go up."

"Up," Ernest said to the automatons. They responded with an almost human alacrity. He waited for Prudence, then started up himself. The fog curled around the base of the stairs, but did not follow them up more than a few steps.

Prudence tried not to count, though her brain seemed to want to. She was not too ashamed to use the railing to help pull herself up, since Ernest was on her heels. The landings were the illusion of respite, since more stairs waited on the other side. The counting helped a little when she made it halfway. When they reached the watch room, Prudence bent, resting her hands on her knees. Gravity hated her in every dimension, she decided.

Close to the light, it was brighter, but not unbearable.

Ernest leaned against the wall, trying to catch his breath, too, though he did try not to look wasted. It was kind of cute. Prudence didn't have the energy to pretend. She straightened, with an inner groan, and pulled up her googles. She positioned them over her eyes, turned on the glare reducers, and activated the scanning program. Through the sudden stream of data in her peripheral vision, she saw Ernest staring. She extracted her spare pair, adjusted the filtering, then handed them to Ernest. A bit dubiously, he put them on, adjusting the fit.

The automatons had placed Ernest's gear to one side of this platform, stacking it neatly. It was hotter up here and the stink from the fuel source was...challenging. She went to the last flight of stairs and looked up. The glass windows up there weren't even rattling. She couldn't hear the wind howling anymore. In fact, it was so quiet, it was a bit...freaky. There was a kind of boom or slam. Like the door closing. A pause, then the hollow thump of footsteps on the stairs.

She extracted the Raijin-ator 5, which she'd stowed in rig strapped to her back, and took a peek over the edge. At first she couldn't see anything. Just heard the steady sound of approaching footsteps. Found herself counting again. Ernest came up next to her, giving her long gun a bemused look. He leaned over next to her. The steps kept coming.

"I think it's Crispin." He straightened and looked at her. Prudence arched a brow. "My other ship handler. The one on the ship."

Prudence didn't find that as comforting as she'd have liked. She kept Raijin-ator 5 directed down.

"It's—"

"Crispin, I know." She looked at him. "How did he get off the ship?"

Ernest was quiet, clearly processing this. "You can't just shoot him."

"I wasn't planning to. Order him to stop." If he didn't obey, then she'd shoot him.

Ernest nodded, leaned over and called, "Crispin, stop at the next landing. Go into maintenance mode and check systems." He leaned back.

One more footstep, then silence. She looked at Niles. "Maybe you should have him give himself a checkup, too. I think I'm having trust issues."

Ernest didn't look happy, but he nodded.

"Have him set up here. He can block the stairway." Or Crispin could have his back. "Maybe have your other automatons set up your stuff over there?" The mechanism that rotated the light ran down the center of the lighthouse. Some weights and such. At least they had the high ground. Overhead there was a raucous cry, unlike anything she'd ever heard. Maybe they had the high ground.

"My equipment was malfunctioning as we approached the storm," Ernest said. "I don't know why you bothered to move it up here."

"Was it malfunctioning or giving you readings you didn't like?" She didn't look at him, her attention still focused up the last stairs.

"But—" he stopped.

She looked at him then, saw thoughtfulness creeping into his gaze.

"Stop looking for the expected and see what's actually there." It was like the first rule of dimensional travel, but he wouldn't know that.

"What are you going to do?"

She put a foot on the first stair. Dang, that was a lot of heat coming down the well. "Going to take a gander at what's out there."

He opened his mouth, either to ask what or protest.

"I'll be fine." Maybe. Maybe not. It had to be done. She pulled the Paraton-ator 20 out of the holster and handed it to him. "This is the safety, that's the trigger." He looked pleased to have a weapon. She just hoped he knew who to point it at. She grinned at him and was startled and delighted when he grinned back. It was such a spontaneous and natural expression. She'd never seen any Ernest do that before.

Then it was gone. His gaze serious. "Be careful out there."

She nodded, even though she was obviously never careful. If she were careful, she'd be back home, working as a teacher or nurse or married to a guy with a normal, 1950s kind of job. So she grinned again and headed up, with the long barrel of her Raijin-ator 5 pointed down, her other hand gripping the hand rail. The heat and smell built with each step up. Of course it would be hot. The sun beat in all day and now the lanterns with their stinky fuel got to weigh in. There were vents, but yeah, still a mostly closed space. She circled around the huge light to the balcony access and eased it open.

Nothing. Not even a wisp of moving air.

She was definitely getting the impression this was The Storm, not *a* storm.

She eased partway out, blocking the door's closing with her body. Just in case the storm changed its mind. She fine tuned her goggles, adjusting them to this light, and studied the scanning data. Still no signs of dimensional travel, though she had to keep a tight rein on her instinct to flee. She scanned the horizon, taking it slow to give her equipment as much raw data as possible. If she didn't make it and someone came after—assuming someone could—they could download the data from the drone.

A shadow passed overhead, and she looked up, blinking as it circled the tower, then appeared to settle on the roof next to the lightning rod, its wings flapping once, before being pulled in against its body. It looked to be the size of a largish dog. Something that looked like claws curled over the edge of the roof, not far from where she stood. As if it sensed her, it angled its muzzle her direction, its eyes glowed red and round, and it blew a golden-red stream against the canopy. A golden-red stream of...fire?

She sensed movement and turned to find Ernest standing behind her, looking up with his jaw a bit dropped. "What in Hades is that thing?"

"I think it's a dragon."

～

A dragon?

"You can't be serious," Ernest said. She'd asked him to believe six impossible things, but a dragon? That was one impossible too far.

"At least there is only one," she murmured. "And it's not that big—"

There was raucous cry, further away, and the dragon lifted its head to answer it with one of its own.

"Oh man, shut my mouth. This day just gets more and more...interesting."

She flashed him a grin, and he wondered if part of interesting was the kiss they'd exchanged. Who was this woman? She wore pants. Carried weapons like nothing he'd ever seen or heard of. Spoke of the impossible and dragons and storm stopping. And she kissed like an angel. She made him feel alive. It would be most unfortunate if he died, just when he finally wanted to live again.

He sounded his heart for guilt and found none. There was not time for guilt or kisses. Even without the dragons, there was the strange storm bearing down on them. This structure, which had seemed so sturdy from down on the beach, now seemed as precarious as his airship. Despite that, he felt exhilarated, happy to be here with her. The danger sharpened all his senses. Made him feel more alive than he'd ever felt before. He didn't prod the old wound, but distantly knew he'd never have been able to share a moment like this with Ophelia. It did not matter. She had no place here. Ophelia belonged to another life, a different time. It was only now, staring into death's maw, that he realized how very little he'd lived the last four years. Or the years before that. All the places he'd been, the things he'd seen, how sad to realize now that he'd done them through a filter that kept him from feeling. One had to live, to learn. To *live*. Not merely exist.

"Look at that."

It was not easy to do, but he dragged his attention away from the dragon. She pointed down, so with some concern he looked down. And blinked. The water had retreated, exposing the granite chunks of rock once more. The roiling surf had also calmed to the point where it was placidly lapping around the pilings of the pier. His airship was still outside the range of the beacon, so he could not tell if it was intact or not. The wind had died down. A shadow passed over, tracking across rock and water in a slow circle, the wing span about enough to keep a large dog—or dog-sized dragon—airborne.

"The equipment has been set up, sir." Fred spoke behind him.

Ernest looked at Prudence. She shrugged.

"Let's go have a look."

To his relief, she climbed back inside, making no demur when he closed the door. They followed Fred back down to the watch room, where he saw that they'd arranged his instruments on the floor in a semi-circle to one side. There were additional crates stacked to one side. He hoped those contained his research notebooks and books.

She crouched down, studying each one in turn. He had that flickering sense of having done this before with her. Like two images superimposed, but one faint and somewhat out of focus.

"They are misbehaving, aren't they?"

They were indeed. His sunshine recorder believed there was sun to record. His hydroscope could not decide if there was or was not moisture in the air. His hydrodeik showed similar issues with the humidity. And his barograph said the pressure was rising and falling, then rising again. His barometer showed dropping pressure, but how was he to know if that was a correct reading?

"What's that one? It's not doing anything."

"That is my Blizablighter 3000," he told her. "It is not activated."

"Really?" She shifted position so she could study it, touching it tentatively with the tip of her index finger. "Bliza-what?"

"Blizablighter 3000."

She turned and looked at him for a long moment, seemed about to speak, but didn't. Redirected her gaze back to the Blizablighter 3000.

"What is wrong?" he asked.

"Name just seems a bit odd for you."

He frowned. Now that he considered the name, it was an unusual choice for him. He felt that flicker again, as if seeing something that could not be, a sense that he had not been the one to name it. Only he had been alone with his automatons when he had built it, then named it, so of course the name came from him. Perhaps it had been an unusual day?

"What does it do?" she asked, her words almost an exact echo of those in the flickering memory.

"It acts somewhat similar to a lightning rod. But instead of directing the electricity into the ground, it collects it, stores it for later use."

"That thing stores electricity?"

"Well, I've only tested it on small strikes and only after testing it with small amounts of artificially generated electricity, but yes, so far that is what it does."

Outside, the dragons roared, first one, quickly followed by the other. Prudence looked up, then at Ernest. "Are these the only instruments behaving badly?"

Ernest pulled out his pocket watch and showed it to her.

"Did it start when you went into the storm?"

He shook his head. "Before."

She looked interested, taking the watch in her hand. She extracted her watch and held it up. It kept time with his.

"That might explain how the storm got here so quickly," she murmured.

He frowned. "I do not understand your meaning." Or her reasoning, if that is what it was.

"You're still assuming this stuff is all wrong. What if it's right?"

"Right...how can that be right?"

"Well, what if time is moving faster? Wouldn't that make all the instruments react differently? It would also explain how you and Octavius got here so fast."

There was no sign she jested. He opened his mouth to protest such an egregious lapse of logic, but heard instead, a distant echo of his own voice doing just that. He clamped his lips together as the words were followed by the sensation that he'd been wrong then. Dangerously wrong. That he could not afford to be wrong again. It was so important he not be wrong...

"I suppose the storm could be causing it. Or something in the storm. Or the storm is taking advantage of time moving faster," she murmured, apparently oblivious to his failure to comment. Her gaze moved slowly from one instrument to the other, then stopped when she came to the Blizablighter 3000. "What's your battery? Your storage device for that?"

The feeling surged once more, the effect almost like that of glass shattering, but was quickly gone. Too quickly. He needed to know what it was he needed to know—

He shook his head and knelt next to her. Just this simple action smoothed, or soothed, that feeling. It felt oddly new. He touched the mass of material he'd suspended beneath the collecting rod. It was multi-colored, but he'd noted that it became more green and gold when holding more charge. "This mineral both conducts and contains the energy."

"I've never seen anything quite like it," she murmured, touching it as well, her hand brushing against his for a brief moment. Her eyes widened. "It's warm. And a bit...tingly."

"That is from the charge I collected in Europe. It dissipates very slowly. It is not safe to touch it right after it receives a strike, even a small one."

"Where did you get it?"

"In...Persia." His voice and thoughts slowed, almost stalled. "One of the drillers gave it to me when he saw it interested me. I believe it might be a meteorite. They found several at one of the sites they were studying." He'd had a sense then that he should have handed it over to one of the geologists, but also had a sense he should hide it. That was the one he'd acted on, though he did not know why. Minerals were outside his field of research. But he did know enough to know it was probably not of this earth. To salve his conscience he'd tested it, discovered its conductivity and ability to hold the charge for so long. He'd been looking for something that would attract and defuse the power of lightning strikes, perhaps harness them into something useful. He'd planned to show this invention to Masterson.

"Persia." With the tip of a finger, she traced the wires he'd attached to direct the strike into the mineral. "How much electricity do you think it can store?"

"I have been unable to determine the upper limit," Ernest admitted. "I had hoped to sail under a larger storm during the crossing." He hesitated, then admitted, "There was considerable lightning activity in the storm. I was...tempted."

"I imagine you were. No sign of lightning out there now." She glanced over her shoulder in the direction of the storm. "Interesting."

"Why interesting?"

She half shrugged. "It seems able to...respond...think...plan. Maybe it sensed that the lightning would be a temptation for you? It did seem rather interested in you, you'll recall."

Though he still felt incredulous, it was getting easier to navigate the logic shoals. He was not sure if that was good or ill. He could admit to himself that the way her mind worked was curiously fascinating.

"You believe it was," he had trouble saying the words out loud, "a trap? That does not seem—" He stopped because using the word possible had lost clarity for him out here in the shoals of this new reality.

Prudence shrugged. "Or a test. It is the only thing here that no other meteorologist would have, is it not?"

He could not dispute this. He had drawings and ideas, but had not felt like he had anything new to offer until the Blizablighter 3000. And truthfully, he was not sure how that helped the study of the weather. Behind that was a truth he had tried to stay ahead of. That perhaps he was not meant to be a weather scientist.

"I am not the weatherman you hoped for," he said, heavily, rising to his feet. He pushed his hands through his hair and down to massage the back of his neck.

She stood up, too. She was tall, but not too tall. Her figure pleasing and sleek in her men's attire. With her back to the center pillar, she lifted her goggles and studied him. "If whatever it is that's out there wants that mineral, then it's possible it's a," she paused, then finished, "a wolf in storm's clothing."

"What is it?" he burst out, yanking the goggles off his face, too.

"No clue," she admitted, "but we need to make sure it doesn't get it. Because what it's doing without it, it's very bad. Not just for you, but for everyone."

He looked at her and asked, because he had to know, because he'd asked it before, "Who are you?" He wanted to stop there, but couldn't. "What are you?"

Chapter Eleven

Prudence glanced at his automatons. Wasn't sure she wanted to have this discussion around a couple of machines who couldn't forget what they heard. "Let's check the lamps," she suggested, gesturing to the stairs. It was not her first choice of a place for a chat, based solely on heat and stench. All that glass, too. But if they went down, they would run into his other machine.

He hesitated, then nodded. She felt oddly conscious of him following her up to the lamp room. Its Fresnel lamp was a thing of beauty, the numerous facets of its glass reflecting and beaming the light out into the night for the ships that might be passing. An engineering marvel, even in her time. The light in the night in this one.

She sighed and put it at her back. Her fingers danced on the buttons of her right arm instrument panel, activating the sound dampening field. It might be detected by whatever was out there, but that seemed a better option than getting overheard.

Ernest grabbed her arm. "What did you do?" He touched it, but of course it did nothing.

"It creates a sound dampening field, so that no one can overhear our conversation."

The scientist warred with man in his expression. "How is that possible?"

She studied him, wondering how much truth he could handle. "Do you have that feeling that we've talked like this before?" she asked, stalling for time, for guidance.

He shook his head. "I did, down there, but it went away."

Okay, that was interesting. "When did it go away?"

He hesitated, then met her gaze with a directness that startled her. "When I started to believe you."

She felt her jaw sag and snapped it up. "Oh. Well, that's...good." Amazing was what she almost said. He'd come further than she'd thought possible. And in a shorter time. The key was the *deja vu*, she decided. If they were in some kind of dimensional time correction, then maybe they'd changed something. But they could still mess up. What was the right move? Right moves? And what would happen if they fixed things? Would this Ernest cease to exist? That was an awful thought. She liked this Ernest better than the others. Liked the kiss. Would she forget again? That was sad, too.

"What's wrong?" he asked.

Everything, she wanted to say. She didn't. "I'm trying to figure out how to explain..."

"The impossible?" He smiled a bit wryly as he said it.

"The wildly impossible."

He appeared to think about this, then said slowly, "I think I can take the wildly impossible as long as it is the truth."

She looked at him. He'd know now. She didn't know why or how, but he'd know if she lied to him. "Okay. The truth then." Chances were, neither of them was going to survive anyway. And if they didn't, would they have to do this again? How many times had they done it?

"The truth then." He looked at her now, his gaze had a new steadiness, a new way of seeing her. "Who are you?"

She meet his gaze, took a breath and said, "I'm Prudence Pinkerton, an inter-dimensional scientist, sent here to stop this storm from eating all of time and everyone in time. For all time." They weren't sure about that, but that's where it seemed to be heading.

He blinked once. Then again. And yet again. The silence grew, but oddly enough Prudence didn't feel awkward. It was a lot to take in. She respected the time he took considering it all. He took a deep breath and blinked once more.

"Inter-dimensional?"

"There will be this scientist in a few years who will postulate the theory that we exist in a multitude of dimensions, each one playing out a multitude of choices. A person goes left, instead of right and a new dimension forms because they made a different choice. Met someone. Didn't meet someone. Instead of the change rippling forward through that time, a new timeline spins off, leaving the—for want of a better word—the original timeline intact and unchanged. For most people, it will remain a theory." She paused, but he didn't speak. He didn't even blink. "For me, for my family? It's not a theory, it's our reality. We, most of us, have the ability to travel through dimensions and through time. We don't know why or how this happened. We're not even sure when it first manifested. All we know is that it doesn't activate until puberty."

He looked...unconvinced.

She made a face. "My family used to call it 'the gift.' When we realized it wasn't always one, someone changed it to the Talent." She shrugged. "If you think about it, one person is born with a talent for music, another for art, and someone else for inventing. No one thinks that's odd." She flashed him a smile. "It's not very comfortable having any talent, is it?"

That hit home and he nodded. "No, it's not." He looked around. "So this is just another dimension to you—"

"No." She shook her head. "This is different." She stared straight into his eyes. "You're different in this one. And the storm, it's different, too." She hesitated again, but in for a penny... "Dr. Masterson postulated the existence of...closed dimensions. Changes that don't spawn new dimensions. One where the changes do ripple forward and change the future. This might be one." She stopped because she was moving into new territory. And he had a lot to take in.

"Masterson?" He swallowed. "He is a dimensional traveler, too?"

"Well, yes and no. He doesn't have the Talent, but he's super smart, so he sometimes travels with one of us." How strange. She'd never wondered when and how he came on board before. He was just there, like her dad.

"How am I different in this dimension?" he asked. He was pale but that could be the bright light. Maybe.

Oh crap. She closed her eyes for a minute, then opened them. "Ophelia. Her dying is different. In all the others, she doesn't. You're married to her. Or jacketed, I mean, about to get married to her."

His eyes widened. He looked like he might speak, but his lips thinned instead. He walked away from her, his shoulders twitching, then he turned back.

"And the storm? How is it different here?"

"It seems to be less...damaging," she admitted. "But—" she

stopped because this wasn't just a wander into the unknown, this was a leap.

"But?" his gaze demanded she continue.

"Your memory of me, of meeting me. That's really new. I've never, ever...ever had that happen."

"But you have a theory?"

"Well, I'm not sure it's a theory yet. More of a speculation, actually. But the fact that you remember something I don't—I wonder if time is...replaying...or...re-setting."

He started to shake his head, but paused. "Re-setting. As if we got it wrong and must make it right."

She nodded, her turn to be bemused. "Is that what you feel, when the memories happen?"

His turn to nod. "It is."

"So if we got it wrong...before..."

"How do we get it right?" he finished.

Ernest paced back and forth for what seemed like a long time. Finally he turned to her. "If the meteorite in the Blizablighter 3000 is somehow the issue, then I should disassemble the machine."

Prudence started to nod, but hesitated. "Does that feel...right?"

It was his turn to pause and consider. His shoulders lifted some. "It feels new."

"Okay, well at least new is different from wrong."

"But it is not known to be right." He rubbed his face impatiently.

He should be used to uncertainty. He was a scientist, a weather scientist. And she really shouldn't have to point out this obvious, but he had taken a few hits in the last minute. "If we've been getting it wrong, then we don't know what's right. All we've got to go on is new."

He stared at her and finally nodded. "You are right." He blinked at that.

"It's ironic, isn't it?" She grinned and he grinned back, though it was one with lots of strain in it. Wow, three in a row. They were on a roll. They started toward the stairs, but Prudence paused to ask, "Lord Henry? Is he new or wrong?"

Ernest stopped, considering. "I only started to have the...sensations...when we were walking. I do not think—I cannot say."

"Fair enough." She headed down, her booted feet ringing on the metal steps as she circled down to the watch room.

Ernest went to his Blizablighter 3000—where had he come up with that name?—and crouched down. He reached for the wires and stopped.

"I did this before."

"So wrong move," Prudence said, sort of asking, but not really. She rubbed her face. A lot of inter-dimensional study involved feeling one's way in the dark, but this certainly had a new, high level of difficulty. "It's not very big, maybe we can, I don't know, I hide it?" She looked around. There really wasn't a place that a determined search wouldn't reveal. But there were some nooks and crannies around that could buy them some time. Maybe.

Ernest knelt, not talking, his expression intent. Finally, he murmured, "Something about the lamp."

"The Fresnel lamp?" It was designed to amplify light, not electricity, but— "Okay. Where do we put it?"

His head tilted to one side, his glance moving from her to the automatons, then finally back to her. His gaze holding hers, he said, "No." He glanced around. "I'll take Winston and Fred with me."

She nodded, not sure she agreed with him. She angled her Raijinator 5 casually, but in a direction it would be easy to target Niles if he made a move, and flipped it to energy charge. She'd seen how fast he could move. She'd get one shot at him. Problem was, it took multiple bullets to take out an automaton. She had to hope a surge would short out his circuits.

She shifted from one foot to the other, wondering why she felt restless and uneasy. Well, beyond the weird storm and dragons. Metal hit metal above her. She didn't like not seeing what was going on up there. She didn't have Ernest's other sense, so this wrong feeling was probably just about being scared to her toenails. She really wanted to look up, even though she couldn't see anything. So she looked down instead. Winston was a dim figure on the last half landing. After that point, the stairs made a complete circuit of the lighthouse before reaching the next landing. He didn't seem to be moving, but she thought she saw the slight glow of his eyes. That was a bit creepy. Her dimension hadn't really gone heavy into automatons when the difference engine was discovered. And it was too easy to mess with their programming, so they weren't used at all inside the Agency. There was no question the ability to travel through dimensions had accelerated the development of other technology available to the Agency, but it was all very carefully controlled. No one wanted to be the CEO who created a catastrophic paradox.

She shifted again, as things grew quieter up top. She wasn't sure she trusted any of the automatons. All four automatons had been out of Ernest's sight at some point, but only the two ship handlers had been outside the umbrella of light. The Storm had appeared during the day, so it wasn't the light that kept it at bay. Was there something about lighthouse lamps? The light they generated that was protecting them? Or was the light an illusion of safety?

She realized even the small sounds had stopped up in the lamp room. What if the automatons had done something to Ernest? There was the clump as first one, then the other descended. But not Ernest.

"Ernest? Are you all right?" She raised her voice to be heard over the footsteps.

"I'll be right down."

His voice sounded fine, a little breathless. The automatons looked the same. Prudence found a niggle of doubt working its way into her certainty that this Ernest was as good and trustworthy as the others. The memory of her missing grandfather surfaced. As far as she knew, they were the two with the strongest Talent ever recorded in Agency history. And he was missing.

What if the trap was not for Ernest, but for her? If someone had been studying her, while she studied the Ernests, how hard would it have been to detect her...lack of distance? The impersonal she'd not been quite able to maintain? All this Ernest had to do was pretend—what had he actually told her? She hadn't told him about Octavius, but if someone had captured her grandfather, they might already know the importance of a familiar. She could transit without him, but without him she could not transit *home*.

She checked her tracking. So far Octavius seemed okay. As long as her connection was strong enough, they should be able to leave. It was not at the maximum range, but it was close. It was tempting, so tempting the portal started to form in front of her again.

But—what if that was—the desired outcome. What if whatever was out there hoped she'd panic and leave? Or...if this trap was for her, they'd want her to have the illusion she could leave—

The boom of the door far below made her jump. If she hadn't been in a lighthouse, she might have hit the roof. But she couldn't jump that high. Close, but not quite. The adrenalin surge almost sent her into a new dimension, though.

"Dr. Warren?" In cultured accents, Lord Henry's voice echoed up the tower, his voice bouncing eerily off the thick stone walls.

She was not in the mood for him. Was it morning in the time... flux they seemed to be in? It was still dark outside, but that did not mean sunrise wasn't happening. And she had told him he could come back. A soft shuffle came from behind her. She turned. It was Ernest padding carefully and quietly down to her level. His gaze was filled with warning.

She got it, but also felt caught between two unknowns, so instead of meeting his gaze directly, she peeked down. The door was open, letting in some light, though she could not identify its source. It could be the sun or light from the lamp. His dark figure filled the opening, laying a distorted shadow onto the rough floor. He had to have checked the house first. If he'd parked next to *The Weatherman*, then he knew they weren't there.

"Dr. Warren? Miss Smith?" Some worry filtered into the suave voice now.

Ernest half shrugged and leaned over the railing. "We are up here, sir." He hesitated, then added, "It is a considerable climb."

It was. It gave them a few minutes grace, depending on how fit he was. Prudence hesitated. "I'm going to go look out again." And possibly have a look around the lamp room?

Ernest did not look pleased, but he nodded. "Keep that close." He indicated her Raijin-ator 5.

"Always." Her smile was a little easier, though she could not say exactly why.

He looked at her suddenly. "It was you."

"It was me...what?"

"The name. Blizablighter 3000." He half smiled. "It was you."

Her smile widened. "I hate to admit it, but it does sound like something I'd come up with." Both the Paraton-ator 20 and the Raijin-ator 5 were unofficial names that had somehow managed to filter through the ranks of the Agency. For some reason, knowing this helped. Her breath seemed to come easier, though doubts tried to peck at this sprout of hope. "I won't be long."

She started up. The doubts lingered, but with less force. Maybe she'd rather believe than not. Besides, if this was a trap, well, the fly never escaped by struggling.

~

Up top, Prudence, with her goggles on active setting, walked all the way around the lamp room. No readings from the lamp, but—her gaze tracked up. There. She blinked and pulled off the goggles. Then lowered them again and turned them to magnify. Slower this time, she pulled them down. Without the goggles, his mineral was almost invisible tucked up there. It looked like the wires from his Blizablighter 3000 now lead up and out the vents to the lightning rod on the top of the lighthouse.

Had he been following his instincts when he put the Blizablighter 3000 up there, or let his scientist out, hoping to test his device while hiding it in sort of plain sight?

She sighed. It might be brilliant. Or not brilliant. Heat and tired sapped at her strength and muddied her thinking. Not that thinking would help that much, since she didn't know much anyway. She clambered out the door, hoping she could pretend it was cooler outside. It was a little better. At least the fuel smell was less. She leaned back, remembering her first transit without a trainer. Just she and Octavius making a leap into the void. She'd had a target, and she'd nailed it. But she'd never forget the first time alone in the space between, wondering where and when they'd land. If they did. They had equipment, but the most essential calculation could only happen in her head. In the mind. Before her Talent manifested, she'd asked Lewis how it happened.

He'd shrugged. "You just feel it. There are lines leading all over, and you pick one and follow it."

"But how do you know it's the right line?"

"You just do." He'd ruffled her hair. "They won't let you and your familiar go solo until you know."

It took skill and training to stick the line. There were so many. So easy to run off course. No one knew why a familiar helped center the mind. There were some theories about animal instincts and such. In the end, it didn't matter. It was a two-part process. First came the Talent, then the familiar found the Talent. If the familiar didn't come, well, there were those who tried anyway. Eventually they were found, sometimes alive, sometimes in a grave. It was a time thing, not just a dimension thing.

If this was what it felt like to lose the line, well, she did not want to go there. And if she was already there? Well, better not to think about it.

She straightened her spine, then her body, positioned her goggles and set them to scan again. She made a circuit around the balcony. The light was warm and comforting. Even in her time, lighthouses were special. Was that what had drawn her here? She did one more round, taking it slower and trying to "see" everything. Maybe the readings would be found, even if—

As far as she could tell, the dragons were gone, or flying somewhere else. On the pier side, there was the shadow of an airship tied down on the opposite side of the pier from *The Weatherman*. Lord Henry's ride, she presumed. The night outside the lamp umbrella seemed less dark than earlier. She reached the door again, glanced around, suddenly uneasy in a new way. Amazing she had a new way to be uneasy. She really thought she'd reached her upper limit.

"My head hurts," she told the night. Her heart felt a bit battered, too. And the sad part? She was the one who'd given it the swift kick. Ernest hadn't done anything. Yet. She sighed, reluctant to go down and face either man. She closed her eyes, rubbed her face. The waft of cool air felt so good, she sighed with relief this time. Cool turned downright cold against her sweaty skin. How could it be cold? Uneasy ramped up to bad feeling. She needed to lift her lids, but man, she didn't want to.

And she wished she'd kept them closed when the prow of an airship emerged from the darkness just ahead of her. It wasn't the fact that it was airborne or even an airship that she found so, well, terrifying. It was the semi-transparent hull, with small pulses of light running along the beams. And the eyes. Thousands of them. Glowing red.

Yeah, those were terrifying, too.

Chapter Twelve

E rnest watched Lord Henry climb the last flight of stairs. The
man showed no sign of distress or breathlessness. In fact, he
might have been strolling on a level promenade. His cane swung
lightly in one hand. His hat held in the crook of his other arm. There
was a regular cadence to the sound of his steps against metal. Like a
metronome. Or an automaton.

Too real.

His mind rejected the connection. He looked human. He had skin
and normal eyes. He was a man, except, no man could walk with that
kind of precision, at least, could soldiers? He did not know. Was that
precise timing possible on a rising stairway? The distance between
the stairs would have to be close to precise. Even a small difference
would throw off the timing.

Lord Henry reached his level and stopped, his chest rising and
falling without distress of any kind.

Automatons didn't breathe. Their chests didn't rise or fall. They
didn't have lungs. Their clockwork hearts took up most of the chest
cavity. There was sweat on his skin. Lines around the eyes. He was a
man, therefore, that kind of precision must be possible. At least it
was not an impossible possible this time. It only felt like it was.

Lord Henry shifted his hat to a position under the arm holding
his cane and bowed very slightly. "Miss...Smith not here?"

Why the pause before her name? "She's servicing the lamps inside
the Fresnel."

His gaze flicked up. Automaton eyes couldn't do that. They couldn't show emotion. Not that Ernest could see an abundance of emotion in his eyes, but there was intelligence. Awareness. His eyes were quite compelling, he realized, and found it took effort to look away.

"I'm surprised you made it back, sir," Ernest said. "The storm seems to have reached this location. Or is imminent. We have already experienced some flooding."

The dark brows rose. "But I have only been gone an hour."

An hour? Ernest blinked.

"We started for the mainland, and the wind came up, and we decided to return here. Without the lamp, we would not have found our way back."

We? "Where is your crew, sir. Do they need—"

"My automatons?" Lord Henry looked surprised. "They remain with the ship." His glance flicked toward Ernest's crew, then back to Ernest, a question in them.

His lips tightened, but he did not respond to the unspoken question, nor would he have had the question spoken. He wanted to protest Lord Henry's callousness, but was aware of his own hypocrisy. He had, several times, put the automatons between himself and danger, but he would never leave them behind when a choice was offered. Though in this circumstance, it was hard to make the case that they were safer here with him.

"Niles?"

The automaton's eyes flickered to active. "Yes, sir?"

"Go down to Crispin, and both of you keep a watch on the water levels out there. Oh and Niles," the automaton looked back, "try to stay dry. I mean, move higher if you need to."

"Yes, sir."

Niles clunked ponderously down the stairs towards his counterpart. As it approached, Winston came back to awareness. For just a moment, it seemed its eyes glowed red, but it must have been a trick of the light. Had to have been because it was impossible. The metal eyes could only be silver. And inside his head, he heard her voice saying, "...six impossible things..."

Had they reached six yet? He was getting rather tired of the impossible.

Now he looked at Lord Henry, his mind returning to his statement that he'd only been gone an hour. Since his watch was not tracking time in a reasonable manner, he had only his senses to track the passage of time. It felt longer, but also shorter. In fact, it felt as if time were speeding up after going very slowly.

"I'm not sure you made the better choice in returning here, sir. If my..." he hesitated, "...instruments are in any way accurate, we are in the direct path of this storm."

Lord Henry looked more pleased than worried. "Do you think it is The Storm?"

"I do not know."

"May I see your instruments?"

"Of course, sir." They were only on the other side of the central pillar, so Ernest led him there. There was a long silence while Lord Henry looked at each one. Finally he glanced at the crates that the automatons hadn't unpacked. They were mostly papers, but also pieces of instruments Ernest was working on. It almost seemed that Lord Henry looked disappointed.

"Is something wrong, sir?"

Lord Henry's lips twisted. "I had hoped to see something...original from an inventor such as yourself."

He couldn't know about the Blizablighter 3000, now hidden up in the peak of the lamp room's ceiling. No one had known until Prudence.

"I have some ideas sketched out, but sometimes one can't improve on what has already been done." He half shrugged, hoped he managed to sound rueful. "Indeed, I'm glad to be spared the embarrassment, since none of these are working properly."

Lord Henry looked disconcerted. Had he not known how to read the instruments? He recovered very quickly.

"Perhaps you...picked something up on your travels that is interfering with them?"

Lord Henry knew about the meteorite. Ernest felt it, though he'd have discounted it prior to meeting Prudence. Had he spoken with the driller who gave it to Ernest? That is the only way he could have known. But why would the man have told him? Why would Lord Henry care? What was his interest? Other than the fact that it was not of this world, it seemed a side issue in the face of The Storm. All he could think to do was play along.

Ernest looked thoughtful, nodded slowly. "I suppose that is possible. Winston, when you and Fred packed these crates, did they have any mineral substances in them?" He knew it was a safe question for his very literal automatons.

"The crates contain your research materials, sir," Winston said. "Books and papers."

Fred pointed to one half empty crate. "That one has a few pieces of incomplete instruments that you were working on."

"May I?" Lord Henry asked, already moving toward that crate. He bent over it, grabbing at the pieces of straw in a manner borderline frantic. He stopped and looked at Ernest, his smile forced. "These devices look...intriguing, Doctor."

"Well, so far they have been mostly frustrating." Ernest picked up a piece of one, turned it in his hand, then dropped it back in the crate.

Lord Henry glanced at the automatons, then the stairs. With lowered voice, he said, "I've come with a warning for you, Dr. Warren. From Dr. Masterson."

Prudence had come from Masterson. Or said she had said. But he'd felt that the knowing he'd felt about her, that sense of doing this before—a knowing that was *not* knowledge, he reminded himself. A trap? With her up there and Lord Henry here? He had only their word they didn't know each other. And her wild story. And honest eyes. Only that and his instincts to put against wealth and eyes that were...eerily compelling. And as calm as his breathing. *Too real?*

"You are in great danger." His gaze flicked toward the stairs again, as if to indicate Prudence was that danger.

There was a clatter of some sort overhead.

"Ernest?" she called out, "Could you step up here for a minute?"

Her tone was in opposition to her words, he noted, wondering if the trap were closing. And who was supposed to be in it.

"Take care," Lord Henry cautioned, grasping his arm with a cold hand.

He should have had that advice four years ago, Ernest thought somewhat ruefully. Despite his concerns, Ernest shook off Lord Henry's hand, and went for the stairs, felt cold air spilling down from the lamp room, as he leapt up two at a time. How could a room that had been stifling and hot now be cold as the arctic?

Prudence stood at the top, gripping the rail, her face so white her eyes looked like black stones.

"What's happened?" It was so cold, he could see his breath and hers, like fog filtered with the lamp light. He heard Lord Henry climbing up after him and grabbed her shoulders, had to tug to get her to let loose the rail. She was cold, even through her leathers. His hands slid down her arms and gripped the chunks of ice that were her hands.

"What's wrong?" he asked again. Instead of answering her gaze tracked past his shoulder. He followed her gaze, half turning them both in the process—

This was one impossible too far. And yet. Hadn't he already seen this? Just before he blacked out on *The Weatherman*. "Wait here," he said, his grip loosening, but her hands tightened.

"No." Pale tongue licked dry, barely visible lips. "I...I'll go with you."

The instinct to protect was strong, but she unslung her weapon, holding it with the muzzle pointed down. He opened the door. It wasn't on the latch, so he only had to pull it back. He bent and stepped out on the ledge. It had seemed generous earlier. Now, it did not.

A raucous cry, quickly followed by that of its mate, sounded overhead. He was somewhat aware that the dragons were back, that they circled above the light, shadows weaving past each other in a regular pattern. The ship was a disturbing sight. Transparent, with pulses of light tracing along its structure. There was fog, but mostly in wisps that clung to the sides of the airship. A bit of fog would push out and then jerk back, as if it hit a barrier or worse.

And there was the eyes. He remembered the eyes. And this cold, he realized. He'd felt this cold during his last encounter with this ship. He wanted to consider the temperature, because it was easier to contemplate than the eyes. So many of them, staring at them. Eyes that glittered. Eyes that pleaded. Eyes filled with fear. Eyes filled hatred. He searched them, afraid to see, and afraid to not see, her eyes.

He didn't realize he'd relaxed some, until Prudence spoke, her voice hoarse. "She's not there."

He wrenched his gaze away, looked down at her. If anything, her skin was whiter than it had been, and tightly stretched across her cheek bones. She shrank back as Lord Henry climbed out next to her. He looked...curious.

"So these must be the specters in the storm," he said. He looked at Prudence, his mouth acquiring a cruel edge. "Do you recognize anyone?"

There was a long silence as she stared at him, then imperceptibly at first, her back straightened, then her whole body. She pushed away from the lighthouse until she stood on both feet. She opened her mouth, but before she could speak, there was a rattle and groan, though not exactly a groan either. The sound was unearthly.

Ernest felt such dread, it was all he could do to maintain his stance. Prudence's grip on his hand tightened. The visible specters appeared to be falling back, or to either side, clearing a path, if it was possible to have a path over nothing. Some of the specters looked as if they cowered back, while others had gloating looks in their red eyes.

"What is it?" she asked, looking to Ernest.

But it was Lord Henry who spoke. "Don't you recognize him? Granted he has changed..."

What was he talking about? Recognize who? Prudence felt both slow and stupid and scared silly. But the warmth of Ernest's hand kept her grounded, well, mostly. If this was the trap she'd have preferred a spider web. Probably. She didn't like spiders either.

A figure began to emerge from the inky blackness at the back of the ship, a gray human-like shadow that moved slowly, each step sending a ghostly rattle that made some of the specters crouch in fear. Others seemed to laugh, black hole mouths opening beneath those red eyes.

In the air in front of her, a portal tried to form. Just a shimmer because she fought it back. She didn't look at Lord Henry, but she felt his pleasure at this small betrayal. The figure reached the prow of the ship. His essence seemed to quiver, then sharpen until she could see it was a man. A man in chains, chains that glowed briefly blue with each step, chains wrapped around him from the top of his head to the feet visible through the transparent side of the ship. Only his face was free enough to see. His eyes were wild and tormented. So much pain in them...the weight of his pain dragged her down. Her knees started to buckle, but Ernest grabbed her, his arm sliding around her waist to keep her on her feet.

Those eyes turned slowly toward her. She wanted to cower from them, from discovery, but she couldn't move. The eyes saw her. They showed recognition. How was that possible? The mouth opened, releasing a scream that reverberated through her skin and bone. And through her mind. With rising terror, she saw fine cracks in the dimensional lines inside her head, saw some of those lines get damaged, some disconnect. If one of those was the one home...

She felt herself being dragged back, away from the chained man, away from the ship, and then she couldn't see him with her eyes, but it didn't matter. The eyes were in her head, looking at her through the lines. The broken lines. She couldn't—and then it hit her, and she knew. Her head fell back. Against a shoulder, that felt so safe and warm, but safe was an illusion. A ruse.

"What's wrong? What has happened?"

Ernest sounded frantic. Not like himself at all. And so very far away. With some effort she turned her head toward him. Saw panic in his eyes.

"What was it?" He gave her a small shake.

"Not what. Who. My grandfather."

"Your grandfather? What—" The color drained from his face. "That's him...but...why?"

"I'd rather die..." she said, surprised at how loud the words sounded in the deep silence.

He pulled her to his chest, holding her so tight she almost couldn't breath. She didn't care. His heart beat against her cheek. He was alive. She was still alive. She wasn't sure that was good.

"You're not going to die," he said. "I—"

She grabbed his jacket lapel. "Promise me you won't let it have me. That you'll kill me rather than let that happen."

"Pru—"

"Promise me you'll use the gun."

His lips thinned, then he set his mouth against her ear. "What if that is what we did before?"

This question cleared some of the panic. She took several breaths. "Does it feel wrong?"

He hesitated. "Of course it does. But I can't tell if—"

"Dr. Warren?"

She tightened her grip. "I don't like him."

His lips widened into the strained version of a smile. "Neither do I."

"Can you help me up?" She honestly wasn't sure she could stand, or stay there if he did help her up, but she wasn't going to cower at the feet of Lord Henry or—whatever it was holding her grandfather prisoner out there. He was a prisoner. The chains confirmed that truth. She managed to get up...just. She gripped his shoulders. "I just want you to know, no matter what—"

She realized he wasn't looking at her, but past her. *I don't want to know.* Despite this, her body somehow turned to look. Her grandfather was still there, but he'd been joined by someone. A woman.

Prudence felt Ernest stiffen as he recognized her, too.

Ophelia.

~

"And now you are finally...finally beginning to understand," Lord Henry said, his tone one who had waited far too long for this moment and was determined to enjoy it to the maximum.

"And yet somehow I don't," Prudence said, her voice thin and strained. "What's wrong with him, with...them?"

"There is nothing wrong with them. They rejoice because their life force serves the Master."

"Yeah, they looked like its the jets. Thrilled to their toes—oh wait, they don't seem to have toes."

Ernest found he could almost smile, even though some of her words puzzled him.

There was a flicker, then the lighthouse lamp lost some of its brightness.

"One of the lamps inside the Fresnel has gone out," Prudence said, almost absently. "I should refill it."

If she felt like Ernest did right now, she could not move. The ice in the air had moved into his bones, into his sinews. As if the lessening of the light allowed it, more of the airship moved closer to the lighthouse tower. One of the dragons dropped through the light canopy, landing on the railing of the balcony. Its red eyes regarded them through the glass, then blew a stream of fire against it. The room grew colder still.

"It's an automaton," he murmured, not sure he'd said the words out loud until Prudence stirred in his hold. "But also more..."

He stood between her and Lord Henry, who held the door open with his body. The dragon dropped down on the ledge and started for the door, its pulsing red eyes seemingly fixed on Ernest. Each step shook the lighthouse tower. The steps seemed to reverberate inside the storm, too, like echoes of distant thunder.

"If you have it, Dr. Warren, now would be a good time to produce it," Lord Henry said.

The dragon was more clumsy on the ledge, but it hadn't far to go to reach the door. It filled the doorway, flexing its wings once and crying out. Its head reared back, the neck elongating, as if it was preparing to spew fire, but a light shot from beside Ernest before the dragon could spew. It tracked toward the dragon, straight and true and cleanly white, striking the dragon in the chest.

Lightning danced across its metal surface, giving flashed views of its mechanical insides and then it tumbled back, crashing through the railing and falling out of sight without a sound.

What the—he looked around and realized Prudence had managed to raise her long weapon and fire.

Lord Henry looked at Ernest, his eyes suddenly turning the same red as the dragon.

"That was unfortunate."

"Maybe," Prudence said, "but it felt good."

From deep within the storm, thunder sounded louder and closer, like a death drum, rising and falling.

"You've made him angry." Lord Henry smiled, his eyes gleaming as if anger pleased him.

Ernest stepped more fully between Prudence and Lord Henry. He laughed. The sound of it echoed again and again, building instead of diminishing.

"You cannot help her," he told Ernest. He lifted his cane, exposing the head. It was a smaller version of the dragon Prudence had shot. Its eyes were red, too, and its mouth opened to expel a smaller spout of flame.

Then the screaming started. Thousands of voices, as if the shot had hurt them, too.

Chapter Thirteen

It was hard to imagine what could be worse, but Prudence had a feeling that worse was still incoming. And then, as if the worst weren't bad enough, another oil lamp went out inside the Fresnel. The lamp's light dimmed some more, and the airship nudged closer, angling so that a ramp—one half wood and half fog—could be lowered to rest in the place where the railing had broken. The brimstone smell intensified, but so did the cold.

And then the screaming cut off, as if someone had flipped a switch.

She felt pinned in place by Lord Henry's creepy human eyes and his dragon head cane. Off to the left, her grandfather's specter turned to face them, his burning gaze both entreating and filled with warning. Not that she needed the warning. The urge to flee was so strong, it took all her focus to keep the portal at bay. Her gear showed a strong connection to Octavius. Ernest gripped her hand. Emergency transit might save them, if her gear was accurate. Had her grandfather faced this horror? He would have followed protocol and tried to transit. Only here he was. Caught like the fly in the creepy web. So that seemed to rule out an emergency transit. Which meant she probably couldn't trust the readings. They might be as messed up as Ernest's instruments.

Was it possible to craft a dimensional transit trap? She glanced at Lord Henry and caught him licking his creepy thin lips in anticipation. He loved what was happening. Couldn't wait for what he thought she'd do.

The analogy of the fly and the spider kept rising in a brain almost frozen with panic. But not quite.

Flight or fight.

If flight was out and fighting was indicated, how did one fight specters? Ghosts? A life force-collecting Master—

The boom of footsteps against ghostly wood yanked her attention back to the ghost ship. Amidst the drifting Fog or mist she thought she saw a figure. Slowly, it emerged from the mist, stopping at the top of the gangplank. Ernest inhaled sharply. Prudence more slowly because her chest was so tight breathing was only barely possible.

It was a specter-distorted-mirror of Lord Henry.

All she could say about him was that he made the human Lord Henry look good. All that was hideous about the man was worse in the specter. And his skeleton was visible through a surface as transparent as his ship. The clothes were tattered and floated around him like the fog clinging to the ship. He didn't doff his ragged top hat. Apparently manners weren't as important after...specter-fying. He leaned on a cane that was a complete twin of the one held by the human Lord Henry. It sparked when the tip touched the gang plank. Through his fingers red eyes glowed, from what she presumed was another dragon head.

She'd never liked horror movies. If she managed to survive this, she'd be a lot less judgmental about what characters did while in them. She knew her thoughts were silly, random even. If she focused on stupid stuff, maybe she could keep from panicking. Because if she panicked, well, she had a feeling that is exactly what they wanted. A fly struggling in this terrifying web. She didn't know how she knew this, and technically she didn't *know* it, but it felt true. If the human-ish Lord Henry liked panic and pain, then how much more would his creepy counterpart be panting for it? Her gaze flicked back to her grandfather. To the chains that contained him. Why was he the only one in chains? Why...no, the question wasn't why. It was obvious why he'd been caught and chained.

He was an inter-dimensional Agent. They were using him—the man with the most Talent ever—to travel between dimensions. To move more than a few people, but a ship. Okay, it was a specter ship, but there was the storm. That's how it could move between dimensions, how it could appear and disappear. That's how he'd been able to play the Dr. Masterson card. Though it didn't explain why it was eating other dimensions—something to do with the life force it required, maybe? Her grandfather's specter looked less than the others. Had they sucked the life out of him and were hoping she could take up the job? Did she have enough Talent to move something that large between dimensions? She wasn't sure she knew how—

The whys and hows didn't matter. They now had the only other Agent as Talented as her grandfather trapped—or almost trapped—in their web. The distinction was small but necessary to keep her from having a hysterical fit.

She glanced at the human-ish Lord Henry. Why two of them? Why—Ernest? And Ophelia? What did he have—

Lord Henry had funded the geologic expedition. While she'd been up in the lamp room trying to get her voice back, trying not to scream like a little girl, she'd heard him ask Ernest if "something he'd picked up in his travels" was causing the problems with his instruments. The only item that fit, and was related to that contact, was the meteorite. Did they want it? Or did they fear it? Or was it both? It collected and stored energy. Might a life force be an energy source, too? Could they collect peoples' souls, their life force, with the meteorite? Or did they hope Ernest could do it for them? Was this trap for both of them?

Lightning began to build around the ghost airship, emanating from the hull, or so it seemed, dancing across the sky and hitting the lightning rod at the top of the lighthouse. She studied the flashes and realized that just as she could see inter-dimensional lines in her head, there were connected lines in the seemingly random flashes. All of them leading from the lighthouse to the ship. Or from the ship to the lighthouse. It was hard to tell. But they were connected flashes, not disconnected flashes.

It was doing something. She wished she knew what, because she had a feeling that it needed to be stopped. She had an idea. Or the ghost of one.

"Doctor Ernest Warren." The specter's mouth opened, but the words seemed to come from the human Lord Henry.

Ernest's grip on her hand tightened. Might have been painful if she'd had feeling left in it. But it was so cold, her breath was a blue mist hanging in the air in front of her.

"I am here," he finally said, his tone so calm, she'd have been impressed if he wasn't smashing her fingers to pulp. "What do you want?"

The red gaze fixed on Ernest, then traveled to Prudence. She lifted her chin, let defiance show in her eyes. She hoped.

"I want the witch."

Witch? Prudence's brows rose. She'd have been offended if she wasn't so busy being terrified.

Ernest's mouth opened, but the Lord Henry specter held up a claw-like hand, the one holding the cane, and pointed the dragon head at Ophelia. Red light shot from it, circling her like rope and dragged her to the top of the ramp.

"Ernest," she cried. "Help me!" She writhed in its hold, as if the rope hurt her.

Hard to believe he could, but Ernest managed to stiffen some more next to her.

Prudence managed to stiffen some, too, as she sensed what was coming.

"Your true love," his voice was thick with derision, "for the witch."

Yeah, not a surprise.

~

Your true love for the witch. The words echoed inside Ernest's head. For a moment, his heart rebounded with joy at the thought—but reason quickly killed the hope. That wasn't, that could not be his Ophelia. And how could he hand Prudence over to that monstrous thing? How could he trade a lost life for a true life?

"It's a lie," he heard himself say. "You lie. You can't resurrect the dead. It's not possible." Even as he said the words, he heard Prudence's voice in his head. *Six impossible things.*

"I am proof it is possible," Lord Henry spoke next to him, using his own voice, not that of the specter. "I am real. Living and breathing. I died," his red gaze flicked balefully toward Prudence, as if he somehow held her responsible, "and came back better than before. She will return, even better than your memory of her. You can have your love, return to your real life, and forget this ever happened. If you give us the witch."

He probed his own senses, hoping for something, some memory of what they'd done before to guide him now. But all he felt was horror. Horror at the thought of Prudence in the clutches of that thing. Horror for Ophelia trapped there. How could he choose? But how to fight ghosts? Specters? Her weapon had destroyed the automaton dragon, and perhaps could kill Lord Henry, but if that thing could bring him back—

"Do it," Prudence said.

He jerked, turned to stare at her. She looked at the specter, not at him.

"Take the deal."

"No." The words were forcefully uttered, so forcefully it shocked him. The specter next to Lord Henry was not his Ophelia and she wasn't his true love. It was a bad time to realize she probably never had been. Oh, had she lived, he would have been faithful, but what he felt for her—he stopped the thought. He had to stop it. Because if he admitted it, if only to himself, then he'd have to take the deal. From guilt. Not because he loved Ophelia so much, but because he did not love her enough.

"Yes." She angled toward him, her smile beyond strained. Her eyes were bruised circles in her white face. "There are so many reasons not to," she managed a sad chuckle, "*three thousand* of them, if we had time to count," her gaze flicked down to his waistband, then back to his face, "and not one good reason to do it. But you need to make the trade. You should save Ophelia." And now her expression was wry, but there was warning and something more in her gaze. "The fly can't escape the trap. You might as well save one."

"She speaks truth," Lord Henry said, amused. "Unusual for a witch."

Her hand seemed to touch him, but instead she did something to the weapon she'd given him, the small click lost in the booming sound of the specter's gloating laugh.

She squeezed his hand one last time, then dragged her hand free from his clasp that wanted to cling, to hold on to her and never let her go.

"I—" he stopped. What could he say? He nodded, to let her know he'd received her message.

"It's all right." She leaned in to press her lips to his cheek, whispered in his ear, "When I reach the top of the ramp." She turned from him to face the specter, ignoring the human Lord Henry. She leaned her long gun against the railing and straightened her shoulders. "Send her down."

The cane head pointed at Ophelia again, the red rope falling away.

"Ernest," she said, starting toward him with her arms out, remnants of flesh hanging from the bones.

All he felt was horror and dread. The dark maw of her mouth, the merciless gaze. The red eyes. He fingered the weapon. He had good aim, even under duress, but never had he needed accuracy so desperately. He did not expect the apparently human Lord Henry to give him more than a shot or two at the Blizablighter 3000. Was this why it had felt right to place it up there? Or was he about to get it wrong again? A shadow moved across the base of the airship. The last dragon, he realized. It would attack, too, mostly likely. In any case, he'd rather reset time and do this again than live his life with that travesty of Ophelia.

Prudence didn't rush toward her fate. One didn't. Not if one had even a smidgeon of survival instinct. In fact, it took all her resolution to step onto that semi-transparent gang plank. She lifted a booted foot and tested it. It held, without feeling solid. She glanced across, met her grandfather's gaze, saw his slight nod. If his free will hadn't been completely subdued, it was a good sign she'd made the right call. Funny how that didn't help all that much. And she didn't know if his free will had survived. He might be part of the trap. Maybe they didn't care if the fly came willingly.

Prudence brought her other foot onto the gang plank. She seemed to sink in an inch or so. She tried to lift her foot, which shifted her weight back and the misty goop tightened around her feet. She couldn't move until she leaned forward, could only go forward, she realized. She leaned forward and was able to take a couple of steps, each time sinking deeper into the goo. Hopefully she wouldn't sink so deep she'd fall out the other side. It was a long drop.

Ophelia didn't rush either. She sashayed, which was not pretty, since she was mostly skeletal. The remnant of her lips curved in triumph, her gaze dismissed Prudence, though Prudence wasn't sure if the dismissal was as a woman or as a threat. If the gal had had access to a mirror, she might not be quite so confident. Because Prudence was a woman and Ophelia was only sort of one, Prudence arched her brows returned the dismissive look, then rolled her eyes.

Ophelia's hands curled into claws and she made a move toward Prudence, but a blast of cold air seemed to push her down the ramp. They passed each other—holy cow the smell—without contact. And, weirdly enough, Prudence began to slide up the gang plank not of her own volition. Like she was on a conveyor belt now, moving toward her nasty fate.

She looked down, trying to see if there was a mechanism of some sort. That's when she saw the fog creeping up the sides of the airship, and then across the gang plank toward her. The flight instinct surged as the white mist crept closer. It took all her willpower to hold the portal at bay. Like icy fingers, the fog wrapped first one ankle, then the other, then it began to wind up both legs. At first it was so cold it ached, a cold burn, even through the boots. She thought she heard a soft clink and felt the additional chill of metal against bare skin, sinking into her bones...

Now panic clawed at her throat. A scream tried to push out. She wouldn't let it, though she choked on it. She felt Octavius's panic. Below her, she saw the dragon circling the water, shooting flames at the surface, as if daring him to come out. She couldn't help him. Couldn't help herself. If Ernest—even if he hit the mark, would it work?

Just because the fly didn't struggle, didn't mean it wasn't trapped. That it could escape.

Her hands fisted at her sides as the fog tightened its grip. The burn was just short of intolerable. She shuddered to hold in the moan. Around her the specters moaned for her, some with pleasure, others in what appeared to be shared pain.

And she drew inexorably closer and closer to the Lord Henry specter.

Like his human counterpart, a tongue snaked out, licking the remnants of lips.

The closer she got, the worse the stench. That's what she smelled, to a lesser degree when close to the human version, she realized. What did that mean? Was a part of him still dead?

The eyes, the other specters behind those eyes, were clustered on the deck, a well-defined gap between them and specter Lord Henry.

The Lord Henry specter smiled, the teeth in his visible skull parting in a rictus grin. He lifted the cane head, moving it in a circle that wrapped her in the red ropes that burned a new way, and turned her like a puppet. At his side, but facing the lighthouse. Facing Ernest and the avid human Lord Henry. A hand, more bone than flesh stroked her hair and cheek, and this time a moan escaped her lips. Despair crept toward her heart, its fingers as icy cold as the specter's touch.

"So warm," the specter purred, leaning close and inhaling—the action and words echoed by the human Lord Henry. His tongue snaked around his mouth again, and the remnants of lips curved up. "So sweet. And all mine. I look forward to introducing you to my ship."

Her stomach roiled but oddly enough, that wasn't the worst pain she felt. They wanted her to see Ernest and Ophelia. They wanted Ernest to see her. They wanted both to completely despair, to feel lost, to lose all hope. That was the power of the lighthouse. Hope. A faint flicker of it pulsed in her heart.

Specter Lord Henry and human Lord Henry lifted their cane heads, directing red light at Ophelia. It struck her like a blow that made her scream, but then flesh and skin flowed in a slow wave up from her feet and across her body. She gasped as her lungs breathed again, her shoulders rising and falling. Her hair, the tatters of blonde turned into a liquid gold flow.

Prudence couldn't see her face.

She could see Ernest's.

His eyes widened with shock and it seemed his hand slackened on the trigger of the weapon that his hand hid from them.

"Ernest." The voice was Ophelia's, richly caressing, filled with charm. "My dearest love..."

Prudence felt that hope flicker waver—and the chains tightened so that she couldn't speak, couldn't breathe.

Darkness began to close in. The ramp turned into a long tunnel with Ernest at the end and the golden Ophelia moving to block her view of him. And to block his view of Prudence.

"I've missed you so much..."

Ernest could not believe what he saw. It was Ophelia, one better than his poor memory. How could he have forgotten her? Thought he was over her? She was perfect. She was real, so real, he only had to reach out and draw her into his empty arms...

So real.

He drew in an unsteady breath. Would he have forgotten this perfection? It was not easy when his thoughts and feelings were clouded with hope and fear, but he tried to match this reality to memory. And as he did, Lord Henry's words came back to mock him. *I am better than before.*

Too real. Too good to be true.

Relief swept through him as his mind cleared. His gaze shifted to Prudence, slowly disappearing into the circling fog. A fog wrapping her in chains, he realized with horror as the fog shifted, exposing legs beginning to fade like the other specters...

The specter Lord Henry stroked her cheek, his eyes gleaming with perverse possessiveness.

"She's mine now," he said, his mouth forming words that came out of the human Lord Henry's mouth.

In one frantic motion, he pulled the weapon she'd given him and pointed it at the shadow that was his Blizablighter 3000 up in the ceiling's peak, pointed it at the meteorite, hoping against the overwhelming despair that he wasn't too late. The pure white light struck the meteorite, or seemed to. He fired again. And again.

He heard the sounds of a struggle below and looked down. Saw Niles and Crispin fighting Winston and Fred in the stairwell. Niles ripped Winston's head off and tossed it aside, then tossed the headless body down the stairwell, too. He looked up and started up the stairs, his arms out. Crispin and Fred appeared to be more evenly matched. He had no time to watch or help him as Lord Henry closed on his other side.

Ernest fired at Lord Henry, then fired again. Light danced across the surface of his body, giving glimpses of bone and a difference engine brain inside his skull.

Overhead, the meteorite flared with gold and white light, veins in the stone picking up that light and carrying it up the wires he'd attached to the lightning rod. The light flashed around the lamp room as well. But most of the energy appeared to surge in a series of masses back along the lightning toward the ghost ship.

One of the flashes inside the room struck Lord Henry lighting him up again. His body shuddered, and he shrieked with rage as his human shell began to disintegrate, the pieces rising and spinning, as if they'd been picked up by a small cyclone. With a final surge of energy, fire and smoke consumed him in a bright, red flash.

The specter Lord Henry shrieked in rage as bright white light continued to build out from the lighthouse, sending more and more masses of light along the connected lightning flashes and back to the airship, hitting it like multiple canon shots.

Ophelia screamed as one of the masses of light hit her, and she vanished in a ball of white and red.

More and more of the light balls slammed into the sides of the airship, punching holes that quickly expanded, as if acid ate at it. Blue sky showed through the holes as the storm began to dissipate, too. He caught a glimpse of the morning sun rising in the east.

A massive ball of light, bigger than the rest, surged up the gang plank toward Prudence and the specter Lord Henry, whose mouth gaped in an unearthly howl of fury. He tried to hold onto Prudence, but his arms turned to dust, and got caught in a small whirlwind that spun the dust away from her.

As the light ate away the ship, the eyes winked out, like stars vanishing with the rising sun.

More light pierced the darkness, the rays of the sun shooting across the water, joining with the last light from the Fresnel and the "storm."

Ernest saw the gangplank beginning to erode away from the lighthouse. In mere seconds Prudence would be stranded over nothing.

"No!" He started toward her, but there was no way to reach her.

The last bit of the specter Lord Henry laughed, the sound choking off as his head turned to dust and then the airship, all of it, including the gangplank, vanished. Prudence seemed to hang in the air for a second. He gripped the railing, his hand out as she started to fall. Out of a low cloud, the dragon screamed towards her, his wings back, his mouth open wide...

The sea boiled to life, multiple arms reaching out and grabbing it in mid-flight, pulling it down into the water. Steam rose briefly from the spot where, a few seconds later, Prudence hit the surface and sank out of sight.

As if releasing one, last act of malice, a shockwave hit Ernest, throwing him backwards into the lighthouse.

Chapter Fourteen

Prudence tumbled helplessly at first, head over heels, the water rushing toward her. From that height, if she belly flopped—with some effort, she got her feet pointed down. Saw the dragon heading toward her—and Octavius grab it. Had time for a smile as it got yanked into the water, and then she plunged in after it.

It knocked the breath out of her. Felt like she went down and down forever, so far she'd never be able to get back to the surface in time. Did she see Octavius struggle with the dragon? She wasn't sure. It was so strange under the water, like a dream and yet—her arms felt heavy and her clothes added to the drag. She managed to raise her arms, though it felt like slow motion. She cut through the water with a weak breast stroke, hoping to stop the descent. Gradually, but far too slowly, she began to rise. Her lungs ached for air, felt as if they'd explode if she didn't inhale.

Strong arms wrapped around her, no, not arms, tentacles.

Octavius. In his hold, she surged up, barely conscious. They burst clear of the water just as Prudence had to inhale or explode. She sucked in the warm, salt-tanged air with gratitude and more than a little surprise. She leaned her head against his dome. "Thank you, sweet baby. I'm so sorry I got you into this."

A tentacle patted her head, while another held her securely. He started them toward the shore. A figure stood there. Not the one she'd expected.

Octavius lifted her onto a block of granite and drifted back. Her chest still heaved. Water ran down her face, obscuring her vision. Water ran out of clothes that felt like weights wrapping her arms and legs. She peered through the slowly thinning stream of water and managed to scramble into a sitting position.

He was still there.

She honestly didn't trust her eyes, her senses, anything after what had happened.

He worked his way across the blocks with surprising nimbleness, until he reached her, helped her to a more secure spot at the base of the lighthouse. The morning sky was deeply blue, but streaked with glorious streaks of purple and blue. As near as she could tell from below, the lighthouse was undamaged. She leaned way back. Even the railing was back to normal, it seemed.

"Why did you jump?" he asked.

She looked at him, this man who looked like her grandfather—a much better version than the chained specter, by the way. She opened her mouth. Closed it. Finally managed, "I didn't jump. I fell."

He looked up, his expression dubious. "Did you?" He looked around, like an absent-minded professor, looking for his glasses. "Well, I'm not quite sure...I daresay we should...this appears to be an island, but I'm sure there's someone..." He stopped, frowning down at her. "Do I know you? Have we met?"

She looked like his wife, or so she'd been told. What she didn't know was how her grandfather could have survived that...whatever it was. If time, or something else, had done a reset, why did she remember—she looked up, where the ghost ship had been, and held back a shudder of remembered horror. Would have been very happy to forget that, but not if it meant forgetting Ernest. Before she could speak, he rubbed his face.

"I apologize. That was quite rude. I'm Franklin Pinkerton the Fourth."

Her dad was the fifth. Did he remember her dad? "I'm pleased to meet you sir. I'm...Prudence Pinkerton."

A frown formed slowly between his brows. "Prudence...I don't —Prudence?"

"Yes, sir."

He studied her curiously. "You have the look of my wife. I thought you might be—but you are too young."

"My father is Franklin the Fifth."

He frowned. "Why don't I remember you?"

"We've never actually met," she said, because that was easier than the long answer that he might not remember. If he was back properly, did that mean they'd done it? She looked around, then up. Where was Ernest? "I'm sorry, sir, but there was someone in the lighthouse, I need to check on him, them. I'll be back, just sit here, okay?"

He nodded, seemed almost happy for the time to reflect.

She ran up the steps and inside, but when she looked up the winding stairs, she found she couldn't rush. Dread added weight to her climb. Or maybe gravity was in a bad mood. Around and around and around some more. What would she find up there? If proper time had been restored, maybe Ernest wasn't here. Maybe he was back in Galveston with Ophelia. She saw a window and looked out. Her knees sagged a bit.

The Weatherman. It was still there at the end of the rustic pier. She could see some automations moving around the deck. She reached the watch room. No sign of Ernest's instruments, or the crates of his notes. Were they back on the ship or lost? She heard movement up above her. Was it Ernest up there? And if it was, what would she find in his eyes this time?

Ernest rubbed his head. It ached so strangely. He explored the source where most of the pain radiated from and found a lump. What on earth? He felt as if he'd wakened too soon from a dream—or a nightmare—but one he hadn't wanted to leave. One he needed to recall.

He touched the back of head now, though carefully. He remembered arriving here, though that seemed strange and murky in some half-remembered way. The light keeper had let him stay, but why had he come up here? The morning was clear and warm. He inhaled the humid, salty air. He felt...lighter. As if he'd left a burden behind. Was this what they'd meant when they had said he would get over his loss?

He could think of Ophelia without pain. And yet, there was still pain and a feeling of loss. But what else could he have lost?

He heard footsteps on the stairs. Not an automaton, so it must be the light keeper. A woman's footsteps. But how did he know that? He turned from the railing and climbed back inside the lamp room, a strange sensation of hope stirring inside him.

First the top of a head came into view. Bedraggled, wet hair, then a pale, worried face. Brown eyes, anxiety in them. An uncertain smile flickering on lips...

Those lips. Surely...

I know her, he thought, but how could he? And yet he did. His heart leapt with joy even as his brain struggled to understand.

"Pru—" For a moment he stalled, then, "Prudence?"

A real smile flowed across her face, though some uncertainty remained in her eyes. Worry as well.

She was drenched, trailing water still. Some trickled down the side of her face, and she dashed at it impatiently.

"What do you remember?"

A frown creased his forehead. "You...fell." He jerked around, pieces floating inside his head. Disconnected. Strange. Impossible. *Six impossible things.* "Impossible things?"

Her hands closed around his. That felt right, so right. He clung, because it helped the floating pieces spin slower. Some of them drifted close, as if they wanted to fit together.

"I'm afraid there were a few more than six of them," she said, apologetically. "Sorry about that."

He freed a hand to push back a damp strand of her hair. "I don't remember you, but I do. I..." he hesitated, but felt it had to be said before it was too late, "how can I love you and not remember who you are?" His grip tightened on hers. She could vanish. He must keep her here. He frowned. "Do you have a giant octopus?"

She laughed then, the sound as bright and hopeful as the morning. "I do." She sobered. "And I love you, too."

He stared at her, absurdly happy, though he should not be. "Why—"

"I think, I hope," she said, moving closer, so that he had to put his arms around her, "that this will help. It did before."

Her chin lifted as she presented her mouth. Before...

He might not remember everything, but he did remember how to kiss a woman...no, how to kiss *this* woman. And he was very eager to do it again...

Chapter Fifteen

"What happens now?" Ernest asked, his fingers entwined with hers and sending tingles up her arm in a way that seriously interfered with her cognitive abilities.

It wasn't easy strolling on Sand Island. So much of it had eroded that they were limited to the boardwalks, which offered no privacy at all. From the *Weatherman* his automatons watched them and the light keeper and his wife had returned, so she figured they had eyes on them. Octavius and Darby, her grandfather's dolphin familiar seemed to be watching them. And then there was her grandfather. He sat rocking on the porch of the cottage. The rhythmic back and forth almost hypnotic. Maybe it helped him recover his memory.

It wasn't just memories in pieces. Her drone was gone. Or her equipment was so damaged it couldn't connect with it. That was possible. Her data storage showed empty. And her goggles were just goggles, no sensors or anything, without a drone to connect to. In some ways, it was as if none of it had happened.

And yet here they all were.

And there were signs it had happened, not just her memory of the events. Ernest had a couple of bumps on the back of his head and she had, well, she wasn't sure what to call the marks on her legs from the ghost chains. They were fading fast, and looked like burns, but thankfully they didn't hurt anymore.

"I don't know," she admitted. She didn't. None of this was supposed to happen, particularly the part where Ernest knew who and what she was. For good or ill, she'd changed his life, changed his future in this dimension. It was possible that this had already spawned an alternate universe. She wouldn't know until she returned to the Base. But if she returned with a guy, she was pretty sure they'd notice, even if she also brought back Franklin Pinkerton the fourth, the lost Talent, slash, grandfather.

She'd be out of the Agency. No appeals. What she didn't know is what they'd do about Ernest. If there was a procedure, no one had shared it with her, probably because they knew that knowledge could lead to, um, worse rule-breaking to avoid those consequences. But considering that they'd proposed erasing Ernest as a way to end The Storm, well, going home wasn't at the top of her list. At least, not without a plan.

She touched her temple. And then there was the other question. Could she go home? It had felt like her Talent lines had been damaged when her grandfather screamed, but she wouldn't know until she tried to transit. The reset, or whatever had happened, may have undone the damage, but the marks on her legs said that it hadn't undone everything. The truth was, she was afraid to look.

"What do you fear?" Ernest asked, stopping so that she had to stop and look at him.

What could be worse than what happened, was probably what he meant.

"Losing you," she admitted. "We're from different times, Ernest, different dimensions."

He studied her for several seconds. "You broke the rules that govern your agency?"

She nodded. Though "breaking" was kind of an understatement. More like broke them, jumped up and down on them, and set them on fire. She looked past him. The sun was higher now in the eastern sky—she frowned and tipped her head to the side. Ernest's brows arched, and he turned to look, too.

"What on earth—it looks like it is bending?"

"It does," she admitted. She turned in a slow circle. The bend extended all around. In fact, it kind of looked like they were in a... bubble? Was that even possible? And why was she wondering if it was possible when she'd just taken a trip through the crazy impossible?

She realized that Ernest was studying her grandfather, who had risen from the rocker. She couldn't tell if he was looking at them or the horizon or something else. He was very still.

"He looks...very well."

He did. *Better than before.* Not that she had a before, other than the specter-fying moments, but she had seen photos of him. Now he looked like a re-touched photo...

"Stay with the ship," Ernest called suddenly.

Prudence spun around. Winston and Fred were climbing over the gunwale. Ernest's order didn't stop them. She saw Niles and Crispin emerge from below and follow them off the ship. Out in the water, it almost seemed like the dolphin's fin changed shape. Franklin number four was on the move, too.

"Do you trust him?" Ernest asked, his hands tightening their grip on hers.

"Don't come any closer," Prudence called out.

Franklin four stopped. "You can't transit."

"Let's find out—"

"Wait." He moved to the place where the boardwalk from the cottage connected with that to the pier. He lifted a hand and the automatons stopped their advance.

Prudence flicked a glance toward Octavius. The dolphin—though now the fin looked like a shark's— was close, but not too close, she hoped.

"You're not my grandfather." Prudence said it, though she wasn't sure. His time on the ghost ship could have corrupted him. *Or he'd been corrupt when he disappeared.*

"You can run, but I'll find you," the possibly fake grandfather said.

"Not an answer," Ernest murmured. "I don't see your weapons?"

"Yeah, they didn't make it out with us here." Had they gotten out of something? Or fallen into something? When she'd been underwater, it had seemed very strange.

She eyed Ernest's ship. The automations were between them and the ship. Was that on purpose? Was it possible that the Blizablighter 3000 was back onboard? Was he right? Were they trapped? Or did they just want them to believe they were trapped. She hissed to Ernest, "See if you can keep him talking. Stall for time."

Ernest's nod was slight.

"Why do you care about us? Unless you seek revenge because we broke your ship."

The bubble edges quivered, as if Ernest had hit a mark.

"The ship was nothing. Only a small part of the plan." Franklin four smiled a mirthless smile. "I tell you again, you can flee, but you cannot hide from Him. There is no safe place."

"The Master?" Ernest asked. He looked around. "I certainly fear the *master* of this place." His tone was scornful, dismissive.

Again the edges quivered.

"Good job. Make him mad, hopefully make him stupid." There was damage. Lines broken and some missing. It made the map unfamiliar, strange. She tried to remember, tried to find the line home —*there is no safe place*. What if home wasn't safe either? With The Storm doing so much damage, with so much danger, in hindsight, it seemed oddly easy that she got approval to come. Was there a traitor in the Agency?

"If the ghost ship was nothing, why have it at all?"

Franklin four chuckled. "Fear is so useful. And He needed it, he needs the lives it carried."

That seemed a telling slip. Had they freed his captives?

"It is obvious why He wants *her*, but you, you were a little mistake. You shouldn't have taken the stone. And now it is lost again." Franklin four sighed, as if he regretted what must be. "And so you must be punished. If you step back from the human, Prudence, then his punishment will be...shorter. Otherwise, I'm very much afraid it will be eternal."

It was then the automatons rushed them, moving much faster than they should have been able to. And out in the water, the dolphin —no, the shark—surged toward Octavius, its suddenly huge mouth gaping wide.

"Hang on," Prudence said. Just before she closed her eyes, she saw Franklin four's face twist in rage, his visage flickering like a bad film for an instant. She thought she saw another face behind his, like an echo of a visage, but there was no time. She gathered Ernest and Octavius, then reached out for ship, felt the weight of it almost stall them out. As if Ernest sensed it, he sent her help as she groped for a line that wasn't broken within the morass inside her head.

She found one. Grabbed it. And with everything she had, and a lot of Ernest's everything, she launched them toward somewhere.

Toward some when.

~

Fire and water. Ernest knew they didn't belong together, but somehow they were intertwined in this place. He felt the singe of fire as they passed out of the bubble dimension. How did he know this? It was as if Prudence's thoughts intermingled, flowed in and out of his. After the fire came the cool of water. This was better, though he felt the drag of a great weight. Prudence was there, her octopus and somehow so was *The Weatherman*. Lights shot past them, as if the thing that called itself Franklin Pinkerton reached in to pull them back.

Now came the wind. Her eyes were wide and fixed and somehow he knew she needed to concentrate to steer them, felt the strain of it in the way she clung to him. He tried to give her his strength, his confidence, but he knew, again, he did not know how, that there was much risk in this transit. That his ship, his beloved *Weatherman*, was part of the problem.

Let it go, he tried to tell her.

But then they hit rough currents. Buffeted from every direction, he hung on with gritted teeth. He felt her gasp, there was a rushing and then they slammed into something and went into a spin that got tighter and faster until the deep, silent dark swallowed them up...

Prudence woke to the soft sound of waves slapping against wood and a huge headache. Her head hadn't hurt this bad since her first transit—

She stiffened. *Transit*. Her eyes popped open. Above her a dirigible tugged at the mooring that secured it to the ship. Ship. Airship. Really big airship. That would explain the rough, hard surface not helping her headache. And how tired she was. She was kind of amazed she'd got it here, wherever here was.

She should sit up, but in addition to the pain in her head, she felt like she'd been run through a wringer. Several times.

"Are you well, Prudence?"

Next to her Ernest eased himself into sitting position. It looked like he hurt as much as she did. She struggled into same position and gave him an anxious once over. No blood or missing parts.

"I expect I will be well soon," she said. "You?"

"I am feeling rather battered," he confessed.

"That's because you were. Battered I mean. Dimensional transit leaves bruises." She flexed her legs. Found they worked, though they weren't happy about it. She was happy to have Ernest's help in getting to her feet, though it kind of felt like they propped each other up in the process. "Oh man, that was a rough one." She arched her back, clenching her hands in the small of said back to ease the pain. It didn't work. She looked around. "I've never transited a ship to another dimension before. Did all of the *Weatherman* make it?"

She got a rather wide-eyed look from Ernest. His mouth opened, then closed. She executed a rueful shrug in answer to the question he didn't ask. Hey, from the outside he appeared he had the parts he needed. She must have looked that question, because he nodded a bit dubiously.

"How about you check the ship and I'll—" her breath caught a little. If Octavius hadn't made it...

There was splash off the port side and a tentacle appeared over the gunwale, rocking the ship slightly. She started to run—but scrapped that idea in a hurry and settled for hobbling over to the side.

"Are you all right, baby boy?" His dome rose out of the water, so she could stroke him. His color was normal. "Got all eight?" He drifted back and waved one at a time so she could count. Ernest appeared her side, giving Octavius a dubious look.

"It's all here." He cleared his throat. "*The Weatherman* is all...it is complete. I am rather amazed."

"I am, too, actually." Octavius bumped her hand with a tentacle, then indicated Ernest. "Sorry, baby. This is Ernest. Ernest, this Octavius."

With a stiff smile, Ernest took the extended tentacle. Another one snaked past and rubbed his head, then Octavius pulled back, sped away from the floating airship.

"He's probably hungry. I know I am." She looked at Ernest. "Do you suppose lunch made it here with us?"

His face shadowed, and she covered his hand with hers.

"I'm sorry about your automatons. I think he must have over-ridden their programming."

"Yes..." he frowned. "But I wonder if it was more than programming. They were more adept than they should have been."

"Really? I thought maybe you'd souped them up." He gave an inquiring look so she added, "Made them work better."

"Souped up." He repeated the words, as if learning them, then asked, "Did you see Lord Henry and," he paused, then continued reluctantly, "Ophelia when they were—they had difference engine brains. Hybrid human and automaton, or so it seemed."

"Were they? I must have missed them going cyborg on us." Prudence looked at him anxiously. How did he feel about losing Ophelia again?

"Better," he said, slowly, "*better than before*. That's what he said."

"I do remember him saying that," she said. "Is that how you knew...?"

He nodded, his gaze distant, as if remembering. "She, they thought I loved her, but it was because I realized I did not, that I never had loved her as much as she deserved, that I would have—but thankfully your plan worked."

She thought about several things she could have said, but cheering was a little insensitive, and she was too sore to cartwheel. Thankfully she had a thought.

"Do you think the automatons were hybrids, too, then?" Had he given them human brains or something? Ugh. None of it made sense, unless she factored in the fact that somehow the—her mind flinched at using the name, but she didn't have another—Master could manipulate time. Or appear to manipulate it? At the very least, he or she had somehow constructed that bubble thing they were in, had scooped them out of the dimension they'd been in. Or just grabbed this small part of the dimension? Real? Not real? Was it illusion or a mix of reality and illusion? The Master had great power and ability and yet had needed her grandfather, and then her...for what? Had the Master been after the Talent or was there some other purpose for capturing them?

"Possibly, though, I wonder, do you recall what he said about life forces?" His frown deepened and was tinged with worry. "Perhaps he knows how to...animate the automatons with the life force of the dead or recently dead? There were reports of people disappearing when the storm passed over."

"Like Frankenstein?" Prudence gave a shudder. Creepy enough to wonder if she would have been given one of the difference engine brains when it got through tormenting her, but sending her life force into an automaton? That definitely boosted the creepy factor. "There did seem to be some sort of two-way thing going on there." She shuddered again. "I'm going to have nightmares for a long while."

"Me as well," he admitted. He seemed to give himself a slight shake. Then he smiled at her, and it was totally the jets where smiles were concerned. She had to smile back, because she had a notion she didn't look the jets after the hammering and the drenching. The look in his eyes, a look she'd never expected or hoped to see *for her*, it took her breath away. It was amazing. It was entirely possible to be worried about the future of humanity and so happy her toes curled.

"So this is your *Weatherman?*" she said, not looking away because she couldn't. "You promised me a tour, I think." She was pretty sure her eyes weren't saying, give me a tour, but they probably should since they were alone on his boat somewhere and some when.

"I did," he agreed. He rubbed the back of his neck, then winced. His chest rose and fell, and his smile lost some of the heat. Though his gaze had a nice simmer in it.

Prudence drew in a shaky breath. To give herself a recovery minute, she looked around, as in around past the airship. There was not a lot of see. Just water.

"I wonder where we are?" she murmured. For the first time she let her brain wrap around the fact that she didn't know where they were or *where* they were. Or much of anything. Felt a bit like stepping onto that creepy gangplank. She felt her hand taken in a strong grasp.

"Let's take the tour, and you can tell me what is troubling you, my dear one."

Oh wow, that was brain-melting sweet. She looked at him and felt the worry melt a little. He led her toward the hatch and helped her down the short flight of stairs. In the narrow passageway, he directed her into a cabin that was obviously his research lab, or whatever he liked to call it. Probably a good thing he didn't show her his sleeping quarters. Not as tired as they both were.

His instruments were lined up on a wooden table built into the wall. They all appeared to be working normally. She looked at him, and he nodded. He pulled out his watch. Didn't know if it was the right time, but at least it wasn't going fast.

"Is the BlizaBlighter 3000 here, too?"

His eyes widened, and he quickly pulled open cabinet doors. His shoulders relaxed. "It is." He stepped back so she could see it, complete with the meteorite.

"He said it was lost," she murmured, touching it with the tip of her finger. No tingle this time. It was tapped out. She knew how it felt. Had she sensed it might be here? She'd grabbed it because it seemed the creepy guy didn't want her to have it, but maybe there'd been some instinct in there, too.

"What troubles you?" he asked again, his hands coming to rest on her shoulders.

"I don't know where we are," she admitted.

"It is a worry," he said, turning her to face him, "but once we see stars—"

"I mean, dimensionally."

"Oh. At least, I think I understand."

"I told you I can travel between dimensions. It's because I have something called the Talent. It allows me to transit dimensions, but the Talent, and with Octavius, well, with us working together we somehow find our way home."

He considered this, his head tilted to one side. "Without him you could not?" She shook her head. "But you are no longer sure you can? Or you don't wish to go back?"

"A little of both," she admitted. "There are good reasons to go back and good reasons not to."

"What are the reasons not to go home?" he asked.

"Well, there's the meteorite that's not lost and the fact that I wasn't supposed to tell you anything about me or us or dimensional travel."

"Oh." He appeared about to ask, then just said, "oh," again. "And what are the reasons to go home?"

"Well, to report what happened. There's obviously something bad happening, that has been happening, only—"

"Only," he prompted when she stopped.

"Well, he said we couldn't hide anywhere. I wonder if there's someone inside the Agency," or more than one, she added reluctantly to herself, "and then there's the fact I'm not sure I can get home again." She added this lightly, hoping to soften the panic threading into her voice.

"But Octavius seems to be..." He stopped when she shook her head.

"The thing is, I see...transit lines with my mind. That's how I move around. Octavius stabilizes me somehow—the scientists that study familiars wonder if an animals' instincts play a part—but it's still about the lines. It's knowing what line to follow in relation to the others." She rubbed the sides of her head, as if that would fix the problem. "Knowing what line and sticking it. That's the Talent."

"Something happened."

She nodded. "When my grandfather screamed, it...damaged my

mental map. It was like a hammer to a mirror. Shattered lines, big gaps. And my tech all got fried." She tapped her arm, the one she'd used to create the sound-dampening field. "I hoped it was an illusion or temporary. But when I pulled us out of that bubble thing, I could see there was a lot of damage still. This line was the only one I could find that was complete. I mean, I think there are more that are okay, but I didn't have time— I had to go. But with the map damaged and my tech all offline, I don't know where we are. I don't know when we are. I'm not sure I can transit again or even if I should try."

"So we might be stranded here is what you are saying?"

He didn't sound too worried. He pulled her into a hug. "We are alive. We are together. We will figure out this place." He lifted her chin so he could smile into her eyes. "It is not so very bad having to live one life in one place—If you are living it with the one you love."

She felt her tension easing, a smile forming on her mouth once more.

"We don't know anything about this world. It could get interesting." She wasn't sure she was dressed right for this place. This made her want to laugh, because it was such a girl thing to think. Her guidance counselor would be so proud.

"We will cross all bridges as we come to them." He bent his head, his lips pressing to hers for long enough to erase most of her worries. He lifted his head. "Things always look different when you are hungry. Let's see if there is something in the galley."

"And if not?"

"Then we will fish for it."

"Octavius can help with that."

"Already I see the benefit of having an, er, pet giant octopus."

She held him back with one hand. "And then?"

"And then we will figure out where we are in this world."

There was something in his voice that made her stop and look at him with arched brows. "And?"

"And how and where a man marries," he said, gathering into his arms, his voice husky as he added, "his one true love."

Prudence slid her arms up around his neck and pulled him close enough for kissing. "Oh, we are *so* going to find out how to do that..."

ISBN: 978-1-942583-07-3

Up on the House Top

About Up On The House Top

Will her Christmas be ho, ho, ho? Or will it be oh no, no, no?

Gini knew Christmas in Wyoming would be challenging as she headed over the frozen crick and through the woods to the family cabin. The lights are going out in her mom's attic, the guy who broke her heart is on the porch...

...and there are aliens on the roof.

According to her mom, it's going to be the best Christmas ever.

Gini's not sure "best" is what she'd call it when the men in black show up. But as she and her ex take the trip to crazy town and beyond, Gini discovers her mom's "present" is also a chance to mend old wounds and remember what Christmas is really about.

Family. Forgiveness. Gifts of—and from—the heart. And maybe even a happy-ever-after...

Have you ever hoped for a ho-ho-ho holiday and gotten something else? Then grab your copy of *Up on the House Top*.

If you like offbeat humor and outrageous situations, you'll love Pauline Baird Jones' first Christmas story!

Chapter One

The drive to crazy town was a good distraction from the Thing that Virginia Prescott did not want to think about. It helped that she needed to focus on the snowy, winding road in the steadily worsening weather.

And if that didn't keep her mind off the Thing, there were her passengers.

It was probably her imagination that inimical gazes bored holes into her back. Gini risked a look in the rear view mirror and caught Isaac looking at her. He met her gaze for a second that felt longer than that, then it slid away with more composure than Gini had had at nine. Her twin sister's new stepson was a little scary.

Gini was still trying to figure out how Isaac and his sister had landed in the rear seat of her rented SUV. There were unmistakable signs they were not willing passengers for this trip. Isaac wasn't openly hostile—yet—but Daphne had made it clear Gini would have to bust an impossible move to rise to the level of pond scum.

Gini didn't blame them. They'd had no say in the very recent marriage of their dad, and it was clear that this absent-minded-professor-ish parent had either forgotten to brief them, or punted that job to her. Bif and Vanessa both worked at NASA, in the same department. It was how they met. But Gini didn't entirely buy into the "emergency" that had left her holding the kids. Not that she begrudged the newlyweds some alone time, but they'd better show up for Christmas. Or sooner. Both of them. Period.

For sure the snow was showing up. From what she could see in the headlights, it was going to be a very white Christmas. It occasionally snowed in Dallas, but for the whitest of white holidays, she'd always had to come home. The swirling flakes had looked pretty dancing around the deer-antler arch at the edge of the small Wyoming town where she and Van had grown up. The sight of it stirred her happy memory cortex. Would Van make it in time to watch *White Christmas* with them? Even if they didn't sing the "Sisters" song out loud—which would probably be an even worse sin than Van marrying the kids' dad—they'd exchange a look that said they were singing inside their heads. It was their song. And in the morning, after the presents and the feast—which could be great or awful, depending how much access mom gave them to the kitchen this year—there'd be deep white drifts for snowball fights and snow angels and sledding and getting so cold hot chocolate was critical for survival—

As if Daphne sensed her happy thoughts and deplored them, Gini heard a sigh—and possibly felt it ruffle her hair—from the teen's side of the vehicle. Sucked to be thirteen. And the two kids lived with their mom, so their dad not showing up at the airport to collect them would have upped the disappointment factor by an equation only Van was smart enough to figure out.

Gini had tried to lighten the atmosphere with some carols—the only music the radio could pick up—but that just seemed to expand the cloud of 'not happy' to the point of stifling, despite the headphones firmly clamped over Daphne's ears. She couldn't remember exactly how it felt to be thirteen, but she did remember not liking much, including herself. In distant memory of that awful time, Gini turned the happy—and the music—off. It was the least she could do. Possibly the only thing she could do.

Ho, ho, ho.

Isaac also wore headphones. Thank goodness she didn't have to hear his game, which gave off an eerie green glow, like it was coming from a war bunker or something.

Ho, ho, ho again.

She was kind of surprised that Bif hadn't responded to her text that she'd collected his children from the airport. She'd even left off the guilt attachment, which was, in her opinion, hugely magnanimous of her. It was possible her timing was awkward. Or maybe there really was an emergency, though she couldn't imagine what emergency

NASA could have that would be big enough to disrupt Christmas. Daphne for sure hadn't believed it, if her extreme eye roll was any indication. Discontent was an almost visible haze back there, though it did go with the green glow.

She saw a familiar half-rock, half-log gate and took the turn. Almost there now. She kinda felt like she ought to warn them that there might be worse than an unwanted step-aunt to face at the cabin, but she didn't know what version of crazy she'd find. Her mom, who had given birth very late in life, had been a solid twelve on a ten-point weird scale, with ten being the most extreme, even before age had started to degrade her synapses. At least the incoming quirky-to-bat-crap-crazy weird was a great distraction from—but she wasn't thinking about the Thing.

Her SUV swept around a corner and the edge of the lights caught a blur of movement. Gini didn't hit the brakes, but she did take her foot off the gas. The thickening swirl of flakes remained mercifully clear of solid objects. She did not need to slam her rental into a deer. Not that—but the light and night must be playing tricks on her. She thought she'd seen a glimpse of something small and green—but that was crazy, even for crazy town.

She'd checked the weather about a hundred times before boarding her plane, but the storm had stubbornly refused to commit until she was on the ground and headed for the cabin—a cabin her mom should *so* not be occupying, with or without a live-in caregiver. And yet here Gini was, ferrying the reluctant step-grand-kids over the frozen crick and through the snowy woods to step-grandma's house. She just prayed that Van and Bif would make it before the storm closed the road.

The eerie glow on Isaac's side of the car faded to black. For no reason she could identify, that made her uneasy.

∽

Dateline: Notes from Isaac's Strategic Planning notebook

I am unable to create an adequate battle plan until I reach our destination. Advanced intelligence is sketchy. Indications are we are headed to a remote cabin. Normally would not object. But situation not normal. Remote might be satisfactory for overseeing exit operations if not for the extreme weather situation. If can't act soon, mom might notice her credit card is missing.

Still undecided about recruiting Daphne. She's been really weird since she turned 13.

Our captor has not left us alone since the ambush at the airport. Though not yet openly hostile, must assume captor is "good" cop, with bad cop due to arrive with dad.

There is also the problem of transportation. Not sure driving simulations enough experience for road conditions...

∾

Dateline: From Daphne's cell phone

OMG, the sister looks just like HER. So creepy. I could just die. Will never forgive dad for this. Never. Losing bars. I am in—

∾

Dateline: Advance scouting party report

Observed the Earth-based land vehicle approaching destination. Storm complicating operations. Unable to ascertain which humans inside. Awaiting report from team at Earth structure. Please report on status of failed cloak and when communications with *XOZYPS&R* will resume.

Chapter Two

Gini pulled in close to the porch with a sigh of relief she didn't bother to hide—since she was pretty sure her passengers wouldn't notice or care. Of course, relief at not ending up in a snowbank was tempered with unease about what came next. The cabin was lit up like Christmas was coming. It always was lit up, since no one bothered to take the lights down. At least Christmas really was coming this time. And it was a good thing mom had left the lights on, because through the last few bends in the road, that had been the beacon she followed. If this wasn't a full-on blizzard, it was the first cousin to one. She gripped the wheel for a couple of seconds, but she had no idea what to tell the kids. She could sort of remember being thirteen, but nine seemed light years away. What grade in school was he in? Third? Fourth? She didn't dare ask because it all depended on when he'd started—

"I need the password to the WiFi," Daphne said.

Gini should have seen that one coming. "I'll try to get that for you." The good news, there was WiFi, though someone—someone probably named Gini—would need to sweep the snow off the dish. Which wouldn't happen tonight. No point when it was still coming down. The bad news, her mom liked to change the password just before incoming visitors arrived. She'd write the new one down on something random and put it in a 'safe' place that could be almost anywhere in the cabin. Or back in the house in town. And just to make matters more interesting, she had little scraps of paper with code looking words written on them that she kept inside the cover of her tablet. Sometimes she hid the new password in there, which meant someone had to go through the scraps every time. Gini never could tell if it was innocent-crazy or her mom yanking their chains.

She saw Daphne make a face at her and decided to let her sort through the scraps this time. It would be good for her character.

Gini pushed open the driver's door and stepped out into blowing snow and a chill that cut through her Texas coat like it was a puff of smoke. At least it wasn't as cold as it could be, since it was snowing, but her blood had thinned in warmer climes, so it felt cold enough—as she told the lady at the rental desk earlier when asked about it. And the lady who had sold them bottles of soda and water. And every person they met heading out of the airport. Cue so many eye rolls from Daphne she looked like a zombie.

She pulled open Isaac's car door in time to see him tuck a notebook and his electronic tablet into his backpack. His gaze was a bit too bland as it met hers. She knew that look, or remembered it, but what could he be plotting up here in the snowy middle of not much?

"I'll get your suitcase out," she said and waded through calf deep snow to the rear of the SUV. Up on the spacious porch, the front door opened, spilling a hopeful shaft of light onto the white drift piled up there. The figure in the square of light wasn't her mother, who had gotten steadily smaller with each passing year and rolled in a wheelchair these days. Did she see the broad shoulders of a guy—

"Gini?" The voice was man-deep and twanged a chord of memory she'd thought she buried too deep to twang.

It couldn't be the boy next door, her best friend besides Van, her first love who'd left without looking back—

He strode forward, the porch light briefly falling around him like a spotlight.

Dexter James Tolliver. In the flesh.

Her head tipped to one side. In the much-better-than she remembered flesh. And wearing the uniform of the local sheriff. Her thoughts did a kind of spin, but considering she had a Thing—a Thing that was kind of a marriage proposal that she wasn't thinking about—pending at home, the hallelujah chorus seemed inappropriate.

~

Of course there was mistletoe hanging in the hall and Dex managed to catch her under it. The kiss was both familiar and different, because he was a man, not the boy who had left her, but familiar enough to make her wonder if she was completely over—

Not going there. With or without the proposal Thing, she and Dex had finished a long time ago—finished because he didn't come back, she reminded a heart pounding a little too briskly for her liking.

She emerged from his embrace to find them under scrutiny by Bif's kids—and an inflatable green alien. Apparently her mom had decided on a space theme for her decorations again this year. This would be the second—or third time. She'd done the first alien Christmas when Van got her job at NASA. The inflatable alien was an interesting twist. It was propped on the entry table with some garland around its neck. It wasn't even a good inflatable alien. It was the requisite bright green, but looked like it hadn't been completely inflated or perhaps had been left out in the sun.

She might think the alien reprise was for her, only her mom didn't know about Gini's secret life as a science fiction romance author. Even if she did, that wouldn't beat NASA. Their mom had been a NASA fan since JFK challenged them to get to the moon. And Van had always been mom's favorite. Gini half smiled, missing her sister's retort that Gini had always been the fav. She might want Van to bust a move to take charge of the step-kids, but mostly she just missed her sister. So that she wouldn't sigh again, she headed into the great room.

If Gini had hoped that one alien was it for the "my-daughter-works-at-NASA" celebration, her hopes were quickly dashed. There was another one, the wide lidless eyes seemingly watching from the massive fireplace as they straggled in. Her mom waited in her wheel-chair in front of a tree littered with spaceships, planet ornaments, aliens, and a NASA cap where the star usually crookedly clung. The only thing really Christmas on the tree were the lights. There was the Spock figurine, its place of honor front and center. Mom had always had a thing for him and kept asking when Van planned to bring him home for a visit. Even Leonard Nimoy's passing hadn't altered her mom's belief that Spock worked at NASA.

"Vanessa," she said, her arms held out for a hug, "where's Buff?"

The meme that a mother could tell her identical twins apart? Yeah, not always true. Gini found herself exchanging a very familiar, very wry look with Dex, just like a thousand or so years and tears didn't lie between now and their last good-bye.

"They are coming in tomorrow, mom." She hoped with all her heart she spoke the truth as she bent to hug the near skeletal remains. She was so thin, Gini was afraid she'd break her if she hugged too hard. She pressed a kiss to paper-thin skin, feeling a familiar swirl of emotional heartburn. Love, worry, frustration—and yes, there was some relief at being *home*, this sense that she'd gotten younger just by walking through the front door. Gini took care not to look at the kids, though she couldn't block out Daphne's derisive snort. She made a vague gesture in the direction of the kids. "Daphne and Isaac, Bif's kids. Kids, this is... your—my mom, Mrs. Prescott."

"Please call me Desi." She beamed at them, not noticing when the beam wasn't returned. "Well, so nice to *finally* have grandchildren." She turned back to Gini, who had known that guilt trip was coming and packed for it. "Wasn't it nice of Dex to stay with me so that Pleasance could go? Since you had to arrive *so* late. He was worried that it might be embarrassing for Van, since she got married and all, but I said that was all over years ago."

This made Bif's two turn to give him speculative looks. Gini had no desire to help him after the kiss, but Dex had always been able to help himself.

"I dated Gini, Desi, not Van," he said easily, his deeply amused gaze holding hers.

She tried not to react, since the kids' attention swung back her way again, Daphne's expression complicated, like she couldn't imagine Gini ever being young enough to date. Then Gini kind of didn't care what they thought as Dex's look—one far too familiar for how long it had been since she'd seen it—kept coming. He'd always been able to tell them apart, she recalled a bit vaguely, as the past stirred up something that might have been embers. Because she was tired from the flight and the drive, she told herself. Christmas was for sentimentality and remembering and, and stuff. It would be strange if her brain weren't wandering down memory lane. Remembering didn't mean anything but, well, remembering.

"I thought I heard you got married or something," Gini said, to remind the remembering that it hadn't all been that great when he left.

"I got engaged," he admitted, "never made it to the altar though."

Since she hadn't either, she didn't call him on yet another failure to follow through on a commitment. She broke the gaze and turned back to find mom watching her with a look that was uncomfortably speculative—and loaded with the potential for more embarrassing to be incoming. She asked with some haste, "So where do you want us to put our stuff, mom?"

"Well, you're in your bedroom, of course. Dex, will you show the children to their rooms? Dinner is Chinese this year."

That could be good or bad. It wasn't like there was delivery up here and her mom's cooking skills tended to come and go—though for the last ten years they'd mostly gone.

"I'm trying a new recipe," mom called as they followed Dex back out into the hall.

"Are you staying for dinner?" she asked, got a wry nod. "No good deed ever goes unpunished."

❧

Dateline: Isaac's Strategic Planning notebook

Have to assume I'm snowed in. Otherwise would already be gone.

These people are very strange. While interesting, I don't trust that old lady.

I wonder if she knows?

❧

Dateline: Daphne's cell phone.

No bars. No WiFi. If a teenager cries in the forest, no one knows because there are NO BARS.

❧

Dateline: Advance scouting party report

Land vehicle arrived despite weather.

Protocol deployed.

Should have gone to Disneyland.

Chapter Three

Her room was the one she usually shared with Van. It was bittersweet to be back, to know that this year they wouldn't be sharing. Gini had been there when they tied the knot, so she'd had a chance to observe her twin's transition to wife, to feel the new distance open up between them. It was, she stared at her reflection in the old mirror affixed to the dressing table, the reason she hadn't outright refused her boss's very prosaic marriage-of-convenience-proposal-Thing tossed her direction a short forty-eight hours ago. It had come at the end of string of pre-holiday, before-she-left instructions, and she'd actually written it down before her brain processed it as something separate from work.

She'd looked up, with a jaw that might have gone a little slack, and caught him looking at her with a hint of amusement in his usually cool and collected gray eyes. In the rank and file, they called Lincoln Graham the Big Chill. Gini tried not to think the nickname, mostly because she was afraid she'd come out with it at the wrong time, not because it wasn't true. The man was not known for being warm and fuzzy, as evidenced by a proposal so devoid of romance she'd have thought he was joking. Only he never joked with his staff. She'd seen pictures of him laughing, so had to assume he could joke, but probably not about marriage. Not when he was one of Dallas's most eligible bachelors, a billionaire romance waiting to happen.

She turned from the mirror wishing it were that easy to turn away from the Thing—which wouldn't even be in the neighborhood of a

Thing if she weren't halfway through her thirties, with a biological clock ticking so fast it made her ears ring. Not that she'd said yes. She'd un-slackened her jaw, mostly to stop questions spilling out her mouth. She could tell he liked that. He didn't want questions. He wanted an answer. So she told him, with amazing composure, that she'd think about it. He'd accepted this with no sign the delay bothered him.

That made it feel more like a business merger than a people merger, so she decided she wouldn't think about it until she had to. Granted, it had turned out to be harder than she hoped, though easier the further she got from Dallas. Until Dex—

She crossed to one of the narrow twin beds and sank down, a small package on the nightstand catching her eye. She picked it up. The tag said, "Open at bedtime." There was one on Van's nightstand, too. Had her mom planned to put the newly weds in the room with twin beds? It was possible. Or she'd planned to show Bif to his own room. That was also possible. It had been quite a few years since Gini could figure out what her mom would do before she did it. Needing a distraction, Gini almost opened it. But her mom, no matter how bad her synapses, had a scary sixth sense for stuff like daughters who didn't follow directions, so she set it down again.

She clasped her hands together, noticing they were already drier. She should dig out her hand lotion—

So what if Lincoln Graham, super driven, super bachelor had proposed like they were planning a business meeting, not a life.

And so what if her old boyfriend had appeared out of the past.

And she was spending Christmas in crazy town without her sister, and with her sister's bitter step-children.

So freaking what.

What was so great about normal? Like she knew what that was anyway. If she said yes to the Big Chill, all that would change was her address. Probably. If the convenience part meant what it seemed to mean. Did it? The thought that it might mean more made her eyes pop wide as she tried not to think about what it might mean if she was wrong. Could *not* imagine doing that with the Big Chill. Since that felt too weird to consider without more input—though how she'd get that input she didn't know—she moved on. The old boyfriend had kissed her, not proposed. Even though she'd practiced writing Mrs. Dexter James Tolliver about a thousand times in the not-quite four years they'd dated in high school. And well, it was Christmas and there was bad Chinese food waiting downstairs.

And an early present to open when she came up to take something for her indigestion before going to bed at a ridiculously early hour because that's how it had always been.

She looked around the room, so familiar in its unfamiliarity to the adult she'd become. Coming here always felt like she'd time traveled to the past. This was the other bedroom she'd shared with Van, the holiday bedroom, the summer vacation one. The place where they'd struggled to fall to sleep in anticipation of the Christmases when they still believed in Santa. Funny how she could remember that feeling so clearly, when so many other memories had faded like old photographs. She'd hung onto belief for a whole year longer than she should have, just because she didn't want to let go of the magic. Her writing had given her back some of that magic. Her characters did impossible things, got happy endings—

She snorted.

Who needed those outside of fiction? Life wasn't about endings anyway. Endings were just the beginning of something different, something new. She gave herself a good shake. And then had to smile, because she couldn't get a lot of angst going in a room where she and her sister had been so very happy. Her ability to up the angst had gone down as she staggered toward fourteen—because thirteen was like the epicenter, the locus, the black hole of angst.

Her lips curved as she saw the faded ghosts of their past selves flitting around this room. They'd giggled, whispered secrets, sneak-read books and kept their cabin toys in the cupboard in the corner. The town bedroom was different, except it had twin beds, too, and town toys. In both places they'd planned and plotted their futures— the ones where they'd become world famous at something or fly to the moon. Van had half made it. She worked at NASA. And Gini, well, she made intergalactic journeys in her imagination. She had a fan base instead of a spaceship. Her pen name was famous enough to be a Guest at some smaller science fiction conventions.

"Oh my gosh." She groaned and covered her face with her hands. What would the Big Chill think about the novels? About the *Star Trek* uniform? Would he know what a Red Shirt was? He didn't know about the geek who wrote romantic sci-fi, who still star-gazed and dreamed of a love that transcended time and space. He'd only met the efficient PA. Would he have proposed if he had known about the geek?

Dex kind of knew, not about the books, but about her geek creds. He was the one who started her reading SF. All of a sudden she wished she were back there, with Van, back when life felt simpler and crazy was slightly less crazy when her dad was still alive. And Dex was there, too, because you couldn't be three musketeers with only two. They'd been the musketeers in space because space was more fun. The future had seemed so...so...

She heard a soft tap at her door and knew who it was. She took a deep breath and stood. Time to boldly go back to crazy town. It's what all good Red Shirts did.

∽

Daphne spent most of dinner not eating. Instead she sorted through the scraps of *faux* passwords and other detritus trying to get WiFi. Gini didn't mention the WiFi was out even if she got the password. No reason to push the teen over the edge until she had to. Isaac would eat a little, then makes notes in his notebook. Gini wondered about that notebook. And she wondered why they had to eat dinner under the watchful platter-gaze of yet another inflatable green alien. At least it wasn't on the table. She must be tired, because it felt like it studied her, and it was kind of like those old portraits where the eyes followed you. Creepy.

Dex watched her, too. That wasn't her imagination. Every time she looked up from her plate, he met her gaze and smiled. She smiled back, then bent to her food, pushing it around on her plate and wondering why she hadn't frowned. Okay, she didn't want him to think she was still bitter, because she wasn't. She was waxing nostalgic, which was totally different from bitter.

No one except her mom talked. Words bubbled out of her, flowing from one topic to another. Updates on people Gini knew and people she didn't. Long detailed genealogies, mixed with health histories and unproven medical treatments that totally worked for this person, but didn't for that person. Who had died. Who hadn't but should have. How excited she was for *this* Christmas because it was going to be the best one ever. Gini could remember her grandma talking in a flow just like this and her mom's hands twitching in her lap while she nodded and smiled and murmured agreement. Gini and

Van had been fascinated by grandma's endurance and their mom's patience. They'd timed Grandma one time and she'd talked non-stop for three hours. In hindsight, she could be impressed her mom hadn't tried to stop the flow. Gini had a horrifying thought. Mom had probably been around her age—

Her mom's flow paused. She angled her head. "Are you all right, dear?"

Gini felt the ruefulness of her smile. "Just glad to be home." She meant it, so it was nice to see a delighted smile spread through the wrinkles on her mom's face. She seemed to be crumpling from the inside out, and Gini felt a pang, wondering if this would be the last Christmas with her. She wasn't, she realized with awareness of how selfish the thought was, ready to be an orphan yet. Maybe she should say yes to the frost-bite marriage. Or she could become a cat lady.

"If you lived closer, it wouldn't be so hard for you to get here."

Hadn't seen that guilt trip coming, though she should have. The funny part? She'd actually been thinking about quitting her job to write full time, and moving home, well, closer to home. Is that why the Big Chill had proposed the Thing? Had he sensed how close she was to bolting? Dude hated breaking in new staff.

She smiled again, bigger this time. "I've missed you, too, mom."

As expected, her mom closed things down early, with a firmness that even Daphne found impossible to resist. When both kids had trailed reluctantly upstairs, Gini bent to hug her mom goodnight. She cupped Gini's face with claw hands, her eyes suddenly lucid and filled with that secret excitement that always seemed to go with Christmas and incoming surprises.

"Don't forget to open your gifts," she said, her gaze leaving Gini's to move to Dex. "Thank you for staying, Dexter. It will be so much more fun with you here. This will be the best Christmas ever."

Gini managed to not frown. Just how long was he staying? Didn't he have some protecting to do back in town? Her mom's gaze moved back her way and Gini smiled a bit too brightly. "Can I help you get settled, mom?" Her mom had moved her room downstairs some years back.

"Tonight I can manage."

"Okay." What was different about tonight? Gini felt a slight frown between her brows as she headed up the stairs. There'd been something in her tone, in her eyes, that made Gini uneasy. But what could she do? When dealing with a mom, no meant no, even when it shouldn't.

"She'll be okay," Dex said, as if he felt her worry.

Gini paused, glancing back but her mom had already rolled out of sight. "Does she seem different to you?"

Dex's brows rose. "Different from what?"

He had a point. What would be different for her mom would be acting normal.

Gini resumed her climb, trying not to show how breathless the stairs made her. She'd been too long at a lower altitude. Dex thwarted her attempt to dart into her room and close the door in his face by stepping into the opening and resting his broad shoulders against the door frame. Dang, she'd thought he was hot stuff back then, but he'd filled out real nice—

Gini gave him a wary glance as he reached inside his jacket and pulled out...a paperback.

Cosmic Calamity by D.L. Prescott.

Her gaze flew up to meet his. Was he about to recommend she read her own book?

"I was hoping you'd autograph my copy." His grin had lots of smug in it.

Her jaw dropped a bit. She snapped it shut. "How did you know?"

"How could I not know?" he retorted. "It's you." He paused. "It's us, the musketeers."

It was true. She'd taken the best of their flights of fancy and woven them into her stories. Just bits in each book. Not enough bits to recognize, she'd thought. She felt color creep up her cheeks, because she'd mixed romance in there, too. In her fiction, the guy always came back for the girl. She took the pen he held out, then the book. She tried to pretend he was just another reader. "Did you want it inscribed to you or is it a gift for someone?" The question was lame, since the copy was worn. He'd probably bought it used—

"To Dex, who gave me my first science fiction book to read, much love, Gini?" he suggested. He sobered some. "It's good. I even re-read it a few times." He flicked the worn edges with his finger. "Though I was a little disappointed you didn't dedicate even one of them to me."

She had in her head. Couldn't count the times she'd typed out the dedications, then deleted them a letter at a time. "No one knows I'm D.L," she said.

"Why D.L.?" he asked, crossing his ankles and settling more firmly against the frame, as if he intended staying a while.

Her gaze shot up to meet his. She lifted her brows and waited for him to get it. Which, of course he did.

"You didn't?" He straightened. "Dumb luck?"

She nodded and he burst out laughing. Every time they'd gotten in trouble, one parent or the other had said it was "dumb luck" they were still alive to tell the tale. Dumb luck had played a part in her writing, too. She'd kind of tripped over her own, well, writing feet and thought, oh. Of course, that's what I was looking for. That's what I was meant to do. She'd always been the one to plot their adventures.

"I'm really proud of you, Gin." She felt her insides warm at the diminutive of her name, said the way only he'd ever said it, but before she could think of a response, he added, "So when are you going to quit that fancy job and come home and be a writer?"

"My boss proposed to me." She heard the words come out and her eyes widened in horror. She'd thought maybe she'd tell Van, but never Dex. Why would she think of telling Dex? As far as she knew he was years and miles away—why hadn't mom warned either her or Van that he was back? Her eyes widened. If she found out Van knew...

Dex's eyes narrowed. "So you're engaged?"

She shook her head. "I...didn't give him an answer." She wanted to yell at her mouth to shut up, but that would be not shutting up. At least she hadn't called him the Big Chill.

Dex's smile was oddly dangerous. Or she had a big imagination.

"Good," he said. He leaned in close, like he was going to kiss her again and she found she kinda hoped—but he just smoothed a bit of hair back off her face and said, "I'm glad you're back, Gin." Then he turned and walked across the hall to his room. He paused, "Sleep well." Then the door closed between them.

Sleep well. Like that would happen now.

Gini shut her door and almost leaned against it, but that was so romance heroine, she resisted the impulse and went to the bed instead. Sinking down, her thoughts spinning like a made-up gravity well, she latched on to the distraction offered by the present still waiting on the side table. The ribbon yielded easily and she lifted the gaily wrapped lid. Inside was a small, glowing crystal. Of course mom had gotten into crystals. She'd gotten into pretty much everything at one time or another, usually after it was no longer cool. She picked it up and turned it in the light. It was warm and her skin tingled, the sensation oddly pleasant. Not quite sure what her mom expected her to do with it, she set it back in the box. For some reason she couldn't explain, she felt better. It was pretty. She touched it once more. She must be more tired than she realized. It almost seemed that light flickered under her skin for a second or two. Neat trick.

She set the box back down on the table and started getting ready for bed and for not sleeping well.

∾

Dateline: Notes from Isaac's Strategic Planning notebook

It's always good to have a plan.

∾

Dateline: From Daphne's cell phone

If fate was kind, I would be dead. And dad would find my body and feel guilty forever.

Fate is not kind.

∾

Dateline: Advance scouting party report

The humans appear docile, except for the large male. Though his attention is focused on the female, as was predicted.

Still no contact with the mother ship.

Chapter Four

The edge of her bed sagged as someone jumped up next to her and gave a bounce. Gini, who had lain awake a ridiculously long time, groaned and pried open heavy lids to gaze blearily at—

She closed her eyes and looked again. Definitely a kid, but not one of the ones she'd brought here. This one looked to be eight or nine. Red pigtails stuck out from her head at right angles. Freckles marched across a small nose and plump cheeks. Her thin body was buried in an over-sized pajama top.

"How many days until Christmas?" The kid gave a wriggle of excitement.

Gini rubbed her face, blinked a couple of times. It was too early for math. She thought about asking who she was, but there was something about her that was familiar, like Gini should know. If she'd arrived this morning—only why pajamas? It hurt to think that hard, so she stopped and tried out her math skills.

"Two, no three nights." That's how they'd counted when they were little. Not days. Days were endless. Nights—except for Christmas Eve—passed in a blink. Her voice sounded odd and she coughed to clear it. She eyed her water bottle, but it seemed further away than it had been last night.

"We should have an advent calendar. With chocolate."

Gini managed a nod. "We always had one when we were little." It was way too early for talking, but this kid hasn't gotten the memo. She tipped her head and studied Gini in an un-kid-like way.

"You're little again, but not little enough."

It was also too early for cryptic. "No," she agreed. It was easier. Her lids started to drift down again, but the kid held out a skinny arm and flexed it.

She smiled beatifically. "It doesn't hurt anymore."

Gini frowned. "Have you been sick?" Her voice still sounded off, so she coughed again, eyed the water bottle. But it would require more energy than currently available to get to it.

The look she got was—odd. A bit like the look her mom gave her when she thought Gini was being dense.

"I got old. But I went young last night." A frown creased the small brow. "I didn't really believe it could happen."

Probably because it couldn't. But Gini could remember being the kid who believed in everything. And everyone. She mumbled something that could be taken as agreement but denied later.

"I like young better." The frown faded to thoughtful. "How old are you?"

"I'm thirty-five." This groan was internal. Why did thirty-five bother her more than thirty-four?

The mite shook her head. "No, you're not, silly." She bit her lip and studied her. "You're old, but not that old. I'll bet you're like eleven or something." She said that like eleven was in the range of ancient.

Gini could sort of remember thinking eleven was old. She rubbed her face again. Was she dreaming? She could be, she supposed. She'd tossed and turned for a long time—she frowned as an awareness of something wrong pressed against the not-enough-sleep haze. The room seemed bigger. Everything seemed further away, but it wasn't just that. She looked toward the foot of the bed and realized that her feet, well, they weren't far enough down the bed. Either the bed had grown or—she lifted a hand to rub her eyes again and stopped. Turned the hand palm up, then studied the back. Had to be dreaming. Because it looked like her hand had shrunk.

Just because she felt awake, well, trending that direction, didn't mean she was. She rubbed a thumb across the back of one hand. Had to be a dream. Her skin hadn't been that soft for years.

"This is one weird dream," she said out loud, realizing now what was wrong with her voice. It had shrunk, too. She held up her hand again, as if she'd find an answer, or wake up. Either would do. The kid put her palm against Gini's, as if that had been an invitation to compare.

"I wonder why it made me smaller than you?"

Gini blinked as she realized who—wow, talk about a Freudian dream. A shrink would have a field day with this one.

"Mom?"

"You'd better call me Desi now that the magic made you older," she said chattily.

"Sure." She struggled to sitting position and assessed what the "magic" had done to her. Based on what she could see—and couldn't see—she was around twelve or—no, she was **not** thirteen in her own dream. She peeked down the too-large nightgown neck. Man, it took her years to get her boobs big enough to fill a bra and poof. Gone. Good thing this was a dream or she'd be so—she frowned. Usually when she realized she was dreaming, it would fade, even when she didn't want it to. Not that she wanted to stay in this dream. Which it had to be because it wasn't as if she and her mom could go to sleep and wake up young. That was just crazy. "This is kind of weird...Desi."

"I made a wish."

"On a...star?"

Desi frowned. "That would be silly. I was trying to explain Christmas to the green men and I told them that Christmas is for children and I wished I was young again and they made it so, just like I was Captain Picard." She frowned. "Or they were."

Oh yeah, dreaming.

The door to her room banged open and Dex—a thirteen-year-old Dex—burst in, his eyes wide and shocked, an oversized robe engulfing a much leaner frame. Desi bounced on the edge of the bed, clapping her hands.

"You opened your present, too!"

"What the—" his gaze landed on the child-mom and he choked back the rude word.

"It was the green men," Gini supplied helpfully, kind of enjoying the dream now that she was sure it was one, even if it was kind of a nightmare to be thirteen again. "Desi wished it and they made the magic happen."

"The...green...men?" Dex's voice did that crack thing that adolescent boys did when they were going through puberty.

Gini chuckled. A pity this was a dream because it was kind of fun seeing Dex rocked off balance. "Your voice is changing again. Wow, what would Freud make of that?"

Was it the Thing? But what had made her send them both back to thirteen? Oh my heck. It was around thirteen that she went from buddies to crushing on Dex. It had taken him longer to catch up with her, partly because he was male and partly because she didn't get her growth spurt until she was almost thirteen. Even though they were the same age, he'd shot past her, with the end result he looked at her like she was a little sister. She rolled her eyes at that memory, then frowned. Was this some weird version of *A Christmas Carol* dream? So she could get over him and move on? Or try to work him back under the mistletoe? Why did dreams have to be so mysterious? She glanced at her mom. And just plain weird?

Dex blinked, gave his head a shake. There was a look in his eyes that was more sheriff than thirteen-year-old. Her brain was really messing with her, well, head. Because this was all in her head. Even though it didn't feel that way, it had to be.

"You seem to be taking this pretty casually." He managed a whole sentence without losing control of his voice, but she saw the effort it took and grinned wider.

"Why not enjoy my own dream?"

"You're not dreaming."

Desi nodded agreement. "This is better than a dream. I hope Santa doesn't change us back when he comes."

"Maybe the green men will talk to him," Gini said.

"Could you, just for a moment, consider the possibility that you're not dreaming?" Dex asked.

Gini looked at him. "I should consider the possibility that green men turned us young? Sure, why not?"

"I didn't say—" He crossed his arms over his chest. "Okay, if this is dream, wake up."

Gini felt a thirteen-year-old's pout form on her mouth. She crossed her arms. "Maybe I don't want to wake up."

"Maybe you can't. Because this isn't a dream."

"It has to be a dream. I am **not** doing thirteen again. I barely survived the first time." She said it half joking, but there was this weird feeling creeping over her. Because he was right. This dream wasn't fading away like it should. She pushed back the covers, slid off the bed, stood up—and her pajama bottoms fell down. Luckily her top covered her to her knees, though it barely hung on to narrow shoulders and the now boob-less front. She looked around, startled anew by how much bigger the room felt. The log ceiling was further away and the furniture had grown. Snow had piled up on the window ledge outside, but the light coming in from the uncovered window's top half was still tinged with gray as the storm brooded outside, probably gathering its whatever for round two. It gave enough light for her to see, and feel, the wrongness of it all. And yet—part of her remembered this. Remembered being this size in this place.

With a huff, she stalked to the mirror. She might have left thirteen behind but Gini would never forget the sight of it. It was the year she felt the worst, looked the worst, was the most awkward person in the whole world, even a world that contained her equally awkward twin. Yup, just like she remembered it. Bony with lots of angles in the places she didn't want them, plump in the places she could have done without, and nothing up front where it would have helped her self image. Everything, but everything was either too big or too small or just not right.

Chapter Five

This could not be real. Fate or the green men wouldn't make her thirteen and her mom, what, eight or nine. No one, even a green whatever, could be that cruel.

Dex went to the bed and picked up the present, though he didn't lift out the rock, just turned the box as if studying it. "You got one, too."

"It's from the green men," Desi said. "We all got one, well, the grownups. Kids don't need one to be kids, because they're already kids."

"Who—where are these green men, Desi?" he asked.

"Maybe they're Santa's elves," Gini said, and got an annoyed look from Dex.

"No, silly. You saw them when you came in," she said. "They said they needed to talk to Vanessa."

The look Dex shot toward Gini was too grown-up for the body currently housing the eyes. It was laced with sheriff and thoughtful and something a thirteen-year-old shouldn't know or feel. But she wasn't really thirteen, she reminded herself. Neither of them were. Her brain was still her brain, even if—she stopped that thought cold. And shot back a look she hoped was equally grown-up and skeptical, because it kind of felt like she'd mentally put out her tongue. "Really, Dex? Mixing a little sci-fi into your—" Well, she didn't know what this was, but it wasn't reality.

"Why did they want to talk to Van?" Dex asked, ignoring her look and, she presumed, the attitude.

"NASA, silly," Desi said, with familiar awe. "She's not as good as Spock, of course."

"Well, who would be?" Gini said. She made more money working for the Big Chill, but *NASA.* They had the same bodies—or had—she cast a baleful glance at her reflection, but they did not have the same brains. Van's had a much higher IQ lurking inside her skull, not to mention better taste in clothes—still, Gini felt she had more alien experience, even if it was all fictional, so the green men should have wanted to talk to her—okay, that thought was *so* messed up she should be embarrassed by it. At least she hadn't said it out loud.

"They said no one ever asks to be taken to a leader. That never goes well."

"That?" Against her will Gini asked the question. "You mean... first contact?"

Desi beamed. "That's what they called it. First contact."

Gini looked at Dex, rising unease nipping at her certainty this wasn't real. Then she looked at her bedroom door. Was the truth... out there? And if it was, Mulder would be ticked he'd missed it.

Dex insisted that they "stack" by her door, even though none of them were armed and all of them were shorter than they should be. He peered out into the hall.

"Clear," he said tersely.

It would have been kind of sexy if he hadn't been thirteen and trying to keep his robe on with one hand. She rested a hand on his shoulder and felt a flashback to when she'd really been thirteen and they'd been sneaking down to watch a critter flick and eat chocolate. She'd rested her hand on his shoulder then, too, following closely on his heels and wishing he'd get a clue—

"We should check on the kids," she said, "the other kids. Bif's kids." Was she starting to believe? Her hands curled into fists.

Dex glanced back and saw the fists. "It's not *my* fault," he said.

Almost she grinned. "I know that."

Dream or not, she knew who to blame. She looked at Desi who beamed back.

"I told you that this would be the best Christmas ever." She bounced on the edge of the bed, her eyes bright stars in the dim light.

She'd said that last night. Did that make the dream theory more or less viable?

"We should stick together." Gini said it reluctantly, uncomfortable with how conflicted she felt about her mom now that she was eight. She'd been a pretty cute kid, was a pretty cute kid, Gini mentally corrected. This version of her mom mirrored the photos she'd seen in the albums, but without the fading. This was Desi in crisp, techno-color. But it, very uncomfortably, also mirrored the weirdness of caring for an aging parent. For years it had seemed like she and Van were getting older while their mom got smaller and yes, younger. Though not in a manageable way. Their mom was an adult and could still make decisions. Even the ones that drove them crazy.

Instead of talking about dates and books or movies, the hot topic at the water cooler these days was how they dealt with their aging parents. She could not escape the irony of this, even in her dreams, apparently.

"Okay." Desi hopped off and trotted over to join them as Dex led them slowly down the hall, sticking close to the wall in a cute mimicry of big Dex. At Daphne's room, he hesitated, then gave a soft knock. Knocked again. Then again.

A surly, sleepy voice finally called out, "What?"

Dex took that as permission to open the door and peer in. Gini pushed past him and walked to the bed. Then looked back at him.

"She's the same." Gini looked around. "No present."

"I told you they didn't get one. They're already kids," Desi said, peering in.

"Excuse me. I'm trying to sleep—" Mild, very mild interest filtered into her eyes. "Who are you?"

"You don't want to know," Gini said. "Did you have a present when you came to bed, a warm rock?"

Daphne stared at her for a long moment, then rolled over, and pulled the covers over her head.

"I'll take that as a no," Dex said, backing up so Gini could close the door again.

They both looked at Isaac's door. Dex didn't knock this time. It was Gini's turn to hang out in the doorway. This room was dim as well, but Isaac—an unchanged version—was sitting up, his face lit by the green glow of his game. Almost, she'd have suspected him of delivering the rocks...

He didn't look up. "What?"

"Just making sure you're all right," Dex said. The words were adult, the timber of his voice was thirteen-year-old boy entering puberty.

Isaac looked up then and regarded them curiously. "Who are you?"

"I'm Dex."

Gini hit his arm. "Dexter James Tolliver! You'll scare him."

"He's going to find out anyway," Dex pointed out, "and he doesn't look scared to me."

He was right about that. Mostly Isaac looked interested.

"You shrunk."

"We all did, except you and Daphne."

"Really?" He picked up the notebook by his bed and started writing. He paused. "Theories?"

"We got a present last night, this rock that glowed and felt warm when I touched it. Did you get one?" Dex asked.

He looked at him, his gaze wide until a slow blink. Then he shook his head. "It was probably the little green men."

"I hope I wake up soon," Gini said, as Dex paused at the top of log staircase. "I can't be be thirteen again. I sucked at it then, and it will be worse now because I know how bad it will be." People joked about going back and doing it better, but no one really believed anyone could do the "glory days" better. All they could hope for was to get out alive and then pretend it had been awesome when they went to their high school reunions.

"Sh," Dex said, peering over the bannister into the deep gloom below.

"They left," Isaac said, looking up from his game, which apparently he could do while walking and talking.

Dex swung around. "How do you know?"

"I went and got a glass of milk when I woke up."

"They could have come back," Gini said, uneasily, even though she didn't believe any of it. At all. Or not much.

"Right, let's go find out." Dex straightened the robe, or tried to, and started down, with half his entourage following at paces commensurate with their ages and attention spans. Gini stuck close because he was the sheriff, the really short sheriff. And he was Dex. Even when he'd really been thirteen he'd been, well, Dex.

It was all way too much like thirteen in her memory. Gripping his shoulder with one hand, clutching the top of her pajamas with the other, she followed him from room to green-alien-less room, though Spock was still front and center on the tree. They ended in the kitchen. The milk carton stood forlornly on the table where Isaac had forgotten to put it back in the fridge.

Gini—because her brain wasn't thirteen—replaced it and wiped up the drips with a cloth that she then hung neatly over the sink faucet. A pity she also remembered the feeling of not quite fitting into her body anymore. She wanted to claw her way out. Instead, she turned and studied Dex, who had gone into mulling mode. Desi began to move around in patterns that made sense to her, but no one else. Isaac got the milk out and had another glass of milk, while apparently continuing with his game on his device. Almost she'd suspect him of having more than two arms. Of course, he left the milk out again, which Gini had to return and wipe up more drips.

They needed help, but who were they gonna call, assuming they could find the phone and it worked? Alien busters? How did they explain this? Who would believe them? Isaac had taken their transition to peer okay, but what kind of authority would any of them have over Daphne? Assuming she could be convinced they were who they said they were. Gini didn't believe it. At least she wasn't willingly believing it. Why should Daphne believe them? "We should call their —we should call Bif."

He wouldn't believe them, but he'd have to come. Might already be on the way, she thought with scant hope. Like Dex, she found herself wondering if their emergency might be related in some way to this alien contact—which was pretty much the only emergency at NASA she could imagine. Not that she believed yet. She could still wake up wondering what she ate last night to bring this on. Couldn't she?

"And how do we do that? I hit no bars on my cell about five miles from here." Dex suddenly looked more his physical age as the enormity of their problem began to dawn on him.

There was no land line up here. "Mom has some kind of phone phone service through the dish." Gini wasn't sure how it all worked.

She looked at Desi, who was still "writing" patterns on the wooden floor, her thin arms outstretched. As far as she could tell, her mom's brain hadn't gotten younger, just her body. "For emergencies. It's got to be here somewhere. Pleasance wouldn't bring her up here with no way to get help, particularly this time of year. I think we have to sweep the snow off the dish though." She glanced toward the window. Piled up snow had collected on the ledges, blocking about half the view. The remaining glass was fogged over. She crossed over and rubbed a circle into fog and peered out. Huge white drifts filled what was usually a meadow or clearing in the summer. Snow weighed down the branches of the pine trees that raggedly surrounded the clearing, giving it a picture postcard perfection—

She gasped and jumped back.

"What?" Dex hurried to her side, glanced out, then wrenched open the door to the back porch.

In the deep snow from last night's storm, they clearly saw the pattern of really, really small footprints going across the rear porch, down the steps and then around the side of the house. As if on cue, they heard the click of something walking across the rooftop.

Gini looked up, like she could see through the ceiling, then looked at Dex. "Reindeer paws?"

≈

Dateline: Notes from Isaac's Strategic Planning notebook

What does it mean that they are up on the house top?

What is their purpose?

Must assume it is hostile, since all adults have been shrunk to a more manageable size.

No surprise they are not taking that well...

≈

Dateline: From Daphne's cell phone, sleep monitor

Snork...

~

Dateline: Advance scouting party report

Protocol produced unreliable results. Studying data. Still trying to contact mother ship....

If we'd gone to Disneyland, we'd could be on the It's a Small World ride about now...

Chapter Six

G ini had been kind of hoping that the aliens got beamed up—
even though it creeped her out to think about little green men
beaming in and out. Had they used the porch supports to climb up
there the way she and Van and Dex used to? She rubbed her forehead
with both hands, as if she could push thinking in from the outside,
but her thoughts remained random and thick.

The sight of the footprints, or foot-ish prints, reminded her of
another problem with sweeping off the dish. "You're not exactly
dressed for snow removal," she pointed out, giving his bare feet a
pointed look.

Dex closed the door, then shoved the lock home. "Do you think
that box of spare clothes is still around somewhere? You know, for
when we were just up for the day—"

"—and fell in the crick," she finished. "I think I remember
stowing some boxes in the attic for mom a few years back."

"Let's hope we can find something that fits better than this." Dex
gave her a wry grin, almost tossing her back in the past again, except
there was more awareness in his eyes than there'd been back then. At
thirteen Dex had been thick as a brick about girls.

"Okay, so if we can get the dish clear we should at least get the
phone online," she bit back a groan. "If we can find it. Be nice to get
mom's computer up, too. And the TV. Like to check the weather.
Because Bif and Van are supposed to come. If—when, their emer-

269

gency—" she stopped again. Reluctant, but it had to be said. Maybe. "What if their emergency *is* somehow related to this?"

If it was, then they wouldn't be arriving anytime soon. Dex grimaced and shrugged. She wasn't sure if that was agreement or not.

"What other kind of emergency could NASA have? I really thought they were sneaking a—" she broke off as Desi suddenly stopped dancing and looked at her. Isaac also looked up from his game, as if sensing this was the moment to pay attention. "Some alone time."

"That could still be where they are," Dex said a bit dryly, the man's awareness boosting signal in the eyes looking out of the thirteen-year-old's face.

It was all a bit then and now, and Gini wished she were brave enough to ask him *why didn't you then and why are you here now?* Because a possible alien invasion wasn't enough to worry about. The writer in her found she was a bit fascinated by her reactions and thought processes. She was all over the map, thinking-wise. Clarity one moment, random inconsequential the next. Or perhaps not relevant to the situation was better description. The past, with Dex in her present, felt more important than she liked. And yeah, there went her thinking straight off the road again. She brought it firmly back to this present.

Not that that helped her thinking all that much. What was it Desi had said? First contact never went well?

She'd sat on a panel on what first contact would be like. When she'd got the assignment, she'd almost panicked until she remembered that no one knew what it would be like. At least no one who would admit it. So they'd all just made it up as they went along, postulating this and that. And now here she was, and none of that postulating felt relevant. She'd for sure never foreseen a first contact where she was thirteen again. And who actually believed in little green men?

"If there isn't an actual emergency and the storm holds off, then they should be heading our way...when?" Dex asked, breaking in on her not exactly productive thinking. Something of her mixed feelings must have shown on her face, because he cocked a questioning brow. She grinned ruefully.

"We really are awake, right? Because this doesn't feel like awake. I mean, I feel awake, but—"

"It doesn't feel real to me either." He pulled out the chair next to her and sat. "Kind of takes me back. I remember this, well, almost this, when I got hit by the realization that you were a *girl* and your mom realized we couldn't be left alone to 'play' anymore."

She didn't blame him for waiting until she was fourteen to notice. If she'd hoped to forget how bad it was to be thirteen, well, this morning had brought it all back.

His rather wry smile was a mix of then and now—the post girls-have-cooties look. She'd fallen hard for him, well, as hard as a thirteen-year-old could fall. She realized now that he'd been a safe place for a vulnerable heart.

Until he wasn't anymore.

She had to bite back—again—the longing to ask him what had happened. This was totally the wrong moment for postmortems on their dead relationship, even if she found the guts to ask. It's not like she didn't know she was the Queen of Denial, or she'd have given the Big Chill his answer before she left Dallas. Though if she were doomed to live her life over, that Thing was no longer a Thing she needed to worry about. She was pretty sure the Big Chill wouldn't want to be married to a thirteen-year-old. Which just showed that every cloud had at least a small silver lining.

Isaac looked up from his notebook and cleared his throat.

"I've been working on a Plan," he said.

Gini wasn't sure why she knew Plan had a capital 'P,' but she did.

"A...plan?" Dex asked the question gravely. Not even a twitch of the lips.

Isaac set his notebook on the table and Gini saw drawings and notes.

"We should probably wake up Daphne," he said, though not eagerly. More resignation in his tone. "We'll need all hands on deck, though not sure." He frowned, considering this. "I figured with her and without her, because it might take her a long time to quit freaking out."

Dex looked at Gini. She leaned back, her hands lifted protectively. "Don't look at me. I'd like to live long enough to not be thirteen."

Isaac ignored this. "As noted, you both need to go get the more suitable clothes, we must locate the phone and, if possible, the WiFi password," he said. "With WiFi we can text, even if it is too dangerous to talk."

Not exactly a lot new in the Plan, though she hadn't thought about the benefits of texting if they were being monitored from above. Gini looked at Desi, aka the keeper of the password, who was now trying to stand on her head.

Maybe she would rather die waking up Daphne.

～

Dex added an action item to Isaac's master Plan. The "men" would "secure" the structure, whatever that meant, and then consider whether or not to wake Daphne, who might technically be the oldest now. But getting clothes was a major priority. Dex did look ridiculous. And she was pretty sure she did, too.

"Desi? Want to go look in the attic?" Desi brightened, then nodded, holding out her small hand with the confidence of an eight-year-old. Gini took it, feeling an odd mix of comfort and not comfort, familiar and strange. She wanted to hold her *mom's* hand. She missed that, more than she had realized, in the bustle of being a grownup.

There was a flash of her mom in the eyes for a moment, before Desi grinned and tugged. "Let's go."

Gini sent a look back at Dex, not happy at this dividing of their forces, but aware they also couldn't move around the house in a clump. If her mom was still in there, Gini might have a better chance of reaching her if they were alone.

"Do you happen to remember where the phone is, mo—Desi?" she asked as they climbed the stairs, then headed toward the end of the hall and the cord that hung down. Desi ran ahead and tugged it, lowering the smaller set of stairs to the attic. Chill air rushed down. And old smells, forgotten-until-now smells. For a moment she rocked back on her heels as the the past rushed over her. She and Van and Dex loved to play up there, even when it was next door to a freezer—

Desi paused halfway up the stairs, a vague—yet familiar—look altering the young gaze. "The phone? It's by my bed...oh look!" She ran up the last few steps.

Gini followed, interested to find that her newly young body was not as bothered with gravity at this higher altitude as her older body had been last night...

Boxes were piled randomly around the opening. She felt a pang of missing her dad. He'd have never left it in a jumble like this. She and Van had done this. *Dad.* He'd seen them off to college, so proud—

"Let's try this one." Desi pulled the top open. "Our snow things!"

It didn't take long to find some clothes that would probably work and there'd always been boots in a variety of sizes because the weather could change in a blink up in the mountains, even in summer. With her arms full, Gini followed Desi down, letting her push the stairs back in place—several times. She stopped by what had been her mom's bedroom, before the wheelchair, as more memories tried to complicate her thoughts. Was this the room Desi meant? It had probably been prepared by Pleasance for Bif and Van. She decided she'd better check, had to push through the past to go inside. Did she still smell her dad in here? For sure, her mom's favorite scent lingered in the air, but she could have sworn—

The phone was in there, for whatever reason. The bed hadn't been slept in. She checked the phone. It had charge, not a lot, but hopefully enough. If the storm got worse, power might be an issue. Desi appeared in the doorway. Gini turned. Questions were tricky when her mom was her mom. Would it be easier or harder now that she was eight?

"Mo-Desi, do you know where the power cord for the phone is? And the password to the WiFi?" She shouldn't have rushed it. Knew it as soon as the words were out her mouth.

The little face wrinkled up in puzzlement. "What?"

The clothes were warmer and fit better, but were far from the sassy that Gini would have liked when engaging in an adventure with her first love. Gini didn't know if she could view this body without the angst attached. As a writer, she knew all about how point of view could affect what one saw, what one felt. But pairing ill-fitting, faded clothing with the awkward body of a thirteen-year-old—didn't see how her point of view could be anything but, "I want to hide in the closet and cry. Or wake up myself again—all thirty-five years of myself."

Yeah, that one.

She looked morosely at Desi, who had sprawled on the huge couch, with her head hanging off the edge, and was now softly singing disjointed bits of Christmas carols. As Gini's now-young body, once again surging into the hormone zone, filled up with angst and thirteen-year-old-ness, it was a bit shaming to realize how much her mom had been the focus of her dark thoughts and feelings. Now, with her mom a kid, angst was a heat seeking missile in a place with no one to lock on to.

She heard the stamp of booted feet on wood, felt a rush of cold air, then Dex appeared in the doorway, shaking snow off his ill-fitting clothes. He had an odd look on his face. Based on all the oddness they'd been forced to deal with since they woke up, Gini found it disturbing. What "odd" was left to put an odd look on his face? Their odd should be all tapped out. She started to ask, but he shook his head slightly, his gaze flicking toward Isaac and Desi.

"I think the dish is clear enough, but we should leave. We can call Bif on our way down." When Gini didn't jump up, he arched his brows like he was still thirty-five. "We need to go now."

"We have a larger problem to solve," she said. "We're not old enough to drive anymore, *Sheriff* Tulliver."

His eyes widened. His legal duty clearly warring with his desire to get the heck out of here. What had he seen out there? "Thirteen sucked then and it sucks now," she added gloomily.

"Leave? Before Santa comes?" Desi's face got a mutinous cast to it. She crossed small arms over her narrow chest and scowled. "I won't."

"We can't leave until we find out what's going on," Isaac said, with more authority than he actually had. She and Dex were bigger than him.

And that was so thirteen, Gini shuddered. Her thoughts paused as another look, not so much odd as wary, crossed Dex's face. If felt very Mulder to wonder what truth was out there.

Isaac, who had somehow acquired possession of the phone, studied it. "While I'm personally opposed to calling my dad—or my mom—if we're going to do it, we should do it before this runs out of battery."

Gini took it, punched Van's cell number and hit send. The call connected—and clicked right over to her machine. Gini bit back something rude. "It's her machine."

"That's something," Dex pointed out.

"And exactly what message do I leave?"

"Here." Isaac took the phone back. Waited a few seconds, then said, "This is Isaac. We need dad to come and get us. Or we're going to run away." He clicked the phone off. Then dialed and, apparently, left the same message for his dad.

Gini exchanged a look with Dex. He shrugged. "That might work." She looked at Isaac. "You don't want to call your, um, mom?"

"She won't be any help," Isaac said, matter-of-factly. "She was freaking out on Facebook before they closed the doors on the plane."

"I wonder who would be help?" Gini muttered. "And what that help would look like?" Did NASA have a men in black division?

Dex looked kind of rueful, though still very worried.

"What?" she asked.

"Do you remember when we used to play first contact?"

"Oh yeah." They had. Had she used some of their play scenarios for the panel? It had all happened pre-angst, was one of those faded photograph memories, but now it all swirled in her head Kodachrome crisp once more. Her lips curved up. "We used to be the ones to save the aliens from the evil whatever that wanted to capture them for research and study. First contact never goes well in fiction," she said the last a bit thoughtfully. When they apparently told Desi "it" didn't go well, they didn't mean here, did they? What if there had been first contact. Did Van know about it, too? Had she *and* mom been holding out on her? Secrecy, blah, blah, blah, but they were *sisters*.

"How come you didn't write that book?" he asked.

"Because I could never figure out how to make it work out for the aliens," she admitted. "Look at how we've panicked, I mean we're not rioting or anything, but we're definitely not happy." Not that she didn't have good reason. Being turned thirteen, in her opinion, was not a good first contact move. Which brought her back to wondering what would be a good first contact move? She traced a pattern in the table top with a finger. "Why do you suppose they picked Van? I mean, it's not just that she's NASA, at least, I wouldn't think." As far as Gini knew, Van's speciality was FTL research. How to get there, not how to say howdy to the aliens.

"She wrote a paper on it," Isaac said. He looked up. "You can Google it. We should probably wake up Daphne—" He stopped.

Gini waited for him to finish, but when he didn't, she followed his gaze to the big doorway.

There was a little green man standing there, regarding them with some wariness in his platter-shaped eyes. Four more appeared around him.

Maybe they could beam in and out. They appeared to be wearing elf suits—Santa's elvish suits—of green velvet with white fur at the collars and sleeves. Little gay sprigs of holly adorned each lapel.

Oh, and they had ray guns. At least, they looked like ray guns.

Her sense they were ray guns was boosted by the fact that they were pointed at them.

~

Dateline: Notes from Isaac's Strategic Planning notebook

If they came in peace, why the ray guns?

I wonder how hard it would be to get one. I've always wanted a ray gun.

I wish I was home alone. Adults turned into kids are more useless than adults.

~

Dateline: From Daphne's cell phone, sleep monitor

...wish I were...snork...

~

Dateline: Advance scouting party report

First attempt at contact with these humans. Hoping friendly elf suits will inspire trust. Bringing grizt-o-nators just in case.

Chapter Seven

In the abrupt and prolonged silence, Gini found her brain going inconsequential again. It was easier than wondering if she was about to get shot with a ray gun. The five green aliens varied in height, and as she studied them, she noticed they were more different than she first thought when they were room decorations.

Even though he was in the middle, because he was the tallest—and the first sighted—Gini called him One. The two on either side of One were almost of the same height—she assigned them Two and Three—and more similar in appearance than the two on either side of them. Four, on the far right, was the only one that lacked the guy vibe, and because there was an elf hat set at a jaunty angle on the green, rounded dome, Gini mentally called her a "her." The far left alien made her think of scientists and geeks, so she added a Doctor in front of his Five. Wide black belts wrapped the comically narrow waists of all of them. And their black boots curled up in front, almost to the point of touching where their knees might be. It was almost as if they'd taken their cue from a children's story book. Four even had a feather tucked in the band of her hat at a rakish angle.

Gini sensed worry from them, though none of the platter gazes had what she'd call expressions. It was possible she assigned them her worry, okay, outright fear.

Dr. Five raised the hand not holding the ray gun. He pointed something at them, a sort of iPad looking thing. It's screen flashed a series of lights, both white and colors, in what appeared to be a pattern. Were they supposed to recognize it? She looked at Dex, who shrugged. Isaac wrote something in his notebook.

Dr. Five's long green fingers moved and the screen changed from lights to binary code. While she could recognize what it was—thank you *Star Trek Next Generation*—she could not read it. She gave a kind of shake of her head and some dots and dashes replaced the binary code. At least, it might be morse, though the noise was a garble of sound like someone twisted the radio dial too fast. After a bit, these changed to a series of discordant tones that made her eye twitch. Out of the corner of her mouth, she whispered, "Do you know what they're doing?"

Isaac huffed an impatient sigh and said, not whispering, but with lots of d'oh in his tone, "They are trying the protocols from the first contact paper."

In a sort of alien flourish, the screen shifted to images, icons of small stick figures. Some appeared to be running with their arms pointed up, while others were sitting. One of them lay on its back. Their was a big circle with a line across it over the whole.

"Oh. Right." She really wished she'd read that paper, though she doubted it would aid her much in comprehending the actual message trying to be conveyed. "I wonder what it—he's trying to tell us?" Seemed like that was need-to-know.

Isaac looked up from his notes. "Don't panic."

Was that a translation, or an admonition? She didn't like to ask. It was getting old being d'oh-ed by an nine-year-old. She studied the stick figures. Okay, that one seemed kind of obvious.

"You won't panic, will you Vanessa?" Desi said, rolling from her back to her stomach and resting her chin on her small hands. It was distinctly weird to see her mom looking at her from out of that young face.

Gini opened her mouth to remind her mom that she wasn't Van, but a cough from Dex, stopped her. If the aliens wanted Van, maybe they should think they had her until, well, until it became really obviously she wasn't Van. She shook her head. It wasn't a total lie. She'd gone past panic by now. The edges of One's mouth quivered.

"It is well not to panic," he said. One green hand rested on the wide black belt, the fingers twitched a couple of times.

His accent was different enough to seem alien, at least to Gini's ears, which were admittedly not that well trained in foreign—or alien—languages. She couldn't help but notice he appeared to have no trouble with the English words. So why all the first contact crap? She'd like to know, but didn't like to ask. The d'oh factor again.

"They are large," Two said, his tone sounding a bit accusing. He held his ray gun with both hands, but his skinny elbows rested on his black belt as if they needed the steadying support. His platter gaze turned toward Dr. Five for a second, before jerking back toward them.

Dex cleared his throat. "Is that why you made us younger?"

His voice was that "let's all stay calm" one that policemen used on *Cops*. It was a bit funny to hear it coming from a thirteen-year-old mouth, because he really nailed it. Not that she watched *Cops*, except by accident, but he sounded just like them. If she watched it. Which she didn't.

One blinked. "Yes."

He was lying. Gini didn't know how she knew but she did. Okay, it felt like she knew.

"Small is better." This came from Three on the left.

Their accents were similar, but enough different to indicate individuality.

Small wasn't better, she wanted to say, not when looking down the barrel of some ray guns, but she wasn't sure she could talk. Or that she should. She was making assumptions, leaps of logic based on her point of view. Author-her knew that. Recently-turned-thirteen-her needed some kind of grounding, a sense of understanding that which could not be completely understood. Or even partly understood. Which led to making assumptions and leaps of logic.

"We'd feel more comfortable if you weren't pointing weapons at us," Dex said, his hands just slightly raised.

"You are large," One said, as if that settled it for him.

"Santa's visit is two, no three nights away," Desi said, her tone one imparting asked-for information.

Based on her mom's reactions, first contact with her had gone just fine. Would have been nice of her to mention it. Okay, so maybe Gini wouldn't have believed her. But at least Desi would have had a told-you-so-moment, something that her mom used to wait and watch for like a cat at a mouse hole.

Another, longer pause. Most of the platter gazes shifted toward Desi. Was it her imagination that the gazes appeared to soften?

"He could come sooner," One said.

Desi's face brightened. "Could he? It's SO long until Christmas. It's *hard* to wait. My mom always used to make me wait."

So did mine, Gini wanted to point out, but didn't. Right then there was no sign of her mom in Desi.

"We will not make you wait."

His companions nodded, though some of them glanced over their shoulders, as if uneasy. Did they fear Daphne? They probably should, Gini conceded, though only to herself.

Desi beamed at them and sat up so she could bounce on the edge of the couch. "Oh, when? When is he coming? Tonight?"

One nodded, though it seemed a bit cautiously. She couldn't tell if One was humoring Desi or something else. Maybe he didn't understand Desi. Gini sure didn't.

Desi flung herself rapturously against the back of the couch. "I won't sleep. Not a wink."

How ironic would it be if her mom did to her what Gini had done for so many Christmas eves. Not that sleeping would be possible with aliens up on the roof. And down in the living room.

"Have you been...visiting a while?" Dex asked.

Gini figured he'd gone into hostage negotiation mode. Could one create a bond with green men and a green gal?

This question appeared to require more thought.

"A...while."

The careful responses were troubling, though Gini wasn't sure why. Okay she knew why. One didn't trust them. Since she didn't trust him, it was probably fair. Though it didn't feel fair. Was that thirteen taking hold? "It's not fair" had probably been her most used words that whole year.

"I have to use the bathroom," Desi said, giving them a bright smile as she rolled off the couch, landing on her small feet.

"Me, too," said Isaac.

All four of them studied Isaac for what felt like a long time. If they'd been studying Desi, then they didn't need to do it again, but it was still unsettling, their singular, intense focus on Isaac. Though it was also smart. Gini was suspicious of his sudden need to pee.

One gave a slow nod. Gesturing for them to go past them. Should they let him out of their sight? Not that they really had a choice. The green aliens held all the ray guns. As Desi and Isaac approached, they shifted back, like a small green ripple. Apparently they were fine with moving around in a huddle.

They were very small. Despite the shrinking, Desi was still taller than them, though not by that much. She could see why their human size might bother them. She'd bet their green heads didn't reach her waist. She wasn't enjoying being smaller, but didn't remember being that little. She tried to mentally crouch and feel small, or at least shorter. That didn't help, so she went for a memory of feeling out of her depth. That was way too easy. All she had to do was bring back the first time she'd met the Big Chill. She'd been so scared and so cold, she'd about wet her pants. She was still surprised he'd picked her—for the job and for the other Thing. For some reason she found it hard to think the 'm' word, let alone say it again, around Dex, or maybe it was the aliens making thinking so hard.

And then it hit her. Her mind kind of...popped.

It was like pacing and pacing, and eating chocolate and ringing her hands and being sure she'd never be able to pull off her plot off this time. The other times were just a fluke. Pure, dumb luck. And then it happened. The mental boom. Like a gift inside her head. The Story. What was supposed to happen next. Only this wasn't an idea or plot boom. It was a "holy freaking cow, I'm looking at aliens. Actual little green men and possibly a little green gal" boom. She didn't know they had gender. Didn't know they didn't. Just knew her mind felt blown. Blasted. Boomed. First her brain bent.

Then her knees bent.

Luckily there was a chair behind her to drop onto. Otherwise it would have been a wooden floor splat.

All five of them tensed, their weapons going from general covering, to pointing at her. Gini didn't have it in her to be scared, to wonder if she was about to vaporized. She was still trying to wrap her brain around the boom.

Aliens.

Not a movie. Not a book. Not the *SyFy* channel. Not fiction. This was the real deal. She'd gone over the crick and through the woods to her mother's house and found...

Aliens.

It would have been easier to come face-to-face with Santa Claus. There was this tiny part of her that still hoped, part of her still wanted to believe—

She gave herself a shake and looked at Dex and heard her younger-but-still-her voice ask, "Why didn't you write me back?"

~

Dex gave her an incredulous look, leaned close to hiss, "Do you really think this is the right time for that?"

She leaned back in the big chair, somehow comforted by its embrace. "I'm about to get vaporized. Think of it as a last request."

He looked at the aliens. So did Gini. They'd all tipped their heads slightly the same direction. Then, very slowly, they tipped them the other way. Getting no help from them, Dex shifted from one foot to the other. Rubbed his face, looked at them, then at her. Gini arched her brows.

"It was your dad," he finally said.

Gini reared back a bit. "My dad?"

The alien heads all straightened. Kind of felt like their eyes widened, though that was also hard to tell. They were already really wide. They might have tensed some at the tone of her voice. But they looked way too interested. Had Desi told the aliens Dex dumped her? So she could be humiliated on two planets?

"He said, well, he reminded me that neither of us had dated anyone else. Ever. That I owed it to you to give you a chance to find out—" he stopped.

"Find out..." she prompted unhelpfully, rather enjoying his obvious discomfort.

"Well, find out if we were meant to be," he said, swallowing rather obviously. "How could we know until we did. Date other people, I mean. He asked me to do it for you," he tacked on with an air of desperation.

"So you got engaged *for me*?" Gini didn't try not to sound skeptical.

He shook his head, but warily. "I needed to know for me, too. That's what your dad said," he tacked this on with the obvious delusion that it would help his case. He looked away, pushed his hands through his hair, then seemed surprised by that. He lowered his hands and looked at them as if they were alien. Which they kind of were. "Not that that's why I got engaged. It's just that, well, we hadn't dated anyone else. When I started looking—it kind of went to my head. I mean, everyone here knew we were a couple, so no one tried —" He stopped, as if he realized he wasn't earning any brownie points. "I was well, flattered I guess, and I thought that made your dad right. Figured you were feeling the same when you didn't write again." He half shrugged. "When it came to it, I couldn't go through with it. I broke it off, but it felt like it was too late. Like I blew it. How could I call you up and tell you I'd made a mistake? I'd almost married someone else."

Gini hadn't started giving off "available" signals until she heard about his engagement. Dumb move, but she'd hoped—like Santa— that he'd come back. "Dad tried to tell me, too," she admitted a bit absently, only realizing it now. That crazy, mostly useless hindsight. She'd brushed off dad's words because, hello, true love. "Did you come back to—" She couldn't finish the question.

"I wanted to come home," he said. "I'd been reading your books and remembering—but I was homesick. Tired of big cities. When Desi told me you were coming—that you weren't involved with someone—" His brows drew together. He half shrugged again. "I wondered—but you are involved with someone?"

His tone made it a question. She wasn't sure she was involved with the Big Chill but—facing down ray guns—she could admit that she had looked at her boss with...feminine curiosity, which he might have noticed and which might be a contributing factor to the Thing-proposal. She was human and the guy was smoking hot. In a chilly way, but yeah, smoking. Like dry ice. She was glad she'd mentioned the Big Chill now, though it had horrified her last night. She hadn't been ready for anyone to know. Now it seemed fair, even if she finally knew why he'd dumped her, why he'd gotten engaged. He should twist in the wind a little. Or a lot. Was that the thirteen-year-old thinking? Or the vengeful thirty-five-year-old?

"I am...hoping to not get vaporized," she said, because she needed to say something before the silence got really awkward. It was possible she was in a very deep sleep, she decided, a bit distantly because of the mental booming, one brought on by stress. She'd had dreams before where she dreamed she woke up, thought she had, and then realized she hadn't when weird happened again. This could be that. Though the detail was a bit troubling. And the fact she wasn't actually waking up. Or waking out of this weird. So she considered what he'd said. "My dad told you to break up with me."

Dex shrugged. "Not exactly. He asked me to back off for at least a semester, preferably two. Said we needed to know. Said we'd both be home next summer—"

He stopped. Because her dad had died that winter and she hadn't come back that summer. She couldn't face home without dad and

Dex. Still felt guilty about it, because mom had needed her. She'd said it was okay, only it wasn't. Ah, guilt, the gift that just keeps on giving. She sighed.

"It all seems so long ago..." she murmured.

"But you are young," One said.

She'd forgotten about the aliens. Wow. Did that make her shallow, asleep, or seriously stressed out?

Dex swung back to face them, like he'd forgotten, too.

"Our bodies are young," he said, watching them closely—with possibly a little relieved in there, "but our minds aren't young. The past, when we were young, is still the past."

One blinked, the movement echoed by his team. He appeared to consider this statement. "It is not enough to be young again? You wish to return to the past?"

"No," Gini sat up straight, trying not to be unduly emphatic. Didn't want to startle one of them into accidentally shooting her, since the ray guns were still pointed at her. "I don't wish to return to the past—" She stopped, because it wasn't completely true. Oh, she didn't want to be thirteen again under any circumstances, but knowing what she knew now about what had happened? Would knowing have changed anything? If she could go back— "You can't—send us back, can you?"

One through Four and Dr. Five studied her. Blinked. Pretty much in synch. She'd written about some telepathic aliens—

"No," One said.

The other four also shook their heads.

There was certainty in the single word, a feeling that he'd spoken the truth. He couldn't send them back. She opened her mouth to ask, but closed it again. Even if they could send themselves back, they wouldn't tell her. And she didn't want to know—

Something rolled into the living room, passing between the small, bowed legs of Four, and rolling to a stop in a small indentation in the wood floor—a dropped bowling ball, she vaguely recalled—almost halfway between them and the aliens. There was a hissing sound, then smoke began to pour out one end.

"Run," Isaac yelled, from somewhere out of sight.

Instead of running, Dex swept her off the chair to the floor. She landed on the rug, with Dex on top of her. Her breath whooshed out of her lungs as they slid forward, somehow tumbling aliens like bowling pins. Bolts of light traced patterns in the smoke, kind of like a disco ball. Their slide slammed them into the wall. Or at least slammed Gini into it. Her head connected with wood and the lights —regular and disco—went out.

∾

Dateline: Notes from Isaac's Strategic Planning notebook

Adults never say thank you.

I did learn some new swear words.

∾

Dateline: From Daphne's cell phone, sleep monitor

Still no bars. Why aren't I dead? I can't live without bars...

Snork....

∾

Dateline: Advance scouting party report

Contrary to broadcasted evidence, I do not think size matters to these humans.

Chapter Eight

G ini stirred, not surprised by the ache in her head. Traveling
yesterday and then Dex—wow, that had been the weirdest
dream ever. And that was saying something. She tended to have some
pretty crazy dreams. She didn't quite give it a nightmare label,
because Dex had opened up—she frowned. Had she scripted his
"confession?" In addition to making her mom eight? Was Dex actually here? What was dream and what was real?

"Gini?"

Her eyes popped open. Dex loomed above her. Thirteen-
year-old Dex.

Not the real she'd been hoping for.

"I need to wake up from this," she said. And go straight to the
shrink without passing "go" and probably having to shell out way
more than two hundred dollars. Crazy town had more insanity then
than usual.

His grin was wry. "Are you all right?"

"Of course not. I'm thirteen." Was she? She studied her arm, her
hand. They appeared to be the same size as when she last woke up.
At least they hadn't made them smaller—she jerked and tried to sit
up. Dex helped her. She looked around. "The bathroom?" The downstairs bathroom, she realized, the one connected to the kitchen.

"What happened?"

"Isaac," Dex hesitated, looking rueful, "somehow got my keys, the
ones to my rig. I have some riot gear in there."

Gini gave him a look. "Riot gear? For Blue Hills? Seriously?"

Dex grinned now and shrugged. "It came with the job."

"What else does Isaac have access to? That came with the job?"

"You don't want to know. Anyway, he set off a smoke canister and, well, rescued us."

Gini thought about this for a minute. Would the aliens consider his actions panic or something else? "That kid is scary." Dex nodded. "Possibly more scary than the little green aliens." Dex nodded again. "So now what?"

"He's reconnoitering."

"Please tell me you got your keys back."

"I got my keys back."

"That's something." Gini struggled up off the floor, sank onto the commode. "Where's Desi?"

"At the moment, she's with the aliens."

"With the aliens? Or *with* the aliens?"

"From what I can tell, she's pretty much with them."

"I wonder if they know that's not an advantage?" Gini asked wryly. She leaned back, rubbed her face for, like, time one thousand. Sighed and met Dex's worried gaze. "Please tell me this isn't real. That I'm going to wake up thirty-five and alien-less."

"I wish I could." He looked thoughtful. "And I wish we could get into the WiFi."

"Why?"

"I'd like to read Van's paper on first contact."

"She probably plagiarized us. I mean, seriously. Who knows how to do it?"

"Well, if they are somehow following it, then maybe we can figure out what they'll do next."

"Except that Isaac panicked," she pointed out. "Or over reacted. Maybe." She frowned. "What do they want? And why here?"

Dex perched on the edge of the tub and sighed. "That's the problem, isn't it? We have no idea what they want. Or how they feel about Isaac's rescue."

"Please tell me he can't get your gun?"

Dex shook his head. "It's in a lockbox that needs a personal code, in case someone gets our keys. He did find my helmet and vest." He was quiet for a minute. "It's like we fell into a *Disney* movie."

"I used to love those things. Did we really used to pretend we had —" she stopped. "Maybe that's our problem. Maybe we should, I don't know, channel our inner kid." She half grinned. "It worked for Picard when he got sent back to kid world."

"Can I just point out that in movies and television, the, the opposition has to follow the script. We're working without a net here. And no matter what our ages may appear to be, we're the adults on the scene, with the responsibility for protecting—" he stopped.

It was hard to make the case for looking out for the kids when they had no idea where either of the actual kids were.

"Well, we can't just wait for Van and Bif to walk into this, whatever. What if this is the first wave of an invasion or something? What if we're the test subjects? What if the plan is to turn the whole world into kids and then, I don't know, rule us or eat us or something." Gini shuddered. She'd always been creeped out by humans-as-food-source stories. "I don't want to get eaten, Dex."

He shifted closer and put a skinny arm around her. "I won't let them eat you."

For some reason, this reassured her, even though there was no basis for believing him. But she did. She'd believed him implicitly until—

She leaned her forehead on his shoulder, memories flooding back at the feel and smell of being close to him again.

"I wish—" she stopped. Because this wasn't the past. It had all happened. Being turned thirteen by little green aliens didn't change anything about the past.

His arm tightened. "Me, too."

She soaked up the comfort for a moment, took a deep breath and straightened away from him. "We need a plan. One that isn't just about hoping Isaac doesn't make things worse."

"I'm more afraid he'll make things better," Dex said, his grin a mix of mischief and wry.

"That would be terribly embarrassing to us both," she agreed. "What do we have going for us?"

"Well," Dex said, after a long pause, "we're not actually thirteen, at least, not inside."

Translation: all they had going for them were their wits. Sobering.

～

They couldn't hide in the bathroom forever, though Gini found that the thought of leaving the bathroom almost took away her ability to stand up. As if he knew it, Dex held out his hand. Everything had taken on a 'then and now' quality. It was if the past shadowed the now, making both feel out of focus. When she took his hand and let him pull her to her feet, the past got sharper for several seconds. She honestly couldn't tell if she wandered into a *Star Trek Next Gen* episode or if this were a crazy version of a *A Christmas Carol*, with ghosts of Christmases past littering up the place.

"You okay?" he asked.

She nodded, even though she wasn't. Her writer brain assessed her critically for heroine creds. And found her sadly lacking. "It's easier to write this stuff than live it," she admitted, managing a wry smile for him.

He chuckled, then directed her to "stack" behind him again.

"Should we go get your gun?"

He hesitated. "I hate to ramp things up that much, but yeah, we should probably try to get to my rig."

He eased the door open, just enough to peer out. He must have felt confident, because he widened the gap and slipped out. She followed him, well, because she always had. Smoke lingered in the air, being pulled from the living room, she'd guess, by the open back door. She shivered, wondering how none of them seemed to have been injured by all the shooting. Could the ray guns have been set to stun? A girl could hope. They inched around the big, battered table, both of them careful to avoid the spot that creaked, and approached that open door. Through it she saw flakes pelting down from the sky again, as if fired from snow cannons. She'd forgotten just how much it could snow. She'd been gone too long.

She opened her mouth to ask about the phone, but closed it again. Bet Isaac had it. Much as it galled, the kid had stayed ahead of them. The question was, could he stay ahead of the aliens? As much as she didn't like to think about it, if they could make them younger, who knew what other technology they had available for keeping them in line? And why had they picked making them smaller as their best option? They couldn't have been around that many real kids. Put more than two of them in a room and the chaos increased exponentially and quickly.

Dex aligned himself against the door frame and took a quick look. Just like the dudes on TV. She might have studied his tush, and felt her thirteen-year-old body shiver a little, even though her thirty-five-year-old brain called her a pervert. He eased out the gap and was gone long enough for anxiety to rise, before a thin arm appeared in the opening and beckoned to her. Mimicking him as much as she could, Gini slid out onto the back porch. The snow was deep back here and more was falling, enough to keep the road closed for who knew how long. The tiny footprints were almost filled in, though the trough from their passage around the porch was still vaguely there.

There was a well-trodden path that was visible in summer, one that led toward the trees and the crick they'd been unable not to fall in, pretty much up until they left—

There was a soft pitter of something overhead. Gini froze, her gaze tracking up, even though she couldn't see anything through the porch's overhang. Dex glanced back at her, gesturing her to stay against the log wall next to the door. More reluctant than she'd expected, she did as he'd not asked. It was nice to have something at her back, but it quit feeling okay when Dex climbed quietly up on the railing and slowly, so very slowly, lifted himself up so he could peer over the edge of the roof...

He gave a yell. It was answered with a sort of screechy squeak. He fell back, landing in the snow bank on his back. Gini ran forward, pausing at the edge of porch. Afraid to stay. Afraid to go. Terrified to look up.

There was the outline of a body carved into the deep white snow. His arms began to flail, forming an almost perfect snow angel. Gathering all her courage, Gini leaned out, tipping her head back just as a green face eased into view above her. She cried out, too, felt herself falling. Heard the squeak and a scrambling sound before she went head first into the deep drift.

It took some flailing for Gini to get her face clear of the snow, or to find which way was up. She managed it just in time to come face-to-face with Dex. White flakes clung to his clothes and face, the light striking the flakes turning him into a sparkly vampire until he impatiently wiped his face, then gave his whole body a good shake.

"Are you all right?" he asked. Gini nodded. Rubbed at her own face, as the flakes melted into her eyes. She blinked to clear her vision. Then, as one, they turned to look at the cabin.

"Is that what you didn't want to tell me about?" she asked, awed.

The oval thing—okay flying saucer—was perched on the peak of the roofline. It was almost a bridge too far, looking up at it. Had they really talked about what this would be like over tall glasses of cold drinks at the cons? Had they hoped for this? Really? Not once had any of them worried about wetting their pants. Not that she'd wet her pants yet. But she was nowhere clear on that either. It was easy to be brave in a bar. One more good scare—

A small green, well, elvish alien scrambled up the snowy roof and vanished around the corner by the chimney. For just a moment, Gini felt satisfaction that it was as scared as they were. It didn't last.

Something black, a SWAT helmet, Gini realized, slowly cleared the roofline from behind the other chimney on the opposite end of the cabin.

"Isaac," Dex said, with a note of despair. "He never listens."

"To be fair," Gini pointed out, "even though I don't actually want to be fair, has he ever been told not to go near the flying saucer?"

This got her an interesting look. The eyes were totally sheriff-Dex, but the effect—being shot at her out of a thirteen-year-old face—was diminished by quite a bit. His mouth worked, like he wanted to say something, but in the end he didn't. Just turned back to Isaac and gestured for him to join them. Isaac gestured for them to join him.

"It is the higher-ish ground," she pointed out, though not because she wanted to shimmy up onto the snow covered roof and then plummet back into the snow. Her body might be young, but her brain hadn't done that shimmy for many years. She blinked. Maybe she was a bit punch drunk.

"He's going to start an intergalactic war, if he's not careful," Dex said grimly—until his voice broke at the end. He coughed and gave her a wary look.

She managed not to react, but felt compelled to point out, "We don't know they are intergalactic."

"A galactic war then," he gritted out. "A war with aliens not of this earth."

If anyone could, it would probably be Isaac. She shivered as the snowed started to chill through her makeshift wardrobe. "So, back in the cabin or up on the rooftop?"

Dex looked at her, his gaze considering. "I don't suppose you'd go inside and wait for me to go get him?"

"In books and movies, the characters always get into trouble when they split up," she pointed out.

He blinked. "You do realize this isn't a book or a movie, right?"

"I...mostly realize it." His brows arched. "Come on, Dex. Really? I've gone so far past reality, I don't even know what to call it." She stood up, because it was that or start freezing to the ground. "My mom is eight, I'm—" she couldn't bring herself to say it again, "so not happy. There are aliens running around dressed as elves—and I know." Dex's mouth closed again. "Maybe that's how they always dress. Whatever. And don't get me started on the baby sitting gig I did not sign up for." Crap. They hadn't checked on Daphne in forever. At least she wasn't up on the rooftop—

It was at that moment that Daphne chose to stroll out the back-door in pajamas, robe and enormous bunny slippers, cellphone in hand. "There's still no WiFi. I can't live like this—"

Daphne stopped, her gaze turning girl-assessing-guy when she noticed Dex, still trying to get clear of the snow drift. Gini didn't like it that her hackles came up. It wasn't...appropriate. Besides, Dex was both too old and too young for Daphne. How many times back in the day had Van told Gini that her crush on Dex was weird, that she should be crushing on older guys who didn't notice her, not Dex who didn't notice her.

"Girls," Van used to say in her most lofty tone, "are more mature than boys, so boys our age are just *too* young for us. It's like he's eleven or twelve in maturity years."

Gini looked at Dex, who wasn't actually thirteen, and therefore mature enough to recognize that speculative look being cast his way. He tugged at the neck of his jacket, a hunted light appearing in his eyes. He looked to Gini for help, which she didn't actually mind. Gini turned her attention back to Daphne, possibly planning to distract her from Dex. She wasn't entirely sure.

Above Daphne's head, though still out of her sight, the side of the flying saucer lowered along the roof line, on the side away from Isaac and—Gini blinked twice before completing her identification—a green Santa Claus, though about half the usual size—was there a usual size for Santa?—came out, stopping near the chimney as if he or it were posing for a kid's picture book. There was a sort of clatter and one of the little green men carried a battered reindeer out the door and set it by the "Santa." Another of them, Gini was too bemused to ID any of them, trotted pulling a sled. It was their old sled, she real-ized. Their *Red Rider.* The harness—which looked like old rope—had some jingle bells dangling at intervals that were probably supposed to jingle, but didn't.

Gini knew her jaw dropped. Was pretty sure Dex's did as well, because Daphne huffed a high sigh. "Wha-at?"

≈

Dateline: Notes from Isaac's Strategic Planning notebook

Since no one has seen the real Santa Claus, I am not sure what to think. What if he is real? I may have jeopardized my chances...

≈

Dateline: From Daphne's cell phone, sleep monitor

I'm surrounded by sub-humans. Though the guy is kind of cute. I wonder how old he is?

≈

Dateline: Advance scouting party report

Strzkinecks said we were trying to do too much. I fear he is correct.

Chapter Nine

They had to split up. Gini didn't like it, but someone needed to look after Daphne, even if Daphne didn't know she needed looking after and if she found out would hate her for it even more than she already did. Inside her head, Gini was in charge and the responsible adult. And Dex for sure needed to regain control of Isaac, if that was even possible. Maybe Santa would help out. Did nine year olds still believe in Santa? Seemed like disillusion set in earlier and earlier each year. And then there was the whole, should my kids believe or shouldn't they, deal. The kids who didn't believe were always bursting the bubbles of those who did. Gini had had a classmate who didn't believe in Santa but was certain Godzilla was for real.

Luckily Daphne realized the boy was seeing her in pajamas and backed into the kitchen before Dex started his shimmy up the porch pole.

Gini scrambled up the steps onto the porch, shedding snow, gave her self a big shake to complete the shedding process, and re-entered —with some caution—the kitchen. The smoke was almost gone, but she was still surprised Daphne hadn't noticed the taint of it lingering in the air. Well, make that kind of surprised. Gini closed the door and leaned against it, not sure what to do or say next.

"You could have warned me." Daphne tugged at her robe, then patted at her bed hair, even though everyone knew patting only worked in the movies.

This was one thing Gini had forgotten about being thirteen, but was now sort of remembering, in a distant and hazy way. This complete and utter self absorption that sucked up the oxygen in a circumference her sister might have been able to calculate. The sheer intensity of the 'if it doesn't affect me then it didn't happen' and 'if it does affect me then it is Life changing and possibly the End of the World as We Know It.' Maybe it wasn't possible to remember that. Or maybe no one wanted to remember. She considered it and decided it might not be possible to remember how it felt, if once one left it behind. There were those who never did, but then their utter self absorption meant they didn't realize they were that self absorbed. These never-left-teens types were annoying and exhausting, so Gini tried to avoid them whenever possible.

Gini hadn't planned on being landed with one, though the fact that she hadn't joined Daphne in the all-about-me zone was kind of reassuring—unless she didn't stop being thirteen. What would it be like to be the "grownup" thirteen year old among a host of them? Would she be forced to do high school again? It was one thing to toy with the idea of doing it all over, while retaining adult knowledge, but the reality of it was quite frankly horrifying. She'd been the geek before. This time it would be worse. She'd be the know-it-all geek. The adult trapped in a teen body. A social outcast before she got through the door. At least before she'd had hope.

Because contemplating that was almost worse than the alien situation, Gini firmly directed her thoughts to the challenging task of briefing Daphne on this new reality. What and how much should she tell her?

"So..." Gini began, but Daphne cut her off.

"Who is he? He's kinda cute. Ish." The tone was snotty, but adult Gini recognized a hint of forlorn buried really really deep in there. Gini was out of her depth, but so was this half child, becoming adult girl.

"That's Dex." She stopped, wondering if Daphne would connect the dots. She didn't have to wonder long.

"Oh." Her gaze flicked toward the closed door. "How old?"

Gini didn't have to think about this one. "Thirteen."

A sort of sigh. "Pity." A faint gleam of interest bloomed in her bored, unhappy gaze. "Anyone else interesting?"

Older, she meant, of course. Gini shook her head. Well, other than the green aliens. They were probably old enough to date. They'd been let off their planet with a flying saucer. But, as they noted, they were very small.

The gaze finally settled on Gini. Another sigh. "Great."

Though it was clear that Daphne wasn't interested enough to ask her name, she offered it anyway. "I'm...Gini."

No sign she remembered Gini's name either. "Daphne."

Oh wow, this moment brought back some awkward memories. Okay, truthfully that moment after the names exchange still intimidated her. The small talk to build some kind of bridge. Since Gini already knew where Daphne was from and the weather sucked toads, she took a breath and dived in. Okay, dipped a toe in. "So we're kind of having a...a...situation here."

Daphne's brows—brows in the beginning of raging out of control at the onset of puberty—arched. "What's the deal?"

"The deal?"

"You're talking like, I don't know, like, you're old or something."

Gini remembered that look. The "you seriously didn't just say that, did you?" That look hadn't gone away until after high school. Or possibly college. Yeah, Gini'd so be a social outcast if she couldn't get back to her own size. Gini searched her brain, and her heart, for young but young from her time, well, it probably wouldn't work any better than old adult and it wasn't like she could Google teen slang right now, so she gave it up as a bad job and tried for less old. "The thing is, things are kind of messed up—"

Did messed up mean what she thought it meant? Who had time to keep up? Or a reason to keep up?

"Well, duh, this rack is zero chill. No WiFi. No bars. My friends will think I died or something worse. It's like so ratchet."

Okay, she did know that ratchet was a major insult. Someone at her last con had mentioned it during a panel on writing for young teens. Maybe Gini should have let the green men vaporize her when she had the chance.

"I will never, ever forgive mom or dad. They are so dead to me." She studied Gini, as if finally somewhat actually seeing her. "I suppose you're related or something, so it's not obv how loathsome everyone here is?" She paused. "No offense." She shrugged.

Gini resisted the impulse to be honest back. Found it was getting harder to care about not upsetting the little dear. Or upsetting her differently? Because so far Daphne'd been in a constant state of upset since the pickup at the airport. Okay, it sucked to expect one thing and get something—or someone—else. Gini had had a lot of that lately, from the Big Chill's proposal to Dex to her mom and the aliens. Not the holiday she'd hoped for.

Ho, ho, ho.

Daphne's eyes suddenly narrowed and her head tipped. Perhaps she sensed an unseen adult presence. She looked to one side, then to the other. She sort of tried not to look worried.

"I suppose they heard?"

Gini nodded. It wasn't a lie. She had heard.

"I thought I'd hear them coming. The way this place creaks and groans, like its haunted or something."

In a way it was. Gini felt like she saw ghosts everywhere, ghosts and aliens.

"Have you ever been in a mountain cabin before?" It occurred to her that Daphne might be scared. Isaac sure hadn't blinked, so she'd kind of forgotten the girl might be a bit freaked out about the isolation, the silence, the crazy. The lack of WiFi.

"Why would I do something so not basic?"

Gini sensed bravado behind the bluster. Great. Now she was back to feeling sorry for her.

Daphne either sensed the sympathy. Or the weakness. Her eyes gleamed. "Who brought you up? Maybe they could get us out of here?"

"We're snowed in," Gini said flatly, though she tried to sound less adult. Not sure she managed it. She was what she was. "Stuck. Not going anywhere anytime soon."

"So dad can't get here?" She added some shrill tones into the rising outrage. "Zero chill."

Speaking of chills...Gini looked over her shoulder at the door, she opened it a crack and stared out for a few seconds. It looked like the wind was starting to pick up again, sending the heavy flakes in at an angle. She saw green legs appear over the edge of the porch roof and abruptly shut the door. Turned around, leaning against it again.

"Only if the wind dies down."

"I hate them. I hate this. I hate everything."

So very thirteen.

"What about the WiFi?"

"Snow will keep that mostly offline, too." Gini braced for it.

Daphne stared at her, her mouth working. Maybe she'd run out of words—nope. Gini wondered if Bif knew his little darling knew those words. While she spewed, Gini went to the fridge, got the milk, a couple of glasses, took it all to the table and poured them both a glass. Started to sip hers, then remembered she needed to pee. Might be a good idea to take care of that before the next shock hit. She'd barely maintained containment during the last oh-my-heck.

Since Daphne hadn't stopped spewing, Gini went to the bathroom and shut the door between them. It was kind of a relief, both emotional and physical. Didn't want to leave when she finished. Took her time washing her hands—a sudden cessation of spewing made her speed up the drying part. But she had to brace herself and dig up some courage to open the door. She peered out. Daphne stood by the table, a half empty glass of milk in her hand, a little milk mustache on her upper lip of her dropped jaw, staring toward the hall doorway. Not eager to move, but aware of her adult responsibility, Gini slowly eased out far enough into the kitchen to see...

Four, her elf hat still set at a very jaunty angle. It might even be more jaunty than their last meeting.

She had the ray gun in one hand and the phone in the other. She held the phone out in Gini's direction.

"For you."

Not exactly thrilled, Gini approached Four. Four appeared to share her not-thrilled. When the antenna of the phone was in reach, Gini grabbed it. Four let go and stepped back, as if she feared that Gini would make a grab or leap or something equally Isaac. Both hands half raised, Gini backed up until she bumped into the table. Only then did she lift the phone to her ear.

"H-hello?" She cleared the roughness from her throat, but couldn't think of anything to add.

"Is this Vanessa?"

The tone was older, but was still a recognizable—and snotty— echo of Daphne's. Had to be Bif's ex. Gini nodded, her eyes on Four who had both those big eyes, and the ray gun, pointed at Gini.

"Hello?"

"Um, yes." She almost added that she was Vanessa, but Daphne would quickly refute that. Possibly with screaming. She looked shell-shocked, but was mercifully not shrieking. Yet.

"Yes, it's me. I. Me. Hello."

Van would not be thrilled at this less-than-stellar response, but Van should be here to take her own phone calls if she didn't want Gini making her sound like a doof.

"I can't get a hold of Bif. He didn't even bother to let me know he got the kids. They aren't getting my texts because of that ghastly remote place. Did he get them picked up? Are they safe?"

"Yes. They are here." This seemed a bit sparse, but since she couldn't verify their safeness, she added, "No bars up here. We're still sorting out the WiFi."

"Is Daphne or Isaac up? I have no idea what time it is there."

Isaac was probably still up on the roof and Daphne? Gini, glanced at her. She was pretty sure the kid couldn't talk yet.

"This phone is about out of charge, but I'll have them call you when—soon. Or—soon. The satellite might be off for a while because of the storm, but I'll—soon. We're all fine though. Plenty of food and...and...such. So we're fine."

Four's ray gun lifted suggestively, the platter gaze anxious.

"Well, have them call me ASAP." Bif's ex huffed, cutting the connection before Gini could.

She pressed the end button and Four held out her hand for the phone. Gini's hand closed convulsively around it, but she slowly made the short journey back in range and handed it over. This time her thumb made slight contact with cool, green skin. They both jumped like someone got shot. Luckily no one did.

Gini glanced back at Daphne. She'd progressed to rapid eye movement. She looked at Four.

"I think she's going to panic."

Four blinked. "I will go to Desi."

And once again, Gini was left holding the kid.

~

Gini watched the teen warily as she circled back to her untouched glass of milk and took a sip. It was like waiting for a train wreck to happen. She wanted to look away. Couldn't.

"What—" Daphne stopped. "Is that Isaac's Christmas present?" Her expression kind of cleared, color inching back into pale cheeks. "He's been asking for a robot."

Gini was tempted, there wasn't a word for how tempted she was. But even a self absorbed teen would have trouble believing her brother got five robots. And a Santa Claus one. Not to mention a flying saucer up on the roof top.

Her silence spoke louder than words. Color drained back out.

"What...are they?"

"Well," Gini sipped some more milk. "I don't know that much, but I'm going with either Santa's elves or, you know, aliens."

"Elves? There's more than one?" This was said on a rising shriek.

"I've seen five so far. Oh, and there's the one in the Santa suit..." Should she prepare her for the flying saucer? Or mention the whole-sale shrinking of the adults on the scene?

Daphne stared at her. "That guy, the one who was here last night, he's a cop, right? What's he doing?"

"Um, trying to get Isaac off the roof." Gini, who had gone into this zone of truth place, considered Isaac and the roof. "He's afraid Isaac will try to take the flying saucer and get shot. He got the keys to Dex's official rig and already threw this smoke thing at them. Your brother is kind of scary, but you probably know that."

For just a minute something broke the panic in the teen's face. She half nodded, but then appeared to process at least some of what Gini said.

"Dex? There are two of them? Who are you again?" she asked again, this time with a huge helping of suspicious mixed with bewildered.

"I told you, I'm Gini. We, um, met last night." Gini hesitated, but it felt like she was already in so deep... "I picked you up at the airport last night."

Daphne stared. Shook her head slowly, but maybe she'd noticed enough last night to feel the truth of it. Or not. Her jaw went slack.

"That's..."

"I wasn't thrilled either. According to my mom, she asked the aliens, or the elves, to be young again and we got the gift, too."

"You're..."

Gini nodded, though warily. Was starting to see some white around her eyes now. The slackness of the jaw turned into a round circle that emitted a low moan, one that had the potential to become a full-on scream. The back door banged open, making them both jump at least a couple of feet.

Dex and Isaac stood in the opening, stamping the snow off their booted feet.

Daphne's eyes went from Isaac to Dex, then moved to Gini, then went back to Dex. They moved into the room, revealing right behind them a trio of green men with ray guns pointed at them. Gini saw Daphne's eyes start to roll back in the sockets and jumped forward. Hadn't expected how dead her weight would be. All she could do was slow her sink to the floor. With Gini on the uncomfortable bottom.

"I told you she wouldn't take it well," Isaac said matter-of-factly.

~

Dateline: Notes from Isaac's Strategic Planning notebook

You'd think a cop wouldn't let the aliens get the drop on him.

~

Dateline: From Daphne's cell phone

I'm not sure why I try. We're cut off in crazy. Or maybe I'm dreaming.

I hope I'm dreaming.

~

Dateline: Advance scouting party report

Did not believe it could go worse than last time.

Should have believed.

And gone to Disneyland.

Chapter Ten

Age thirteen hadn't been perfect for Dex either, she recalled now, studying him from the couch where she'd been directed to sit next to a still unconscious Daphne. He and Isaac were kneeling in front of the Christmas tree with their hands clasped behind their backs, an alien with a ray gun behind each of them. It was his unhappy expression that unearthed yet another sepia memory.

His mom had been really sick. Gini had been too young, too thirteen, to really understand what he'd been going through. It was something that happened in the world of grownups and his mom had gotten better. She'd looked great the last time Gini saw them. She half frowned. His parents hadn't mentioned Dex might be moving back either, but maybe they hadn't known last year. They never talked a lot about Dex to her. It was as if they knew—there was nothing to know, she reminded herself, was there? She frowned. Did all her inner confusion have more to do with the holiday and the stress of seeing little green men? Or were there still embers at the bottom of their old fire? He'd broken her heart once. Looking at him now, getting pelted with memories of how it had been, it was hard to believe he'd done that.

She trusted him now, in some ways, like she had then. Felt like it would be okay because he was here, too. Was she turning into thirteen in her head, not just a body thing? Or did knowing why sort of help restore some of the trust she was totally surprised to still feel? Not with his getting engaged part. Nothing could erase that. Even now she could feel that choking sense of disbelief. The feeling she'd walked into a waking nightmare. Not her Dex. He couldn't. He wouldn't. But he had. She was old enough now—on the inside anyway —to realize that what happens in high school should sometimes just stay in high school.

In that one way her dad had been right. They'd been too young, too wrapped up in each other to really know much. Had it been about comfort and feeling safe? Or had they missed their chance at love?

If she could go back, but they couldn't. The green dude had been emphatic about that. But she couldn't help but wonder about the "what if." What if they hadn't broken up, would they have made it all the way? Would they be together now? What was what road not traveled would have looked like? If she could go back...

"I don't want to," she said, shocked to hear her voice break the silence. Dex shot her an inquiring look. She felt her cheeks heat. Because here she was doing the romance heroine introspection instead of figuring out what to do about the little green people. Even if she couldn't do anything, she should try. She owed it to all the characters she'd put in harm's way. And got them out of trouble, she reminded herself. Jeez Louise, she was acting like she really was thirteen and stuck on an angst cycle that was spinning its wheels in the past. "I'll tell you later." *Maybe.* "So now what?"

"It's Christmas," Desi said, as if Gini had asked the question of her. "We sing Christmas carols and read Christmas stories and get ready for Santa to come and make all our dreams come true."

Gini met Dex's wry gaze. She didn't know whether to be afraid. Or very afraid.

Ho, ho, ho.

So, her mom was working with the aliens. Or with Santa's elves. Was it possible they really were on Santa's team? That this was the moment she'd dreamed of until the revelation that Santa was an in-your-heart-deal, not an actual magic man in a red suit. What kid didn't want to be the One who got to meet him and know he really was for real? What if they were muffing it? It was as if Dex heard her thoughts. His brows arched and his head tipped to one side as he gave her a classic "really?" look. She half shrugged. Which was more ridiculous? Believing in Santa or aliens? At the moment, it was a toss up. Though there hadn't ever been ray guns in the stories...but would the authors of the stories know Santa's elves didn't have ray guns? It was a dangerous world. And supposedly Santa knew who was bad—

Desi trotted over to the big upright piano in the corner and lifted the lid. She looked at it, a flicker of her mom appearing in her eyes. She flexed small hands, as if realizing they weren't the size they were supposed to be for playing the piano. Could mom play again, now that she was young? Arthritis had sidelined her hands from doing a lot of things some years back. Van, who hadn't quit her lessons, had taken up the baton of providing the musical accompaniments. Gini, who had quit, could pick out the tunes with one hand, well, some of them. If her mom deputized her to play, it might be an "outing" of her non-Van-ness.

"I need my music books," Desi said, her tone tracking between old and young. She looked at Gini. "Why aren't they here?"

Because there had been no one in the house to play them. The present went out of focus again as she saw all of them, even her dad, standing around the piano and singing...

Desi's small face brightened. "I remember. They are in the big cupboard in the kitchen."

"Do you want me to get them?" Gini asked, half rising.

She shook her head. "Stygrx will help me."

It sounded like her mom choked on something, but One nodded, leading her to believe her mom had said his name. There was something in his expression that Gini found comforting and uncomfortable. He obviously liked her mom, so he wouldn't want to hurt them, would he? On the other hand, did her mom have a thing going with an alien? Or an elf? Either was kind of ick. She waited until Desi and One were out of sight, then looked at Dex. Her mouth worked a couple of times.

"This can't possibly be happening." Gini thought she thought this and didn't say it out loud until she heard the words come out her mouth and kind of echo around the high ceilinged room.

"You were large. Now you are not. What is not to believe?" asked Two. Or possibly Three. She still couldn't tell them apart, even after, what? A half an hour's exposure to them.

"Well," Gini said, even though she was pretty sure she shouldn't, "people generally don't get little around here. Well, they shrink sometimes," she flicked a look in the direction her mom had gone, "but they still get older."

"Christmas is for children," Dr. Five said.

"Yes, it is," Dex jumped in before she could, "but we all had our shot at being young. We...step aside for the next generation. It's our, our way."

"You are not fond of your way," Three pointed out. Unless it was Two. "You complain about it. You complain about it a lot."

The others nodded.

Just how long had the little green aliens been watching them? Dex gave her a look that seemed to suggest she could take this one. She started to say that they didn't always say what they meant, when it occurred to her that was probably not the best thing to say with the ray guns in play. She licked her lips.

"It's complicated," she said. "We...look back at when we were young, because being an adult is complicated and challenging and it feels like life was simpler back then." Except for thirteen, she could have added, but she didn't really want to be made younger than she already was. "So we wax nostalgic, but what we're really saying is that this grownup thing is hard." Desi appeared in the doorway with One. They both had music books clutched in their hands. Gini met her childish gaze and added—not sure if she said the words to her mom, the aliens or herself, "Holidays stir up a lot of emotions, a lot of memories. It's natural to look back. To remember. To wish..." She hesitated, glanced at Dex, but not for long. She turned back to her mom, "To wish you'd done something different, but who we are, what we are, it's because of, well, everything. All the choices. All the mistakes. All of everything. The good and the bad. If you take out this or that, you aren't you anymore."

"This feels like me," Desi said, another, longer flash of her mom in the very child-like gaze. "I wish..."

When she stopped, Gini prompted, "What do you wish, M—Desi?"

Her mom had had dreams. She must have. Gini knew this logically, but it was hard to *know it*, to feel it for one's mom. Moms were moms. They were just there except when you needed them and then they were *moms*. Not someone with needs and wishes. Seeing her like this, well, it felt different. Confusing and scary, like a rug had been pulled from beneath her feet. Was this what it would feel like to lose her?

Thin arms tightened around the music books and the small mouth pursed. Her head turned toward One and Gini knew there was something, something longer and deeper than she personally felt comfortable with, between them. Desi shifted the books so she could hold out her hand. One shifted his burden so he could take it, the long fingers closing like long green stems around Desi's, his fingers wrapping at least twice around her thin wrist. It was both creepy and sweet. But mostly creepy. It was kind of immature of her. Maybe. But she was stuck in a thirteen-year-old body watching her mom hold hands with a green alien. She felt entitled to be immature. To feel a bit betrayed.

"You wouldn't have believed me," Desi said, but her voice was mom's. This was her mom from several years ago, before her memory began to sputter and pop. It was filled with certainty, wisdom, some humor and more resignation.

Gini opened her mouth to defend herself, to protest maybe, but her mom was right. "No, I wouldn't have believed you."

"They never believe," One said, sadly.

"Mulder did," Gini said, a bit weakly.

All of them gave her Looks. Even Isaac who shouldn't have known about *X-Files*.

"No," Gini felt compelled to admit. "They don't believe. We don't believe." They talked the talked, but they didn't believe down where it mattered. Even with a flying saucer up on the house top, part of her didn't believe. "We hoped…"

One gave her a skeptical look.

"We do hope. That's why I—we write about it and look up—"

"I believe," Isaac said.

All eyes turned toward him, but no one knew quite how to respond, since his belief, while not exactly panic, had morphed into an attempt to take the flying saucer. It had certainly contributed to their current crisis *vis a vis* the ray guns.

"Maybe you can only believe when you are little," Desi said. "But then you are too small to know what to do with that believing."

Gini had the sensation of listening in, or coming in late, to a conversation. Like she was eavesdropping on something she had no part or place in.

"When did you, when did…" she gestured toward the aliens. "How…"

"They borrowed me when I was little," her mom said. Color surged into her thin cheeks, and it almost seemed that she got a little bigger. She looked at One. "I was afraid at first, but Stygrx was little, too, littler than now, I mean. He helped me, he was my friend. I

307

should have forgot getting borrowed, but I didn't." She looked pleased with herself.

Her mom had always liked doing the unexpected.

"Did you tell...anyone?" Dex asked.

Gini thought about her mom's parents, trying to imagine that conversation. The cabin had originally been theirs, though her parents had updated it several times over the years. It was just a cabin. A bit of a cliche really, not the locus of a failed first contact.

"Stygrx said if I did, either no one would believe or if they did, it would be bad. I didn't want to be studied or get in trouble. Or anything. I slipped a couple of times, but my mom and dad thought it was my imagination."

It was the logical conclusion.

"Grandma told me you had an imaginary friend," Gini said. Had this...encounter...made her mom quirky or had her quirky been there and appealed to the aliens for some reason? Had Gini's own geekiness begun with her mom's alien abduction? It was very hard to be Desi's daughter *and* be original. And wow, wasn't that a thirteen-year-old thought?

"And Stygrx didn't want to be cut open."

"I still do not want that," One said, emphatically. The others nodded, their platter gazes getting wider with alarm.

"*It never goes well.*" Gini said the words slowly, looking at each of them, and then finishing at One. "Have you tried this before? Tried to talk to us, not just Desi?"

"Always they panic," Dr. Five said sadly. "So we make them forget, or mostly forget."

"You wrote the paper, you who are the child of our friend, Desi, and we had cause to hope again. And we wished to see her once more." One smiled at Desi.

Gini was not sure which was more, well, disturbing. The alien crushing on her mom or the realization just how much she wasn't the sister they were looking for.

～

Dateline: Notes from Isaac's Strategic Planning notebook

I was hoping for Santa and his elves. But aliens are next best. Wish

I'd gotten in the flying saucer, though. Looked pretty sick before they tackled me.

∾

Dateline: From Daphne's cell phone

If I keep my eyes closed, this will all go away...

But I will never, ever forgive dad...

∾

Dateline: Advance scouting party report

We have hope again. Oh wait...

Chapter Eleven

"So, how about those Christmas carols?" Gini winced inside at how over bright she sounded. Her smile was strained. She felt it, saw her mom study her. Had she realized that Gini wasn't Van? She'd had trouble telling them apart for as long as Gini could recollect. But she eventually figured it out because they weren't alike, not inside. For a second the longing swept over her to be small enough for the "it will be better in the morning" hug. Or the "mom will take care of it" reassurance. She wanted to tell her about the Big Chill and what she'd learned about Dex and that she was sorry she didn't come home that summer after dad died. And yes, she was also sorry for all the times she didn't have a clue. Especially sorry for the things she still didn't have a clue about and when she finally did, it would probably be too late.

And for all the things that could never ever be again.

Thirteen. It all seemed like it started then. When puberty forced them into taking their first tentative steps toward becoming adults. It was the way it was, the way it had always been. Everyone grew up. Was that why she'd been knocked back to thirteen? So she'd learn what she clearly missed then? Little green ghosts of all her mistakes past, present and future? She was supposed to learn...what? That she hadn't understood her mom any more than her mom understood her at times? Did they think she never had regrets? Felt sorry for the things she'd gotten wrong?

Desi flexed fingers that had been bent and twisted for so long, turning them so the palms were up, then running one hand down the back of the other. It wasn't Gini's imagination. Her mom was getting —not bigger exactly, because she'd been shrinking for years, but older again. She could still move her hands, but the skin was losing its youthful look, lines beginning to spider along the backs. One reached out and smoothed a green hand down her hair as gray threads sprouted like weeds in the red.

Dex made a sound. His eyes widened and he looked at his hands, too. As she watched it seemed they got longer. It was seriously creepy to watch.

She felt a ball of heat in her middle. It wasn't awful, in fact it felt kind of good, but also a bit like wetting her pants. It spread out into her extremities, the sensation indescribably odd, as her fingers seemed to stretch toward the light. Felt a bit like one of those camera views where the space seemed to shrink some around a character. She occupied a different amount of space in the room. Relief mixed with worry. Would she forget? What was the point of having lessons you hadn't figured out yet if you couldn't remember them? How could she finally figure them out and learn to be better...

"Will I forget?" Gini looked at Dr. Five. Felt like all this was his doing based on the slim evidence of his attempts at first contact with them.

"Do you wish to?"

Did she? This wasn't just about a bat crap crazy life lesson. She'd also have to remember the aliens. Could she handle the responsibility of *knowing*, of being one of the crazies with an alien abduction story? Not that she planned to out herself as one, but she'd know inside. And she wouldn't mind forgetting her mom had a thing for an alien.

But if she took the out, if she opted to forget, then she'd forget Dex's confessions. She'd never know her mom had a Desi side. She'd lose what she learned about them, about herself. Not that she was totally thrilled with her performance. But she hadn't wet her pants. That was something.

Even if she never said a peep about all this, she could go to the conventions and *know*. That might be kind of cool. Painful because she'd have to resist the temptation to argue about how it really is, but still cool. It was almost as "insider" as having met the real Santa.

Heat formed in her middle again, surging out. Felt a bit like the Grinch's heart growing, though she hadn't reached two sizes from thirteen—at least she didn't think she had—and technically she couldn't know how a Grinch felt, but still...

She met Dr. Five's gaze with one that she hoped was filled with conviction and, well, not panic or anything else they needed to worry about. Did she believe she'd get the final say if she did choose to remember? If she wanted to, she needed to make her case, she realized. There was no alien crushing on her like Desi had had.

"I guess I'm like my mother before me," she played the "mom" card without much shame, then might have felt a little when her gaze connected with Desi's. "I don't want to forget."

Dex cleared his throat. "I don't want to forget either."

He smiled at her and she had to smile back. She sighed. Part of remembering, part of learning from that remembering was taking responsibility for the choices made. Yeah, Dex had walked away, but she had let him. They hadn't dated during the covered wagon era. She could have called him. She'd been afraid. She hadn't trusted him or herself. So her dad had been at least partly right. They'd both needed to grow up. Yeah, she wished she'd done it a little faster. Embarrassing it had taken her seventeen years—and getting knocked back to thirteen—to look him in the face and ask the question.

Daphne sat up with a jerk, almost knocking Gini off her perch on the edge of the over sized couch. Apparently she'd been playing possum or been in a state of denial.

"Well, I want to forget. All of it. I want to not be here. And I don't want to be here ever again. And if thought my dad would believe us, I'd so tell on all of you."

"If you forget, then you won't be mad at dad anymore," Isaac pointed out.

Daphne looked torn at this realization. Thirteen-year-olds could be very vindictive.

"It's Christmas," Gini said, trying to ignore a little voice in her head saying that thirteen-year-olds weren't the only vindictive ones. "Maybe you don't need to be mad at him." Interesting that she looked at Dex as she said this.

Daphne stood up, her arms akimbo and her mouth open to reject this craziness, but Desi spoke first.

"Christmas is for giving, not getting. Forgiving. For remembering the good things." Desi climbed up on the bench and opened one of the songbooks. "Nobody's perfect."

Daphne appeared ready to dispute this as well, so Desi added with an adult firmness still at contrast with her appearance. "Nobody. Not even you." Her hands settled on the keys, trying out a few notes.

As if this were their cue, the little green aliens left the captives, and formed a circle around Desi. Gini had a weird feeling they'd done this before. Dex and Isaac cautiously lowered their arms and then got up. Desi looked at them over her shoulder, the authoritative mom tone to her voice when she said, "Well, get over here. It's time to sing."

With some unease, the humans joined the alien circle while Desi played an intro. Not a bad job either. A few wrong notes never hurt a Christmas carol. It was Desi's favorite, something else Gini had almost forgotten.

"It came upon the midnight clear..."

Alien voices—slightly off key in an alien way—joined with slightly off key human voices, but somehow, in spite of, or perhaps because of the somewhat inexpert playing, it worked. Even Daphne's face softened some as the words called to her heart instead of her head.

It was a pity that the short green Santa Claus rushed into the room with his beard hanging off one green ear.

"Santa!" Desi's fingers hit the keys in a discordant chord. "Look Virginia! There is a Santa Claus!"

Instead of a ho, ho, ho, he gasped out something that sounded very alien. It ignited a round of alarmed gasps from the alien portion of choir. Desi's eyes widened and she grew older some more.

"What?" Gini asked.

"The men in black," Desi said.

~

Gini wasn't sure what bothered her more. That her mom spoke alien or finding out the men in black were headed their way.

"You must speak to them. Explain," One said, quivering with fright, his platter gaze fixed on Gini. "They will listen to you."

"To me?" Gini put her hand on her chest, but then dropped it as a bit over the top. Even if she felt a bit over the top.

"Can't you just beam out?" Dex asked, his body making another age adjustment. His shoulders broadened some. His arms stuck out now from the sleeve of the shirt that had fit him a few minutes earlier. He'd fit in his uniform soon. That may or may not help. Who knew what the men in black would respect?

Gini looked at her arms and realized they were starting to extend beyond the edges of her sleeves, too. Probably not the time for a hallelujah, but she wasn't eager to be a lab rat for the men in black. Not that this was all about her, but still...

"Our mother ship sustained unknown damage. Its shielding cloak partially failed. We have not been able to contact it for many hours."

Gini looked at Dex. The NASA emergency? But what had brought the men in black their way? Other than the flying saucer up on the rooftop. Had they somehow spotted that? Through the blizzard? Dex grew some more and his back seemed to straighten.

"What do you say, Gin? We could at least try to help them?"

She was kind of more interested in helping herself—apparently thirteen still lingered in her bloodstream—but Desi and the aliens looked so imploring, and honestly? She and Dex and Van had played this "save the aliens" scenario when they were kids. Which made it a no-brainer. Maybe it had been programmed into her DNA—though hopefully not during some kind of weird alien abduction moment. She nodded, helpfully she hoped, and not as unwilling as she felt. Dex looked at the kids, one brow lifted.

Isaac nodded without even thinking about it, which kind of surprised her. Daphne hesitated, but she was at that "follow the crowd" age and finally nodded, too. There was a gleam in her eyes, though, that showed there was still little bit of kid left in there.

Apparently Gini had some, too, because unwilling began to melt in the excitement of possibly outsmarting the men in black.

"How long have we got?" Gini asked. For the first time, she realized the wind had died down. Great, now it decided to quit storming.

"Possibly an hour. Possibly less," Dr. Five said, after consulting the pad he'd used to confuse them earlier.

Maybe precision was challenging when one was used to counting in plus or minus light years?

"How functional is your mother ship?" Isaac asked, pulling out his notebook and pencil.

"It functions well," One said, "but we need our mother ship to alter mem—I mean to go home."

"Oh please, don't let me forget," Gini said involuntarily. "I promise I won't tell!" Okay, that sounded very thirteen still.

Dex's lips quivered. "We should both change. Quickly."

Gini looked down. He was right. Her legs stuck out the bottom of the pants far enough to look odd.

Isaac didn't look up from his writing. "I'll work on a plan while you change." He paused and now he looked up. "But hurry."

She and Dex exchanged possibly their thousandth look of...something. Did Isaac create plans to feel in control? She couldn't say he'd succeeded—or failed—at any of them. She could give him chops for having flair.

Gini found it a bit unsettling that a couple of aliens attached themselves to she and Dex. At least they gave her the one she thought was a girl. Four's feather had lost its sass, as if it too feared the men in black. Gini made a pass through the bathroom. She did not want to pee her pants in front of the feds. Then she changed, stopping with some dismay when the arm's of her favorite sweater hang down over her hands.

"I'm not completely me yet."

Four blinked without comment, so Gini went out in the hall and found Dex rolling up the sleeves of his uniform shirt.

"I know," he said. "Can't be helped."

They started down the stairs and had just reached the bottom when there was a knock at the front door.

Four gasped in fright and leaped up on a table, assuming the inflatable alien position, her feather quivering where it curled into her face. Dex's alien guide ran into the living room as if the hounds were after him.

Gini's heart was pounding, as Dex reached out and opened the door.

It wasn't a man in black.

It was the Big Chill.

Awkward.

~

"Merry Christmas, Virginia," Lincoln Graham said, his voice not as chilly as usual. He held a bag of gaily wrapped presents and a bottle of something that looked expensive, like he'd stepped out of an ad or a Christmas movie—one of the romance ones from *Hallmark Channel.* Everything about him was perfect, from his airbrushed hair to his "casual" winter boots. His cashmere coat fell perfectly open and his jeans and tee shirt probably cost more than her car.

Gini put a hand up, wondering if she'd remembered to brush her hair. She relocated her dropped jaw to its proper position. "Merry Christmas..."

She should probably call him by his first name, but she never had. At least, she hadn't had a chance to get past 'sir' since the Thing. She stepped back and almost tripped over Dex, who still had one hand on the door.

"Dex, this is Lincoln Graham, my um, boss." Her voice was higher than usual, with a hint of shrill that might be panic or the fact that she wasn't her real age yet. "And this is Dex, Dexter James Tolliver, our local sheriff." She swallowed. "And family friend. Of course. He's a friend. Too."

The Big Chill was no fool and never had been. Couldn't be one and get where he had in life. His gaze tracked from her to Dex, then back. At least it hadn't stopped at the alien on the entry table. There might have been some narrowing around the eyes, but he held out his hand. Dex did, too. Some sizing up, but neither gave away their conclusions about each other. No sign they did the "whose grip is the strongest" deal either.

No reason they'd fight over her. She studied them again, just to make sure. Nope, no sign of battle lines drawn. Not sure how she felt about that. She glanced back. Four seemed to be the only alien in sight.

"Come...in..." Her smile and greeting felt stiff. "We were just...just..."

"Singing some Christmas carols and hoping for news of Gin's sister and husband getting here. We've been cut off, you know," Dex said, leading the way down the short hall to the great room.

Gini didn't know if the aliens and Desi had beamed out or what. Only Isaac and Daphne were still in there. Daphne sat on the bench with her back to the piano, her eyes a bit wide. Did she have sense enough to fear the men in black? Maybe Isaac had filled her in. Daphne's gaze alighted on the Big Chill and went from anxious to interested. Then she gave Gini a "what the what?" look and smoothed her hair down. Gini didn't blame her. The Big Chill might be light years older than Daphne, but he was definitely high end.

Isaac had sunk to the floor and was still writing in his notebook. In the sudden silence, he finally looked up. He took a long minute to study the Big Chill. The kid really was scary. Interesting that the Big Chill studied him back with equal something. And why was it easier to call him the Big Chill inside her head than Lincoln? Or Linc? His girlfriends called him Linc. Only she wasn't a girlfriend or his fiancé yet. Or ever? At least she wasn't greeting him as a thirteen-year-old.

Small mercies. Though the mercies weren't quite thirty-five yet either.

She held back a gasp when she caught sight of one of the aliens on the mantel. Until she got deeper into the room, the tree had hidden Three or Four. She still couldn't tell which was which.

The air was so thick with stuff, the Big Chill would have to be thick not to notice. And he wasn't thick. Daphne gave him the eye, mentally adding up the cost of his wardrobe. She shot Gini another incredulous look. The Big Chill noticed and his lips twitched. He managed to look at ease, which was impressive, but not a surprise. The real question was, would he be able to keep his cool when the men in black arrived?

A tiny choke escaped her compressed lips. Both men turned and looked at her. Dex's eyes held a warning. The Big Chill looked curious. And alert. His gaze tracked up her. Then down. A bit of puzzled appeared in the dark depths. How old was she right now? Or better yet, how tall was she right now? Was it a height thing or an age thing? The ball of heat formed in her stomach. Thankfully he looked away before she surged closer to her real height. Not there yet, though. She unrolled one of the cuffs. Two to go.

"Do you play?" the Big Chill asked, indicating the piano.

Daphne shook her head so he looked at Gini.

"Only a little. Very little." She lifted one hand. "One hand and even then..."

"Gin's mom was playing," Dex broke in. "I'm sure she'll be back—"

"I am."

Gini spun around and she was back. Completely back. No, not quite. The fingers were bent again, where she gripped the arms of her wheelchair, but she wasn't as bent as she'd been when Gini arrived. Her eyes were different, too. More alert. Still the contrast between the eight-year-old and the eighty-year-old was startling. Even Daphne gave a small gasp. Desi looked more, Gini hesitated, frail, almost transparent. As if she were fading from this life in front of their eyes. But the lines carved by pain were there. Not as deep but there. Gini resisted the impulse to reach out to her. To hold her here. Small Desi's words echoed in her head, "They don't hurt anymore."

"Mom." She swallowed back the wrong words, at least wrong for the moment. "This is Lincoln Graham, my boss." She made herself look at the Big Chill. "This is my mother, Desi Prescott."

Desi studied him carefully even as she held out her hand. Was it Gini's imagination that the hand quivered, then became more bent? The Big Chill blinked and seemed to give himself a slight shake, before he took her hand and murmured something polite. Neither of them seemed to know what to say after that. Finally the Big Chill held out the bag of gifts. Gini jumped forward and accepted it.

"That's so sweet of you..." she faltered to a stop. Dex took the bag and set it next to the tree.

The silence that pooled around them was not a comfortable one.

"I think it's time to bake some Christmas cookies," her mom said, turning her wheelchair. "Come children. Dexter."

Daphne's face resumed its more familiar discontent. Isaac glanced at the mantel, at the alien there, then followed Desi out of the room.

"Come on, Daphne." Dex took her arm when she seemed inclined to linger. "Gini needs to talk to her, um, boss." He steered her out of the room.

Gini wouldn't have thought it possible, but the silence got more uncomfortable.

Finally the Big Chill broke it. "I did try to call."

He studied her again, a faint crease forming between his perfectly marked brows. Standing next to him, she knew she wasn't the same height she'd been when she left Dallas. The difference wasn't huge, but she felt it. He was perceptive enough to know something was different.

Gini gave him a wry, uncertain smile. "No service up here and our satellite has been covered in snow." She hesitated. "I'm surprised you made it. I thought we were snowed in."

"I followed a snow plow in. And a bunch of official looking vehicles. There's some kind of training exercise or something taking place further up the road. Helicopters and everything."

Training exercise. Almost Gini looked at Two. Or Three.

"Training?" She tried to keep her tone light. Wasn't sure she managed it.

"That's what one of them said when he tried to stop me coming in."

"I'm surprised they let you," she said, her throat suddenly dry. The Big Chill arched his brows and she was less surprised. They might be the men in black, but he was Lincoln Graham.

"I get the feeling you wish I hadn't." His tone was more statement than question, but there were question marks in his eyes.

"It's not," Gini managed to stop herself from saying 'you,' which would give the wrong impression. Or the right one. "My mom...she's always...interesting. And this year, well, she's pushed her own boundaries." Gini ran a hand through her hair and tried a smile that was probably a grimace.

"And the cop?"

For a minute Gini didn't know what he was talking about. She blinked. "Dex? Oh right. I didn't know—he came up to mom sit until I got here. I was delayed. And then there was the blizzard—" She stopped, trying to find her way back to his efficient PA. "I had to wait for Bif's kids at the airport. He and Van got stuck at work. Some kind of emergency."

"A NASA emergency?" He sounded more amused than skeptical.

Gini was kind of impressed he'd remembered her sister worked for NASA. She'd mentioned it maybe once. She felt some color in her cheeks but managed a chuckle. "Yeah, they are newlyweds, though. I am hoping they'll get here soon. Bif's kids aren't real happy with him right now."

His gaze managed to pin her, snagging her gaze with ease and holding it.

"What's wrong?"

"You mean besides my aging mother, the bitter step-kids and—" she stopped, but it didn't help.

"And the old boyfriend?"

"We went to high school together." Why did she feel guilty? She'd arranged flower deliveries for his dates. And she hadn't said yes. Her mouth firmed. Found a bit of her backbone. "Why me?"

Her timing had been off pretty much from the beginning of this adventure in who knew what, so why change that now?

To his credit he didn't look away for about fifteen seconds. His lips straightened. She recognized the look. Did he think she'd be a tough negotiation?

"I had a feeling you were getting ready to bolt."

She blinked. "And decided marriage was the solution?"

He shook his head. "If it was only about your job, I'd have offered you more money." His head tilted a bit. "But I have a feeling that wouldn't have taken it?"

Gini, a bit surprised at herself, shook her head. "I liked working for you."

"But..."

"I've," she hesitated, but decided author confessions were better than first contact and the men in black, "been writing. And thinking of moving back to you know, be closer to my mom. She's getting on and there's just me and Van."

"And the boyfriend?"

"I didn't know he'd moved back." Oops. That was an admission he had at least been one.

He hesitated. She braced for more questions about Dex.

He surprised her. "Writing what?"

"Novels. Science fiction." She took a breath. "I'm afraid I'm a geek. I go to the cons and everything."

"Everything?"

"I might have a *Star Fleet* uniform."

His lips twitched. "That is something of a blow." He studied her, as if trying to fit this new information into what he knew of his PA. "You must write under a pen name?"

"D. L. Prescott."

He considered this. "Why D.L.?"

"When I was little, our—my parents used to say it was just dumb luck we survived."

He laughed then. It warmed his whole face and might have made a flicker of something happen in her middle. A flicker she so did not have time for, she realized as Two or Three gave a tiny twitch. That's when she heard it. The sound of helicopters approaching.

The Big Chill, *Lincoln*, she mentally corrected herself, looked up. Then his chin dropped and his gaze laser focused on her. She'd seen that look before, too, though never directed at her until now.

She gave him as innocent look as she could manage. "How...odd. I hope the, er, exercise isn't going to run over us?"

~

Dateline: Notes from Isaac's Strategic Planning notebook

I hope we are on right side.

Too bad they aren't really Santa's elves.

∾

Dateline: From Daphne's cell phone

I think I need to forget. Even if it lets dad off the hook.

∾

Dateline: Advance scouting party report

And once again first contact goes horribly wrong.

∾

Dateline: Most Secret - No One's Eyes Only

Finally we have them...

Chapter Twelve

The kitchen was a scene of floury—though alien-less—chaos when Gini and the Big Chill entered to the sound of circling helicopters. Though Gini still clung to faint hope the helicopters weren't filled with men in black and would go somewhere else, she didn't have to see one land to know she'd been clinging to broken straws. And, apparently, bad analogies.

If Dex and her mom had hoped to blow smoke up their black pants, they'd made pretty good progress. There was a huge blob of white dough in the middle of the table indicating cookies in progress. Isaac had a smaller, flattened blob that he was attacking with a snowman cookie cutter. Daphne, floured to her elbows and sporting a Santa hat and a pretend smile, was whacking inexpertly at it with a rolling pin.

The Big Chill stretched a hand toward a wayward clump.

"I wouldn't," Dex said, his lips twitching. Based on the amount of time they'd had to mix the blob up, Gini figured it was just flour and water.

Dex's gaze tracked between them, possibly noting the tension indicating unresolved issues. Or not. The guys in her books noticed stuff like that but that might be wishful writing with no basis in reality.

Christmas music channeled into the room from an old-style boombox on the counter and there was even a half-sliced fruitcake on a wooden cutting board. Bet no one would try a taste of that. It looked authentic enough to be scary. And bore a remarkable resemblance to the one they hadn't eaten last year.

If the Big Chill or the men in black didn't look below the surface, they'd see a scene of ordinary Christmas activity.

Her nerves stretched taut, she decided she couldn't wait for trouble to come to them. And honestly, wouldn't they be curious? Sounded like the end of the world out there. So she went to the door and yanked it open, letting in a blast of cold and noise.

The man standing there with a half raised fist wasn't wearing black, at least not where it could be seen. He'd gone woolly mammoth with his outerwear. Even had a face mask and goggles. It was kind of sad. Yes, it was cold, but this wasn't the North Pole. Maybe he'd thought that's where they were going and been hoping for Santa, too? There was an idea for a book. The men in black versus Santa.

As if he realized he was over-dressed for the cold, he lifted mask and goggles, revealing a stereotypical Fed face, one straight out of the movies. Clean-cut and crisp. Statistically they couldn't all be that way. Maybe the guys in black got first pick or something. He held a weapon, but it was pointed down. More figures leaped off the helicopter in the clearing, its rotating blades kicking up its own small blizzard of snow. As soon as it disgorged its passengers, it lifted off, allowing another one to take its shot at the spot. The rotating blades moved enough snow to almost drill down to dirt. She had to assume there were more choppers in the front. The racket was incredible with the door open. Like swift ants, they flowed in either direction, clearly intent on surrounding the cabin.

Talk about overki—she cut off the word in her head, but the sight of so many armed men, well, it didn't matter if she didn't think it. The risk was there. Gini had to fight not to let her gaze look up, like she could see through the porch roof to the rooftop. Fear kept her from moving to look. She for sure didn't want to get them interested in what may or may not be up there.

So she looked the guy in the eyes and slowly raised her hands about shoulder height, but letting her expression speak incredulous volumes. A tinge of red crept up his cheeks. Interesting that she could make a man in black blush. That would never have happened in the movies.

She leaned out, just a bit, and glanced around. "Is something wrong?" She had to shout to be heard. Okay, not her brightest comment ever. She could do better when she had time to edit.

"Are you all right?" He managed to shout without looking like he was.

Gini let her brows rise. "I was." She looked past him again, then said, "What's going on?" The question seemed logical, normal. Did she know what that was anymore?

"There's been a prison break."

"Prison?" She didn't have to fake that shock. "What prison?" The man in fur looked taken aback. "Rawlings is, what?" She half looked back at Dex. "Over two hundred miles from here, isn't it?"

"Closer to two-fifty," he agreed, joining her in the doorway.

The racket began to ease. Apparently all the choppers had done their thing and retreated to a circling-vultures position. Now the Christmas music could be heard again, boosting their festive creds, or so she hoped. Behind her Desi sang softly along as she cut cookies out of the somewhat flattened blob. Daphne lifted her rolling pin. A clump of dough still stuck to it. She started pounding it against the wood table.

The guy blinked a couple of times, or possibly he winced, as he took in the scene, then finished his survey with Dex's uniform. The rolled up sleeves looked normal and logical, given the cookie making going on. Dex had added some floury touches to his hands and hair.

"How long have you been here?"

Dex's brows shot up, but he answered with unruffled calm, "Since mid afternoon yesterday. Why?"

Man in fur blinked some more. "It was actually a...prison...plane. It...went down. Not far from here we think." He straightened as if someone had barked at him. "We need to search this structure. All structures, actually."

Dex shrugged and stepped back, his body nudging Gini out of the way. "Sure. Come on in."

Gini wasn't sure what he knew that she didn't that made him look so unworried. She just hoped he knew what he was doing with what he knew that she didn't. And that what he knew that she didn't was true. Because she'd left at least two aliens back there.

"Is there anyone else in the house?" The guy asked, as a group of men formed a line behind him, clearly intending to be part of the search party. This did not appear to deplete the numbers surrounding the house all that much.

"As far as I know, we're all right here," Dex said. "I can show you around—"

The man held up his hand. "No offense, but no."

"None taken," Dex said easily, turning back to the table. "What was it you wanted me to find for you, Desi?"

"The sprinkles, dear," her mom said, placidly. "And I think there are some more cookie cutters in that drawer there." She pointed to a drawer and Dex headed toward it.

The man in fur's gaze lighted on the Big Chill. No surprise his shoulders straightened some, as if he'd come to attention. The Big Chill had done more to erase slouching than the military.

The man in fur cleared his throat. "We should be out of your way soon, sir."

After a long, unnerving pause, the Big Chill let his chin dip a millimeter or so. Man in fur ran a finger around the neck of his furry coat. Gini was pretty sure that didn't help.

"The rest of the house is that way." Gini indicated the opening. "Oh, except for a bathroom over there."

The man in fur blinked, nodded, then, for some reason looked at Isaac who had looked up from his labors giving him that look that Gini found so unsettling.

His snowman cookie appeared to have suffered some kind of mortal wound. "Can I have a ride in your helicopter?"

It would have been an uncomfortable silence version three point four, but for the music and stamp of booted feet as the men spread through the cabin. Conscious of the Big Chill's gaze on her, Gini tried to look curious, instead of on the verge of mind melting panic. It wasn't just Big Chill looking at her either. She felt the concentrated attention of Dex and Desi. Did they think she was the weak link in a room that contained Daphne? She'd have been offended but there was no room left for any more emotions. Where were the rest of the aliens? What about their flying saucer up on the roof top?

Oh how she wanted to ask, but of course, even if the men in black weren't in the room with them, that didn't mean they hadn't left someone—or something—lurking out in the hall in hopes she'd be just that clueless. Or dropped a bug on their way by. She glanced around, but didn't see anything obvious. Because it would be. D'oh.

So much depended on what the men in black knew, or thought they knew, and the measures the aliens had taken to protect themselves. Now, when she couldn't ask, she wondered why their mother ship had a cloak but not the flying saucer up on the housetop? Could their capabilities be connected like the ships in *Independence Day?* It was an unfortunate connection to make because then she wondered if she'd picked the right side. What if she was helping to prepare the way for their whole world to be conquered?

Her gaze collided with Dex's and his lips twitched, as if he knew what she was thinking. Easy for him to be chill when he was packing heat. Only they didn't call it that anymore, did they?

Floor boards creaked as the search moved upstairs. She stiffened as she remembered the "magic" rock presents by their beds. Had anyone thought to remove those? She knew the old cabin's creak points well enough to know exactly where they were. If she hadn't been stiff with fear, she'd have been upset with the idea that her personal space was being searched. She heard the distinctive squeak of the attic steps being pulled down and much of the stamping boot sounds moved up and away. Almost imperceptibly, she relaxed. There was nothing in the attic for them to find. And if they'd found something, wouldn't someone come—

"Ma'am?"

Gini turned toward the opening. Who—the man looked at her, not her mom, which should have been a relief, but wasn't. She wasn't *that* old. And no it wasn't situation appropriate to be annoyed at being ma'am-d, but why be appropriate now? The man—a different man in fur than the first one at the door—looked directly at her. Gini fought back the longing to flee. She arched her brows in what she hoped was an unworried question. She didn't speak because she wasn't sure she could. It felt like multiple squeaks were stuck in her throat. With a scream or two behind them.

"Could you come into the other room with me, please?"

Dex made a small move, quickly checked. It seemed the Big Chill went unnaturally still. He'd made his fortune riding undercurrents and this room was thick with them.

She nodded, flicking a quick—hopefully reassuring—glance at Dex, then at her boss, then her mom, before moving to the opening. She followed him out into the hall. The alien she'd dubbed Four was still on the table, the feather quivering now and again as stray currents of air lifted it. Or she shivered from fear. The man directed her to the great room. Inside Gini found the first man in fur standing in front of the big tree. In a kind of weird twist, it looked as if Spock stood on his shoulder giving her his "live long and prosper" sign.

He indicated the couch, probably as a power play, but whatever. She'd almost forgotten she still hadn't returned to her full size, but was reminded when she perched on the edge, sort of leaning against it to keep her feet on the floor. No question the big couch and the dude looming over her made her feel extra short, even without the alien shrinking in the mix. Was this how her mom felt sitting in her wheelchair and getting steadily smaller? It was an uncomfortable thought and she shifted uneasily.

The man in fur stepped to one side of the tree and gestured behind him. "What is this?"

Gini's carefully didn't look at Two or Three on the mantle.

"A Christmas tree?"

He heaved an impatient sigh. "It's covered in—you all seem to be very fond of aliens." One finger flicked an *Enterprise* ornament, boosting the sneer factor in his comment, as if there were something sinister about this fondness. Had the man in black seriously never been to an SF convention?

Gini licked her lips. "The tree is kind of my mom's ode to NASA. She's been a fan since the first guy orbited the earth. And my sister and her husband work for NASA."

"And you? Where do you work?"

This did not seem like a good time to admit writing about aliens. "I work for the other guy in the kitchen, Lincoln Graham. I'm his personal assistant." She didn't elaborate. Didn't feel she needed to, since the Big Chill had won the point in their gaze clashing.

He looked at her for what felt like a long time. With some panic, she felt a ball of heat form in her middle. Was it wrong to pray it was a hot flash? The heat spread out toward her extremities as the hard gaze drilled into hers—

There was a plunk as one of the ornaments fell off the tree and rolled over to bump against the man in fur's booted foot. He looked down just as Gini felt another growth spurt. He looked up, then frowned slightly, as if he sensed a difference but didn't know what it was. She jumped up and bent to pick the ornament up. Chewie from *Star Wars* stared at her from a sea of silver gilt.

She found a branch to hang it on and looked straight into the platter gaze of Dr. Five. Almost dropped it again, but managed to hook it over a branch despite shaking hands. Dr. Five winked. When eyes that big winked it was impressive. Gini's lips twitched, even as her heart gave a frightened leap. She flexed her hands to get the shakes out, or at least better controlled. There was another gap where sleeves didn't quite hit where they were supposed to. She smoothed both arms down. She was almost back to her normal arm length. One more growth spurt ought to do it. Unless, what if her whole body wasn't growing the same? Be embarrassing if her parts weren't properly aligned. And possibly autopsy inducing. That dried her throat.

She swallowed, took a deep breath and faced the man in fur. "Your escaped prisoners must be uncommonly short."

He frowned. "What do you mean?"

"You seem to be looking for them under my mom's ode to NASA Christmas tree?"

He hesitated, a hint of uncertainty in his steely gaze. "That's quite the Christmas display on your roof."

Gini felt her stomach drop. "You think they are hiding in my mom's Christmas display?" She bit back a snide remark about frisking Santa. It was always talking too much that gave the game away. And she had no clue what the "display" looked like.

"No." He paused again. "Seems a bit much."

Gini didn't blink, mostly because her eyes were too dry. "My mom likes to go big or go home with all her holiday displays." She swallowed, managed to add lightly, "You should see what she does for Halloween."

He seemed to consider this. "In the middle of nowhere?"

Gini managed a wry lip twist. "She thinks the space station can see it. It's, well, her...gift to whoever is up there." It helped that this was actually true. Her mom really did think she had a thing going with the space station. Or she'd been blowing smoke all these years when it was really her green men she'd—

"A flying saucer and a green Santa sitting in a Red Rider sled being pulled by a flock of pink lawn flamingos?"

It was her turn to blink. She nodded, half shrugged. Gave him a "what can you do?" look.

"But—"

Gini felt a bunch of alien autopsies—and possibly some human ones—hanging in the balance. She leaned in, as if confiding a secret.

"My mom thinks Spock works for NASA. She was hoping he'd

come for Christmas this year." His eyes widened a bit. She nodded and grimaced. "At least she doesn't get up there herself anymore."

His gaze flicked up, widened and he almost grinned. He stopped himself, but it almost happened. He suddenly became almost human, too.

"Right." He hesitated and Gini had that sense he was getting orders from somewhere. "We're sorry we disturbed your holiday preparations. We'll have some men on the road for a while, until we catch the, um, escaped prisoners or get new intel on their movements."

"Well," Gini's smile felt more normal, "if we find them in our presents, we'll give you a call." He didn't smile. Not that she expected him to. She felt better for it though. "Oh," she had a thought, "my sister and her husband are probably heading this way. She looks like me." She got a look. "We're twins. So we look alike. Identical...twins." She clamped her lips shut. "Please let them through. My brother-in-law's kids are pretty ticked off that he's late. Though if you were to give Isaac a ride in a helicopter..."

He stepped back with some haste. "Wish I could but..." He turned and booked it out of the room. Like double time even. Out in the clearing there arose quite the clatter as the men in fur withdrew from the various parts of the house and exited from doors front and back and lined up for collection.

And then there was a...profound silence. Slowly, so slowly it was almost slow motion, the branches of the tree parted and Dr. Five clambered out, giving a wince or two as the branches caught at his green skin.

"They thought your flying saucer was....was..." she couldn't say it.

He nodded solemnly.

"Slap Santa on it and they'll think it's a blow up display," said a tiny voice behind her. "That's what Isaac said. So we did."

It was Four, her feather still bobbing. Her skin seemed a somewhat lighter green, too.

"Well, okay then." Couldn't argue with what had worked. "Now what?"

There was a choking sound from the doorway and Gini saw something she thought she'd never see, not her lifetime or in the next life.

The Big Chill rocked back on his heels with shock.

~

After ten novels, Gini felt she ought to be better at words, particularly since most of her books dealt with some kind of alien interaction. And now that she'd had real first contact, well, that almost made her an expert, or should have.

She tried for a PA type smile, but it wasn't easy. "I did mention we had a kind of...of...situation here." Had she had time to mention that?

The Big Chill stared at her. Blinked. Stared some more. Blinked some more. He looked back toward the hall, as if he wanted to bring back the men in black, but Dex and Desi were there. Dex channeled his total cop stance, his hands at his waist—one of them very close to his handgun. She thought it interesting that her mom managed to look "don't do it" while sitting in a wheelchair.

He turned back to face her but didn't manage to find his voice. Desi rolled past him and the aliens clustered around her chair, two of them taking one of her hands with obvious and tender affection.

"Our mother ship has contacted us," Two, or possibly Three said. "Its systems are functioning well once more."

Four trotted up to Gini, and with an oddly formal solemnity, removed the feather from her hat and presented it to Gini. Gini smiled at her and took it, letting her hand close over Four's this time, giving the green hand a gentle squeeze.

"Thank you. I don't—"

Four shook her head, the green mouth turning up at the edges. "It is well."

Desi nodded and Gini could have sworn she faded some more, her body shrinking as she returned to her true age. She looked up and smiled at Gini, the eyes so very much her mom's that Gini caught her breath. Gini went to her, kneeling between two aliens and putting her hands on top of the green ones. The skin was cool and soft and well, green. Unsettling, but she owed it to her mom not to flinch. Gini met her gaze, finding some comfort in the fact that the vagueness was gone for now. There was something else in there, too. Gini's head tilted.

"You're...leaving?" Was her mom leaving? Or *leaving*?

Desi freed one hand and reached out and smoothed Gini's hair back from her face. "You'll tell your sister good-bye? That I love you both very much." Her hand lingered. "I'm so proud of both my beautiful little daughters."

"Mom—"

Desi shook her head. "We all have to...go. I've been—going for a long time. Dexter will watch out for you."

Involuntarily, Gini's gaze jerked up to meet the Big Chill. While still pale, he'd recovered enough to give her a wry look. He didn't look uncomfortable. He never did, but he'd distanced himself some.

"I can only be put together for the work day," she admitted, as if he'd asked. She'd created, she realized now, a fictional PA to show up, a persona for the real Gini to hide behind. It was weird she'd only now figured it out. Oh, she was good at her job, but the polish, the crispness? So very much not her. The real her was the writer, the geek, the gal not afraid to don a *Star Trek* uniform with her geek friends. "This is the real—" she stopped. "Well, the cabin is real. This is my first nonfiction alien encounter. But the real me, even before this was not, well, that calm."

The Big Chill nodded slowly and she bit back the impulse to ask again why her? Now she'd probably never know. A pity that.

Dr. Five put a green hand on her head. Kneeling, her gaze was even with his platter one. He might have smiled.

"You have done well once you ceased to panic. You are indeed like your mother before you."

The ball of warm formed again, surging out and she felt her last growth spurt happen. The Big Chill's eyes got wide again. She almost told him it wasn't her fault, but managed to not to.

Dr. Five leaned close. "He won't remember."

It was probably better if he didn't, but she hoped she would't have to turn him down again. Wasn't easy to turn her back on the romance novel, billionaire proposal moment, even if she'd never really planned to say yes. Made her feel a bit dubious when she realized it. But she'd needed the proposal to come home, even before she knew Dex was here. Probably needed to add it to her list of character flaws she needed to work on.

Dex stepped up to Desi's wheelchair and he bent to plant a kiss on Desi's wrinkled cheek.

"You're one of a kind, Desi. Thanks."

Desi patted his cheek. She looked at Dr. Five. "Is it time?"

He nodded. "You should both distance yourselves."

Dex held out a hand and pulled her up. He didn't let go as they distanced themselves. There was a hum that started softly, then began to build until she felt it in her teeth. It wasn't exactly painful, but it wasn't comfortable either.

"Mom!" She half reached out, then let her hand drop. "I love you! We both love you!"

There was a bright flash, and, just for a moment she thought she saw her mom young again, not eight, but young and happy and her eyes bright with excitement at the coming adventure...

∿

Dateline: Notes from Isaac's Strategic Planning notebook

This Christmas vacation has turned out better than expected. Santa Claus, aliens and the men in black.

∿

Dateline: From Daphne's cell phone

Cookies? They made me make cookies? And aliens? Seriously? Dad so owes me for this one.

Though that fed guy wasn't half bad...

∿

Dateline: Advance scouting party report

Closest near miss yet. But we are pleased our friend Desi travels home with us again.

Chapter Thirteen

Gini jerked awake, disoriented for a few seconds. She stared at the wooden beams overhead trying to figure out—oh, right. She was at the cabin. For Christmas. She rubbed her eyes, pushed the hair off her face and sat up. Everything looked the same as it had last night. Suitcases open, contents spilling out, snow piled up on the outside window ledges, and their teen/crush posters on the walls, so why—she gave her head a shake and got up. Why would anything be different?

She rested a hand on the bedside table and reality shifted for a minute. That was her hand. Did she think it would be different? Different how? Her water bottle sat where she'd left it last night. All was as it should be. Just having a little trouble shaking off sleep. And that dream...why couldn't she remember it? Oh well. It happened sometimes. She shrugged on her robe, made a pass through the bathroom and then headed downstairs.

The sight of the green alien on the entry table stopped her in her tracks, about four steps short of the bottom. She glanced around, not sure exactly why she felt uneasy at the sight of it. After a pause, she approached it, though cautiously for some reason. It looked like an inflatable alien, not—

"What's wrong?" Dex asked from the kitchen doorway. He had their youngest on his hip, her tiny face still glistening from being recently washed. Her head was nestled against her dad's broad shoulder and Gini's heart turned to mush in her chest at the sight. Two kids and he could still curl the toes in her slippers.

"You're both up early. I didn't hear a thing." Not like her, but she had been tired last night after spending a long day chasing kids and getting the cabin ready for Van and her family to arrive. This was the first time they'd been back for Christmas at the cabin since Desi— Gini blinked—since their mom had disappeared in a blizzard four years ago. Dex had been more than their rock during that hard time. He'd been the shoulder she learned on and cried on. Plus he knew Desi—knew her mom almost as well as she did. She could talk about mom and he knew, he understood. It was a bit weird they hadn't found her body in the spring, but there was some rugged areas not far from the cabin and, in a way, she was glad they hadn't. Without a body, she could pretend her mom just left—

"You were pretty deep asleep." Dex transferred the baby to his other shoulder so he could pull her close for a hug and a kiss.

"Where is young Desi?" Of course they'd named their first daughter after her mom. She even kind of looked like her grandma, though her hair wasn't long enough for red pigtails yet. Gini blinked because she could see them so clearly—

"She's still working on her cereal."

Their three-year-old was probably smearing it all over the table. But both table and kid could be washed.

Four years and she was still amazed they were together. And so grateful she hadn't given the Big Chill an answer before she left for the holidays that year. He'd found a PA—and wife—much better suited to his perfect life than imperfect, geek Gini. Her thoughts flickered, as a memory of the Big Chill here, in this hall, danced briefly inside her head. That was weird. He'd never been here. He'd thought about it, he said, obviously relieved when she turned him down.

She snuggled into Dex's shoulder, loving the long limbed guy-ness of her sweetheart. And wished that her mom has lived long enough to meet her grand kids. She wanted some so much—

"You okay?" Dex asked, his voice rumbled in the chest her cheek pressed against.

She nodded. "Was just wishing D—my mom could be here." Why did she keep calling her mom Desi? She'd never—the inflatable alien caught her eye and a shiver of unease danced down her spine.

"Where did that come from? It wasn't here last night, was it?"

Did it seem Dex tensed?

"No."

She lifted her head. There was something in his eyes that made her lean back and study him. She glanced at the alien and then looked at him again. She rubbed her face with the hand not resting against his back.

"Is anything wrong?" he asked, almost hopefully.

"It's just—I had the strangest dream last night—" she stopped when his brows lifted. The fuzzy details of the dream sharpened. "I had a *dream*." And in the dream she'd insisted she'd been dreaming. Weirdness. The heater kicked on, sending a gentle surge of air through the room and dislodging something. It floated off the table and drifted to the floor. Gini bent and picked it up.

A feather. A *feather*. She turned to Dex with, she was pretty sure, a slack jaw. He grinned.

"It took you long enough to remember. I've been biting my tongue for four years."

"But that's not—" she stopped, with the feeling she'd said that before. And been wrong then, too. She dragged the feather between her thumb and index fingers. Had it been waiting for her to remember or—she eased the inflatable forward and checked the back. There was a tab to release the air. She sighed and Dex chuckled.

"Is the SF author saying she doesn't believe?"

"But..." her voice trailed off as memory of that Christmas four years ago unspooled in her dead, memories quite at odds with how she thought it had been. "...four years? Why did you remember?" She straightened. "Did they mess with my memory?" The lack of trust kind of hurt.

That earned her a look. "You think I know how any of this worked? I'm just the sheriff, not the whatever I'd need to be to know how it all worked."

"When did you remember?" He didn't speak and more outrage surged. "You never forgot, did you?"

He looked rueful. "Well, someone needed to manage Desi's disappearance."

"So you knew, you always knew—why didn't you say anything?"

"Would you have believed me?"

She stared at him, unwilling to admit she might not have. And if she'd thought he was crazy...

"But Van and Bif, the emergency—"

"Turns out they were studying some interesting space debris. It kind of looked spaceship-ish, but wasn't anything after all."

"Do you think they messed with their memories, too?" The Big Chill sure hadn't seemed to remember—

"I didn't ask. I was just glad to have a second chance with you. I didn't want to mess it up."

He took her hand in his and led her into the great room. Somehow, he managed to get her seated on the couch, the baby tucked between them. She stared at the big tree covered in her mom's ode to NASA ornaments, glittering in the dim light filtering into snow and frost covered windows. And there was Spock, in his usual spot, urging them to live long and prosper.

"Did you ever, before, I mean, think about coming to see me?"

"All the time."

"Well, why didn't you?" She wouldn't have been hard to convince. She hadn't been hard to convince. She'd played hard-to-get for maybe a minute.

"I asked Desi how you were doing and she told me about this big job you had—" he stopped. "I hadn't found your books then. If I had, nothing would have stopped me. I only found them earlier that year. Stumbled onto one in a used bookstore. I had this feeling of knowing something—so I bought them all. And as I read them, I knew. I *knew*. So I started the ball rolling to get here, to be here when you came."

Gini stared at the tree. "Do you think she knew—"

Dex shook his head. "I honestly don't know. I just know she was right."

"About..." Gini prompted, wondering which right he referred to.

"She said it would be the best Christmas ever."

It had been a great Christmas, despite her mom—not going missing in the snowstorm. Had some part of her known, way down deep inside, that her mom was okay? That she wasn't lost in the storm but off to the stars with One? Good Christmases had followed that one, though they'd been spent elsewhere. A wedding, two kids. So much happiness. There'd been sorrow, but it had been tinged with the sense that her mom was now one of the happy ghosts lingering here with their dad. Had their dad known about the aliens?

Young Desi chose that moment to trot in, dripping cereal from chin and hands. Dex jumped up, scooped her up and, holding her away from his clothes, carried her out for cleaning.

Gini hugged her baby close, inhaling her sweet baby scent. This would be the best Christmas ever—until the next one. And the one after that. From this old couch she could see a long line of happy Christmases stretching into a future that would hold, hopefully, a couple more kids sledding and skating and drinking hot chocolate and watching for Santa to come.

Though she'd be totally okay if Santa stayed mysterious and invisible—and out of their Red Rider sled.

~

Project Enterprise Short Stories

Introduction

The journey is not over in the Project Enterprise Series. Two complete stories that feature guest appearances that you don't want to miss are currently available. You'll want to collect the complete set in this award-winning series!

First up is "Men in Jeans."

Richard Daniels thinks life can't get any stranger than working at Area 51 until he gets assigned to find out where Houston area SF writer, Jilly Smith, gets the ideas for her books. Should be an easy assignment—if it weren't for the dead guy in Jilly's back yard and the non-business related ideas she's giving him.

And then dive into "Steam Time" to find out what happened to the mysterious (and sometimes bad guy) Dr. Smith.

Tobias Smith hadn't planned to ride along with Dr. Everly and his Medicine Show, but they were heading in the same direction - Marfa. During the journey, Tobias quickly uncovers another surprising revelation - that Everly's 'son' is not who 'he', or should he say 'she', appears to be! Tobias soon discovers he might not be as bad as he thought - in a good way - when he and Ani find themselves bumped into an alternate reality complete with an automaton gang and airships.

Could Tobias be the hero, save the day and get the girl? Stranger things have happened in the award-winning Project Enterprise universe! Ride along as two mysteries are solved and hearts are changed!

Steam Time

The man formerly known as Tobias Smith hadn't planned to ride along with Dr. Everly and his Medicine Show. Grifters gave him a pain their elixirs couldn't heal. But he was headed to Marfa, too. And Everly's son turned out to be a really a fine looking damsel—one in distress when the ghost lights of Marfa bump them into an alternate reality complete with an automaton gang and airships. Could he be the good guy? Be the hero, save the day and get the girl? (Originally appeared in *Dreamspell Steampunk Vol 1*)

Steam Time

T*exas 1892*

Ani called him stranger inside her head, because he sure wasn't a "Joe." To his face she didn't call him anything cause she couldn't call him what he wasn't. Hadn't said much of anything to him, not since he'd ridden over the rise three days ago and Pa invited him to ride along with them. He was headed to Marfa, too, though that was all he'd shared about himself of a personal nature. He didn't talk much, which suited Pa, since he talked enough for all of them and a few more besides.

Wary for reasons she hadn't figured out yet, she'd watched him through her lashes, mostly at night around the campfire, though her gaze might accidentally stray his direction now and again in daylight. She took care not to meet that hard-as-a-drill gaze, since she was supposed to be a boy and she didn't feel like one when she looked at him. And if he looked too close, he'd know she wasn't that young. Good thing she took after her blessed Ma, who had looked young until the day she went to her reward.

Ani'd exchanged skirts for pants when they took to the road selling the elixir from the rear of the wagon. Like her Pa, their wagon walked a fine line between serious and spectacle, as did his English accent. He claimed to be gentry, a younger son who'd eloped with the under housemaid and been shipped off to the colonies to remove the stain of his disgrace from the family name. Sometimes she believed it was true. She could talk gentry like him when the situation called for it, which it didn't that much. Mostly she looked peaked and moaned so her Pa could heal her. Her gaze skittered the stranger's way again. Not sure she could do either in front of him.

A lot of men had passed by—or even stopped to buy—since that day they took to the road, but none as interesting as the stranger. Big and likely looking, with a huge helping of tough in him, he had a cool gaze that saw things, though he was also a gentleman—or as much a one as her Pa. She saw it in the way her Pa reacted to him, how much it pleased Pa when the stranger called him "Dr. Everly" with just enough respect so as not to be obvious, heard it in the way he spoke, too.

Pa didn't seem to see the danger that lurked below the stranger's surface though he should. Danger clung like his clothes, fit him as well as they did, mingled with his scent that the night breeze sent her way every now and again. And lurking behind the danger she sensed a deep well of sad.

Unlike her Pa, Ani saw it all. One of them had to. Not everyone liked finding out you couldn't buy a miracle for a dollar. That's why they'd had to avoid the Paisano settlement this year. No, what surprised her was how it felt to see those things in him. Made her feel all strange and sad, too, made her want to do something about it, despite the danger. Didn't think the stranger would let her do anything for him though and a good thing that was. Wanting to do something about a man had caught her Ma in the tangle of Pa's life. Ma had loved him to the end, but she saw him clear and told Ani to see him clear, too.

"Illusions are for magic shows," she'd said more than once, "not for living."

Pa, well, he preferred illusions and more than a few delusions. Heaven knew his amazing elixir was mostly both. The stranger? If he'd ever had illusions, she had a feeling he'd lost them long ago.

So Ani kept her head bent over her book, though she peered through her lashes, trying to see the stranger clear, to see past the odd stirring in her chest at the sight of the long limbs stretched toward the fire and the broad shoulders settled against the wagon wheel. Tried not to note that the shadows on his face weren't all from the need to shave or the low hanging moon. He looked relaxed, well, as much as he could when he looked like he could whip his weight in wildcats.

"Jules Verne?"

It took her a few seconds—and her Pa clearing his throat—to realize the question was for her. She lifted her lashes, taking as long as she could before she had to meet his gaze. Felt a bit of a jolt when she did, a strange mix of cold and hot shivering through her. She nodded her answer, cause her voice caught in her throat and she wasn't sure it would come out low enough for the boy she was supposed to be. Another cough from her Pa got her to hold the book out for the stranger's inspection. He took it, keeping her gaze captive during the exchange, his hand brushing hers long enough to send another round of shivers through her. A relief when the gaze shifted from her to the book, though not enough to unclog her throat.

"*The Steam House.* Interesting choice."

What did he mean by that? It was sure the right choice for the boy she was supposed to be. Lucky she liked everything Verne wrote, wanted to write something like it, but with a griffin. Pa thought it made her look more like a boy to have a book in hand, boosted her peakedness, too.

The gaze lifted, slow like, and grabbed hers again. Made her want to run, though she couldn't say if it was away or—he couldn't *know*, could he? The high desert night was chilly, but Ani felt heat storm her cheeks and was glad for the darkness that hid most of the blush. Boys didn't blush, did they? Truth was, she didn't know as much as she should about boys or girls. When they hit a town she had to go into her act. Even after the healing, folks tended to keep their distance, just in case.

Beyond the stranger, the first ghost light appeared, down toward the Chinati's. Didn't take it long to split into two, then into four. Showing some color this year. Felt the stranger's gaze pulling at her own, so she pointed at them to distract him, or maybe she needed it. The way he looked at her, made her feel odd, kind of discontented with how things were, how they had to be. How they'd always be? Sad mingled with discontented at that thought.

By the time he looked, there were twelve in the sky. The stranger's brows arched just a bit. "The Marfa lights. So that's what they look like."

Almost seemed he spoke to himself, but Pa grabbed the opening anyway, did some expounding on the differences they'd observed their last three years in the area, on how they didn't always show up in the same place. Her Pa did like spectacle, and so, it seemed, did the ghost lights, as they began to scoot around. They didn't always, and this was her first time to see color, though the locals had told them it could happen.

The stranger rose, moved away from the fire, taking her book with him. Ani bit her lip, fighting the urge to go get it, when she knew she should keep her distance from the stranger. *I want to finish the chapter* is what she told herself when she scrambled to her feet, fighting—for the first time in a long time—to keep the girl from her walk as she eased in beside him.

Be a good thing when they reached Marfa and parted company. *A good thing*, she repeated, not sure why she felt the need.

This was the first time she'd stood this close, could compare his height with hers. Didn't know why the ways they were different felt kinda right, kinda nice even. He was a border ruffian and dangerous to boot. But she'd lived safe for so long, it felt like life had passed her by. Been put on the shelf before she had a chance to be off it—

"Have you ever followed them to their source?" The stranger shifted to look at Pa, the movement putting a bit more distance between them, though Ani caught a glancing blow as his gaze passed her on its way to Pa's.

Pa rose and came to stand next to her. "Some have tried."

Ani heard the change in his voice, half amused at the notion of chasing lights, half tinged with a bit of longing to try it.

"As a man of science, I would, of course, be able to unravel the mystery, if I didn't have responsibilities to those unfortunate sick who need the healing that I bring to this blighted region."

Translation: *he was tired, the night was cold, and the fire helped a mite to ease the ache in his bones from the wagon's jolting.*

Pa moved further from the circle of light cast by their fire, as if the ghost lights drew him. Before she could stop it, Ani sent a huffed look the stranger's way. If they started chasing the ghost lights, they'd most likely come in at the little end of the horn this winter. Though, she half glanced at the lights, they did kind of seem to beckon. Almost teasing-like.

"I think I might just take a ride that way," the stranger said, though it sounded like he was talking to himself again.

She felt a pain in her chest at the thought of him leaving. And a good thing, she reminded herself, rubbing the pain spot.

His gaze slanted her way, catching her at it. "Want to ride along?"

Shock, longing, and a desire to hide widened her eyes and muted her voice again.

"Boy would like that." Pa's words didn't help her speaking problem any. "You wouldn't mind a little adventure on this fine night, would you? See the elephant, so to speak?"

He wanted her to go with the stranger? Then she figured it out. Didn't want the stranger finding out anything Pa couldn't. If they discovered something, he could take credit later. She half sighed as that odd feeling welled up in her chest again. She had seen the elephant more than she liked with Pa, but—and this was the odd part—seeing it seemed a mite appealing with the stranger at her side. Or maybe she was just weary with being safe. Be better if the elephant turned out to be a griffin though.

～

"You can take Delphine," Everly said.

He meant the horse—the man formerly known as Tobias Smith presumed—since he'd already agreed to let his daughter ride off into the night with a stranger.

"Joe" hadn't meant to ask the question, then told himself it was a test, since the words were out there and couldn't be taken back—cause he was ninety-nine-point-nine percent sure the boy was a girl. One thing he'd got right was Everly's total lack of common sense, which was why he shouldn't have asked the question. Clear as day Everly didn't want to go racketing around in the dark, but didn't mind if the girl rode along, just in case there was something to find.

"Joe" wanted to shake his head or shake them both—not feel a spurt of pleasure at the thought of spending time with the girl. He hadn't been thinking right since he'd spotted the medicine show wagon leaving Alpine and heading in the direction of Paisano Pass. He'd figured he'd pause just long enough for courtesy and then ride on by. He was a mite sensitive about grifters after getting caught in the net of one of the worst in several galaxies. And then Everly's "son" lifted her chin and he caught sight of those big, blue eyes. His polite refusal turned into a yes that dismayed her almost as much as it did him.

Do no harm was the creed he lived by in this place, in this time—nothing in the creed about rescuing a damsel in distress, in particular a damsel who didn't seem to know she was in distress.

The girl was the opposite of Olivia, which was a relief. A grey-hound lean, strawberry blonde who was not that good at being a boy and who had, at first, looked to be a bit on the cowed side. And then she set her chin his way and he knew that all the life hadn't been stamped out of her. That the traces of red in her hair weren't for show. The hint of defiance might have reminded him of Olivia—and sent him on his way—but where Olivia's eyes had dismissed him with more than a hint of scorn, this waif's...didn't. She was curious like a woman about him but—and this wasn't a surprise since she'd been a boy a while—she didn't have a clue what to do about it.

He felt some sympathy for her. And more for himself. He'd thought he was done with women. Seemed he wasn't, quite, but he was bad news for her or any woman, which was why he usually kept his distance. *Do no harm.* Of course, her father was worse than bad news—if he'd done the math right on how long Everly had had the girl traveling about being a boy. He'd shared their life story the first night, some of which might have been the truth, all about *his* broken heart and taking to the road to forget.

"Joe" knew more than he wanted to about broken hearts, and Everly's wasn't *that* broke. Might be a bit dented, but Everly was too in love with himself for real grief. If he'd been half the man he should have been, he'd have sucked it up for his daughter, given her the life she was supposed to have. Not this.

No place for a woman with only one crazy old man as protection, but it wasn't a bad place for a man alone, one who needed to forget. The Paisano Plateau had a sort of raw, bleak beauty that matched the raw, bleak places inside him. During the day, the sky was as blue as the girl's eyes, at night a blanket of stars lay over the land, giving the illusion of safety, of being invisible. As if to belie the thought, a coyote loosed a long, lonesome howl in the distance.

Empty had a whole new meaning in a place like this.

He studied the ghost lights, torn about his reason for riding this way.

He'd been down by the Rio Grande, a sentimental trip he shouldn't have taken, when he heard someone talking about the ghost lights outside Marfa. He'd recalled wondering about them when he'd been here in the 1940's. He knew that when large time events happened, traces of the disruptions could show up in odd ways any where and sometimes any *when.* Were these lights the traces of time cleaning up after that intergalactic grifter he wanted to forget or remnants of the disruption that took him to the 1940's?

He'd had a chance to get back to his own galaxy, though no way to make it to his own time, so he'd passed on it, thinking here would do. Less chance of running into someone he'd pissed off. He knew it fairly well, since he'd been in and out of it more than was right. And truth was, the shorter life spans of this time had some appeal to someone whose life had been unnaturally stretched by the time travel. Didn't want to live that long with his memories of what he'd lost, what he'd done against his will. He might have gone looking for trouble that would speed that demise when he headed for Texas. And then he found himself near the last place he'd seen Olivia—knowing that she was just ahead of him in time somewhere—and well, he knew it had been a mistake to stay here.

You can't have what was never yours.

It was the one thing he'd done right. It gave him a little peace knowing that. That he'd cared enough to let her go. Didn't much matter *when* he went after this, or where, as long as it was far from the temptation to look her up...unless...his gaze slanted back to the girl saddling her mount. Could rescuing a damsel in distress rescue him? His mind called him delusional, but his gut said...maybe...

Everly fussed around both horse and girl, giving the illusion of helping without doing it. "You'll be back by sunrise," he directed.

Had he processed the fact he planned to send his daughter off with a man he'd known for only three days?

"Of course, Pa." Her voice was low, pitched to be plausible for a boy, a fact the vulnerable nape of her neck disputed. Strands of blond hair, lifted by the breeze, caressed skin turned to milk in the moonlight.

"I'll look after the...boy." Hard to get that word out when she slung a long leg over her horse, settled into the saddle with an instinctive, feminine wriggle.

She slanted a look at him that seemed to say she could take care of herself and he'd best not forget it. He almost smiled. Couldn't remember the last time he'd smiled, let alone almost smiled. She had guts, which brought him full circle to—she deserved better.

He might not be what most would term better, but looking around this place? He kicked his horse into a slow jog down the trail after hers. He was all there was.

∼

They rode in silence, passing through deep shadow, before emerging into almost bright-as-day moonlight as the horses picked a path through a dry wash in the general direction of the moving lights. When they were distant enough from the camp that Everly couldn't hear them, "Joe" kicked his horse to a jog that put him next to the girl. Felt her struggle against looking, waited until she gave in, before he spoke.

"You shouldn't be out here."

That lifted her chin and her brows. "And where should I be?"

She might have meant to sound defiant or even indifferent. She didn't manage either. The tone did edge into provocative. Seemed to be some female left in there.

"Back East. Somewhere safer, for sure." She opened her mouth to object, so he cut in, "You're not a boy."

She looked more resigned than surprised, though she shot back quick enough, "And you're not a Joe."

He grinned, surprising them both. "True enough. How did you—"

"You look *nothing* like a Joe."

She tried to be irate but failed at that, too, when a grin twitched the edges of a mouth that looked like it needed kissing. As if she felt his interest in getting up close and personal with her mouth, the lower lip pouted an invitation that her brain might not recognize as one. Maybe he should pass on the ghost lights and where they might take him—but if they turned back now they wouldn't be alone. Going forward seemed the better option for now and truth was, the chances of the ghost lights doing anything but taunting him with false hope were slim.

"What do I look like?" It was an opening she could use to slay him if she were inclined that way, but if she didn't, maybe she'd come up with a name he could live with. He'd tried out a bunch of them since he left Smith behind with the broken remains of the crate he'd landed in. And Galfrioni? Well, it might have worked in another time, another galaxy, but here? It would just get him shot.

That brought her big-eyed gaze full bore his way. She took her time, studying him from top to bottom, seemed like she enjoyed the looking because she sure didn't hurry either direction. Her head tilted the other direction and she did the top-to-toe examination again, maybe even slower than before. He liked that she didn't hurry, found it an encouraging development. Another thing he could like about this time, or at least this place in this time, courting could happen as fast as it needed to. If she didn't want him, he could find out and move on with only his pride dented a little this time. Her gaze found his and something stirred in the ashes of his heart. Yeah, he needed to move fast. Didn't need to have it cracked twice, that was for sure.

"Chance. You look like a Chance."

She hadn't gone for the jugular, another encouraging development. The name fit better than his boots—or his grandiose Garradian moniker—and the words with the name were apt, too, though she didn't know it yet. He was her chance and she, well, she might be his chance, too.

"Clever—" He stopped as he realized, "Your Pa never said your name."

She might have hesitated, or just paused to give him a look.

"Analisse." She hid shy in a very female sniff, her cute little nose lifting a bit, but not so much she lost sight of him. "I suppose you don't use your real name because you're wanted by the law."

Didn't sound like it bothered her. He grinned again. A new record. "Not by the law—" In this time, anyway. "Just...private."

"Pa says the same thing—after he shares our life story with everyone who comes by." Her tone hovered between rueful and annoyed.

"Analisse. I like it." It suited who she should be.

"My Ma used to call me Ani." She eased it out like it was information, not an offer, though she might be persuaded otherwise.

"Ani." He'd never been one for a lot of persuading, continued before she could pretend to object, "If you could go anywhere you wanted, where would it be?" Maybe he assumed facts not in evidence. Maybe she liked the life, liked being a boy. He could adapt to a lot of things, but wasn't sure about a traveling medicine show, though—she shifted giving him a glimpse of her shape as the round circle of the moon backlit her—there'd be compensations.

"Anywhere?" Her gaze turned dreamy in the moonlight. "I'd probably go home. Put on a dress, see if I could stand it."

Her smile was unexpected, mischievous and loaded with charm. Animated her face from fine to beautiful. Had she been given the chance, she'd have had no trouble snaring a husband.

The wind went from merely persistent to a hearty gust. Delphine whinnied a bit and tried to turn off the trail toward what looked like a tumble of rocks.

Ani held her mount in, though she didn't turn her back to the trail. "Probably a *tinaja* close by. We can water the horses there."

It was a chance to talk, to find out what she wanted from life. He felt his horse shift under him, trying to turn, too. He let the animal have his head, pondered doing the same for himself. *Do no harm.* What if he could do some good for both of them?

≈

Moonlight bathed the rocky enclosure, deepening the shadows, though the *tinaja* gleamed where it formed a rock pool. She started to dismount, not averse to taking a drink, too, but Chance was there next to her, his big hands circling her waist and lifting her clear of Delphine like she was a baby or something.

A brief sense of soaring through the cool air didn't end when she landed at his feet. With the horse at her back, the big man fencing her in, she should have felt worried, scared even. They were so close she almost brushed against him when she breathed. Not that she could breathe. All of her felt caught, not just by the hands at her waist, but by emotion welling up from a place so deep inside, she hadn't known it was there. Was this how her Ma felt about her Pa? This wild, reckless yearning that dried her throat and sent her heart a racing? She should have been terrified. An odd time to realize this was the safest she'd felt since Ma passed.

His hand, his big man hand, drifted up to brush against her cheek, his touch light—though the skin had been roughened by work—and mighty gentle. Was this what it meant, to take the rough with the smooth?

"Have you ever been kissed, Ani?"

She shook her head. No reason to lie. He had to know she hadn't. His hand slid across her face, across skin that heated at the touch, and around the back of her head, pushing her cap off on the way, then it found purchase on the back of her neck, his fingers threading into her hair, turning her soft like mush. She'd have dropped at his feet, but the hand at her waist kept her up. Gentle pressure changed the angle of her head, perhaps as a prelude to a kiss, because a man didn't ask unless he meant to do, did he?

She should stop him. She may not know much, but she knew that. Only...she was twenty-eight years old. A spinster who'd never been kissed. So she waited, hoping, still not breathing, as his mouth made a slow approach. Guess he wanted her to know she could stop him anytime she wanted. She wanted all right, she wanted for him not to stop, and she wanted something she didn't know how to name, something that twisted her insides in a way that felt sort of good, sort of scary.

The first touch of his mouth against hers was gentle, like his hand had been. Felt like he tasted, maybe explored a bit, then firmed. Rough and smooth again. Felt the quiver of it in her stomach and right down to her toes. She sighed into it, into him, but didn't know how to tell him she needed more—

His other arm slid all the way around her back, drawing her in against the hard wall of his man body, one so different from hers. She'd known men were different, but she hadn't known how different until she relaxed against him. He didn't push or force, just...invited her in. She accepted, pushing up on her toes, her hands inching around his back in tentative exploration. Muscles rippled under her hands, the skin warm through his shirt.

Something strange and scary and wonderful spiraled up and up inside her, like setting a horse free on a long stretch of desert. Faster and faster and then, slowly at first, he reined them in, though they were both still breathing faster when he lifted his head. She'd have died on the spot if he'd stepped back, but he didn't. He held her like he knew she needed it.

A shudder lanced through him. Did she do that to him? She explored the line of a muscle on his back and he shuddered again. She smiled at the power of it. "Now I've been kissed."

"You're long overdue."

She leaned back, glared at him. "Is that why you did it? Cause you felt sorry for me?"

"Sorry for you? Feel sorry for me. This is the second time I've had my brains scrambled by a woman."

Ani felt a pang, one not as nice as the other feelings. "Who was she?" Did he love her? Did she care? Not clear. It was the coming in second that stung, though what did she expect? A declaration of marriage? She was a spinster in boy clothes. Helped some to know she'd scrambled his brains.

He eased away some more, rubbed his hand across his hair, looking almost flustered. She felt cold. Had she always been cold and not known it? She leaned against Delphine, feeling the need for something at her back.

"Someone from my past. My distant past." He rubbed his face now. "Can't believe I brought her up. Even I know that's lame."

Lame? Odd, but she got the meaning, felt her power—her female power—to her toes. Ma had told her women had it. She thought she didn't get any. Didn't mind being wrong. He looked almost vulnerable, or maybe just worried, when he shifted, spilling some moonlight across one side of his face. He seemed to gather himself in, maybe braced a bit. Did he think she'd make a scene because he kissed her?

"I should have waited, but you looked fine in the moonlight, Ani." He half reached out to her, stopped. "Meant to wait and ask before I kissed you. If you said yes, I mean." He stopped, rubbed his face again and looked at her, with lots of sober in it. "You deserve better than what your Pa's given you. You deserve better than me, but I seem to be it. This place, you know people make up their minds fast, because there isn't much time, and your choices are limited. You don't have to decide now, but I'm declaring so you can think about it until we get to Marfa. Figure out what you want. Decide if you want different from what you have."

Her first proposal. At least, "You're offering to marry me?" He nodded. So it was her first. Probably her last. He was right, only offer she was likely to get out here or anywhere. She saw her Pa clear enough to know he was not going to do what was best for her, but she hadn't had a choice. Until now. "I'm twenty-eight." Her chin lifted. Not many men would take on a woman her age, lessen they had kids that needed a Ma.

He didn't look away or flinch. Just nodded like it didn't matter. "I'll deal fairly with you, I give you my word."

It was sudden, but she'd seen faster courtships wandering around the west, a few after several doses of Pa's elixir. At least he wasn't drunk. Out here, she'd had to learn to judge fast, and hopefully judge fair. See real, as her Ma had said. Hard to know if she saw him as he was, with her heart pounding, no way to know unless she took a chance. She could continue with her Pa, with how things were, continue going nowhere until Pa passed and she had nothing or she could take a chance. Almost like his name was the answer. *Take a Chance.*

"Your word's fine." She swallowed dry, wishing she'd had time to drink some water, too, so she'd sound less scared. "I'd be pleased to accept." The moment the words were out, she wanted to call them back—and then he smiled, some tenderness in it, and she didn't want to call them back. She wanted another kiss, though she held out her hand to shake on what felt like a bargain.

He took the hand, leaned close, his mouth briefly touching hers. Too briefly. Maybe she looked disappointed. "Better not kiss too much until we tie the knot. You're a serious temptation, Ani. I'm grateful for your trust. Wouldn't want to abuse it."

A temptation? The words were fine, the way he said them better than fine.

"I'll ask your Pa when we get back. Like to do it when we get to Marfa, if that's acceptable."

"No reason to wait."

His eyes glittered out of the dark, and she knew, though she didn't know how, that he wanted her. Not that she was clear on what that meant, without a Ma to explain things, but she felt it coming from him. Neither had had time to fall in love, and maybe they never would, but wanting was, she hoped, the prelude to being friends at least. She could use a friend, especially one who thought she deserved better.

Off to their right, the ghost lights flashed, or maybe it was a storm starting up in the distance. The ghost lights didn't usually flash like that. The air crackled like a storm, but out here that didn't always mean rain was coming. Sometimes the lightning came without the rain, as if taunting them with the promise of water it had no intention of delivering. If there was rain, could make the washes at risk of flash flooding. They should probably move out of this draw. Another surge of something, something new in the air made Chance stiffen like the horses when a coyote was near. Lightning flashed, close and bright enough to blind her for a few seconds and when she could see again, she saw something on the rise, something that hadn't been there before, something that gleamed like metal and had two red circles where eyes might be.

"What's that?" She shifted closer to Chance, as unease made a cold path down her back.

He turned—felt like he turned to stone next to her. "It's an automaton."

～

Chance stared at the automaton, as his focus shifted from romance to defense in the space between one breath and another. Not for the first time, he missed his ray-based weapon. It could be taken down with his Colt .45, if all six shots hit their mark—tough to do in this light—and that assumed it was alone. He'd have to let it get closer, though it was odd it hadn't moved. Maybe it hadn't seen them yet. Had to have been a reality shift. Not just the 'ton had changed. The moon was lower and the temperature was higher.

He needed to get Ani safe, but how? He couldn't send her back to her Pa. He might not be where they left him, if he existed in this reality. He looked down toward the valley. The ghost lights had settled some, and twinkling in the distance were fixed lights that had to be Marfa. Once she got clear of the foothills, it was a straight, fairly easy ride across the desert. She could be there by morning.

He bent and grabbed her cap—she'd need it when the sun rose—pulled out a roll of money and shoved both into her hands.

"Chance—" She began, though she had sense enough to keep her voice down.

Before she could finish, he lifted her onto Delphine's back, handed her the reins. "That's our stake, Ani. Keep it safe until I come. Ride for Marfa."

"My Pa—"

"We're not where we were. The lights, they did something to time. He could be anywhere. Ride for Marfa. Check into the Paisano Hotel." If it existed in this reality. "I'll follow you there when I'm sure its safe." *If I can.*

Maybe she sensed the qualifier, maybe that's what distracted her from the rest of what he'd said. When she had time to consider it, what would she make of it?

"I've been more boy than girl. I can help."

The words warmed him. "This creature isn't something you should mess with. Ride to safety. Do this for me, please." He had to be honest. "If I don't come in a couple of days use the money to go home. To live your life. Let your Pa live his. Just...live. Be happy." He pulled her down, pressed a hard kiss on her mouth, then stepped back. He glanced back, but the 'ton hadn't moved. He almost straddled his horse to go with her, but if it were after him, he'd suck her into his nightmare. He had to be sure this wasn't about him. "Trust me."

After a pause, she nodded, though with obvious reluctance. "Make sure you come. I'd like fine to be your wife, Chance." She stuffed the money down her shirt, pulled on her cap, turned herself and her mount in the direction of Marfa, and kicked her horse away from the 'ton, toward the valley. Too soon the darkness swallowed the sight of her. He secured his horse, close to water and food, then turned back to the 'ton, from the temptation to ride after her. He would follow her when it was safe or die here. He was not going back into hell. It hadn't moved, though the eyes still glowed red. The ghost lights were quiet, too. No way to know if the pulsing was regular or not, or what would happen to him, to Ani, if they pulsed again. He shifted sideways, moving at an angle from the 'ton, trying to feel a change coming or sense this reality going unstable, a skill he'd learned passing through a bunch of them, as he scrambled over the tumble of rocks around the *tinaja*. If the 'ton had motion sensing capability, it wasn't working.

He clambered over the last fall of rock, then ghosted down the small wash, choosing an angle that would bring him behind the automaton at what he hoped was a safe distance. It stood in full moonlight on the rise, so he'd know if it moved—Chance stopped. Something odd about its head. Curious, he eased closer, pausing at intervals in case it reacted—the back of the automaton's head was open, a tangle of wires trailing out the opening.

What the—he climbed up on a tumble of rocks next to it, coming at it from the side just in time to see the eyes pulse bright, fade, pulse again, then fade to dark. He moved in, walked around it, still careful, but almost certain it was disabled. Questions swirled in his head, but did he care about the how and why? He could follow Ani—his thoughts fragmented again.

An airship.

Silent like the automaton, not even a hiss of steam coming from it, it squatted on the trail they'd passed on their way to the *tinaja*. He frowned. Airships existed in many realities, but as far as he knew, automatons existed only in one place—and in fiction. If trouble was incoming from his past—well his past was actually his future—he didn't want to lead it to Ani. The deep silence made his senses twitch with all kinds of warnings he knew better than to ignore.

Soundless, Colt .45 ready, he approached the silent airship, circled it twice before slipping aboard. He paused at the prow to process the quiet, letting his instincts lead. The envelope creaked as a small breeze whispered the length, but nothing else broke the silence. So why did he sense he wasn't alone?

Could be getting paranoid, though he had good reasons for it.

He used the engine house to cover his back as he drifted along the length. It wasn't exactly like the others he'd seen. This one was longer, seemed to have some seating—the feel of a cold barrel against the back of his head confirmed his gut, though he'd have preferred to find out he was right from the other end of the weapon.

~

Ani spent the first hour of the ride trying hard not to think about what she'd seen, what Chance had said. But as the moon climbed—again—not thinking got harder and harder to manage.

We're not where we were. The lights, they did something to time.

She'd write him off as crazy, but for the moon. And the feel of the night air, it was different from how it had been when they left the camp. And that thing. And the way it had felt before things...changed.

Could be dreaming, which would be a pity, cause then she wouldn't have her first ever proposal. Or the faint hope of an actual wedding. She touched her chest, where she'd shoved the bills into the corset that helped flatten her chest. The thought of it did help—if it were real. It felt real. Could she dream—or even imagine a kiss like that? Warmed her up nice even now, just thinking about that kiss. Course, thinking about that thing killed warm. If she was dreaming, it was a powerful clear dream. Didn't seem to be waking up if she were asleep.

Should probably worry more about Pa, but he hadn't exactly put himself out for her. He'd sent her off into the night with Chance and then most likely gone to sleep—after imbibing some of his elixir for his aches and pains. She'd wait the couple of days for Chance, but if he didn't show, if he couldn't show, she'd take the chance he'd offered and take the train east. Pa might waste a few days looking for her, but then he'd make his way to Marfa. She'd want to be gone before he got there. Be better for her if his "son" was lost in the desert.

Instead of the hotel, she'd go to Angelica. She'd been kind to them last year, might even suspect Ani was a girl. Could help her get some proper clothes. Pa'd never suspect that. Angelica could take a note to the hotel for Chance, tell him where to find her. Or her Roberto could. They both worked at the hotel, though Roberto dreamed of working for the railroad. He did like steam engines and such. Be easy for either of them to leave the note in a way that no one would know where it came from, just in case Pa got the notion to ask a few questions. Was it wrong to hope Chance did come? Cause she did, she hoped something fierce.

Hope. Been a long time since she'd felt it.

~

The angle of the barrel, the feel of the air, told Chance the assailant was above him, crouched on the steering platform. An awkward angle. He should have kept his distance.

"Give me a good reason not to pull the trigger right now." The voice was familiar—and not.

Ani? Made sense there'd be another of her in a new reality, though it always felt strange when it happened, stranger now that he was engaged to his version. He made his turn with less than the lethal force he'd originally planned, knocking the barrel up and pulling her down from her perch where she hung in his hold, struggling like a wild thing.

"Let me go!"

Didn't see the point of holding her when he had her gun, so he did. She staggered a few feet, then faced him, all of her on defense. This Ani wore a dress and her hair had probably been up before he grabbed her. Now it hung to one side in an untidy, blonde mass. So this was how his Ani would look in a dress, as a woman. Had a few more curves than his—or Ani'd done something to minimize them. The idea intrigued—and gave him another reason to survive and make it to Marfa to claim his bride.

"I'm not going back!"

That got his mind back in the moment. "Back? To Marfa?"

"Where else? You can tell your boss I'm not marrying him no matter what he does!"

The hairs on the back of his neck lifted. There'd been no sign of any man in Ani's life in the other reality, but then she'd been dressed as a boy. "Where's your Pa?"

"My *Pa?*" Her brows rose. "My *father* is, well, he's in Marfa and, as you well know, perfectly happy to let me pay his gambling debts."

Now the hairs went on high alert. "Who is this boss?" He smelled trouble incoming. Her brows arched higher. "Let's pretend I have no idea what you're talking about."

She huffed out a sigh, half glanced around like she expected someone. "Doc Smith, of course. He runs Marfa since he got control of the 'tons."

Smith. He tried not to jerk at the name. It was a common one on Earth. Didn't mean it was his Smith. Or even the ancestor of his Smith. But he *was* someone willing to force a woman into marriage.

And he'd just sent Ani—this one's twin—right to him.

Chance opened his mouth to tell this version of Analisse that he had to leave, but they both heard the sound of a horse approaching at a fair pace. She tensed and he for sure tensed. Was this his Ani returning or the person Analisse expected?

"Analisse?" It sounded like Everly. Chance shifted into the shadows.

Her shoulders slumped a bit, but her chin set in a way that reminded him of his Ani. "Please—" She cut off the rest of what she'd intended to ask, when Everly rode into sight and pulled his horse to a stop.

"This was a foolish move, girl. All you've done is put Roberto in danger, too."

"What do you mean?" She tried to sound tough, but her voice quivered.

"He's not coming. Doc knows about him. Had him arrested. He's going to hang him in the morning if you don't come back."

"If I don't marry him, you mean."

Everly shifted and looked away.

"He'll kill him if you do marry him," Chance said, stepping out of the shadows weapons ready. Didn't matter if this was his Smith or a version, anyone who forced marriage on a woman wouldn't keep his word.

Everly jumped, making his horse skitter sideways.

"Do you think I don't know that," she snapped, shoving her hair back. "But I have to try—"

"That's wise—"

"I can help," Chance cut Everly off. If he was in the business of rescuing damsels, he couldn't draw the line at just one, particularly when he suspected this one and had put his in the cross hairs of her problem.

"Why would you help us?"

"You remind me of someone I know." If he were lucky, he'd save both damsels and settle a score, maybe get to be the hero instead of the bad guy.

Hope kept her upright in the saddle for the long, silent ride through the night. The ghost lights, the arrangement of the mountains, and the lights from the Marfa settlement kept her on course until she ran on to the railroad tracks. She followed them after that, half dozing in the saddle. She saw the windmills first, helped by the rim of sun topping the mountains at her back. Ani reined in Delphine and considered. The one thing she couldn't do was ride the horse into town. Pa'd know his own horse, probably better than he knew his daughter. She slipped to the ground, took her canteen and had a drink, tied it back to the saddle. She resisted the urge to loop the reins around the saddle horn, instead let them trail and slapped Delphine on the backside. Felt almost put upon when the horse trotted off without a backward look. Ani angled away from the tracks now, heading for the side of town where Angelica lived.

We're not where we were. The lights, they did something to time.

The feeling of danger she'd sensed in the wash, it rose again, chilling her insides. What if Angelica wasn't here? Or was that different, too?

She pulled the cap down so it shadowed her face, slowed her walk as she passed the first of the windmills that pulled water from the ground for the town. There were some signs of stirring, of day's beginning for some folks. She passed into the shadow cast by the first adobe, moving quiet as she knew how, though trying not to look like she was creeping or anything.

The adobes were closer together here, made it easier to stay hid. She was glad for those shadows, though she didn't know why. Pa would tell her that her imagination was getting the better of her. And maybe it was, but this time Marfa didn't feel as peaceful-like. The few people she glimpsed looked sullen and fearful. She stopped, leaned against a corner like she had nothing better to do and studied the adobe that should be Angelica's, then the area around it. Saw someone lurking in the shadows across from it. Red eyes gleamed out of those shadows.

It's an automaton.

Whatever an automaton was, it had turned Chance from lover to hunter in the time it took her to blink. Heard a grinding noise—and the thing moved into the light. It wore the clothes of a cowboy jeans, cotton shirt, chaps, hat and guns, all dark and kind of sinister looking. Moved with a jerky precision that should have been silly, but wasn't. It was like he was a copy of the hired guns they'd run into every now and again—run ins that always ended with Pa giving them some of their earnings and free samples of elixir. Pa called it the cost of doing business where the arm of the law didn't reach, buying protection. Pa didn't like buying anything that didn't earn him a profit but a gun to the head was mighty persuasive.

He approached the door to Angelica's hut, banged it once, then again. It swung open and she stood in the opening, her hands on her hips. She looked the same, brown skinned, her dark hair twisted into a knot on the back of her head, her dark eyes flashing defiance, though the thing topped her by a considerable bit.

It didn't speak. Did gesture for her to come out. She pulled her shawl more tightly around her, tossed her head, then stalked out, slamming the door behind her. She set off in the direction of the courthouse, the main street of Marfa, her skirts swishing with her anger, that thing clunking behind her. There was a chugging, like a train incoming, but it came from above. A shadow passed overhead, drawing her gaze. Above her, a strange flying machine passed by, no, several of them, like a flying train, only with strange bloated tops and their bows like ships, plumes of smoke streaming back from each of them, not just the lead one. It turned in the direction of the train depot.

We're not where we were. The lights, they did something to time.

After a brief hesitation, Ani followed, not sure why she felt the need, because she wanted to flee, not just Marfa, but to Chance, back to the *tinaja*, back to where she belonged.

Something hung over the settlement, hung thick over it, something not happy or good. And with the rising sun, came the sounds of a commotion of some kind, but it wasn't until she crept close to the square that she saw the gallows. She did not want to see a hanging. Giving in to the urge to flee, she turned, just as more dark shadows fell across her. Only this time, it wasn't a flying train, but two of the automatons.

~

"How did you take down the 'ton?" Chance asked Miss Everly, raising his voice to be heard over the chug of the airship engine. Calling her that helped separate her from his Ani—and she'd insisted on it, much to his amusement. Clearly her life had been different from Ani's, though her father was still a nightmare, since he was willing to force her into marriage to settle a gambling debt.

They'd tied him up in the engine room, and then launched the airship, since they needed to reach Marfa before dawn. Thankfully this one traveled at a good speed. They should reach Marfa shortly after Ani, hopefully in time to keep her from being mistaken for Miss Everly. She'd briefed him on the layout of the town and the nature of the opposition. A 'ton outlaw gang was a new twist.

"Roberto told me about the flaw in the design. Doc doesn't know about it, or he'd have killed Roberto before now."

"Flaw?" Flaws were good. Flaws in automatons even better.

"The latch on the back of their heads is weak. You just bang it real hard, it opens, then all you need to do is grab a handful of wires and pull. The trick is reaching the head, cause they're tall and if you don't get it right the first time, well, the 'ton has time to turn around. I stood on a rock and just banged him as he went by, but that 'ton isn't too bright. My father bought it before Doc came or he'd not have had it. Now no one gets a 'ton unless Doc says so."

This one talked a bit more than his Ani, her accent more refined.

"Doc Smith." Chance hesitated, but he'd put the question off, not sure he wanted to know. Now he needed to know. "Is he a big man? Ugly? Compelling eyes and plumy voice?"

"I thought you said you hadn't met him?" She started to puff up again.

"I was hoping it wasn't the same man." Or hoping it was? He needed to be careful, keep his thoughts cool, focused. If he let his anger loose, his longing for revenge off the leash—could be bad for Ani. This was a rescue mission. And if he got a chance for some closure, well, he wouldn't say no.

She subsided some, though retained an air of suspicion. He mulled telling her more, but she wouldn't believe him. He didn't believe this most of the time and he'd lived it.

"There it is," she said, her voice tightening with tension.

The sun was more than a bit above the mountains behind them, the light creeping across the desert toward Marfa. Still too murky to spot Ani. Hopefully she'd made it to the hotel by now. Above the settlement, an airship train chugged toward what was supposed to be a train depot. It was an odd sight, even factoring in all the odd he'd seen. Looked like they'd connected about ten airships, as if the notion of a train persisted but with a twist. It was fortuitous though. He steered them toward the rear, not coming down until they'd cleared the windmills that provided water for Marfa, and followed it in, using it to get the lay of the land below.

"They're prepping the gallows." Her voice broke a bit. She looked at him, hope and despair warring for supremacy in her eyes. "Looks like he's got all his 'tons on duty, too."

Chance eased their airship down a short piece from the depot and shut the engine off. "If you told folks how to take down the 'tons, would they do it?" It would be a good diversion and even the odds a bit. "Anyone you can trust to fight back?"

"Everyone hates him, even the men who'd usually help him, since he replaced them with 'tons. Don't have to pay them, you see." She frowned. "Roberto's got friends. If they knew they could take on the 'tons and win," she paused, then nodded with determination, "whole town would be against him."

"Then go, talk to them. Stay out of sight as much as possible. Here," He pulled off his long coat and tossed it at her. "Cover up or you won't make it four feet."

"What are you going to do?" she asked, as she pulled on the coat, tucking her wayward hair under the collar.

He'd check at the hotel for Ani, but, "Best way to kill a snake is to lop its head off."

"You're going to take on Doc?" She sounded incredulous. "Good luck with that." Her look said *nice knowing you* as she went over the side like a pro.

"Miss Everly?" She looked back, her brows raised. "I'll need that diversion before they start the hanging." She paled but nodded and disappeared into the shadows by the depot.

If Ani was safe at the hotel, he put their future at risk with this move on Smith. It was a tough gig, being the good guy. And it was a bad time to remember that every time he'd taken on Smith, he'd lost.

A night that started with her first proposal should not have concluded by getting snatched by automatons, though at least she kinda knew what they were now. Kinda. The two metal men lifted her feet off the ground and swept her forward, right into the people milling around the gallows like a bunch of cowed ghouls. While she'd like to believe it was a bad dream, the unforgiving grip of their metal hands felt too real. And she didn't seem able to wake up, though that didn't stop her trying.

The crowd—funny how a gallows attracted the whole boodle even in a little town like Marfa—parted at their approach, all of them avoiding looking directly at her. Some she recognized from previous years, some she didn't. She'd liked to blame them for ignoring her plight but the automatons were big. They were metal. They had guns. She'd have probably looked away, too. The metal men most likely explained why no one looked happy and a lot of them looked scared. Kind of seemed like they'd been herded to the square for the hanging, now that she considered it. But who was supposed to swing?

Didn't seem to be an obvious candidate, when she looked around, as much as she could what with the jarring gait of the metal men rattling her teeth. At the end of town, the big courthouse cast a long shadow down the road. Churches weren't where they'd been, looked gone in fact, and there was a big saloon where the mercantile had been. Fancy women in their bedclothes leaned on the gaudy balcony railings. No surprise it housed a bawdy house, but the fancy women weren't usually so bold. And the men, instead of looking interested, well, they all stared at the courthouse with what she might call a fair bit of hatred at the man waiting there.

He stood on the steps watching her and the automatons approach, clear that he thought he was a big bug. He didn't look happy, but he didn't look unhappy neither. He wore a suit and tie, unlike most of the men gathered about, and stooped a bit around the shoulders, kinda like a vulture, now that she considered it. Had a fine mustache, the only fine thing about him. Rest of him was downright ugly. Eyes sunk back under bushy brows, beak of a nose and thin cruel mouth. He stood, one booted foot slightly forward, one thumb stuck in a pocket, the other hand holding a timepiece. When he saw her, his brows rose like he was trying to look surprised. He tucked the watch away and smiled. It was ugly, too.

"How prompt you are, my dear Analisse. I might almost call you an eager bride, despite," his gaze traversed her person in a disconcerting manner, "the wardrobe adjustments."

Bride? She'd kinda worried she was for the gallows. Not a relief to be wrong. She might not know much, but she did know a Bad Egg when she saw him. She'd seen his ilk in their travels, though this was the first time she'd attracted the attention of one.

"A new look for you, though please don't take it as a complaint. It's charmingly practical choice for your little excursion." His voice was finer than his face, but threaded through with evil. "And I can get used to the hair until it grows back."

Ani blinked. Silence had served her well in the past, so she kept mum and waited. He knew her name, but she didn't know his, a mite disconcerting. He signaled to someone, prompting a scuffle that sounded like it came from the direction of the jail, then two more automatons dragged someone—no, not someone, Roberto, into view. Was he the one they planned to hang? Was that why the automaton had fetched Angelica?

The Bad Egg shifted slightly, gestured toward Roberto, the move graceful, but not in a pleasing way.

"I'm not as heartless as you seem to think I am, my dear. Conclude your little flirtation and we'll move on to the nuptials." His expression hardened. "Unless you'd like to swing with him."

She might be floundering a bit on the names of the players, but she recognized the melodrama. She'd seen plenty in her travels. Eased her some to know her lines at least.

We're not where we were. The lights, they did something to time.

If there was a Roberto and Angelica in this place, then could there be an Analisse, too? It seemed there had to be, because they'd certain sure never met. Even a Bad Egg needed to know a gal before trying to wed her. If the Bad Egg was the villain that must mean Roberto—she realized he looked a bit longing, a bit anguished even. Saw puzzled enter in when she looked at him. Spoke well of him that he could tell she wasn't his Analisse. The Bad Egg could take lessons from him, but wouldn't. Bad Eggs never did. She gave a tiny shrug, then turned back to the Bad Egg. Felt the waiting nature of the people behind her, one might even call it bated. The limelight was usually Pa's, except for her brief bit of ailing and getting cured. Didn't mean she didn't know how it was done.

"I have to thank you for your...*kind*...offer, sir," his gaze narrowed, cause she might be playing to the gallery a bit, "but I must decline on account of my previous commitment to another."

It wasn't a lie. She was for Chance, whether he made it to Marfa or not. The gallows made her gulp a bit, but—looking at the Bad Egg —she preferred hanging. One thing she'd learned from Pa was how long and challenging life could be with a person who didn't give a bean what you thought about anything. At least with a hanging the pain'd be short. She hoped.

You deserve better. This wasn't better, but if she had it to do again? If she said no and didn't ride into the dark after the ghost lights? If she'd known it would end like this, would she have chose different? And then she thought about how he'd looked at her, how he'd kissed her, the sound of his voice when he asked her to trust him. And she knew, not only would she do it again, she might, she just might...love him. She looked at Roberto, but saw Chance. Saw him the way she'd seen him the first time, saw him the way he'd looked that last time. If he were standing there instead of Roberto? She'd be pleased to die with him. And in a way, that's what she'd be doing.

Roberto opened his mouth but closed it again. What could he say? He had to know that no matter what Ani did or didn't do, who she was or wasn't, he was going to swing.

Bad Eggs always went back on their word.

The Bad Egg's face didn't change, in fact, he half smiled like it didn't matter that she'd given him the muffin in front of the whole town. His eyes showed her it did, though. They chilled like the ice on a winter river. If he could have forced her, he would have. Teach him to strut his pride before the whole boodle of them.

"So be it." His chin jerked, and the automatons dragged them both to the gallows. A wail from Angelica, a rising murmur from the people, made the other automatons around the edges move their metal hands to rest on their guns.

Roberto's hands were bound, but no one thought to bind her hands. It gave her a smidgeon of hope, though she wasn't certain what to do with it. She had a knife strapped to her leg, had started wearing it there when some border ruffians stole the one she wore at her waist. Knife wasn't much use against all those gun-toting bad— automatons. Human hands took over from automatons. They were a mite big for the wooden structure.

Ani reached the top, found facing the rope loop more than a mite unsettling. Looking at her audience wasn't much better. Never been quite so much the center of attention. Tipped her head a bit. Did it seem like a breeze or something moved through. Stiffened some spines, it seemed. The Bad Egg didn't seem to notice, as one of the fancy girls sashayed up a cooing and a billing. The Bad Egg didn't object. Typical. Wanted his cake and to eat it. If he thought the sight would make her fractious, well, he could think again.

Though, she considered the crowd again. A most timely distraction.

The hangman cleared his throat, and Ani realized he was waiting for her. Guess it was the polite thing to do, ladies first and all, though it didn't feel it. Not that she wanted to watch Roberto hang. No reason to pile on the agony.

Hangman didn't seem to want to look at her. Made it hard to get the rope over, so she did it for him. Rope felt rough, scraped her neck some, felt a bit streaked by it, which had a chilling effect on her spirits. The hangman stepped back to the lever that would drop the trap, his gaze on the Bad Egg. Ani lifted her chin. Only good advice she ever got from her Pa: show no fear.

The Bad Egg started to raise a hand.

Someone shouted and rowdy spread like greased lightning through the people. Seemed they'd been beaten down a mite to let her rip like that. Groups of folks, even the women, surrounded the automatons, taking them down with considerable enthusiasm.

"Do it," the Bad Man yelled over the noise.

The hangman reached for the lever, but a shot rang out and the rope around her neck went slack. Another shot dropped the hangman across the lever. Ani didn't have time to react, just dropped down, hit the ground hard enough to rattle her teeth. Started to tumble, but someone caught her arm, steadied her. She stared into eyes a match for hers. Took a longer look. Saw longer hair and a *dress?* Ani frowned. Was she wearing Chance's coat?

Some shouts, sounds of scuffling overhead and then Roberto dropped through, too, almost knocking both of them down. He staggered, and the other Analisse let go of Ani and wrapped her arms around him, near choking him to death. Didn't look like he minded much, though he couldn't hug her with his hands still tied.

Ani sighed a bit, extracted her knife and cut him loose. Not a practical sort of girl. Her Pa—her thoughts kind of stalled out on that thought, but it felt odd to ask about him when they'd just met. Couldn't be a whole lot of use if he was the sort to let this Analisse marry a Bad Egg. Besides, she had a more important question, though she hated to ask it of...herself.

"Where's Chance?" He had to be here. This had the feel of a Plan. Riots didn't accidentally start, nor did hanging ropes get fortuitously severed.

"Smith."

The word wasn't shouted, though it sounded clear over the chaos. Quiet spread as fast as rowdy had. Ani dragged the noose off her head, pushed her way out from under the gallows, climbed the steps again, her gaze searching for—there he was. Standing dead center in the road and looking mighty fine, mighty tough. Ani saw the Bad Egg. He looked like he'd been about to leave, since his gang of automatons all had stuff poking out of the backs of their heads. The people parted, making a path for him toward Chance, kind of blocking his escape. She'd seen a few gunfights, enough to recognize one about to happen.

~

Chance had seen Smith trying to slip away when the last of his 'tons went down. Miss Everly had done a fine job of marshaling a resistance. Seemed Smith had no friends in Marfa, not even with the scum class. There was a lesson there, though he'd need to ponder it later. Almost let him slither away. Ani was safe but a snake could grow a new skin and make a new set of people miserable.

Guess if a guy wanted to be a hero, he had to sometimes save more than the damsel, or even two. And if he were honest, which he tried to be these days, he might get a bit of closure from taking this Smith down, even if he wasn't *the* Smith who'd made his life hell for so long. Helped that he looked just like him.

He could admit he'd felt a bit of doubt when Ani had begun her response to Smith's "proposal." How could he expect her to choose him over a hanging? But she did. Made a man feel proud, made him feel like he could do what was needed. Had felt something odd happen around his heart, or maybe when she put that noose over her neck. Didn't need to tell Smith that she'd rather be dead than married to him. It was implied. Best implication he'd heard in a long while. It changed him from the inside out. If Ani didn't doubt, then he couldn't.

He used a long rifle to shoot the rope, didn't feel it was an exaggeration to call it the most important shot of his life. Now he faced the second most important shot.

He had a feeling Smith was the best gun around.

Didn't matter.

Looked into Smith's eyes. Saw his confidence, his evil.

That didn't matter either.

He felt...bulletproof.

Chance relaxed his shoulders, loosened his stance, wriggled his fingers a bit, though it was mostly for show. He'd been ready for this for what felt like forever.

Smith swept his coat back behind his guns, his hands out, stance alert, ready.

Chance watched his eyes. Eyes were where a draw started.

Dead silence in every direction except for faint creaking from one of the windmills. Then the small sound of a child quickly hushed. Felt the support from everyone around him. Didn't need it. He planned to walk away with his woman.

Chance didn't blink, didn't look away from that cold, dead gaze. Just waited.

Saw it.

The slight shift to the right.

Gun was in his hand, trigger pulled before the thought traveled to his brain.

Smith had his gun out, too. Shots must have been close cause they sounded like one and an echo.

Something plucked at his arm. Started to sting. Ignored it. Waited.

Smith started to smile, maybe some relief in it, then the smile faltered. He swayed for two long seconds, then fell forward onto his face. Dirt puffed into the air around him as if it wanted distance from him, too.

He did a sweep for further threats. Didn't see any. Smith had had no friends here. He holstered his .45 and went to get his woman, who had climbed back on the damn gallows.

She went down a step, then another. Hit the ground and sped up a bit.

People fell back for him, started to smile, though also a good bit of puzzled in there. Then Miss Everly and Roberto popped out from under the gallows, confusing things further. Chance didn't mind the confusion. Just minded not having his woman in his arms.

Ani started to run, jumped when she reached him, her arms and her legs coming around him. Good reason to keep her pants, he thought, though a bit hazily as her mouth found his. For a girl who'd been kissed once, she showed a remarkable aptitude. He spun them because he could, because he had to, because he'd defeated the bad guy and got the girl. When they both needed air, he lifted his head.

"You got grazed," she said, examining the slight wound.

"I'm fine." He looked around. "Who does the marrying around here?"

~

Ani didn't come face to face with herself again until after her wedding. And *her* wedding. It was a bit confusing, but at least the guys they married were different. Analisse seemed a bit fazed by it all, but then she hadn't been in the wash and got switched out of her place. Of course, she hadn't almost gotten hung either.

Ani might have been intimidated by the gentry talk and pretty dress, might have wondered if Chance speculated a bit about Analisse, except for the kiss. He'd shown a proper enthusiasm for it and for the wedding to a bride with a dusty face and dressed like a boy.

"I feel like I should thank you, but I don't know what for," Analisse said, maybe making an effort to sound friendly. Her Roberto showed a bit more enthusiasm and gratitude, but he had been on the gallows with her. It did focus the mind to almost swing.

"You going to stay in Marfa?" Ani asked, looking from one to the other. It was bold of her to marry a Mexican, but he was a fine looking boy. She glanced up at Chance, her Chance. He made Roberto seem small and young, though they were of a height. Still got a thrill remembering how coolly he'd faced down the Bad Egg, though she did intend to speak to him about putting their wedding in jeopardy twice in one day. Didn't want him to make a habit of it.

"We will see how it goes," Analisse said, after exchanging a look with her husband. Angelica hovered close, glowing with relief and joy.

Ani had to resist the urge to try to chat to her. She wasn't this Angelica's friend.

As if Chance heard or felt her uncertainty, he said, "We should go."

"You could stay," Analisse said, though with a noticeable lack of enthusiasm. Both them looked relieved when Chance shook his head.

"We could use a ride back to where you found me," Chance said.

Ani loved the airship ride and she and Analisse compared family notes, more relaxed now that they knew they weren't going to be living side by side. Didn't meet that Pa, tied up in the engine room.

Didn't want to. Bit of a shock to find out Pa had lied, that it was Ma that was gentry and Pa a gentlemen's gentleman. Though not a total shock. He'd always had an uneasy relationship with the truth.

They reached the wash at dusk, helped along by the never-ending wind. Bit of a surprise to find Chance's mount still there, more of shock to find Delphine there, too. Seems she'd formed a bit of a bond with her husband's stallion.

Her husband.

She was married. Thankfully neither Analisse nor Roberto seemed inclined to draw out the leave taking. It was their wedding night, too. Ani did pause to wonder if Analisse knew what that meant, be nice to know, though Chance would most likely explain. They finally chugged away, the sound fading into the soft moan of the wind and the snuffle and stamp of the horses. Ani looked around the darkening wash, maybe felt a bit of unease, considering what happened the last time they were here.

Chance took her hand, led her to a rock big enough for them to sit side by side. A seat was nice, but she'd been hoping for a kiss. Didn't quite know how to ask for it, though.

"We could try to stay here in this reality, but most likely it won't work, because there's already a version of you here. Time has a way of setting things right, so thought we'd sit a spell and see if the lights come back tonight, see if they'll shift us back to your time. Or," he hesitated, "a different time than this. I can't promise we'd get home. No way to know for sure where we'd go. In my experience, it's pretty random."

In his experience.

"You've done it before."

He nodded. "I'm not from this time, or your time, so it's you that time will shift, taking me along for the ride."

"Where are you from?"

He hesitated. "From the future. From another planet. In another galaxy."

Ani blinked. It was preposterous, but she'd seen automatons and airship trains, had almost swung today. If he'd told her that before, she'd thought he was plumb crazy. Now...

"Oh."

"It's a long story, one I'd like to forget, leave in the past." He clasped her hands, half turned her to face him. "I came here to forget, to die, and found a reason to live when I met you. When you faced Smith like that—I thought I was too damaged to love anyone, too dead inside. I was wrong. I know it's soon, too soon for you to feel it, too, but I love you. If you'll let me, I'd like to prove it to you."

Ani's mouth curved up at the edges, taking it slow, as she felt her woman power surge again. "You're a fine man, Chance, a good man. When I faced the Bad Egg, when I climbed that gallows, I knew it, too. I knew I loved you and always would. That I'd have died for you on the gallows."

His smile had been fine before, but this one lit him up like the sun coming out as he pulled her close and finally kissed her. She thought she'd been kissed before. Well, that was nothing on this one. It was like flying in the airship and galloping and the best day she ever had, all rolled into one.

"Then we'll need to stay real close until it happens."

"Close sounds fine to me." She hadn't a clue what happened next, but she was powerful curious to find out.

Men in Jeans

A romantic suspense mystery

Richard Daniels thinks life can't any stranger working at Area 51until he gets assigned to find out where a Houston area SF writer gets the ideas for her books. Should be an easy assignment—if it weren't for the dead guy in her back yard and the non-business related ideas she's giving him. (Originally appeared in the *Death in Texas* anthology)

Men in Jeans

When Richard Daniels started working at Area 51, he figured he'd see some weird stuff, but he never thought he'd get sent out on a gig with ET as his sidekick. They were Area 51's version of *Men in Black*, though they dressed in tee shirts and jeans. Blended in better.

Well, Rick blended in better. He flicked a glance at Kiernan Fyn, his extra terrestrial companion. He looked more biker than space guy. According to the guys who'd know, Fyn could kick ass in at least two galaxies. Maybe that's why no one had made him trim his dread locks to conform to military regs.

"Quiet," Fyn said, staring at the house.

He should know. Rick shut off the engine, adding to the silence in the clearing. When he'd picked Fyn up, his wife said he was excited to get out of Area 51. He didn't look excited then. Didn't look it now. If his expression had changed in the last twenty-four hours, Rick had missed it.

"Yeah." To fill the silence he added, "Maybe she's not home."

No way to tell with the garage door closed. Place looked and felt isolated, though technically it wasn't. There were houses all around, but the lots were large, some close to half an acre. And the freeway was about five hundred yards through the trees. Not to mention freaking huge Houston, Texas, in every direction. According to one of the local guys, the neighbors were "Texas close." Guess that meant they were in the same time zone.

"Maybe."

That doubled Fyn's output from yesterday. Rick almost made a joke about him talking too much, but yesterday's joke hadn't gone well. No one could say Rick didn't learn from his mistakes.

If they'd been tracking terrorists, Fyn was the guy Rick would most want at his back. He was like seven feet tall, all of it solid muscle. A bit of overkill as backup for a visit to a writer, though.

Unless she was ET, too.

Or a traitor.

Or both.

Rick contemplated Fyn. No, even if she was all those things and more, he was still overkill.

Though it was hard to make the case she was innocent when her books nailed the Garradian history so perfectly. Only the names had been changed. Been better for her if *The Harradian Chronicles* had been less popular.

Still, Rick couldn't figure out why Area 51 was interested. It's not like anyone outside of Area 51 knew about the Garradians—except the *Project Enterprise* expedition. It was scattered over a couple of galaxies, so he knew they weren't talking. They might be emailing, but they weren't talking, well, except to each other.

Rick turned his attention back to the author's house. It wasn't anything special. It huddled down in the trees and Texas scrub as if it weren't sure it had a right to be there. Looked a bit shabby except for the front door—a bright, unapologetic red.

J. E. Smith had only recently bought the property, so maybe it was her way of making her mark. Or maybe she just liked red. According to her driver's license. Jillian Elaine Smith was thirty years old, five foot six inches tall and weighed 135 pounds—though she'd probably skimmed a few pounds off her real weight. Rick had never met a woman who was honest about her weight. She had black hair and blue eyes, and the official photo, well, he'd have been hard pressed to pick her out of a lineup, based on that photo.

Not that he'd find her in one. No criminal record, not even a parking ticket. She had the normal amount of friends—male and female—and none of either had stayed overnight since the surveillance started. She appeared to be the right amount of reclusive for an author—or a person with something to hide.

Like the fact that Jillian Elaine Smith had died at birth.

Who was she really? What had compelled her to write the books?

She'd never have popped up on the Area 51 radar but for the books. The ID grab was almost flawless. She'd even managed to create a false grade school trail. The geeks were still trying to figure out how. It's not like she could have stolen the ID in kindergarten.

Early surveillance had failed to unearth any connection to Area 51, but that didn't mean it wasn't there. It was their job to figure out just who and what Jillian Smith was—or wasn't. Someone further up the line would decide what to do about her. No one had told them exactly how to do anything without giving away what they knew, but no one had ever said his job would ever be easy. It helped to have low expectations. He just hoped they were low enough for this gig.

They slid out of the car and Fyn shadowed him up the walk. Guy cast a long shadow. Rick applied some pressure to the doorbell. When nothing happened, he applied some more and held it for a twenty count. Just before they could consider their next step, they heard footsteps approaching the door.

There was a peep hole, so Rick held up his ID so she could see it.

The door didn't open.

"What do you want?" The voice sounded muffled coming through the red door.

"We need to speak with you, Ms. Smith."

The door opened a crack, the chain still on. Part of a face peered out the gap.

"Let me look at your ID."

Rick put it in her hand. They weren't FBI but she wouldn't be able to tell. It was an authentic forgery.

"He doesn't look FBI."

Rick looked at Fyn. She was right. He'd crossed his arms over his chest and planted his feet, like someone who meant to stay as long as needed. If he'd really been FBI, the dreads would be long gone.

Rick tried to look safe and trustworthy. "You can call that number on the badge, ma'am. They'll vouch for us."

"I'm sure they will." Her voice sounded a bit dry, a bit cynical.

Lady wasn't a fool.

Another long pause, then the door closed—and opened again, this time without the chain. She stood in the opening. She had a cordless phone in her hand, her thumb on the speed dial. Just a guess, but he had a feeling nine-one-one was the number. Very smart lady. Pretty, too. Way better than her driver's license photo, but then most people were. Green light spilled into the dim hallway, highlighting the fact that she was, well, hot. Great features, great body in shorts and a tee shirt. Bare feet, the toes painted same red as the door. She had gathered her hair into an untidy mass on top of her head, but silken strands escaped to curl against creamy skin.

Her eyes were so blue, they almost looked purple.

Not what he'd expected from a writer. Or ET. Now if she was Mata Hari...

The eyes narrowed in suspicion and her body language was defensive.

"Why would the FBI be on my doorstep?"

Her gaze met his. Her chin lifted. Slid Fyn's way. Fyn stared back without speaking. Huge shock that. After what seemed like a long time, his shoulders lifted in what might have been a sigh. Or a shrug. A slight, a very slight frown formed between his brows.

"We'd like to talk to you, ma'am." Rick smiled in a friendly way. Whether he wanted it or not, he'd been cast as Good Agent. Fyn was tailor made to be bad.

"So, talk."

Since no one could see them, it was hard to make a case for taking it private. At this rate they wouldn't be inside before she wrote and released another book. Speaking of which...

"We were wondering where you get the ideas for your books, ma'am?"

Her jaw slackened. Her eyes widened. It didn't reduce her hotness factor at all.

"What?"

Rick wished he had a tie to tug on. Not that he liked wearing ties, but the moment seemed to call for a good tie tug. "We need to talk to you about your books, ma'am."

"Is this some kind of weird joke?" She looked past them, as if she expected a camera crew to pop out of the underbrush. "A new reality show?"

"We're not allowed to joke, ma'am." It took some work, but his lips didn't twitch.

She didn't try to keep hers from twitching.

"I—you..." She sighed. "You'd better come in."

Finally she stepped back so they could enter. She kept the phone in hand, though.

Nothing unusual, or even that interesting, about the hall or the Great Room at the end of it. Rick wasn't sure what he'd been expecting, or would that be hoping? Maybe a picture of her home planet on the wall? Alien furniture. Her certificate for passing spy school? Garradian artifacts?

"I understand you only recently moved here?" He looked around. She'd settled in fast. He'd been at Area 51 for two years and he still had some unpacked boxes lying around.

She arched her brows, her body language still defensive. Or annoyed. Hard to tell those two apart sometimes.

"Can we sit down?" Rick had had twenty-four hours to come up with a plan. Twenty-four years wouldn't have been enough. He was basically winging it. So far couldn't feel any lift. More like they were running along the ground. Hitting stuff.

"Of course." A pause. "Can I get either of you something to drink?"

Lot of reluctance in her voice, a bit of polite.

"Water would be nice." Rick smiled.

"Yeah." A pause from Fyn. "Thanks."

He kept that up, he really would be talking too much.

She disappeared into the open plan kitchen that butted up against the Great Room. Fyn settled on the edge of a chair, like it was a hot seat, his hands clasped between his splayed knees.

When she returned, both men stood again and she handed them each a bottle of water. Rick twisted the top off and took a drink. The cold water felt good going down. Nevada was hot, but that was a dry heat. Texas was damp hot.

"Thank you, ma'am." He waited for her to perch on the edge of a rocker, before resuming his spot on her couch. He let the silence grow, hoping she'd give him an opening.

She didn't.

"You been writing long, ma'am?"

She rubbed her temple as if it ached before she answered. "About five years."

"You were a librarian, weren't you?"

"Yes."

Most people would be babbling by now, spilling their guts. She just looked at him, her violet eyes wary.

Okay. He thought a bit, then tried, "Any reason why you chose science fiction?"

She looked away. Looked back. "It's what I like to read."

"Really? You read science fiction? Why is that?"

Her lips tightened and he thought she'd lose it.

"Because I like it."

Point to her. "Right."

Fyn shifted restlessly. "Why'd it take you so long to answer the door?"

Wow, a whole sentence.

"I was reading. Science fiction. With my headphones on."

He could see temper simmering in her eyes.

Fyn looked around. "Where's your book?"

Her fingers tightened around her bottle of water. "I was outside. On the deck."

Fyn rose, pointed out the patio doors. "Out here?"

"Yes." She snapped the word off.

"Mind if I look?"

He got a look that might be permission.

Fyn pulled the glass door back and stepped out. Rick could see the foot of a lounger, saw Fyn pace toward it and stop. He turned. Retraced his steps.

She stood up, her arms crossed again. "It's called *Games of Command.* Do you need me to tell you the plot to prove I was reading it?"

"Actually," Fyn said, "I was wondering about the dead guy."

He had to be joking, but he wasn't. Jilly could see a dead guy, lying on his back at the foot of the stairs. He was dressed in a *Star Fleet* uniform—kind of ironic because it was a red shirt one—and had on a pair of Vulcan ears. He also had a huge scorch mark in the middle of his chest. This was in the center of a round body and below rounder surprised eyes.

"Do you know him?" Agent Daniels, the "good" agent, asked.

She heard him through an odd rushing in her ears, kind of like the surf going out and coming in. Should she call a lawyer? He asked the question again and finally she nodded.

Jilly looked at Daniels, sort of aware he was a nice looking guy, in a distant kind of way. He filled out the jeans well. And the tee shirt. Had great eyes. Green. Her favorite color. It was his eyes that convinced her to let them in. Now she wished she hadn't.

Bad agent was hot, too, and kind of wild, like one of the characters in her books. He looked great in jeans but would look better in leather and packing space guns.

"His name?"

She rubbed her temple. "I don't know."

"You said you know him."

This question came from bad agent. Something Fyn or Fyn something.

"He read my books. He'd show up at signings." He'd dress like Jusan, one of her characters, and used that name when he sent her fan email. Did they realize how many people showed up at her signings? Her head started to ache.

"He was stalking you?" Daniels jumped on it like a cat on a mouse.

"In a benign way." Jilly rubbed the sides of her arms. She turned abruptly and went back inside, but it felt like "Jusan" came with her, his image tattooed to the inside of her lids. She massaged her temple, feeling the ache sharper now. She really needed to get that checked. It seemed to be happening more often. Headaches had been the norm after the fender bender, no surprise there, since she'd banged her head against the steering wheel, but they'd eased up until recently. Now the pain wasn't enough of a distraction from her dead fan.

How had her personal stalker ended up dead in her backyard?

This had to be some kind of record for a bad day. First the FBI shows up at her door asking weird questions about her books, then they find a dead man in her backyard. Maybe not the worst day ever, but surely in the top ten?

She could tell the big guy thought she'd done it. Daniels just looked surprised. He'd called the police, but they were taking their time. She didn't know whether to be offended or relieved. The two men crouched by the body, talking. Fyn gestured, then got up and walked toward the tree line. Daniels seemed to hesitate, then he came back inside. She turned and sat at the table. She couldn't see the deck from the table. Daniels sat down opposite her, and she could see him trying to figure out what to say. She decided to help him out.

"Why are you really here?"

He studied her for what seemed like a long time. "You appear to have—come into possession of classified material."

"What? What classified material?"

"I can't tell you that. It's classified."

"You can't tell me what classified material you think I already have?"

"That's right."

"And where is the evidence of this classified..." She stopped. "My books? You think my books contain classified material?"

"Have you been in contact with anyone in the government, ma'am?"

"Only the IRS. They're fans of my money since my books started selling well. I don't know if they read them."

He actually smiled. A nice smile. Might have curled the toes in her shoes if he weren't *freaking crazy*.

"It's in your best interests to cooperate with us, ma'am."

"Kind of hard to cooperate when I don't know what your problem is." She huffed out a frustrated sigh, fought her way to calm. "I write *science fiction*. I *make it up*. How could making up stuff be classified?"

"That's a good question. But..."

"The answer is classified?"

"Yes, ma'am." He was quiet for a minute. "What about experts who help you with technical stuff?"

"Experts? You mean experts in scientific advances that haven't been discovered yet? Or are fictional? Those kind of experts?"

He didn't blink. "Yes, ma'am."

Jilly leaned forward, hissing through clenched teeth. "Aren't any. Don't exist. I make it all up." She leaned back, taking a couple of deep breaths. "Have you read my books?"

"I read one of them, the first one." He smiled again. "It was good."

"But somehow classified."

"Well, yes."

He shifted, as if uncomfortable, but he didn't look uncomfortable.

"You know, your comedy routine would play better with your straight man here instead of patrolling my back yard like Sherlock Holmes."

He grinned. His gaze seemed admiring, but that might have been part of the routine.

"Seems to be taking the cops a long time." Had he even called anyone? Maybe they killed "Jusan"...

She heard an odd, thumping noise. What the...

Helicopters. Several of them.

She gave Daniels an ironic look. "I'm sure that's the HPD. They always arrive by chopper."

~

He liked her, Rick realized, more than he should. She had spunk and a good eye for bull. She'd seen right through them, even before the real *Men in Black* swarmed over her place like ants on cake. Though they also wore jeans, just more expensive ones.

She still sat at her kitchen table, her hands loosely clasping her bottle of water, staring at the wall in front of her. One or two times, Hitchens, the guy in charge of the team, had stopped to ask her a question. Each time, she'd turned her gaze toward him, stared at him for a full minute, then looked away without speaking.

She hadn't asked for a lawyer. Yet. He hoped she didn't, since she wasn't getting one.

Fyn emerged out of the woods at the back of her house and gestured for him. They met in the center of the backyard.

"Found something."

Apparently he'd used up his allotment of full sentences. Rick signaled for a couple of the guys to come with them and followed Fyn into the woods. It was cooler under the trees but somehow more humid, which felt like it canceled out cool. The heat made the smell back here more pungent.

Fyn stopped and pointed to one of the trees. Rick stepped around, staring at the scorch mark on the tree, about chest high if the man was as short as the dead fan. They moved deeper into the wood and found more of the marks until they reached a small clearing. Fyn paced around, pointing out his finds. Some trampled flowers, a mix that clearly wasn't indigenous. More scorch marks. Tire tracks. Footprints. A dead ferret.

A ferret?

Rick crouched by the critter. No scorch marks on the visible side. He turned it over and realized it was still warm. Its heart was still beating. Okay, even in an odd situation, that was pretty strange.

He stood up, stepping out of the way of the photographs being taken.

"What if he just walked in on something?" If he'd been planning on an unscheduled visit with his favorite author, sneaking through the woods might seem logical, particularly to a guy dressed like Spock.

"See if you can find our victim's vehicle."

Rick didn't wait to see the guy nod, just headed back toward the house. When Fyn joined him, Rick wasn't totally surprised to see him carrying the ferret, which was starting to wake up. He hoped they found an owner. Fyn appeared to be bonding with it. And Rick would probably get the blame when he wanted to take it home. Fyn's wife could kick some serious butt.

When they got back to the house, more show and tell.

The victim was one, Oscar Redding. According to his Texas driver's license he was taller and thinner than he looked. Couldn't fudge his age, which was forty-three. He was a card carrying member of the *Star Trek* Fan Club, the *Stargates* Fan Club, the *Star Wars* Fan Club, was president of the J.E. Smith Fan Club and had an ID badge for Consolidated Weapons Systems, Inc.

Crap.

CWS had provided some of the weapons systems for the *Enterprise Project* ships. Some of their people had helped with the repair and refit of the *Doolittle's* weapons arrays. It was hard to see where he fit in, but it was also hard to see an innocent connection when the man was dead—apparently shot with a Garradian type ray gun, if Fyn knew his stuff.

Rick had no doubt Fyn knew his stuff.

Rick phoned home. "I need to know what information Redding had access to and I need to know it yesterday." He'd always wanted to say that. A bonus that he meant it and that it was true.

"Sir?" It was one of Hitchens' bright young men. "Mr. Hitchens was wondering if you could join him in the garage. With Ms. Smith."

There was a small Ford pickup truck parked to one side of the double garage, but that wasn't what had caught Hitchens' attention. No, it was definitely the workshop on the other side, complete with welding equipment. On the shelves, Rick could see all kinds of what appeared to be alien technology. On a workbench lay a ray gun. Did ET have a workshop?

Smith crossed her arms over her chest, her expression cool and closed.

"Can you explain this, ma'am?" Rick asked.

She stared at him for several seconds. "It's obviously my secret laboratory, Agent Daniels."

"This isn't a joking matter, ma'am."

Hitchens did sinister and threatening better than anyone Rick knew.

"Am I laughing—what was your name again? I don't think I caught it."

No one said anything.

"Let me guess. Classified."

Time to be good cop. Rick eased up next to her.

"Ma'am, if you could just explain? You have to admit, this is rather...odd."

"You mean more odd than a bunch of Feds swarming my house and asking about my books?"

Seemed like a good time not to say anything.

Finally she sighed. "I like to—build some of the stuff I use in my novels. They're mock ups. Models, so I can picture it, describe it, visualize how it would be used if it were real. Which it's *not*."

Rick stared at the ray gun. "So that's not real?"

"Of course not!" She picked it up, pointed it at the wall, and squeezed the trigger. A flash of light surged out of the tip, slamming into the wall. Flames flickered for a few seconds, before they went out.

Smith walked forward, looking just a bit dazed, and reached out to the big, black mark left on her wall. Before Rick could suggest she not do that, she pulled her hand back.

"It's—hot." She looked at Rick. She opened her mouth. Closed it. Opened it. "Do I need a lawyer?"

Rick sighed. "Tell me you checked that thing for prints before she picked it up?"

A tech nodded. "Been wiped clean, sir."

Rick studied the room again, his gaze stopping on the door. He nodded toward it. "Have you checked the door?"

Hitchens nodded. "It leads out to the backyard."

So, someone could have come in here while he and Fyn were talking to her. That didn't explain why someone would leave a piece of alien tech in her garage. Or the dead guy in her back yard.

It was clear that the clearing had something to do with the dead guy. But it didn't clear Smith of involvement in whatever was going on. Rick really wanted to clear her. "Was the door locked, ma'am?"

"Probably." Her chin lifted.

He looked at the tech.

"There are scratches on the lock. It could have been picked. No way to tell when, sir."

He took the ray gun from Smith, looked at it, and handed it off to Fyn. Fyn studied it carefully. Looked at Rick. Shook his head.

So it might have been made in the U.S.A. Or here in this garage. Could someone develop a working ray gun in a garage?

Was he even asking himself the right questions?

Jilly was back at the table. The feeding frenzy seemed to have died down, but it didn't help her headache. How had her space gun mockup been replaced by one that actually worked? Who had killed "Jusan?" The two events had to be related, but thinking about it without full disclosure from these people just made her head ache more. She rubbed her temples, fighting back a feeling of falling that seemed to be a side effect of the headaches.

Bad cop Fyn intrigued her for some reason. She shifted in her seat to keep him in sight as he paced restlessly around her house, a ferret around his neck. She didn't remember him arriving with a ferret, but then she'd been more interested in good cop Daniels at the time. She got that odd, almost-shift in her vision and felt a longing to be at her computer. These were her most creative moments, when it seemed like her vision split between what was and the place where her novels happened.

Daniels sat down opposite her again.

"You said Redding brought you gifts," he began.

"Was that his name?" It seemed important to know his real name, though she couldn't have said why.

"Oscar Redding. What kind of gifts did he bring you, ma'am?"

"I wish you'd call me Jilly," she said, then wished the words back. This wasn't a social occasion and he wasn't her friend, even if he acted like he was. He was good cop and it was his job to trap her into admitting she'd killed—Oscar.

His smile warmed the cold places inside her, even if it shouldn't.

"Jilly. The gifts?"

"Flowers. Chocolates. Jewelry—nothing expensive. Trinkets. Like charms related to my books."

"Flowers. Any special kind?"

"Usually a mix of types, the kind of thing you could pick up at the grocery store."

"Not your favorite flower?"

Jilly frowned. "I didn't really have one." That wasn't true, but the flower she saw in her mind existed only in her novels. It was a lovely, waxy red, the color of her door and her toenails and the scent, she didn't know how to describe its scent. It—soothed. She'd missed it when—when what? How could she miss something that didn't exist? Why did she sometimes feel homesick for a place that wasn't real? She rubbed her temples again.

"You have a headache, ma'am, sorry, Jilly?" He looked worried.

He did good cop very well.

"I'm fine." She didn't want to like him. She wouldn't like him. He was just playing her and he wouldn't tell her why.

He studied her, as if considering what to tell her, but he was really doing it to break her.

"We found some flowers scattered around on the ground in a clearing back there." He nodded toward her back yard. "And we found his car parked just off the freeway on a dirt road. I figure he was coming to see you."

She shook her head. "No, not to see me, not dressed like that. If he was planning on seeing me, he'd have been dressed like Jusan, my character."

Daniels straightened. "You think maybe he meant to leave the flowers?"

"Yeah, I do." She rubbed her face. "He wouldn't realize how creepy that would be. He'd probably think he was being thoughtful." She hesitated. "I had mentioned I'd moved in my blog. Maybe it was a—house warming gift."

"Did you know he worked for a company that makes experimental weapons?"

She had a feeling the question was supposed to shock her.

"I didn't even know his real name." She hesitated. "I suppose on some level I knew he had a job. I mean, he bought me stuff, but not expensive stuff. I might have vaguely thought he was a computer geek or something. When I thought about him. Which wasn't that often."

She rubbed her face again. "I had lots of fans. Some of them also give me things."

"Like what?" He looked curious. No more, no less.

"Pillows and tee shirts with my book covers silk screened on them. Souvenirs from their vacations. Plush toys. Space toys. It was— sweet. Friendly."

"You've written four books, but the stuff in your garage, it didn't look like a lot of stuff?"

Jilly felt pain stab her temples again. She fought the urge to rub the spots.

"When I finish a book, I hold a contest for most of it. It clears the decks. It's something I can give back to my fans. Might even be valuable when I'm dead."

"Do they keep it?"

"Some do. I've seen some of it turn up on eBay." Tiredness tugged at her concentration. She'd been up early writing. "I've donated a few things to charity auctions and they've done pretty well. They're unique. More valuable since I hit the NYT."

"NYT?"

"*New York Times* bestseller list. I was on there with J.K. Rowling." A few books down, but still there. She couldn't hold back the smile or the thrill it still gave her to remember seeing her name there with Rowling's.

"Cool." His smile took some of the edge off her headache. "Did anyone come with Redding to your book signings?"

She frowned, thinking back. Finally she shrugged. "It's hard to say. People visited while they waited in line. I was usually busy talking to the person in front of me. Readers are mostly friendly. They don't just talk the the book they are getting, but about other books they like. I can hear them. If you like this novel, then you might like this one. And some of them knew each other online, but not always in person." She looked at him. "I'm sorry."

He leaned forward. "Let's assume that Redding's death in your yard is a coincidence, Jilly. That it's about that weapon and not you. He's coming by to leave you a house warming gift before he goes off to the *Trek* convention downtown."

"That's easy, since it's true. I'm not involved."

A quick smile from him. He shifted, leaning toward her, though he didn't move closer.

"He starts through the woods and runs into—something to do with that weapon."

"Something?"

"It—appears whoever was in that clearing was shooting it. There were scorch marks on several trees. And the ferret."

"The ferret?"

"The weapon appears to have a stun setting. They stunned the ferret."

"That's pretty cold. It would still hurt, and the pain lingers for several hours."

Daniels looked at her, blinking slowly. "How would you know that?"

It was Jilly's turn to blink. "I guess I don't. That's actually what mine does. In my book. Sorry."

"Right." He paused, as if collecting the threads of his story. "Suppose Redding recognizes someone or several people in the clearing? There's some—confusion, maybe. Possibly even two of the weapons."

"How could you tell?"

"The scorch marks on the trees, leading to your house. They go both ways and are of varying heights. I think Redding—and someone—took one of the weapons. Redding gets shot and someone—breaks into your garage. He or she sees your replica and makes the switch, then leaves."

Jilly studied him for a moment. "Clever. You could be a novelist, Agent Daniels."

"Call me Rick."

Was his smile friendlier than the last one? More—intimate?

"Rick." As soon as she said it, she knew it was a mistake. It forged a link between them that she liked too much—and that made panic flutter in the back of her throat.

She had to get away. It was the only way, they said.

Who were they? Four books and she still wasn't sure. She just knew she had to keep pushing toward it, toward them, whoever they were. When she found out, she wouldn't be worried anymore. She wasn't afraid. Just worried. She didn't need to be afraid.

Well, not until a man died in her back yard and she got invaded by—whoever these guys were. She might need to be afraid now.

"The other story is the one where you're in the clearing, getting classified equipment and that our arrival was—unfortunate."

"That one isn't as well developed. If I'd been running from the clearing, wouldn't I have been out of breath when I answered the door?"

"That's why I didn't spend as much time on it," Rick said, looking a bit wry. "Hitchens likes that one, though."

"Hitchens being the man in black." As soon as she said the words, she felt a shiver of something dance down her spine, helped by the slight twitch Rick gave at her words. "Now that I know his name, will you have to shoot me?"

She kept her voice light and ironic, to hide her sudden, possibly rational fear.

Rick looked puzzled. "Shoot you?"

"He implied even his name is classified," Jilly prompted.

"Oh, right. My bad." Then he grinned, looking remarkably unrepentant. Did that mean he was actually the one in charge? "So..."

He stopped, met her gaze with a steady but determined one.

"So, Fyn and I are going to stay here. We don't want you to be alone if someone comes back here looking for the weapon. And if they do, we'd really like to meet them."

"And if I say no?"

"Then we'd have to assume you're part of it and—arrest you."

"Right." She found herself wanting to smile when she should be angry. Furious maybe. "Then I guess you can stay."

When he got up and walked over to Hitchens, she wondered why they were letting her stay. But she didn't really have to ask it. It was obvious they didn't really trust her. And it had started long before they found a dead man in her yard and a working space gun in her garage.

~

Hitchens and his boys melted away, taking the body and leaving the ferret. They'd wanted to take the ray gun, too, but Rick needed bait. If the killer was watching the house and had seen them arrive, he wouldn't be back, not even for a ray gun. But it was possible whoever had switched the guns had led the chase away from the house. It was even possible he or she got clear. Or got caught and talked.

Either way, someone would be back to make the switch or they'd be in contact with Jilly.

Before Hitchens left, they'd wired the place from stem to stern. An ant wouldn't be able to pass gas without them knowing it. If they'd had more time—but time seemed to be the one thing they didn't have. Events had moved rather quickly since he and Fyn arrived to scope out a possible alien.

And Rick still didn't know the answer to *that* question. And, worse, still didn't know how to find out.

For the first time, he wondered why they'd sent him. And why Fyn?

When they went out to their car to add some armament, Rick asked Fyn.

He was quiet for a long time—no surprise that. The surprise came when he spoke. In whole sentences.

"There is evidence that some of the Garradians had," he hesitated, "nanites in their bodies. Among other things, they—communicate with each other."

"Okay."

Another silence.

"I have some. I was injured during the battle with the Dusan. Nanites were used to heal me. If she had them, I should have sensed them."

Rick didn't even have an okay in him. Felt more like a *hot damn*. But he wasn't confident enough to say it out loud.

"Does that mean she's *not* Garradian?"

"No." Fyn gave him a look. "Just means she doesn't have nanites."

"Do you think she is?" He'd spent a lot of time staring at her. He must have an opinion.

"Sara thinks she is."

His wife thought Jilly was Garradian. He almost asked why her opinion mattered more than, oh, everyone else's, but somehow couldn't. Maybe it was that surge of menace that flared in a gaze already fully loaded with threat that did it.

"Then she's a really good liar," Rick muttered, more to himself than to Fyn.

"Maybe she doesn't know."

Rick looked at Fyn while he considered the words and the implication: that Fyn didn't think she was lying either. It was kind of a relief but also disturbing. How could she write about the Garradian history and not know it was real? Even though he had a pretty wide definition of weird that was pushing it.

"I don't see how," he said, again more to himself.

Fyn shrugged. Maybe he'd just run out of words. He tucked his ray gun into his waistband and covered it with his tee shirt. He picked up his night vision goggles and handed the other pair to Rick.

A few hours ago, Fyn and his armament had seemed like overkill. Now Rick wondered if they'd brought enough.

~

Jilly cooked them all some dinner, not because cooking was her thing or to be friendly. Mostly she needed something to do with her hands. She longed to be sitting at her computer. She longed to be alone to *think*.

Her mind wanted to flash back to the space gun, the way it had felt in her hand. She should have realized it wasn't the mock-up. Now she remembered the mock-up was a lot lighter, but at the time, it hadn't felt wrong. What was even stranger, when it fired it had surprised her, but—not. She had this vision of standing next to someone—Kamen—and he was pointing to a black mark just like the one on her garage. Who was Kamen and why did he seem not made up? Why could she see a screen with what looked like specifications for the weapon on it? It felt weird to even think in terms of specifications. She was an author, a former librarian. Not a weapons specialist.

And why did the switched weapon look so much like her mock-up?

Oscar Redding aka Jusan used to email her questions about the weapons in her books. He liked the tech talk, the theory behind her stuff. Sometimes it surprised her that it felt like her answers were real, so real she pulled back from saying too much. There were actually three fans, slash, readers who liked to talk weapons tech on her email loop. Dragonslayer, "Jusan," and skywalker8524. A lot of "Jedi" loved her books, too. She hadn't known they were "space operas" until someone told her after her second book released. Some of her fans got defensive about the label, but it didn't bother Jilly.

"Everything all right?"

Until Daniels spoke, Jilly hadn't realized she was staring at her cupboard door, her hands idle on the raw chicken. Jilly hesitated, not anxious to throw any of her fans to the feds, but Oscar had died. If one of them was involved...

She turned to face Daniels, no Rick, he'd asked her to call him Rick. She propped a hip against the edge of the counter.

"I have this fan loop online. I was just thinking..." She hesitated again, wishing she knew if she were doing the right thing. Rick was smart enough to look encouraging, but not speak. "There are three of them that like to talk weapons tech more than the others. Sometimes to the point of being annoying. Oscar was one of them. I don't think of them together, because it's online, but they did know each other. At least, they went to the same SF cons."

"You ever see them together—now that you think about it?"

His tone wasn't condemning, which it could have been.

"How can I explain what it's like? There's a camaraderie when you're on a loop. You feel like you know people, but you really don't. Sometimes you put names to faces, but not always. Some people are bold online but shy in person. Jusan, Oscar, didn't start really stalking me for several years. And it was always benign." The pain in her head dulled to a steady throb. "If they have websites, some of them post pictures taken with me. There's a place online for them to post websites. Might be worth checking out."

"Let's do it," Rick said, taking the knife from her hands.

"The chicken..."

"I'll finish it," bad agent said, sounding almost friendly. Or hungry.

Jilly washed her hands and led Rick to her study. Her computer was already booted up. She had a feeling her hard drive had been copied. At least they hadn't taken the whole thing with them. She pulled up the website and went into the links section. All three of the tech talkers had websites. She pulled up each one for Rick, then let him take her chair.

All three of them had at least one page of pictures taken with them and favorite celebrities. It gave Jilly an odd feeling to see herself in a picture next to those of William Shatner and Amanda Tapping. Like she was famous, too.

Rick made a call, feeding the names and websites to someone. After a bit, some information came back to his Blackberry that made him look thoughtful.

But not enough to share.

Jilly considered the two men left alive. Dragonslayer was a tall, cadaverous looking man who probably should have been an undertaker—and might very well be one. Skywalker8524 was the medium one of the trio, medium height, build and coloring. Short, medium and tall. She couldn't have planned it that way if she wanted to. In fiction, it would be too obvious, she thought with a wry smile.

"Do you keep records on where your mock-up tech went?" Rick asked.

Jilly pulled open a file drawer and removed a thick file. Four books and a lot of tech. She handed it to him.

He flipped it open and studied the first sheet, which included a name, address and a photo of the item.

"Impressive."

"IRS," Jilly said. They didn't like her claiming her welding supplies as tax deductions. They'd lost.

"I see you've made one of the space guns for each book."

"It's a popular item. And my characters use them a lot."

"Were they all the same?"

"Mostly. The last one and this one were modified because that's what happened in the book. Even in a fictional world, progress is necessary."

Even as she said the words, she had that flash again of a lab in her book and specs on a screen. It felt so real, like she could reach out and touch them. Like she could actually build one...

With the flash came the pain, so sharp she almost gasped out loud. It hadn't been this bad since the accident...

"Are you all right?"

Through little lights that danced in front of her eyes, she could see him, could feel his hand on her arm steering her into the desk chair.

"I think I've got a migraine." She took several deep calming breaths.

"Do you have some medication?"

She almost shook her head, but thought better of it. "Used to, after the accident..."

"You were in an accident?" His voice was almost as sharp as the pain.

"A minor fender bender. Or should I say head banger?" She tried to smile but wasn't sure it happened.

"When was this?"

"When?" She leaned her head against the chair rest, wishing he'd go away and leave her alone. "I don't know, a few years."

"Before or after you started writing?"

"Before." The pain began to ease as her thoughts shifted in a new direction. Weird how that worked. "It's kind of what got me started. It was a small accident, but it made me realize my life was passing so quickly and I wanted more." She straightened in the chair. "I liked being around books, but I also wanted to write one. Then one became two and two become four."

"Interesting." His voice was a low murmur.

What was so interesting about it, she wanted to ask, but he seemed almost unaware she was still there.

Her glance strayed back to the screen and the photographs. A figure in the back drew her attention for some reason. Also made the pain spike again. She clicked on the picture, enlarging it and stared at the man standing to one side.

"He came to one of my book signings," she said, feeling almost faint from the pain washing through her. It went way beyond her head. "He was strange. Looked at me like I should know him..."

Rick crouched by her chair, clasping her hands in his. Warmth crept up her arms and through her body.

"And did you know him?"

"No..." Her voice was as uncertain as she felt. At the time, she'd felt like she should know him. "He just has one of those faces." That's what she'd told herself at the time. "I didn't like him."

Before Rick could speak, her phone rang, the sound shrill in the small room. They both jumped. She looked at the caller ID. It showed a private name and number.

Rick's gaze went from thoughtful to intent in a single blink.

"Answer it."

She depressed the call button. "Hello."

"You have something of mine and I have something of yours, Ms. Smith." The voice sounded like it was being filtered through one of those voice things. Metallic and sinister. The way a person would sound who killed with a space gun. "We can do this the easy way or the hard way."

Jilly cleared her throat. "I've always been a fan of the easy way."

Rick looked at the seedy warehouse and almost sighed. Couldn't the bad guys ever try to be less stereotypical? Just because they always had meets in places like this in the movies, did that mean they had to take it into real life?

"Nervous?" he asked, trying to decipher Jilly's expression in the dim light and failing.

"Duh."

The lady had spunk.

Fyn had already exited the car before they pulled to a stop outside the warehouse. It was possible he'd already rounded up the bad guys and was just waiting for them inside where he'd ask what took them so long.

"They told me to come alone."

"They always tell you to come alone and they know you won't. They know we won't let you. He's got his backup, too, which he hopes will trump our backup." They could have a whole squad of Marines and not trump Fyn. Rick planned to stay out of his crossfire.

He handed her the ray gun. "You go in, show them the weapon, then hit the deck and let us clean up."

"Sounds simple."

"Don't make it hard."

"Okay." Her voice sounded wry in the humid darkness.

As soon as she opened the door, the stink of old wet stuff rushed in. She slipped out, slammed the door, and he heard the crunch of her footsteps as she walked toward the slightly open door.

He looked at his watch. His backup was slow but should be here in five.

He waited until she reached the door, then started around the side of the building away from her.

Fyn slid through the darkness feeling comfortable for the first time since he left Area 51 and Sara. The night vision goggles made it easy to move around obstacles and see the opposition before they saw him.

He picked a guy up and threw him against a wall. He crashed through it. Cheap wall. His weapon was quiet, but someone might notice the flash. Besides, he needed the workout. He looked down at the guy. Not that he'd given him much of a workout. He paused to tap into the satellite system, the way Sara had taught him. He found one passing overhead and focused in on the area around the warehouse.

Ten heat signatures outside the warehouse, strategically positioned to cover any approach. Only four inside. Interesting. He made a mental heads up display, a HUD, to work with, lined up his angle of attack and started forward again. There should be a guy right —there.

Bingo. Only nine more to go.

Jilly moved toward the faint glow coming through the slight gap in the door. Rick had given her a flashlight and she used it, pointing it at the ground as she picked her way through the alley's debris.

The night air was thick and humid and weighted with the scent of old dead *everything.* She reached the door and widened the gap enough to step through. There was just enough light to see her way clear to a barrel about five yards ahead. She assumed that was her mock-up space gun lying on top of it.

It was hard not to think of mice and cheese, particularly in this place.

"Hello?" Her voice echoed around the high ceiling.

"You wearing a wire?" The voice was still metallic, like on the phone. He'd probably gotten a voice synthesizer at one of the SF cons. Despite the disguise, there was something in the voice that tugged at her memory—and stabbed into the place in her head where her migraines started. *Great. Not now. You can ache later.*

"I'd never be that obvious." She sounded cooler and calmer than she felt. Probably because she was being that obvious.

A pause and he laughed. She was sure it was a him.

"True. You never go for the obvious."

Jilly couldn't believe he fell for it. Or he didn't care. Rick said he had goons. They had guys. Well, they had guys incoming. For now, they had Fyn. Actually, thinking about Fyn calmed her. He looked like he could kick some serious butt.

"You have my item?"

"Yes. I see mine there, if it is mine?"

"It's yours." A pause. "Mine's more valuable."

"Certainly more dangerous." Her turn to pause. "I accidentally fired it. I should make you pay for the paint job."

"I guess you could try." A sinister pause this time. "I wouldn't advise it."

That sounded a bit too sinister for comfort. "I suppose not."

"Make the switch and you can go."

She almost believed him. He knew she hadn't come alone. And he knew she knew he hadn't come alone either. But she didn't think he knew about Fyn. Or he wanted her to think he didn't know? Her eye twitched. Maybe it would be better not to think too much until this was over.

"You get to see me, but I don't see you?"

"You can see me, but then I'd have to kill you."

Okay, that was definitely sinister.

"How long you been waiting to use that line?"

A laugh. "Feels like my whole life." Another pause. "I don't want to hurt you. I like you. I like your books."

She knew, to her toenails, that he was lying. He didn't like her. He didn't like her books. But she had to play her part, pretend she believed him. She started toward the barrel, toward the mock-up, but something, maybe a gut deep instinct stopped her in her tracks.

"What are you doing, Ms. Smith?" Metallic anger in the voice.

"I'm having trouble suspending disbelief." She licked her lips, then added, "Don't feel bad. No one gets the plot right the first time through."

She shifted closer to the shadows.

"Stay where I can see you!"

I don't think so.

She dove for the shadows, the flash of energy heating her back as she went down.

Rick eased around a corner, then pulled back at the sight of the heat signature at the end of the corridor. Nothing happened, so he eased an eye out of cover and studied the figure. His posture was alert, but he had his back to him. Rick wasn't sure he could cover the distance without the guy hearing something. He wanted to keep it quiet for now, even though he was worried about Jilly.

He couldn't see what the guy hoped to gain from the meeting. He knew they were here. They knew his guys were there. He had to know their guys were surrounding this warehouse.

So why had he exposed himself like this?

Unless he wasn't in there? Could he be broadcasting from somewhere else?

He started to swear, but then stopped. Okay, if he wasn't going to show up for the meet, why set it up? If he wanted the weapon, then he wouldn't stop until he got it...right?

Unless he had another agenda...

It hit him all at once. He ripped off the goggles, jumped around the corner and downed the heat sig with one shot from the ray gun. Sweet.

"Fyn, move in now! We've got to get Jilly out of there. It's a trap! All teams move in! I say again, move in now!

❧

Fyn saw their signatures pop up on his HUD, even as he heard Daniels shouting in his head set. He'd cleared two sides and the back of the warehouse. Only three guys—make that two. He saw a door ahead and kicked it down, then rolled through the opening, firing right, then left, then straight ahead. In the sudden silence, he heard the thump of a body against the floor. He checked the HUD. That was odd, now he saw only one guy. Maybe Daniels took out someone. Guessed it was possible. Fyn jumped up and started making his way through barrels and crates toward what he assumed was Smith's position. He could see the one guy left moving in on her, too.

What made Daniels think it was a trap? He adjusted the satellite tracking tighter, looking for anything in the area around Smith that didn't look right...

"Bomb. I think we got a bomb."

❧

Rick moved into the main storage area of the warehouse at the same time Fyn gave the bomb alert. His gut kicked like a mule. The bright flare of an energy beam just missed him as he dove behind a crate.

"Jilly! He's going to kill you!" He popped up and fired to one side of the location the ray had come from, then to the other. Got a muffled yell for a reward.

"Like I didn't know that!" Jilly's voice sounded too calm. "I would like to know why, of course."

"Why?"

The metallic voice seemed odd, like they'd wandered into an SF movie instead of the cop show more suited to the setting.

"You don't write mysteries, Meli. You peddle our secrets for this stupid world, pretending you created something."

Okay, that was definitely SF.

"The book signing..." Jilly's voice sounded strained now and Rick could almost see her rubbing her temples. "You thought I'd recognize you."

"You pretended you didn't. Your mistake. Maybe you should have been an actress instead of an author. Now you have to die."

"Don't believe him, Jilly," Rick called out, trying to draw the guy's attention. Hoping she'd use the time to work toward the door. He eased down an aisle, trying to work his way toward where he'd heard her. Light slammed into a support beam ahead of him.

An answering beam came out of the shadows across from him, hitting that spot. There was a thump, then a crash as a body tumbled to the floor.

"That's everyone, Daniels," Fyn's voice came through the head set. "Only our people left..."

∾

The pain was worse than any she'd ever experienced. *Meli.* That name pounded through her head. She knew that name. Rick said to get out. She needed to try to get back to the door. The rest of it, all of it waiting to crush her, that could wait. He was trying to kill her. *He—* his name was Ambrel. A paper pusher. A jerk, even before they left the outpost...

No, don't think. Just move.

She felt the grit from the rough floor grinding into her hands as she crawled through a tunnel of crates and pain. She heard voices, saw flashes of light, but through it all, she saw her home, saw her people—before the scattering.

She hadn't written books. She'd told their stories, shared their history. How could she not know what she was doing?

"Jilly! It's clear!"

His voice was a light in the fog.

"Run! Run to the door! There's a bomb..."

That cut through everything like a beam slicer. Jilly pushed up, looking around to get her bearings. As she started toward the door, a bright beam of light cut through the air in front of her.

Transport beam.

She raised the weapon, waiting for the light to clear, then pulled the trigger. Ambrel only had time to look surprised before the beam hit him in the chest, knocking him back one step. She fired again and he staggered, then he tripped over something and fell.

Jilly ran forward. He was lying on top of another body.

Dragonslayer.

Ambrel's mouth moved once, before he managed. "You got me, but you didn't save yourself, bitch."

Suddenly Rick was on one side of her, Fyn on the other.

"Nice shot," from Fyn.

They grabbed her arms, swept her toward the door. Her feet didn't even touch the ground. As they pushed through the door, Jilly heard the explosion, felt the heat, saw the light, just before they went down...

Rick lifted his head cautiously and looked around. Hitchens' team saturated the area and he could hear sirens in the distance getting closer. Beneath him, he felt Jilly stir and rolled off her. Flames from the warehouse licked the night sky, sending smoke in huge puffs to hide the moon.

Fyn was already up, his arms crossed like he was bored and none of any of it had anything to do with him.

"It was a transport beam," Jilly said, as she took the hand he held out to her. "He's—he's—an alien."

Rick kept a hold of her hand. The other still held the ray gun. It was pointed at her head. He eased it out of her grip and stuck it in his waistband

"How do you know he's an alien, Jilly?"

She sighed, rubbing her head. "Because I'm one, too." She looked at him, her eyes huge in her pale face. "I came here to escape people like him..." She rubbed her head again. "I forgot. I hit my head and I forgot, not completely, but enough. That's why you came, isn't it? To find out if I was—Garradian?"

"Yes."

"I felt it, even with his voice disguised. I—knew him. I started to remember. I knew he was going to kill me, I felt it, even before my memory came back."

"You got good instincts." He brushed some dirt off her cheek.

"What happens now?"

"Area 51."

Her brows arched. "It's for real?"

He nodded, gave a half grimace.

"Wow." She was quiet a minute. "So, you and Fyn, you're like *Men in Black?*"

"Yeah. Only we wear jeans. I've never been big on suits."

They started toward the car.

"So, you work there? When you aren't tracking aliens?" Her wide gaze looked his direction, almost shy, a bit hopeful.

He smiled. "Yeah."

"So, maybe we'll see each other around?"

He stopped and faced her. "Oh yeah, Jilly Smith. We'll see each other around." Her smile was his reward. He grinned, started to turn, but stopped. "What's your real name?"

"Melischodira."

Rick blinked once, then again. "So, Jilly, do you think you can help us find your friend's transport—station?"

She shrugged. "Maybe. And he's not my friend. He killed Dragonslayer."

His hand brushed against hers and he grabbed it, liking the way her hand felt in his. Dry heat and Jilly. Area 51 was looking up.

~

Ebook Bonus: Time Trap

As a special thank you for buying this digital edition, I'm including this short story that originally appeared in *Embrace the Romance: Pets in Space 2,* a *USA Today* bestseller. The anthology was also picked as a *Library Journal* Best Books for 2017 (e-Originals).

Introduction

Hiding in time is not as easy as you'd think...

USAF Engineer Master Sergeant Briggs—only his mother called him by his first name—is not enjoying his birthday. A year older and ordered to recuperate on a quiet bay away from the Garradian outpost, he's ready to mutiny and go back to his beloved engines. When his friends send him a gift from Area 51, he figures it will relieve his boredom for an hour or so.

Until he turns it on and he gets his second present of the day.

Madison, and her parrot partner, Sir Rupert, are on the track of a traitor to the Rebellion when they time travel into a trap. Their only way out is via an old transport pad, but instead of sending them somewhere, it sends them back in time. Straight into the arms of the one man who could kick her tires and light her fires.

She would like to get to know the handsome engineer, but the trouble following her can get people erased from existence. The fact he's a hero, like her lost brother, just makes her want to protect him more.

Briggs doesn't trust time travelers—with good reason—but now he has to work with the unlikely pair because trouble is coming. Trouble that puts an outpost filled with geeks and ancient technology at risk. It's not the first time he's worked with a woman to save the universe, but it's the first time he's wanted to keep her for himself.

If only she were a little older...

With a Time Service Interdiction Force on their heels, can the three craft a plan that will save a base full of geniuses and technology and get them the happy ending they deserve?

Chapter One

Master Sergeant Briggs—yes, he had a first name, but only his mother had ever used it—stared somewhat balefully at the crate delivered to him by the lowliest Airman currently stationed on the so-secret-they-weren't-even-supposed-to-think-about-it Garradian outpost. No one had wanted to be the one to bring it to him. Rumor was, there was a no-fly zone over his "recuperation sector." What a bunch of wimps. So he was kinda grouchy about being side-lined for his *health*. And turning a year older.

Who wouldn't be? Jeez, he'd been banished to a freaking hut. So he'd gotten shot. It was a graze. That maybe got an alien infection, but he'd kicked that to the curb. And what do they do? They park him on a bay overlooking a freaking ocean. It was hot, but it wasn't the heat bugging him. It was all this freaking fresh air. Like he was some kind of beach bum or suffering a mid-life crisis, instead of a guy who lived and died for planes and spaceships and the motors that made them move. His lungs needed engine fumes, not tropical breezes. He needed work, not a birthday present.

He glared at the crate. It didn't flee. Just sat there. Only two people he knew would be brassy enough to send him a birthday present, especially right now.

Sara Donovan and Doc Clementyne.

He could hear them laughing all the way from the Milky Way. They wouldn't be laughing when they turned forty five. Five years to fifty. How the hotel did that happen? He wasn't supposed to get older if he took a trip to a galaxy far, far away. He was pretty sure someone had promised him he'd get younger if he signed on the dotted line. Or if not younger, then that he wouldn't get older. Some kind of paradox or something.

About to stomp away from the crate, he hesitated. Donovan and the Doc did know him pretty well. Were they busting his chops? Or sending him a lifeline?

If they didn't want to drop and give him twenty when he got back to Earth, there'd better be something interesting in there. He pulled out his army knife—one on steroids—and selected a chunky blade. He applied this—with force—to the nails holding the lid down. Yanked the lid back and tossed it aside. There was a note on top of the straw. At least they'd been smart enough not to send him an actual birthday card.

We found this in the Area 51 garage sale and immediately thought of you.
Cha-cha-cha,
Donovan and Doc (and their significant others)
P.S. According to the files, this was collected on 2789645. Ring any bells?

Area 51 garage sale. He chuckled. He should have known. Those two did know the way to make his engineer's heart happy. He dug through the straw, tossing it aside. The late afternoon wind would clear it away. The wind was like the tide. It came. It went. Every freaking day. Weren't even any damn birds chirping on this blasted place. What kind of island didn't have birds?

His hand struck metal, he felt around for the edges, and lifted it clear. Heavy little sucker. It pulled at his wound, but he ignored that and carried it over to the rough table he'd built on his second day of exile, using some of the driftwood washed in by foxtrot tide. The local doc could tell him to take it easy, but she couldn't make him do it. If he'd had the parts, he'd have given the table an engine. And driven it back to the base.

He set the big disc down on top of the table and stepped back to study it. Not exactly promising. Looked like a manhole cover. Maybe those two were jerking his chain. Only his knowledge of Donovan and the Doc kept him from heaving it into the surf.

And the fact that Area 51 did not save man9hole covers, not even for garage sales.

2789645? Actually that did ring a few bells.

He pulled up the stool he'd also made, and considered the item, rubbing his chin thoughtfully. If memory served—which it might not now that he was so foxtrot old—that was the first planet they'd dropped a team on back in the early days of Project Enterprise, when they weren't sure any of it was going to work.

The planet had had a barely habitable atmosphere, some algae that only excited the botanists and this. The geeks had studied it for a while, but had lost interest when it didn't do anything. No one had asked him to look at it then, and he'd had other priorities, so he didn't care.

Now? He might care a little.

He'd gotten that desperate.

Why had they sent him this thing? Something about it must have interested them. He leaned back wondering how they got their hands on it, and then how they got it to him for his birthday—all without getting him or themselves flagged and hauled in to explain. Until he remembered who they were. Alone, those two were dangerous. Together? Lethal. He liked that about them. And they could dance. He'd always hoped to find a permanent dance partner—but he didn't hang out in the right places for that kind of woman.

He sighed. Reached out a finger and flicked the edge of the metal. He wasn't worried about touching it. If there'd been any danger in touching it, someone would already be dead. Or turned into an alien.

It was thicker than a manhole cover. No sign of a seam on the sides. He ran his hands across the top. It was rough, mostly from mild corrosion, he decided. His fingers found indentations that could be an alien version of screws or bolts. He lifted it up and studied the rim, rolling it left, then right. Lines were cut in the rim, not unlike a coin, but then his fingers found two depressions, side by side. He pushed them both. They gave, but nothing happened. Not a surprise. The geeks had probably done that much. He pulled out his cheaters —one of those gifts that keep on giving for crossing into over-forty range—and studied the rim. Was there a seam?

He turned it over. The bottom was dotted with multiple ovals that formed a circular grid across the surface. He touched one of the holes. It indented about an inch. He felt around. Was that wiring he felt in there?

"What do you do?" he muttered. The wind and the tide didn't know.

Time to see if he could open this bad boy up. Be nice to put one over on the geeks of Area 51.

Chapter Two

They dropped through the time tunnel in a dark rush, the landing a jolt that shook Madison all the way from her toes to the top of her head. Good thing she knew how to stick a landing. She didn't move and thought she wasn't breathing until her nostrils filled with the pungent scent of cleaning supplies and the dust their arrival had stirred up. With her knees still bent from the landing, she wiggled her nose, trying to head off an errant sneeze.

The fear of getting shot helped. This was their most vulnerable moment. It took a few seconds for all the molecules to settle, during which they were an easy target.

When no one shot them, she eased her weapon free and flicked it to stun. She wasn't supposed to kill people for fear of messing up the timeline. But they could kill her. So not fair.

After another moment of assessing silence, she pulled out her handy little scans-for-almost-everything device with her other hand, and flicked it on. The scanner had a fancier name but even its initials were too long to remember. With her weapon extended, she lifted the scanner up next to it and studied the faintly glowing screen, looking for something she might have to shoot, well, stun. No other life signs, at least in the immediate vicinity. She adjusted the settings with her thumb, scanning wider. No one but them so far.

Of course, the opposition could be wearing a fancy heat-blocking suit, too. But for now the intel that had sent them here looked to be decent. She didn't let herself get optimistic. There was still a lot that could go wrong.

Sir Rupert's claws dug into her shoulder, as he poked his beak up out of his specially designed-for-him backpack. He wasn't good at whispering, so he used his claws to ask for an update. She felt the soft brush of feathers against her neck and lifted her index finger, her signal for "just a minute." She changed the settings again, this time scanning for threats inside this room. Found nothing, which would be one of the reasons she'd chosen to arrive here. Even the tightest security types didn't think about teching up the janitor's closet. Not that they really needed to double down in this room when this outpost was thick with beyond-the-latest in protection and detection technology—if their intel was right.

There should be—yup, there they were. The master security feed wires ran into, and out of, a box in the corner of this room. This would be the other reason she'd chosen to arrive here. One really didn't want to land in a motion-sensor-rich zone to take out, say, the motion sensors.

She navigated around a bucket, then a mop. Man, you'd think people would come up with a better way to clean in the future.

She scanned the junction box for alarms, then felt along the sides with her fingers—she liked to use high and low tech—and when she was satisfied there were no trip wires, she shone her light on what looked like a keyhole. She looked closer. Amazing. It was a keyhole. She shook her head, pulled out a lock pick, and popped it open. The guts were high tech again, so she used her handy dandy line-tapping thingy, and soon she was looking at the station's video feeds on a small screen. She shifted between the various views, looking for signs of trouble. This station was, according to the intel, a kind of safe house and time travel research center.

As she studied the feeds, she also noted the arrangement of hallways, sleeping areas, offices, a couple of labs, the arrival and departures room, and the inevitable time command center. It pretty much matched the map she'd been given prior to her briefing, and according to her time chronometer, she had nailed her time landing.

She gave herself a mental thumbs-up because her hands were full.

Once she was sure of her route, she fired up the recording program, just in case anyone was monitoring this particular time. While that was doing its thing, she went into the guts of the programming, studying their scanning and blocking tech. She wasn't a geek, but thanks to good briefings, she played one during time ops. She frowned. It wasn't at the level she'd been told to expect. A niggle of unease created a nagging, unreachable itch between her shoulder blades. If she could have, she'd have flashed out right then, but how did she explain the niggle to the very tough new guy, who probably had something to prove since he'd just been promoted?

Still uneasy, she turned off anything she couldn't false feed, then started her recordings looping. It was kind of old school, but Madison was really old school. And she liked to throw in curveballs so the opposition couldn't get a good file on her. Being predictable was the kiss of death in the time travel biz.

She went super high tech on the motion sensors. Motion sensors were evil. And sneaky. The motion sensors were easier to mess over than she'd expected, too. Her niggle went up a notch.

Sir Rupert must have felt her stiffen. He emerged from his pack and perched on her shoulder so he could ruffle his wings. "Well?"

"Too easy," she told him. Of course, there was no way to know if anything she'd done had worked until they opened that door. At that point they'd either get shot or not. Their geeks could jump forward in time and get the latest devices, but so could the Time Service. It was a quiet battle of wits fought across the whole canvas of time, though neither side culled much tech from early in time. Wasn't much call for catapults in a time outpost, or anywhere else she'd been. Though she remained hopeful. In her opinion there was something kinda majestic about hurling large objects long distances.

"One or two niggles?" Sir Rupert asked.

They might have done a few too many ops together. "I'm up to two."

"Tell me when you hit three," he said.

"Roger that."

For a parrot, he had some big, brass ones. And like her, he knew that so much access to so much tech meant these outposts were getting harder and harder to crack, even with good intel from their spies in the Service. They both knew that the quality of the intel had been declining. Hard to pinpoint exactly when with time travel in the mix. All that bouncing around in time, sometimes she forgot what she knew and when. It was the new guy, a former security chief on a space station, who had figured out they had a mole. Which could mean their spies had been erased or reprogrammed.

She closed the panel and turned toward the door but wasn't quite ready to cross the space between. She reminded herself this intel was supposed to be solid as a rock—one traveling through space and time. Which meant it was solid until it wasn't.

She still had doubts about a mole, or so Madison had heard, but *She* must have approved the mission. Madison also knew that the details had been tightly controlled. Only Madison, Sir Issac, the new guy, and *She* knew about it. Even the geek who'd talked her through the tech didn't know when or where they were headed.

And Madison was the only one who had picked the exact time and place. Knowing that didn't help the niggle, in fact, it made it worse, but not quite to a level three yet. Had Madison somehow given them away? She trusted everyone but *She*, but not because Madison thought *She* was a mole. It was *She's* utter ruthlessness that made Madison uneasy around her. It was probably a good quality for a Rebellion leader, but it did make a lowly minion uneasy. Madison could admit that this prejudice could also have something to do with when she'd been born, at a time when heroes beat the bad guys by being heroic instead of ruthless.

She hesitated, trying to pinpoint where her uneasy originated from. Madison had been told it was almost impossible to jump back in time and change the outcome of an op—there was even an equation for it. But "almost" wasn't for sure, and that didn't mean the opposition hadn't learned how—or that *She* would tell her minions if the opposition had closed that loophole. Frankly, the way both sides had agents bouncing around in time, it was miracle they didn't collide in transit.

So Madison had two rules. She never believed everything she was told, and she always expected the worst—without going full on pessimist about it. More in the vein of "it was what it was," with a little of "what will be will be" thrown in there.

She'd escaped the Time Service agents more than once because of her rules.

And because she believed the niggles in the middle of her back.

According to their intel source, the mole had been, or was here on this outpost right now, only in another time. Dwelling on him being here, but not *here*, made her head hurt. She worked better without a headache. The science said that because all of time was aligned somehow—blah, blah, complicated equation—there were echoes, that these echoes could bleed through both time and space. There were certain species that could perceive these echoes. Wasn't it a nice coincidence that Sir Rupert was one of those species?

All they had to do was get in, let him look around, and leave without getting captured or wiped out of existence by the Time Service.

Easy peasy.

In other words, just another day—or millennium—in the Rebellion.

She realized Sir Rupert had left her shoulder. He was standing in front of a large disc that had been propped up against the wall, partly concealed by some cleaning paraphernalia.

"I haven't seen one of these for, well, for a very long time."

Madison directed her pinpoint beam at it. "What is it?"

"It's a transport pad. This is the precursor to the time travel launch pads."

"Seriously?" She shouldn't take the time, but they were in what the geeks would call a minor time flux. Which meant they had lots of time until they didn't. She joined the bird, running her light over what looked like a manhole cover. "You've gotta be kidding. Who had the nerve to use that thing?"

Sir Rupert regarded her with some amusement in his dark eyes. "I did."

"Oh. Well." She grinned. "No one ever said you lacked nerve."

He ruffled his wings, like he might be pleased.

"Let's get going," he said. He fluttered back up onto her shoulder, and worked his way back into the pack, his moment of nostalgia for the good old days over.

"You're the boss," she said, then added. "Keep your beak down." Maybe if he dug his claws into her niggle, it would go away. Or at least give it a nice scratch. She activated the door and when it slid back, she peered out. The silence—and lack of shots fired at them—were somewhat reassuring. She stepped out and turned left, padding silently down the hall toward the command center.

Chapter Three

Briggs fitted the outside cover back in place. It had been an interesting exercise getting it open. A mix of WD-40 and a magnet did the trick. Sometimes you had to go low tech on high tech crap. The interior had been interesting. Not as interesting as an interstellar engine, but better than an inanimate table.

He was pretty sure he'd found the break in the wiring—some duct tape fixed that—and then he'd traced said wiring back to what had to be the on/off switch on the outer rim. The power source had been the most interesting thing about the disc. Even almost depleted, it looked like it packed a lot in a small space. He'd almost taken it out—that would interest the geeks more than anything about the disc—but he wanted to see if he could turn the sucker on first. If he could get one over on the geeks at Area 51, well, that would be his second birthday present.

He tightened everything down, then turned it over so the dots were facing up. He had his cellphone—he couldn't phone home, but they'd launched a small satellite because the geeks missed being able to text—set up to record some video. Geeks always wanted proof. He adjusted it using the selfie stick he'd gotten as a joke gift at the Doc's bachelor party. This he'd rigged into a crude tripod. Now he carefully zoomed it in on the disc and turned on recording. He circled back to the device, careful not to block the video. He looked at the camera, he should probably say something, but he was better with tools than words. Didn't they say pictures were worth more anyway? He depressed the switch on the side and stepped back.

This time something happened.

There was a low hum that slowly built to just shy of annoying. He heard the moveable parts inside start to move. First one of the dots turned faintly red, then red flowed across the top of the disc. More humming and moving parts sounds, and the circles turned from red to green all at the same time, sending beams of green light toward the sky at least six feet in the air.

Interesting. Still not sure what it did.

He was tempted to stick a finger into one of the beams, but he knew better. Funny how knowing didn't stop the wanting.

Oh, the human condition.

He looked around, found a stick, and carried it back to the beams. He poked it into one of the green lights. The stick glowed green, but nothing happened for a count of three, maybe four, then the end of the stick vanished.

Okay. Birthday present number three. Got to keep all his fingers. And he now knew this thing did something. Wasn't sure what, but something. He went and shut off the video, then turned back to do the same to the disc, but right then the hum increased in intensity and the green lights began to pulse.

Chapter Four

Thanks to a sudden increase in her niggle—and a minor change in airflow—Madison ducked before the first shot sizzled past where she'd been standing. Crouched behind a control panel, she fired back and was already changing position before that shot reached the other side of the room. She might have heard a muffled thump, as if someone had dropped to the floor. Hopefully it was not of their own freewill. Fire was returned where she'd been, then tracked to each side.

That would be why she kept moving.

Sir Rupert, who had poked his beak out of the pack so he could use his super power, now ducked back down, so far it felt like his claws were digging into her rear. The pack had some deflective qualities, which she hoped they wouldn't need.

Memo to self: if it niggled like a trap, it was probably a trap. It could be a fluke, she reminded herself. Maybe someone dropped in and found everything off. Bad luck happened, too. It wasn't always a trap. Only time would tell which it was, an irony she wished she had time to appreciate.

She got a dig in the back, which meant Sir Rupert thought it was time to go.

Good idea, might be hard to make happen. She didn't have time to check, but she had a feeling all the station's stuff was back on. Supposedly this suit would mask their location and could do an emergency flash out even with blocking tech deployed, but a failed flash out would mark her position for them like a big arrow in the sky. Not even she could tumble and dance herself out of the kind of fire that would attract. And—there was that thing about not believing everything she was told. A stench was growing around this op that was making her question everything. But Sir Rupert would have told her immediately if the mole was in the op information chain.

They might still be able to jump out from the closet, if they could get there. Unless that gap had been left open on purpose, a gap in coverage designed to lure them in. All roads led to this being a trap, but that should have been impossible. As if she hadn't learned that the impossible was only impossible until it wasn't.

She kept her body between Sir Rupert and the incoming—he was more important than she was—as she began to retreat along the shortest route back to the closet. And—this is why she got picked for these missions—as a former gymnast, she knew how to move in ways even highly trained Time Service agents didn't expect. She initiated an intricate and random series of tumbles, leaps, and rolls—careful to keep her pack from coming close to touching the ground, or any other objects, or being exposed to enemy fire. Music in her head helped, though she missed hearing the real thing.

As opportunities presented, she fired back and even went high at one point. No one ever expected that. She fired down on them from some kind of file cabinet, and then dropped down, using it for cover while she got her bearings.

Lots of shots incoming. And they were blue, which meant they were trying to stun her. For now. But the color of the shots told her something else.

This was a Time Service Interdiction Squad. Their best and brightest. Could it be Boris out there—she shut that thought off at the root. *Don't go there.*

If they caught sight of Sir Rupert, they wouldn't settle for knocking her out. They would not risk him getting off this outpost with what could be in his head. Would their scanning be able to separate his profile from hers? The pack was supposed to prevent that, too. But...oddly enough, sometimes the super tech got too sophisticated for its own good and missed the small stuff. Like a parrot. She would have liked to figure out what gave them away—apparently still hoping this wasn't a trap—but she was too busy dealing with what was.

She had a slight edge, or so she hoped. Unlike many of the

other rebels, she'd never been a Time Service agent, so their intel on her should be limited to those scans taken during past ops, which varied based on the sophistication of the tech used at the time. With time travel in the mix, she never said never. But at least they'd never had a chance to dig around inside her head. People could try to be unpredictable, but they tended to be unpredictable in ways that sophisticated tech could predict. Yeah, another equation.

She reached the hallway opening and flattened against the wall in a low crouch, angled so that Sir Rupert was protected as much as possible. She felt the vibration as more station systems came online. Didn't have time to see if they'd found her video loops. She was pretty sure they'd be able to track her soon, if they weren't already.

Just in case they weren't, she dug in her pocket for one of the pebbles she invariably kept there for moments like this, and tossed it well away from where she wanted to go. It clinked against the metal floor and a flurry of shots crisscrossed the spot. Still blue.

The volume of shots confirmed her suspicion she was up against a squad. Kind of flattering. In a not wonderful way.

None of the shots had come from the door she wanted to go through. Apparently she was supposed to just dive through. Because the best and brightest the Time Service could muster would leave one door unguarded.

She did a crouching roll across the opening—she did have a bird on her back—and fired multiple rounds through the opening, laying down a wide spread to clear her path ahead, then she was up, following her fire down the hall. It was a nice narrow hallway with no alcoves to hide in. Hopefully the hostiles on her heels would be just far enough behind to give her time to get to the closet.

The doors lining the hall were all metal, so any that were partly open she lit up as she ran past. Amazing how hot a metal door got from even one energy blast. Her weapon wasn't set to stun. Not anymore.

She heard cursing, and at least one body hitting the ground. Shots came from behind now, tracking after her like angry bees. She was still doing her gymnast thing, but the hallway was narrow. She needed to get out of it and fast. She returned fire from a low position, her flip taking her into the shallow protection of the closet door. Her shoulder was out just far enough to catch a blast that almost spun her away from the door. That wasn't a stun. But not a kill shot either. She staggered from the hit and pain, but managed to stick it. Sir Rupert gave a soft squawk.

"You hit?" She pressed in closer, angling to protect him, fired off some shots and hit the control to open the door, ignoring the pain spreading out from her shoulder and trying to cloud her thinking.

"No."

She fired another spread, then the door opened at her back, and they were inside the closet. The door closed and she fired on it, aiming at the handle and hinges until they glowed bright red. Only then did she reach up and try to flash out.

Not a huge shock when they didn't.

Might be damage from the hit, but most likely the opposition closed the hole they used to get in. Also meant their intel on the suit was wrong. Or they'd upgraded for it already, but—

"Blocked?" Sir Rupert asked, making his way back to her shoulder.

"Yeah." She should have tried to jump sooner—

"They locked this place down before they started firing," Sir Rupert said, as if he knew what she was thinking. Which he probably did. He was that smart. He didn't waste time bemoaning the failure of the suit to perform as advertised.

Multiple shots made the metal door rattle in its frame. They had maybe thirty seconds. Probably less.

"The transport pad," Sir Rupert said.

"Why did I know you were going to say that?" Had she had the same thought? Was that why she'd retreated here? Sometimes if felt like even she didn't know what she was thinking. She crossed to it and started to lower it.

"Not that side."

"Heavy bugger." She flipped it over, wincing as pain flared brighter in her shoulder. She blinked spots away, kicked the bucket and mop to the side so there'd be room for it to lay flat. She glanced back. Red spots were appearing on the metal door. Spots that glowed and expanded as the metal began to melt.

"Turn it on here." Sir Isaac's beak touched the spot, then he hopped on the device.

She depressed the spot. There was a hum, but it felt like a long time before the circles turned red.

She glanced back again, maybe ten seconds, and they'd be through. She pointed her weapon at the door, preparing to take a stand if she had to. Sir Rupert was the one who had to escape. She took a quick look back, but he was gone. Just a pattern of green beams shooting up from the disc and piercing the ceiling.

"Man, I hope you know where we're going."

A pinhole opened in the door, growing rapidly as they concentrated fire on that spot. The shots were red now. One red beam skimmed by her other shoulder as she scrambled onto the device. The door burst open, weapons firing at, and sparking off, the green beams—then the room vanished in a tunnel that was both familiar and not familiar. Just a transport pad, she reminded herself, but the ride felt like more than that. It was beyond rough. She tumbled and bounced around in the tunnel. Saw the white light coming and tried to slow down. Couldn't. Tried to aim for the center. Didn't think she'd nailed it.

She might be about to find out about catapults, though...

The transit sped up. Wasn't going to stick this landing. Be lucky she didn't break something. With a spin she flew head first through the center of the circle of light...

Chapter Five

S omething catapulted out of the green beams of light like it had been hurled, something that squawked loudly as it tumbled beak over claws, just missing Briggs' head. The spinning tumble continued unchecked toward a stand of palm-like trees. Somehow it recovered, made a narrow pass between two tree trunks, then circled back to a landing on the peak of the cottage. It ruffled its feathers as if annoyed, then began to preen itself.

A parrot? He blinked. The green body, with a band of red just above the beak looked parrot-like.

"That's not something you see every day." Particularly in this bird-less place. Too bad he'd already turned off the video. No one would believe he really saw a parrot shooting out of that thing.

The bird looked up and Briggs had the odd feeling it had under-stood him. He'd heard parrots were pretty smart. He glanced back at the disc. At least now he was pretty sure it was some kind of a trans-port pad. Definitely needed to get the power supply out—

He heard the hum build again and turned fully around, just in time to catch what flew out next. Instinctively his arms wrapped around the very humanoid—very female—form it ejected. He stag-gered a few steps and then went down. The sand was harder than he'd have thought. His breath rushed out as they slid toward the water, his arms still wrapped around the woman.

When they hit wet sand, they slowed, and finally stopped. He felt water soaking into his shirt and heard the waves hitting close to his head. Took him a couple of tries before he could grab some shallow breaths. Each one was filled with the smell of salt, woman, and singed something.

He could feel the female struggling to catch her breath, too. Yeah, she was definitely female. Almost every inch of her was pressed against a lot of him, creating a different problem in catching his breath.

In the sudden silence, the bird squawked once.

Over on the table, the disc's beams flickered, there was a popping sound from inside, and it went dark, smoke puffing out the holes on the top. Great. Now he didn't even have a depleted power supply to show the geeks.

"Ow."

Her voice was pained, but, well, nice. She took a couple of deep breaths that increased Briggs' male holding a female problem. He wasn't as old as he'd thought. He would have shifted her off, didn't want it to get embarrassing, and he would like to catch his breath, but the thing digging into his ribs felt a lot like some kind of gun. If she twitched wrong...

She muttered something that could have been a cuss word.

"...that hurt."

It was something of a relief she spoke very American sounding English, but also a worry. What was she doing on this top-secret outpost? He'd bet real money this was not what Donovan and Doc had had in mind when they sent him the disc to play with.

The weapon retreated as she rolled off him and onto the sand. She didn't get up, just lay there staring at the sky, her chest rising and falling quickly.

He yanked his gaze off her chest and sat up. Only, the changed angle made her harder to see. Was that some kind of high-tech camo? If it was, it was damaged. One second she was part of the horizon, next he could see her very nicely put together figure encased in a black suit.

She muttered again but all he heard was, "...buggers shoot better than I thought they could..."

She lifted the hand holding the weapon, then looked at it as if surprised to find it in her hand. It was impressive she'd kept hold of it during that landing. She stared at it then looked at him. She seemed about to say something, but instead she rolled over and got up, the movement of her body smooth and graceful.

Oh yeah, she was a girl. If he'd had any doubts after the close proximity check. Almost idly, he thought, bet she could dance a great cha-cha. And he wished he could get a better look at that weapon. It wasn't like anything he'd ever seen, even around this outpost.

"You're flickering."

That sounded like it came from the peak of the hut. Briggs got up, not nearly as smoothly as the woman. Because he was a guy, and he had his pride, he kept the wincing to a minimum. His wound had not liked the slam against woman or ground, though other parts of him hadn't minded the woman-slamming part. He thought he saw her touch something near her shoulder, and the camo faded, leaving just the black suit. Now he could see it had lines of silver running through the tight fitting black. He gave a half tug at the neck of his tee shirt. Very, very tight fitting. He'd have spent more time matching brief memory with reality, but, as if she just realized he might be dangerous, she lifted the gun and pointed it at him.

His gaze narrowed. He was not in the mood to get shot again. He made a half move toward her.

"Don't." She flicked something on the weapon.

He assessed his chances. He could take it from her. Did he want to? She looked like kind of cute standing there and the look in her eyes said she really didn't want to shoot him. There was definitely a glint of humor in her chocolate-brown eyes.

Her lips twitched. "Stun hurts almost as bad as getting shot." She rotated one shoulder. "And getting shot is the pits."

He couldn't argue with that, his hand lifting to cover his own protesting injury. He should have just taken it from her while they were on the ground. His gut said she was dangerous, but something else told him she wasn't dangerous to him—at least—he backed away from finishing that thought. Took a tug at his tee shirt neck again. Damn the heat in this place.

"You okay?"

He started to answer, but realized she wasn't talking to him.

"I am fine." The bird squawked once, then flew down, making a neat landing on her shoulder.

All she needed was an eyepatch to look like a pirate, standing there with her shoulders back, her chin up, and her feet planted. Her grin was sassy.

"Thanks for breaking my, um, fall," she said.

More heat bloomed where it shouldn't. He opened his mouth to answer, but she holstered the weapon like a pirate. Then she reached up toward a now visible line of buttons situated just below her shoulder blade and pressed one of them.

There was a distinct pop and smoke jetted out of her suit from the back.

The bird glanced back. "Well, that's embarrassing."

Chapter Six

Embarrassing didn't quite cover it. At least the big guy, the very nice looking big guy—she flicked her gaze up and down—seemed pretty unfazed by their abrupt arrival—and failure to depart. He might even be kind of amused.

Madison might be impressed.

And, by the way, she'd totally lost her fascination with catapults. She was lucky he'd been there to catch her. Of course, he was big enough to catch two of her. She studied him. He had looked annoyed when she first pointed her ray gun at him, but now? Hard to say. Was that a twinkle buried deep in his eyes? She liked the eyes, with or without a twinkle. Even drawn in a line, his mouth was—she ran a fingertip along hers and sighed. Made her gaze move on. Military haircut and bearing. The tee shirt was stretched across a chest she had good reason to know was well-muscled and unyielding. And yet, the landing had managed to be pleasant for all that.

His denim shorts exposed tree-trunk legs planted in a way that should have made her nervous. Okay, he did make her a little nervous. He could probably take her down with his pinkie finger. She felt a little color steal into her cheeks as she recalled how it felt to be held against him. All of him. The iron bars of his arms around her. His afternoon beard had been nicely rough against her cheek, his mouth temptingly close.

Did he date older women? Who pointed ray guns at him?

Sir Rupert's wings brushed the side of her head, as he lifted off, circling the clearing, then landing on a rough-hewn table parked in front of a rustic cottage. Had she landed in *Robinson Crusoe* land? The guy sure looked the part.

Sir Rupert gave a small squawk, his version of a snort, perhaps, his claws lifting briefly. So what if the big guy was the only non-time traveling male she'd met in, well, she didn't know how long. It wasn't that relationships were discouraged in the Rebellion. The new guy had a wife. But it was tough to get involved with someone who could be years younger than you, or crazy ancient, when you finally had that date. At least it was easy to shake off the bad ones. Don't call me, I'll call you took on a whole new meaning in time travel.

As if he sensed her random and inappropriate thought processes, Sir Rupert ruffled his fathers and walked around the manhole cover. Still troubled by the rustic setting, she considered the big guy, then decided he could have already taken her down if he were so inclined. She let her hand drop away from her weapon—oh yeah, that hurt—and walked over next to the boss.

"Won't that just take us back," she stopped, slanting a glance at the guy, "where we came from?"

The big guy appeared to hesitate, too, then walked to the other side of the table from her. "If I was asked, I'd say you depleted the power source and that thing won't take you anywhere."

He was a pretty cool customer. Despite the, um, rustic surroundings, he'd clearly had contact with tech. Fixing tech was not her skill set. Breaking it? Yeah, she had that down pat.

"No," Sir Rupert said, continuing to circle the disc as if that would somehow make it work again. He angled his head to look at her. "They knew right where to shoot."

Now that he'd mentioned it, she felt air from what must be a hole in the shoulder of her suit. And possibly some sluggish bleeding. And just like that the pain rose in a wave. This made the horizon waver for several seconds and her stomach gave a nauseous bump. She firmly pushed it all to the back of her brain. Because the niggle was back between her shoulder blades.

The squad couldn't use the manhole cover to follow them here, so that might be a relief, but could they track them some other way? She looked around again. Where was here? She turned back to the big guy, tried out a smile. It felt like it hit a deflector shield and fell into the sand at her feet with a painful plop. He crossed his arms over his chest—man, that was a great chest if his tee shirt wasn't lying—and she knew it wasn't.

"We don't care for Time Service agents around here."

Madison looked quickly at Sir Rupert. He was the boss.

"Neither do we," he said.

The big guys brows arched skeptically. If he'd had dealings with the Service, which he clearly had, she did not blame him.

"You're not Time Service...agents..." The sardonic tone faltered a bit as his gaze fell on Sir Rupert.

Okay, so he'd run into agents, but not Sir Rupert's *Militarian* species. That was interesting. What would he think when he found out the bird was in charge of the op? Sir Rupert gave her a tiny nod, though his glance also advised caution. Like she didn't know that.

"We're, well, I guess you'd call us the opposition." Tip-toeing through minefields was her thing, assuming it was an actual mine-field. But emotional mine fields? Not so much. Her ears were starting to buzz as the pain indicated it did not like being ignored. "Do you mind if I sit down? I don't feel that great."

She got a hard stare from the big guy and a very brief nod. She gripped the table as she sank onto the stool. She leaned an elbow on the table and tried to slow her breathing. Cause each breath hurt like a son of a gun. Been a while since she'd taken a hit this bad. If it had hit her somewhere else—but Sir Rupert was right, whoever fired it had known right where to point and shoot.

Must be frustrating when he or she saw Madison vanish via the manhole cover. She would have chuckled, but that would hurt, too. Through a growing haze she met the big guy's hard, distrustful gaze. So why did she sense something else from him? Why wasn't she that worried?

"I'd let you point my ray gun at me, but it only works for me." She lifted it clear of the holster and set it on the table top, then shoved it toward the big guy. Sir Rupert let out a muted squawk that she took to be a protest. Or agreement. Sometimes it was hard for her to tell.

"DNA or handprint?" The big guy asked, managing to keep one eye on them, as he snagged her ray gun and studied it with what she'd call professional interest.

"DNA," she told him, her voice oddly distant from the rest of her.

He quirked a brow. "Ray gun?"

"It has a fancy name that I can't ever remember," she admitted.

And that's what they'd called them in the books and movies from her time, a time where a girl like her wouldn't have got to look at one, let alone get to point and shoot one at bad guys.

She could tell by the way he handled it, he was comfortable with weapons. If her head would clear, she'd figure out what that meant for them. Beads of sweat began to track down the sides of her face and the wavering horizon began to blur. She needed to stay awake, to stay focused. There was her niggle...

Sir Rupert fluttered over to the edge of the table with a worried squawk. "You are injured. I should have realized..."

His words kind of faded so she missed the end. The horizon steadied for a second, long enough for her to see two moons, dim in the late afternoon sky, but definitely two moons hanging there over the big guy's shoulder.

She rubbed her mouth, her hand coming away damp with cold sweat. "This isn't Earth."

The big guy lowered her weapon, his gaze sharpening.

Sir Rupert looked up, his feathers ruffling.

"What year is this?" She tried to look around, but that was a very bad idea. Spikes of pain shot up from her shoulder, stabbing into her brain and everything spun fast enough to ramp up the nausea. From a long way away she heard her voice say, "Usually I can make a good guess, but this place doesn't give much away." She tried to grin, but it felt like it wavered more than the horizon. She was talking too much, but couldn't stop herself.

"Who are you?" He had his Sphinx on, though he did glance at the bird this time.

"I am Sir Rupert." He ruffled his feathers importantly.

It might actually be his real name. Birds didn't have the same risks with sharing their real names. It was hard to track down a flock and pick out the one bird who could erase you from existence. Time was not only fluid, but apparently had a sense of humor. Let's make sure, it said, probably snickering somewhere out there, that you remember people you can never see again, because they didn't exist anymore. And then let's put you in position to fix all kinds of time paradoxes. But not that one.

Never that one, thank you so much, Boris.

The big guy was looking at her now, she realized, though it seemed his expression had softened. Or her gaze was getting blurrier. Probably that one. He wanted a name, she realized fuzzily.

"Scarlet Doe." It embarrassed her to say it out loud. Even about to pass out from pain, she blushed. She met his ironic gaze. "I told them it was the worst fake—"

"Code name," Sir Rupert interposed.

"*Code* name, worst code name ever." The big guy's brows rose and his look said, give me something better than that if you want my help. She couldn't give him her real name, so she gave him the one she'd used in her head for so long it felt like her real name. "Madison. You can call me Madison."

Her insides tensed, despite the pain that caused, as the name dropped into the gentle sea breeze and rose through the air toward the warm, high sun. The horizon didn't tremble or reverberate, at least not in a time-ish way. That's how she would have known that somewhere that name had registered with someone. Real names in time travel were dangerous, existence threatening, but so was time travel. Besides, all they could do now was kill her. For her, well, she didn't exist, though it had been a near thing, a fluke in time. But even she needed something to anchor her to her past, even if it was gone. It was so easy to lose yourself in time. And for someone who had been doing it as long as she had? That anchor was as critical to her survival as staying hidden.

They all knew it, so they were careful about using those anchors outside their own minds. Until now, not even Sir Rupert had heard the name Madison. Which begged the question, why had she told the big guy? And the answer came back in two parts.

He would know a lie if he heard it.

And for some reason she was too foggy to figure out, it was important he believed her. She wanted him to trust her.

"And you are?" she asked, then was sorry because he probably only had a real name.

"Briggs."

It felt like her chin sank deeper into the palm she rested it on. "Briggs." She smiled at him, felt the cloudiness of her gaze, even as she worried at how much their arrival would put him at risk. "Nice to meet you, Briggs."

He frowned and stepped closer. "You are hurt."

"Yes." She felt the clouds going dark, felt herself listing to the side —felt those strong arms lock around her for the second time. "Thanks again," she murmured, her head dropping to rest against his truly wonderful chest as her lights went out.

Chapter Seven

Briggs carried Madison inside the hut and settled her on his bed. Her waist was ringed with a belt loaded with neatly slotted equipment. The only one missing was her ray gun. He removed the gear, then the belt, and tossed it aside. Only then did he lower her—feeling something stirring inside himself, a something not appropriate to the situation, as he did so. But doing it felt oddly familiar, as if they'd done this before. Which was not possible. So—maybe it just felt right, the kind of right that he hadn't felt for a long time. It hadn't been so long that he hadn't recognized the look in her eyes, an interest she hadn't tried to hide. Was it a tactical move? Hadn't felt like it, and the interest had stayed in there as the fog closed in, and took her down.

Before he could stop himself, he smoothed the hair back from her face, noticing how her lashes fanned across the upper curve of her cheeks. Her skin was pale beneath her tan, revealing a sprinkling of freckles across a nose that tipped up on the end. His gaze lingered on parted pink lips, noted the rapid rise and fall of her chest. He pulled his hand back, though his fingers wanted to linger on the soft skin and trace the lines and curves of her face. And then move lower...

She'd never make it onto a magazine cover. She was short, her body more compact than thin. Very fit, with signs of strength in her limbs and body. That was okay. He'd never been interested in half-starved waifs with big, sad eyes. What he'd seen of her eyes, they for sure they hadn't been sad. Serious, sassy, amused, and interested, but not sad.

She did interest him. He faced it because he needed to take care. If this was some kind of move on the base here, well, he had to make sure that didn't happen.

Madison. Even as he considered how this might be a play, his hands moved down her arms, then flexed her legs, trying to assess her injuries. He checked her ribs, but was defeated by the suit. She seemed to have been sealed inside it.

"Put your fingers here," the bird said, tapping its beak between her breasts.

He gave the bird a wary look.

"To open the seal on her uniform," it added.

Briggs decided he didn't want to know what the bird was thinking when he hesitated. He touched the suit, careful to keep his fingers in the center. But his knuckles brushed curves as he tried to find a seam. Felt like a creepy guy, even when his thumb finally found something. He pushed and a gap appeared. He pushed a little harder and his fingers brushed against soft, firm skin. He didn't yank back. That would be obvious, even to a bird. She didn't stir. Breathing a bit easier —okay, nothing was easy about this, but he doggedly worked to open it wider.

The vulnerability of her situation called to his sense of honor, the reason he'd joined the Air Force. To serve. To protect. But then there was that other call. It wasn't just a guy and a gal call, though it had started that way when she slammed into him.

There was something about her that had made a stealthy pass through his defenses, not just the base's. She was wrong for him in every way—including too young. He could be her father. Maybe if he repeated that enough, if would finally sink in. But that wasn't going to happen while he was sitting here opening her suit while the warm, clean scent of her filled his nostrils. Here he'd thought it would be better to smell anything but fresh, sea breezes. It was a reminder to be careful what you thought you wanted because the universe was listening and happy to show you where you were wrong.

He tried taking a deep breath, but that just made it worse, so he held his breath and finished exposing her from waist to neck. Underneath she wore a light weight tank top that hugged her skin and revealed the fact that the suit had seriously compressed her...chest.

Briggs massaged his temple, but stopped when he caught the bird looking at him in a way that was kinda unnerving. Like it knew exactly he was thinking. The skin he could see was smooth and also lightly tanned. No sign of tan lines—not that he was looking. Much.

He averted his gaze from the danger zones and eased the suit off her shoulders—sweat beading on his skin and hers—dang tropics—until the suit was folded down around her waist. Normally he'd have been interested in that suit. Of course, he'd left normal when the parrot bounced out of the disc. His gaze accidentally tracked across her tee shirt and he found one reason to be glad it wasn't cold. Just the one, though. Because the heat outside was not helping him at all with the heat stirring inside.

"Where did she get hit?" His voice came out husky, but maybe the bird didn't notice.

"Back left shoulder."

He shifted her onto her uninjured side and all heat fled in the face of a cold rage that wasn't any more appropriate than the—his mind rejected lust. Oh, he wanted her, he admitted reluctantly, but well, he needed to move on. She needed his help. He studied her injury.

It was an ugly, sluggishly bleeding gash high on her back, partly inside, and partly above the rounded edge of her tee shirt. The force of something had driven bits of wires, small pieces of metal, and cloth into her skin, but—he studied it carefully—he didn't think it was deep, despite the debris. He could probably patch it up, but—his thoughts strayed to the alien infection that had put him in the infirmary for several days....

"She should see a doc." And what would that involve? Their presence was a security breach that was going to be hard to explain. He glanced at the bird, who was perched on the bed examining her injury with a bird-like, but oddly professional, interest.

"It could have been worse," the bird said, relieved. "Can you apply first aid?"

The bird said. Had he just thought that? It wasn't a shock that a parrot, or parrot-looking bird, could talk. It even had the croaking overtones of a parrot. But this was *talking*, not just talking. He shouldn't be surprised. They'd been looking for non-human, sentient alien life from the first flight of Project Enterprise. It was even possible this wasn't the first contact with a non-humanoid, since there were other ships out there nosing around. It was his first, however. Until now their people had had contact with only humanoid aliens.

Briggs nodded, dug his first aid kit out of his duffle. and opened it. He found the supplies he needed and started cleaning and disinfecting the wound. He didn't hesitate, even when she stirred and muttered in pain. He'd tended battle wounds before. And this was a battle wound, no question. He might have cussed under his breath, but he kept going. It had to be done. When he was sure it was cleaned, he studied the injury carefully. There were signs of scorching around the edges. His lips tightened. Someone had used an energy—a ray gun—on her. And she'd fired back, he reminded himself. Still pissed him off someone had hurt her.

He doused the area with antiseptic, waited for it to dry, then carefully applied Super Glue to close the torn skin. He sprayed on some pain killer, then covered it with a light bandage and eased her onto her back again. Only then did he look at the bird, trying to decide what to ask.

The bird hopped up on the headboard and looked around. "Are you marooned in this place?"

Briggs sat back, shifting to ease his wound, which was complaining about the workout, now that he wasn't busy focusing on Madison's injury. *Madison*. That probably wasn't her real name either, but it meant something to her. He'd felt it, felt truth in it somewhere. "I'm recuperating." His annoyance with this broke into his tone. "The base..."

He stopped that sentence unfinished. For all he knew, these two were attempting to infiltrate the base. Just because they looked like time travelers and she'd asked what year it was, and they'd appeared out of a disc, didn't mean they'd traveled through time. It could be a simple transport pad. A decoy? Donovan's handwriting had looked genuine, but it wasn't like he could give her a call and ask. And it might have been an unintended consequence. He had been the one to fix it and turn it on—something no one at the base or Area 51 would have approved. In his boredom, he'd been careless. He could face the uncomfortable truth now that he was forty-five and probably more mature.

"You are wise to take care. The people hunting us are ruthless and highly trained. If they find you useful, they will take you, and reprogram you to serve their needs." The bird moved one way along the headboard, then moved back.

"And if they don't find me useful?" Briggs asked, his gut tightening at the thought of the "useful" people at the base, including Doc

Clementyne's brother, Robert. Robert, who had finally found happiness and purpose in his life.

"They will erase you from time. It will be as if you never lived."

He frowned. "But wouldn't that..."

"Do you think they care about fallout to others?"

"The time service—"

"...has changed," the bird said. "Absolute power corrupts absolutely. They began trying to fix and repair time breaches, but at some point their focus changed. And now it ripples back through all time in an unchecked rotten flow."

"But—" he started to protest, but how would he know that big events hadn't changed? Or if this bird spoke the truth. They were the 'opposition,' but that didn't make them allies. Even if he had a built-in prejudice against the time service thanks to Doc. The bird could be talking to earn his sympathy and turn him into a weapon against its enemy.

"The only place they take care is around large events, because these anchor time and time will push back."

If the bird could have smiled grimly, Briggs sensed it would have.

"They learned that lesson the hard way, but they did not learn enough."

Briggs studied the bird, but it was not like he had experience reading a bird's face for truth or lies. Odd that his gut felt it spoke the truth—the truth as the bird knew it, he decided.

"Why are they after you two?"

"We are hunting a traitor and they seek to stop us before we can return to our base with that information." The bird ruffled its wings and stepped lightly along the headboard again. "They did not factor in the transport pad or they would not have left it for us to find."

Was the bird sure about that? That thing didn't seem like the kind of thing you left lying around in an unsecured area.

"We found it in a storage closet, shoved into a corner," the bird said, as if it heard Briggs' thought.

Had it had the same thought?

"I can not be sure it was not part of the trap," the bird conceded. It looked around. "I do not think it meant us to come here, however."

Yeah, a trap that depended on him turning that thing on at the right time wasn't a very good trap. More like a lucky chance if these people were as bad as the bird thought they were.

The bird looked around now. "I did not expect to arrive here."

Briggs let himself grin. "Where did you think you were going?"

The bird regarded him solemnly. "Anywhere that wasn't where we were." It paused, then added, "But more useful than here."

Briggs' grin widened. He was kind of starting to like the bird. He grinned. "Yeah, I'm not thrilled to be here either," he admitted.

The bird regarded him in a way that might be thoughtful. "You should leave."

Briggs' gaze narrowed. There'd been a warning in there. Did it expect trouble to follow them here? He looked at the bird. "How do I know your trouble won't follow me?"

"It is our job to contain it," the bird said.

Briggs didn't try to hide his skepticism. Then his brows lowered in a scowl.

"They can't get here on that," Briggs pointed out, already sure that wasn't how trouble was gonna arrive.

"No," the bird's head bobbed as if it was aware of the irony, "but nevertheless, they will come."

Chapter Eight

"I'm afraid I have to agree with Sir Rupert." Madison's voice was husky, but calm.

Briggs twisted around to look at her. The fog was clearing from her eyes, revealing worry. He saw something else in there though, something he recognized because he'd seen it many times during his years in the USAF.

The look of a warrior preparing to meet the enemy.

"And thank you for the third time." She shifted her shoulders. "It feels much better."

Better wasn't fighting fit, but he also knew when someone couldn't be talked out of a fight. Not someone with that stubborn jaw line.

"You're welcome." He kept his tone even with an effort. He wanted to argue with her. He wanted to grab her and change her mind the old-fashioned way. Not that he wanted to get caught with his pants down when the enemy arrived. If they arrived. And when had her enemies become his? A smile tugged at the edges of her mouth, and regret filtered into her expression. She could be his daughter, he reminded himself. It didn't help as much as he'd hoped it would because she didn't look at him like he was her dad. Was it because he wanted her to be older that it seemed like she was older than she looked?

"You never said what year this is?" she prompted softly.

He hesitated, but couldn't think of a good reason not to tell her. "2017."

Her eyes widened. "Really?" She glanced up at the bird. It ruffled its wings, which could be its version of surprise. "But I thought—" She stopped, then asked, "Where..."

"That's classified." His non-disclosure agreement didn't say he couldn't mention the base to time travelers, but there were all kinds of clauses about not talking to anyone—including yourself—and getting shot if you did. So it added up to not disclosing to time travelers in his opinion. And the kind of shooting in the agreement? It wasn't the kind that required recuperating in a hut or anywhere else.

"I need to get up." She reached out and he did, too, maybe to stop her, but her fingers slid between his, her palm brushing against his and he forgot about stopping her. Might have made him think about pushing her back down. Warmth surged from where their hands touched and it felt like they'd always held hands and always would. There was the heat of desire in the mix, but also the warmth of a wood fire, the kind that invited you to settle in, to stay, and make something that lasted—

His fingers tightened involuntarily on hers. There was no fool like an old fool...

For several seconds, it felt like she returned his grip, probably just so she could swing her legs over the edge of the bed and rest them on the floor. Side by side, her head barely reached the top of his shoulder. He waited for her to free her hand, but she didn't. If anything her grip tightened. Her breath came in quick bursts for several seconds and she bit her lower lip. He had to stop himself from reaching for her as she lost color, but after a moment or two, her breathing slowed and some of her color came back. Her lips formed into a thin, stubborn line.

She looked at him, her smile wavering a bit, and finally there was some sad in her eyes. He didn't mind because there were other things in there, too. If he died right now...well, he wouldn't be happy, but it would be better than seeing her walk away...

The bird flew over to the top of the rustic dresser, breaking into whatever was happening between them. It walked one way along the top, then back, almost as if it were pacing.

She hesitated, her shoulders stiffening as resolve pushed out every other emotion in her eyes.

"How big is our possible risk zone?" she asked.

It stopped, a wing came up, as if rubbing the lower part of its beak. "They'll come in on a tight beam because they won't know what they're jumping into."

"They won't like that," she said with a grin. "Couple of hundred yards? More? Less?"

The bird appeared to nod. "Less, I think."

Madison shifted a bit, so that she half faced Briggs, their hands still linked.

"Is that enough to keep your people safe?"

"If it wasn't, could you do anything about it?" he asked, though without heat. He figured she was trying to find out what she needed to know, without actually finding it out. He appreciated the effort, even if he wasn't sure it would work. She had no idea what this island contained.

She nodded. "There are some things we could do." She glanced around. "Defensively, this isn't the best location. Or the worst."

"The structure will give them something to focus on," the bird pointed out, his tone in the range of 'it was what it was."

Wary and trust contended for the upper hand inside his head. Last time he'd felt like this, he'd been trying to decide if he could trust Doc Clementyne—but he hadn't felt like this around Doc. Then he had needed to only believe his head, not his heart. Could he trust either when all he wanted to do was sit here and hold her hand? Okay, not all he wanted to do. His lips twisted wryly.

"That should be enough," he admitted. If he'd put Robert Clementyne at risk, there was nowhere in time or space he could hide from Doc Clementyne.

She squeezed his hand one last time and then released it so she could stand up. This time she didn't face him when she said, "You need to go."

She didn't know he couldn't, even if he wanted to, which he didn't. He'd never walked away from an important fight in his life. But there was more to it than this girl and his uneasy feelings for her. More that was both complicated and simple. It was his fault the base and its people were at risk. He'd opened the door these two came through. And he had to close it. He couldn't die trying. He had to live and do it. That was the simple part. The complicated part? He stared at her profile. He sure as hotel wasn't leaving her—these two to face the incoming alone. That wasn't in his DNA—though it was the first time he'd felt the need to protect a bird.

"No," he said, his tone mild, but firm.

She spun to face him, her head tipped to one side as, he guessed, she assessed his resolve. Finally she glanced at the bird. It almost seemed like it shrugged.

"We could use the help."

"The risk—" she said, but her protest lacked force.

"I'm guessing we don't have a lot of time to argue. Is the ray gun your only weapon?"

Her posture changed. Kind of reminded him of Donovan when she was preparing to toss someone on their ass. He rose, towering over her with his brows arched. Not that Donovan had ever managed to toss him. After a pause, she nodded.

"How many hostiles incoming?"

She wasn't the one who answered him.

"At least six. Highly trained and outfitted with dangerous and deadly technology they've stolen from the future."

Briggs mouth straightened into a line, and he shot a look at Madison. She seemed startled, but not annoyed. Was she surprised by what the bird had told him? Who was in charge? Who got to decide what? He could take orders, but—as if she sensed the question, she spoke.

"Sir Rupert is my," she hesitated, "...boss. I'm his bodyguard. It's my job to get him safely back to our base." He knew his gaze narrowed sharply because she added, "But it is always in my brief to protect innocents from hostile actions of the Time Service squads. You do not have to believe me, but I am as committed to protecting your people as you are."

"We are committed to that," the bird amended. "It is why we do what we do. To protect all living things from the damage done by the Time Service."

Because he couldn't do it to the bird, he directed a drilling gaze on Madison, using all the technique he'd learned during his years in the military. She didn't flinch or look away. Her lips might have twitched once.

"So," he said, finally, "six hostiles incoming?" That didn't seem too bad, even with fancy dancy technology.

"There might have been more than six who attacked us," she cautioned with a frown. "There was a lot of incoming fire, but they could have upgraded their weapons from our last, um, encounter."

She rubbed her forehead. "I didn't get a look at any of them. Just heard one or two go down."

"So what's your highest estimate?" Briggs pressed.

Her lips twisted wryly. "They might wait to reconstitute their squad before they come after us. Or they might call in backup. Twelve is the most I've ever seen them risk on a single op." She frowned. "It depends on what they think they'll jump into."

"If they believe you are alone, injured, and cut off from assistance," the bird said, "they will not wait for backup."

"But..." she started to protest, then stopped. "They would have brought a full force if they thought we jumped back to our base. But they know the manhole cover wouldn't take us there." She looked more hopeful.

Briggs grinned at the "manhole cover."

"But..." she murmured, the look she exchanged with the bird was interesting.

"What?" he asked, adding impatiently, "I need to know."

"He is correct. He does need to know."

Madison shifted her shoulder as if it pained her, but she met his gaze with sober determination. "If they saw Sir Rupert during the op, they will come in at full strength and loaded to kill. They can not afford to let him return to our base alive."

Did he need to know why?

"I told you we were seeking to identify a traitor, a mole in our organization," the bird said.

He frowned as a thought occurred to him. "How will they track you?" From where he sat, the disc looked dead out there on the table.

Once more it seemed that Madison looked at the bird for permission.

"He needs to know," the bird said again.

"I do," Briggs said grimly.

Madison patted her waist, then looked around, found the things from her belt he'd tossed onto the bed, and went over to them. She sorted through the small pile until she found the one she wanted. She activated it and directed it at the suit, watching a small screen. She finally made a face, speaking to the parrot, not him.

"Yeah, it's got an active tracking beacon."

"What...the suit?"

She nodded.

"Can you turn it off?"

In normal circumstances no one could find this outpost, since it had cloaking technology, but these two had made it in, so that probably wouldn't keep out their incoming squad. He could summon help, lots of it, but he had a feeling that conventional defenses wouldn't work in this situation.

"Maybe," she said, but once again she looked at the bird. "They might already have a fix on it."

"You want to use it to draw them in," he said, because it is what he would have done.

"We could try to leave, but if they already have this location..." She shrugged and did it very well.

He'd meant he had to be a grownup and not look—more than once. Apparently he was not as mature as he'd hoped. He glanced up, found her watching, humor and something else in her eyes. If she weren't younger than him...She met his gaze steadily.

"It's the best way for us and for your...for anyone here. They don't know the terrain, won't know what they are jumping into, but if they follow the beam in, they'll be less likely to look around, at least until they've got what they want."

He frowned. "A couple of hundred yards isn't that narrow." Had she seriously thought she could cover that much ground?

"I assess they will come in at considerably less than one hundred yards," the parrot said. "Their scanning will see the trees as obstacles to avoid, so the clear space on the beach is where they will most likely land."

Madison nodded. "And they'll know, if I'm conscious, they won't have that much time. I will have sensed them incoming."

Briggs blinked, not sure what to say. She could sense that?

"She's a very good time jumper," the bird said. It began to pace once more. "I do not believe they saw me. I transported before the door was breached. They'll know you were injured and that your suit was damaged and that the pad was the only way out."

"You think they'll be overconfident," Briggs suggested.

"Not a good reason for us to be overconfident," Madison said. "Their tech will be formidable, even if they think I'm down or almost down."

Her worried gaze met his. He should care they were up against some scary dudes with scary stuff, but words lost their power when she looked at him like that. He was treading in deep water, no question, but if it came down to a choice, he had to choose the base, its people over her.

She gave a slight nod, as if she knew it and agreed. "So we fight."

"Was there ever any doubt?" the bird asked.

"How long do you think we have?" Briggs asked now, his brain kicking into strategy mode.

Madison frowned. "That thing wasn't supposed to send us through time, just space."

Briggs blinked.

"What happened before your transit?" the bird asked.

"There might have been some shooting," she admitted. "More shooting, I mean," she added, with a sidelong glance at Briggs. "While I was in the beams."

"The concentrated weapons fire must have boosted the power and the signal, enabling that pad to connect to this one," the bird said. It fluttered over to the back of the chair, and moved back and forth on this now. "It is only thing that explains it."

"I'm not going to ask what would have happened if there'd been no pad to connect to," Madison said.

Since she hadn't asked, the bird didn't appear inclined to answer.

It was nice to know he'd been right about what the disc did. He might be forty-five but he still had it. "The other pad must have had a better power source," he mused, then gave himself a shake. It didn't matter now. "How long do we have to plan?" It was need-to-know.

Madison hesitated. "Oddly enough, the trip through time will give us more time. We might get three hours, but safe number is more like one hour."

One hour? Briggs tensed. "Then I need to make a call."

"I need to walk around, get a feel for the location," Madison said. She started to turn.

"Wait." She stopped, one brown lifted. "This is my turf. I know the terrain," Boy, did he know it. "I'm in charge."

She hesitated, glanced at the bird and nodded. "But Sir Rupert leaves the area. He can't be seen."

"During your call, could get me access to a computer," the bird asked. "I could endeavor to send out an SOS."

"You think help will come in time?" Briggs asked, not thrilled at more time travelers arriving.

The bird moved its beak from side to side. "There is not enough time, I know, ironic, but these are the limitations we live—or die—with."

"He could get the word out about our traitor," Madison said.

"I don't like it," Briggs said.

"Then I will go find some birds to, um, hang with."

Briggs blinked, not sure whether to laugh or grind his teeth. "There aren't any birds on this...in this place."

"No birds?" Madison looked shocked, then shook her head. "We're running out of time."

Briggs hesitated, then went with his gut and prayed it wasn't letting him down. "I'll arrange a safe place and a way to send your message." But he'd also make sure Robert was warned.

"Your plan," the bird said, "you must disable, not kill them."

"That's not—"

"Not all of them are willing," Madison said, clear reluctance in her voice. "And we don't know what impact their deaths would have on the timeline."

"You're in one batcrap crazy business," he said. "Okay, I know how to disable."

"Thank you," the bird said.

He shook his head. "I'll go make my call."

He stalked out the door toward the water. His chest heaved twice, then he lifted his radio.

~

Madison stared at Briggs' back for several seconds, then turned back to Sir Rupert, but she didn't know what to say or even ask.

"Trust him," the bird said.

"I do." She glanced out the door again. "He doesn't trust me, us."

"No." His wings fluttered and he lifted off, coming to where he could look out the door, too. "You should collect your things and get out of that suit."

"If they don't see a heat signature connected to the suit—" she protested.

"Trust him to work something out."

She looked down at the bird, but he wasn't looking at her. He hadn't done this once already, had he? Not that he'd tell her if he had. He would try to steer them away from where it went wrong—she rubbed her temple. It always ached when she tried to think her way through the paradoxes of time travel. She was tired of it, she realized. Tired of doing the same operations, tired of looking for Boris—the one who had changed her life for all time. She chose to be happy, as happy as possible, because why give up more of her life to a faceless nosebleed waste of space. But she felt out of juice.

This place, that man, had made her realize how very fast she'd been running, trying to stay ahead of how alone she was. And how very much she wanted to not be alone anymore.

I don't know how many more fights I have in me. Even thinking the words made her realize she did know. She had one left, because she couldn't let that man down. She couldn't let him die because she'd made a mistake. She hadn't trusted her niggle.

That couldn't, it wouldn't ever happen again.

Chapter Nine

Briggs had told Robert not to get out of the chopper, but he was too much like his sister. The impossible not only didn't scare him, he thought it could be beat. He grinned at Briggs, his curious gaze tracking past him to Madison and the bird. His eyes widened in delight and he passed Briggs, his hand held out.

"Robert," he flicked a glance back at Briggs, "and I'm not supposed to ask your name."

"Madison," she said. "And this is Sir Rupert."

Her smile was so natural for Robert, Briggs felt a stab of something that couldn't be what it felt like because Robert had a wife. But then he processed the fact she'd told him their names. Trust. She trusted them.

"How do you do?" the bird said, waving a claw in greeting, Briggs supposed.

Briggs lips compressed when Madison shot him a questioning look. He trusted her, he realized, but Doc—this was the brother that had been lost to her. Nothing could happen to Robert.

"We were wondering if you could take Sir Rupert with you. He kind of needs to send up an SOS to our base."

If anything Robert looked even more curious. "How do you do that?"

"Facebook," the bird said.

Both he and Robert did a double take.

"Facebook?" Robert slanted a look at Briggs.

"We all have an emergency account," Madison explained. "We use Facebook memes all the time to send messages. And those quizzes. Sometimes we use the quizzes."

"I don't," Briggs admitted, a bit dazed, "have an account. But—"

"It won't be instantaneous," Robert said, "but we should be able to get you connected. Emily loves Facebook."

Madison half opened her mouth, then closed it.

"His wife," Briggs said. She needed to know what was at stake here. And to know he trusted her.

She met his gaze, gratitude in the worried depths.

Robert half turned toward the chopper. "Let's get your stuff unloaded." He hesitated. "Sure you won't need more help?"

"We'll be fine. Just help," Briggs had to swallow, "the bird with his meme thing."

Robert laughed as the bird flew a small circle then landed on his shoulder. "I always wanted to be a pirate," he said, stroking the bird.

Briggs could be wrong, but he thought the bird rolled its eyes.

Briggs stared out over water reflecting light from the waning sun. Night was incoming, probably at the same time as the bad guys—the guys he hoped were bad guys. It had been a busy almost hour, one far too short, since Robert had left with the bird.

Madison had traded her suit for some camo, though not without a protest.

"If you're in there, we won't have enough fire power." She was not going to be bait on any op with him.

So they'd filled the suit with bags of hot water and arranged it on the bed. He'd hesitated, then looked at her. "We may not have a choice. If we can't stop them—"

She nodded.

She wanted to kill them, he realized. There was more than getting shot in the shoulder that drove her, but he didn't have time to find out. He snorted silently. Time. What a mess time travel made of things that should be simple, straightforward. "Can you do this?"

He kept his tone neutral, but with a layer of hard he used when he sensed an Airman on the point of wavering.

She looked at him then. "I can do what has to be done."

She might as well have said, *I can do what must be done one more time*. She was at her limit. Maxed out. But she'd do it. He wanted to—but they both needed to get under cover.

"Will you do one thing for me?" she asked, her voice so quiet, he almost missed her words.

"If I can."

Her lips trembled into a small smile. "I promise it won't hurt."

She turned until she fully faced him and reached out with one hand, settling it lightly on his chest close to his heart. Her chin lifted. "There's not much time..."

She lifted onto her toes, her lips parted, but she was too short. His lips quirked, Briggs bent his head, and met her halfway. She didn't seem to know what she was doing, but it didn't matter. He hadn't forgotten how to kiss a girl. His arms found their way around to her back and he pulled her close and maybe off her feet entirely. Desire tried to surge out of control, but he didn't turn it loose.

There was no time. No time...

He felt her stiffen and lifted his head.

"They're coming."

For half a second, he couldn't let go. Then his arms slackened. She stepped back. He couldn't, not until she created the distance. His hand shook slightly as he touched her hair one last time. He dropped his arm to his side, his fingers clenched.

"Right," he said. "Let's do this."

Briggs had helped Madison slide into the sniper's blind they'd built, one on either side of the target zone, then he piled foliage across the opening. She dug deeper into the dead leaves and other debris as she heard his crunching footsteps taking him to his position. Plants gave off a heat signature, too, so the dense foliage should muddy hers, particularly when they had a nice clean one inside the cottage to focus on.

Their positions would also provide a good crossfire situation. She had two weapons—a tranquilizer rifle and one with real bullets, already positioned for sniping. She only had to shift her hand to grab a stun grenade.

She considered her instructions again, making sure they were clear in her mind before things went hot.

The plan was good. He knew strategy, was just the kind of person the Time Service liked to acquire. She had to make sure that didn't happen.

As the clock ticked down to zero, she felt calm settle over her mind, her body alert, but not tense. If this was her last performance, she intended to make it a good one.

They wore headset radios, tuned to a frequency his people were unlikely to stumble across, but they were only useful until the shooting started. Her headset crackled.

"Romeo Tango Golf," she heard Briggs say.

Ready to go.

"Mike Tango," she answered. *Me too.* She felt the change as the time bubble formed. "Hotel India," she said. *Hostiles incoming.* She lifted the tranquilizer rifle, tucked it into her shoulder, and prepared for her first target.

~

The horizon shimmered a bit, and then Briggs saw six dark figures appear along the beach line. Almost immediately they were gone. They'd activated their camo, he realized but they'd be moving in toward the hut. In the moonlight falling across the beach, he saw footsteps appear in the sand and grinned. No one had come up with a way to hide footprints.

They reached the table and stopped, probably looking at the dead transport disc. He activated the drone. It rose slowly, until it was about chest height, hovering in the shadowy doorway of the hut.

"What's that sound?" one of them asked. The footprints turned, first one, then all of them angled toward the hut. They began to track forward.

Keep coming, he thought, *just a little further.* When they were close enough, he sent the drone out of the doorway and activated the EMP device the drone carried. There was a flash of bright light. *Hello, electromagnetic pulse.*

The drone went dead.

But so did their fancy tech.

They went from blending into the horizon to dark shadows backlit by the rising moons.

Madison fired her first shot, then a second. Nice. Two shadows down. The other turned toward the shots, giving Briggs a chance to lob a stun grenade into the middle of them. Another bright, blinding flash. Followed by the sound of muffled thumps into soft sand.

Don't move, he wanted to tell Madison. But their radios had been taken out by the EMP, too.

He waited for his night vision to return. There were dark lumps around the hut's doorway. But were they all down? He lowered his night sight and their heat signatures popped them out. No sign of movement. With his weapon ready, he kicked out of his blind and approached them.

Madison appeared out of the dark on the other side. He lifted a hand to stop her before she stepped into the light.

"Cover me," he ordered. He pulled out the plastic zip ties and secured the first guy, feet and hands, then moved to the second. One figure shifted a bit and a shot hissed out, hitting its target. The moving stopped. Even as Briggs secured each one, his mind was repeating over and over, "Too easy..."

A sharp cry, cut off before it was complete came from Madison's position. Briggs dropped down between two of the prone figures as something blue sizzled past, close enough for him to feel the heat. A bright cage of lights dropped over him and the figures. He heard the crackle of it, felt its heat maybe two inches above his head. And from Madison's direction, he saw another one appear, trapping her inside.

Madison felt the niggle too late to escape the energy trap. The heat of it traveled along her weapon, forcing her to drop it. Then two figures emerged from either side of the hut, both with their camo already down. One circled the cage that held Briggs trapped.

"Sometimes it pays to be late to the party," the one closest to her said. His voice was icy cold, crisply devoid of anything that might give away his origins. He stopped and looked at his downed team. "We need to know what happened."

Briggs wasn't down in the sense this agent meant, but he was not moving. She did not see how it would help, but she clung to the faint hope as the man's attention shifted to her. She was the only one who appeared to be standing. He walked over until they stood a few feet apart. His gaze traveled up, down, and then back up to her face. His gaze narrowed. His hand lifted and it took all her resolve not to flinch, but it was just a light. With her night vision lost, she couldn't see his reaction, but she heard his sharp intake of breath.

"Not possible," he said. "You're...not possible."

Her vision clearing, she studied him now.

"Boris," she said. "You're Boris. You're the one who erased my family." It was the only way he could have recognized her. Because of him, they didn't exist. She didn't exist.

"Boris?" The man seemed puzzled, though it was hard to be sure in the moonlight.

"Boris Karloff. The always bad guy."

Now he chuckled. "That depends on your perspective, I suppose. I did what had to be done."

"You erased my family, my brother, and the people he was meant to save died. You had no right to do any of it."

He shrugged. "Apparently I missed my target."

"I was away," preparing for the Olympics that had never happened for her, she thought painfully, "they came for me first. But they were not in time to save..." She couldn't continue. Didn't need to. He knew what he'd done.

His quiet laugh chilled her to the bone as he came closer. Stopping only when he was just shy of the shimmering cage that held her back from killing him with her bare hands. She'd tried not to think about meeting him, because it would have eaten her up inside, but now that he was there? She wanted him dead.

"You really believe that? You believe they were too late?" He laughed again.

Madison felt cold go deeper into her bones as she stared into his cold blue eyes. Funny how fear changed the cold. Cold should just be cold.

He shook his head, his gaze mocking. "You were young, but surely in time you must have realized you were the one they wanted. It was never about your family. It was always about you."

The one true thing she'd learned during her time with the rebellion was how to hide her feelings. It served her well now. She stared at him from blank eyes, while her brain raced, trying to feel her way to truth. His words would hurt later, if she lived, if she found out he was right. This moment, the talking, it wouldn't last. He couldn't erase someone who didn't exist, but he could kill her. She was human.

And if she died, so did Briggs. And when he died, they'd search this place and find his people. She didn't know what was here, but she could tell Briggs believed there were people here the Time Service would want. Somehow she had to keep him talking. Time, almost she laughed, they needed time.

"And why was a thirteen-year-old gymnast such a threat to the Time Service?" She was impressed with the bored scorn that infused the question. Girl gymnasts weren't that big of a deal when she was training. But she'd lost that dream, too. And why had she mattered to the Rebellion? No, now was not the time for those questions. If she wanted answers, she had to live.

"You don't know, do you?" His laugh held surprise. "You are one of the most gifted time sensitives in, well, history."

She didn't even blink. "And you didn't want that?" She didn't try to hide her disbelief. *Never trust a Time Service agent.* It was the first rule in the Rebellion.

"Oh, we would have, but your other gift was a deal breaker. They didn't tell you that you have a complete, built-in resistance to the mind wipe, did they? I'm sure it was just an oversight. There you have it. You couldn't be turned. No use to us, but very useful to the Rebellion. We couldn't risk you or any future heirs being out there, so you had to be erased." He paused. "How every clever *She* was to hide you from us. We never even had a whiff of you in all this time."

"Are you so sure you weren't mind wiped?" Madison asked, as hope faded. She could see death in his eyes. He was going to kill her. She couldn't think her way out of this cage. If Sir Rupert had called in help—it was possible they'd get here in time to clean up the scene. But she wouldn't make it. Briggs would die—or worse, be taken to use.

He shrugged. "I never needed to be persuaded to join. I like my job." He walked around her cage, looking her over like an animal being assessed for slaughter.

He was drawing out the moment so she'd suffer, she realized. He did like his job. "It's a pity," he said.

"What's a pity?" she asked, knowing he wasn't capable of feeling pity.

"That you won't live long enough to ask her if I've lied to you." He lifted his gun, letting her see as he flicked it to the kill setting. His other hand held the cage control.

He'd have to drop it to shoot her.

She might be able to move fast enough.

He stepped so that the tip of his ray gun almost touched the cage and was pointed at her heart.

Her breaking heart.

I'm so sorry, Briggs.

Chapter Ten

Briggs froze, keeping his head down, his body slack. As he went down, he'd felt something hard pressing into his thigh. If it was the drone...inch by careful inch, he eased his hand down. His fingers brushed against it, then curled around it. He traced it. Yeah, that was the drone, the EMP device still attached. He'd left the trigger back in the blind, but that would be dead anyway. There was a chance, a slight chance, that the device had enough charge left. He'd not set it to full charge, just in case. Didn't want to cause any problems on the base.

His guard moved closer and Briggs lowered his lashes, feeling the dull thud of his heart as Boris spoke to Madison. It was clear he meant to kill her.

Don't think about it. Deal with it later if we make it. His fingers traced the shape, found the device. He was running out of time. There. His finger found the manual trigger.

"It's a pity you won't live long enough to ask her if I've lied to you."

Briggs pressed the button, praying at the same time. The flash was smaller this time, but the cage disappeared. His guard was close and slow to react. Briggs took him down and out and was already headed toward the two figures silhouetted against the rising moons. They disappeared into the shadows of the trees. He could heard the scuffle, the panting breaths of a desperate struggle. A grunt of pain and then silence.

Afraid to hope, Briggs darted toward where he'd last seen them—

Madison stepped out of the shadows, her face white, her eyes haunted.

He grabbed her and pulled her close, his hands running down her back, then up, as if to assure himself it was her, that she was alive.

"Is he dead?" He spoke matter-of-factly into her ear. A contrast to the frantic beat of his heart and hers.

She shook her head. "I...no." She inhaled shakily. "I wanted to but..."

She stopped. His grip tightened.

"Wait here. Don't move." He headed into the shadows, found the guy she'd called Boris, and dragged him out into the moonlight. He had a nasty swelling bruise on his chin and was bleeding sluggishly from a wound in his side. Briggs used more zip ties on him and his sidekick. He angled his head and studied Boris's partner. She did look a bit like a Natasha...

Once he was sure they were all well secured, he went back to Madison.

She hadn't moved though now her body shuddered with shock. Now the words she'd exchanged with Boris came back with echoing force. He didn't know what to say or do, other than to hold her again. He wanted to tell her it would be all right, but the words stuck in his throat.

How could anything be all right for her? She'd lost so much. Questions formed and were discarded before they were uttered. Nothing sounded right.

"I'm sorry," he finally said. "I'm sorry."

She looked up at him then. "I am, too."

~

Madison shuddered with the adrenalin that had carried her through the fight with Boris. He was a good fighter, but a lousy gymnast. The super power he hadn't seen coming. And the knife strapped to her leg.

She was still surprised she hadn't killed him. He'd been worse than she'd imagined. A cold, killing machine.

Maybe that was why she couldn't do it. It took her too close to the edge of becoming like him, becoming him.

"You," she was close enough to feel Briggs swallow, "could stay here, you know. We're a motley crew, so you'd fit right in."

She was surprised to hear, to feel herself chuckle. Knew she'd find him grinning, felt her own lips stretching into something like a grin. It was a relief to feel the drama ratchet down. She'd never wanted to be one of the drama girls, not with the team or without. It was even a relief to feel the pain in her shoulder and the slow creep of blood from the wound she'd reopened—

She started to answer him, but stiffened instead, spinning to face the rippling horizon once more. As *She* and the new guy's cells settled into this time, she stepped protectively in front of Briggs. *She* noted the movement and her lips twisted wryly. The new guy moved forward to examine their catch.

"Nice work," he said, his wary gaze moving between Madison and their boss.

"That's Boris," she said, adding, "the one who erased my family."

"He's dead?" *She* asked.

"No." Madison lifted her shoulders in a sigh. "I'm not like him. I'm not a killer."

The new guy straightened, eyeing Madison carefully. "What do you want me to do with him?"

"I want you to keep him away from me," she said. Briggs stepped up next to her, his hand on her shoulder.

"You had help, I see," *She* said. Her gaze returned to Madison. "You can't trust them, you know, him least of all."

"Even a Time Service agent will tell the truth when he knows it will cause more damage than a lie," Madison said evenly.

She's gaze flicked toward Briggs. "We can talk about this later—"

Madison felt Briggs grip on her shoulder tighten, then loosen, as if he'd forced himself to do it. She shook her head.

"I'm not going back. I can't do it anymore."

"You could still be a target—"

"I don't exist, remember?" Her lips twisted wryly. "And according to him, you can't rearrange my brain. So you're going to have to trust me. And leave me alone to get on with my life."

She didn't like it, but the new guy was watching.

"We're supposed to be the good guys, remember?" Madison said.

She thinned her lips, but she gave a half nod. "Sir Rupert..."

There was a raucous caw-caw from the trees, then he sailed into view, landing lightly on Madison's shoulder.

"I think this island needs birds," he said. "Not to mention someone who can make sure you don't interfere with...anyone's future."

Madison reached up and stroked under his chin. "Thank you," she said softly.

The slightest slump in *She's* shoulders was the only sign he'd tipped the balance. Her blank gaze tracked between Madison and Briggs. "I don't suppose you're going to introduce us."

"Not a chance." Madison met and held her gaze. "I've done more than enough time. You know that's true."

The new guy spoke again. "We are the good guys, are we not, ma'am?"

"Of course." *She* gave a shrug that was not quite casual. "You did good work. We'll all miss you."

"You'd better," she let iron filter into her tone, "miss me, I mean."

She glanced at the new guy and finally did sigh. "You have my word." She nudged one of the men with a toe. "You have no idea how good she is...was," she said. "You will miss her."

The new guy grinned. "At least we got our mole."

Madison's smile was real this time. She glanced at Sir Rupert. "Good job."

Now that it was decided, *She* turned brisk. "Tag them for transport," she ordered. With a half salute for them, she vanished in a shimmer of horizon.

"I'll keep an eye on her," the new guy promised, before he and the catch of the day vanished.

Madison tensed, reaching out with her senses, but there was nothing but the night breeze and the light from the two moons. And a man and a bird. She gave a small chuckle, then laughed with sudden joy. It had been a long time...she sobered thinking about how long.

She faced the man. "I hope you meant it, because I can't go anywhere now."

Sir Rupert, as if he realized he was a bit in the way, lifted off, circling the clearing before landing on the table. Madison would have liked more space than that, but it was what it was.

The man rested his hands on her waist and she saw joy in his eyes, too, manly joy of course. But also hesitation.

"What's wrong?" she asked, lifting her hand so it rested against a cheek roughened by the beard he hadn't had time to shave.

"Today was my birthday," he admitted, with a rueful scowl. "That thing was a present sent by a couple of friends."

"Happy...birthday?" She couldn't remember the last time she'd been in real time to celebrate a birthday, or been with anyone who would have cared.

"I'm forty-five," he muttered.

Madison looked at him, trying to understand his problem.

"I'm a lot older than you," he muttered, even lower than before.

Her eyes widened and she couldn't help the half chuckle, half snort. "Sorry, but," she bit her lip. "You said this was 2017, right?" He nodded warily. "Briggs," was this the first time she'd said his name out loud? "I was born in, um, 1946."

She could see him doing the math.

"1946?"

She nodded. His hands slid further around her, moving up her back, then down her shoulders while heat built swiftly inside her. Heat and longing and an aching restlessness. His mouth turned up slowly, the smile sexy with lots of hot in his eyes.

"You're in really good shape."

"I try to work out and...and...eat right," she said, breathlessly, her lips aching for his. Had she only known this man a few hours?

"Do you know what my friend, do you know what Robert said, before he took the bird away?"

Madison almost lost her breath at this sign of trust and at the way his hand trembled as he smoothed the hair back off her face.

"What...did Robert say?" she asked.

"He said, you should keep her."

"Did...he?"

He bent his head toward her mouth. She pushed up on her toes, but his mouth was just a bit out of reach.

"Can I keep you, Madison?"

"Please," she said and finally his mouth covered hers. His arms banded around her, so that all of her was pressed against a lot of him. He was a big guy. But now there was time to get to know all of him. Lots and lots of lovely time.

~

History of Women in Gymnastics

While the most famous women gymnasts competed on the Olympic stage in 1972, women began to compete on the same apparatus as men as early as 1928. The floor exercise was added in 1932, and in 1952, the bar, beam, floor and vault events for women were added, making it entirely possible that thirteen-year-old Madison could have been training for the Olympics when the nasty Time Service messed with her life in or around 1958.

~

Afterword

~

Thank you for reading the collection. I hope you enjoyed it. :-)

To find out about all my releases, be sure to sign up for my New Release eZine and get a free eBook.

Or hop over to my website and check out my series:

Project Enterprise The Big Uneasy Lonesome Lawmen

Browse my complete backlist by visiting my website. :-) I have some stand alone novels, too.

And if you want to talk books, you can find me here:

My Blog Facebook Fan Page Twitter Pinterest Goodreads

If you enjoyed this book, I hope you'll consider leaving a review. It's not just because I'm needy (even though I try not to be!). Reviews help other readers decide which books to buy. :-)

~

Also by Pauline Baird Jones

Available in print, digital and audio.

Science Fiction Romance/Paranormal

Project Universe Series:

The Key (book 1)

Girl Gone Nova (book 2)

Tangled in Time (book 3)

Steamrolled (book 4)

Kicking Ashe (book 5)

Found Girl (book 6)

Project Enterprise: The Short Stories

Time Trap: A Project Enterprise Series Short Story

Nebula Nine (time travel adventure)

Open With Care (Christmas collection that includes, "Riding For Christmas" and "Up on the House Top"

Specters in the Storm: A paranormal/steampunk/science fiction romance novella

Out of Time (World War II Time Travel Romance)

An Uneasy Future

(A science fiction romance mystery series set in future New Orleans)

Core Punch (1.0)

Sucker Punch (2.0)

One Two Punch: An Uneasy Future Bundle

Short Story Collections

Project Enterprise: The Short Stories

Do Wah Diddy Delete

Let's Fall in Love

The Real Dragon and other short stories

The Real Dragon

Romantic Suspense

The Big Uneasy Series:

Relatively Risky (1)

Family Treed (Short Story)

Dead Spaces (2.0)

Louisiana Lagniappe (3.0)

Worry Beads (4.0) Coming soon!

The Big Uneasy Bundle

Lonesome Lawmen Series:

The Last Enemy

Byte Me

Missing You

Lonesome Mama (Bonus short story)

(The *Lonesome Lawmen* is also available as a digital bundle)

Do Wah Diddy Die

The Spy Who Kissed Me

Perilously Fun Fiction Bundle (includes *The Spy Who Kissed Me* and *Do Wah Diddy Die*. Bonus: *Do Wah Diddy Delete Short Story Collection*)

A Dangerous Dance

About the Author

Award-winning, *USA Today* Bestselling author Pauline never liked reality, so she writes books. She likes to wander among the genres, rampaging like Godzilla, because she does love peril mixed in her romance.

To find out more about Pauline or her books:
http://paulinebjones.com